THE EX-CON

THE ACCOUNTANT

AND THE WOMAN IN THE TRUNK . . .

"She had a good two-handed stance, the barrel lined up with her dominant eye, pointing, not at his head, but his chest. No one-eyed squinting. No hysteria. This was a woman well acquainted with firearms. And she'd know her rights too—know she'd be well within them to blow five or six inches right out of the back of an ugly intruder like him."

JOHN D. BROWN
BAD PENNY

A THRILLER

BLACK
SWORD
BOOKS

BAD PENNY

Copyright © 2013 by John Brown

Published by Blacksword Enterprises, LLC

Cover design copyright © 2013 Shai McDonald

ISBN 13: 978-1-940427-05-8

ISBN 10: 1940427053

First edition: December, 2013

Revised May, 2014

In memory of George Obrist,
one of the good guys

Contents

Prologue

Coalville, Utah

JESUS GOROZA, the man with tats running over his limbs like demons, thought the woman they were following on this deserted piece of interstate was FBI.

Ed Meese, the driver, the man with the scar on his neck, didn't think that was the case at all. She was in her early-twenties, a bit young for the FBI. And she was driving an old 1990s Buick without another soul in sight. Wouldn't the Feds have sent backup at the first sign of trouble? Of course, maybe she'd convinced her bosses she was clear, convinced them that the big FBI agent had everything in hand, and they'd pulled back the cavalry.

Meese shook his head. Cops were idiots.

The two men had been keeping back, playing it safe, giving the woman plenty of room. It was just after four a.m., the sun still more than an hour off. Hardly a soul out here. Just them and her driving in the dark, the two men waiting for her to make her mistake.

Up ahead the woman slowed, then took the exit to a small out-in-the-middle-of-nowhere Utah town called Coalville. In a big city, there would have been cars. There would have been some bustle. There would have been witnesses.

There were no witnesses here. Not on these streets.

There were hardly any homes. Meese figured there were at most a few dozen, and they were all strung out along a main road that stretched for ten miles or more. All of the houses were dark. A bunch of hick farmers dreaming about cows.

A brightly-lit Best Western hotel and a Texaco gas station stood on one side of the interstate. A lone Sinclair gas station stood on the other. The woman came to a stop then accelerated up and across the overpass toward the Sinclair gas station on the other side, the side that you couldn't see well from the interstate. The side she obviously thought might give her cover.

"Bingo," Jesus said.

In a big city, the Sinclair would have been ready for business. In this know-nothing town, it was dark and locked. The pumps, of course, were on. And the station's sign with a green dinosaur on a white background towered above the place and shone out into the fading night.

But there was no attendant standing guard over the cash and cigarettes to observe the woman. No one to see her stop and start the pump. No one to see her go try the bathroom door around the side. No one to see the two men pull up to the station a few seconds later.

Meese said, "Looks like your offerings to the White Lady paid off."

Jesus opened the glove box and pulled out the semi-automatic. "I told you she wanted mescal."

Prayer, mescal offered up in a glass five days in a row, and cigarette smoke blown into the Lady's skeleton face.

Meese pointed at Jesus's gun. "You remember: this whore isn't worth anything to us dead."

"She's worth *less* dead," Jesus corrected.

"A lot less. Hand me some ties."

Jesus reached into the glove box again and came up with a bundle of long white plastic zip ties and a roll of duct tape. These weren't garden variety ties; these were nice and fat and designed for human wrists.

Gas stations always had cameras. Meese spotted two here. So instead of rolling up into the well-lit area by the pumps and the woman's car, he pulled around the corner into the dark night shadow below some trees, threw it in park, and cut the lights. He and Jesus put on their ball caps and pulled them down low so their faces would be in shadow. Then they got out and quietly hustled up to her piece of crap Buick just to make sure nobody was in it, then silently moved to the side of the building to surprise her when she came back from the bathroom.

Meese slipped the ties into his back pocket and took a position by the corner. Jesus stood back with his gun to head her off in case she tried an end run.

High above them the green and white dinosaur sign buzzed with electricity. In the distance, someone in a pickup with some pipes got a little frisky and floored it. The roaring motor echoed from the other end of the still town. Whoever it was might have had the opportunity to witness the one exciting thing to happen in that farming town that day, but they were headed in another direction, and the roar of that motor faded in the distance.

The woman came around the corner. She saw Jesus. Her eyes went wide. She turned to flee, but Meese was right there. He lunged for her.

She swung for his face. Connected. But he had taken plenty of blows from men a lot bigger and stronger. He'd taken harder blows as a kid.

He tackled her. Right there on the asphalt. Slammed her down hard. She was a fine little thing, slender, and strong.

She cried out, threw an elbow, kicked, almost wriggled free. But he outweighed her by at least seventy pounds. And he was strong. Years of strength built up in prison.

Meese grabbed her by her dark hair and smacked her head into the asphalt.

She screamed, but Meese rolled her over and punched her hard in her slim gut. A pounding blow like a sledge hammer that knocked the air right out of her.

The scream cut short. Her eyes went wide with the shock and pain.

Meese reached around and grabbed one of the zip ties. It was almost eighteen inches long. It took him only a second to loop it around her ankles and feed the one end into the locking mechanism. Took him no time to yank it tight.

By this time the woman had her breath back, but she wasn't going anywhere. He rolled her back onto her stomach, wrenched her arms behind her back, and zip-tied her wrists.

The woman screamed.

"Tape," Meese said.

Jesus ripped off a length of duct tape, then knelt down and slapped it over the woman's mouth.

She tried to scream again, but found it just didn't work the same when her mouth was shut. Sounded more like a growl.

Meese patted her down, checked her pockets. No guns, no knives, no hidden microphones. Just a man's wallet with a driver's license and a piece of plastic. Where was her phone?

They hauled her up. Meese hefted her slight weight over his shoulder. He was happy their quarry had turned out to be a woman, and not some fat cholo with a death wish.

Jesus ran to the Nissan. Meese followed, lugging his cargo through the light by the pumps to the dark street.

Jesus opened the trunk. The trunk light came on, and Meese stuffed her inside. She fit pretty well. A lot better than some big guy would. But she was going to kick and growl and that wouldn't do. It would be annoying if nothing else.

"You ready?" Meese said.

Jesus fished around in his shirt pocket then nodded.

Meese said to the woman, "I'm going to rip this tape off. This is your last opportunity to scream for help. I figure you deserved a sporting chance. Here we go."

The woman looked up with desperation and anger in her eyes.

Meese grabbed her by the forehead to hold her face firmly in place. "One, two, three," he counted and ripped the tape back.

The woman opened her mouth to scream, but Jesus was there with a bottle of grape flavored Benadryl. He deftly grabbed her nose with his fat fingers and pinched it shut, then he glugged a great quantity of the medicine into her open mouth.

The woman choked and swallowed and coughed and came up for air like she'd almost drowned.

"You think that's enough?" Jesus asked.

"It will have to be for now," Meese said, because he was starting to feel the prickles on the back of his neck. Starting to feel his early alert system sounding a warning. "Time to go."

Meese wiped her mouth roughly with the sleeve of his shirt to clean off the Benadryl, and then he brought the duct tape back across the woman's mouth and sealed it shut. Jesus snapped the trunk down.

The woman bumped and growled inside.

"We're going to have to drop her car," Meese said. If they didn't, whoever opened this station up would see the car, wonder about it, and go to the camera recordings to see who'd left it. And then they'd call the police. On the other hand, a car dropped on the side of some road far away from the station might not attract any attention for days. And when it did, chances were nobody would be thinking of looking at gas station recordings.

Jesus put the Benadryl back in his pocket.

"Keep your prints off that car," Meese said. "Use a couple of those blue towelettes above the squeegee bucket."

Jesus nodded and turned back to the Buick. Meese skirted around the back of the Nissan. His alarms were in full swing now, sounding like a fire drill. He threw open the driver's side of the Nissan, slid in, and shut the door, safe behind the dark tinted glass.

A few seconds later the Buick appeared in his rearview mirror, bumping out onto the road. Meese put his car in gear, made a U-turn and headed back toward the main drag, Jesus following in that Buick. Fifty yards later he came to the intersection and signaled with his blinker as a good citizen should to make a right turn. As he did, an old guy in an old pickup approached the intersection from the cross-street, turned, and drove right past him. Meese waited and watched in his rearview mirror with curiosity.

A few moments later the pickup's brake lights flared. And then it turned into the Sinclair and pulled up to the pumps.

"Cheese and crackers," he said. He did have a sixth sense alarm. No doubt about it.

Meese smiled, gave the car some gas, and made his right turn.

They dropped the Buick a few miles away on the curb by a church then rode south for a few miles to the next little hickville and found another entrance to the interstate. Jesus fiddled with the woman's phone, trying to force it to reveal its secrets.

The woman in the back kicked.

"That's going to drive me crazy," Jesus said.

"Twenty minutes and the Benadryl will chill her out," Meese said. "If not, we'll take care of it. The next hour we've got miles and miles of empty road." He was thinking of her slim hard body. Thinking of what she might be wearing underneath. Thinking about how sweet she'd probably feel. They wanted her alive and ready to talk. Meese could deliver that and still handle the merchandise. He hoped she was a cop because that would just be the frigging cherry and whipped cream on top.

Jesus reached into his bag of Red Vines, pulled out a couple of whips, and took a bite. "How's the temperature?" he asked.

Meese looked at the gauge on the dashboard. "It's out of the red for now, and that's all I care about." Then he turned and accelerated along the on-ramp. He switched on his blinker again and pulled out onto the dark freeway.

Miles behind him one pair of headlights moved toward them along the interstate. Miles ahead of him a pair of red taillights zoomed away. Alongside the interstate, the town slept on. The whole thing had lasted all of fifteen minutes, in and out, and not even the cattle in the fields had taken notice.

* * *

In the trunk, the woman breathed in through her nostrils and tried to calm herself. Her heart was beating like a bird in a cage. She fumbled around behind her with her zip-tied hands for the emergency trunk release and found nothing but the bones of the car.

It was close and dark like a coffin. Except you wouldn't smell motor oil in a coffin. You wouldn't hear the drone of the tires on the road or see the pinpricks of red leaking around the housing for the rear lights. But it was a coffin nevertheless.

She'd known they'd find her. Eventually. Just as they found the others. The faces of those she'd worked with appeared before her and stabbed her with a pang of regret.

She adjusted her position, took slower breaths, tried to keep the panic away. She told herself she'd known the risks—they all had. Told herself she'd do it all over again. Told herself this wasn't over until it was over. Then she prayed to the Holy Mother. Prayed for eyes to see her chance.

Prayed the men would make a mistake.

1

Cowboy Donut

ONE STATE AWAY and seven hours later, Frank Shaw sat in the back office of Cowboy Donut and silently prayed that God would overlook his many sins and give him a break. But it appeared God was out this morning because Frank was facing the owner of the Cowboy Donut, watching yet another job interview begin to swirl the toilet.

Trying to get a straight job as an ex-con was a lovely experience. Kind of like being dragged behind a bus. No matter how tidy you looked or how sharp your resume was, it all came down to two questions: "Have you ever been convicted of a crime" and "What were you in for?"

Ms. Mary Rogers, the sun-cured owner of the Rock Springs, Wyoming doughnut establishment, had just popped the second question. She was probably in her fifties and had two-tone hair that seemed to take its inspiration from a badger—all bleached on top and dark underneath. She was no nonsense. She reminded Frank of the hard-nosed sergeant who played a guerilla chief in Robin Sage, the culminating, four-week-long, large-scale, unconventional warfare exercise that he and about 300 others had to pass to join the Green Berets. There had been no pulling the wool over that man's eyes.

No pulling the wool here. And he'd be an idiot to try. First of all, he was going straight. Second, any employer who didn't have a carrot for a brain was going to run a background check. And it was clear Ms. Mary was not running on carrots.

So Frank dropped his bomb—voluntary manslaughter, a security job gone bad. He'd been protecting the wrong kind of noun for the wrong kind of people, which led to six fine years in prison.

First interviews were like first dates. And Frank had basically just told this date he had an Ebola monkey virus that would make her eyes bleed and then asked her for a kiss. That, of course, was yummy to women everywhere.

Ms. Mary narrowed her eyes. "What else am I going to find on your RAP sheet?"

"That's it," Frank said. "Just the one unfortunate incident."

"Murder is a pretty big incident."

"Manslaughter," he corrected. "Not murder."

She made a noncommittal sound and looked down to study his resume a bit more, like maybe something new would pop up there.

He'd done this now a couple dozen times and knew the best thing was just to keep quiet, let them peacefully work through their Judas-Priest-there's-a-killer-sitting-across-the-desk-from-me moment. As he waited, he looked around the office and back out to the kitchen. The shop reminded him of a Starbucks, except instead of the mermaid logo, these folks had mounted a pair of longhorns above the menu board. The horns must have been almost seven feet from tip to tip. The place smelled nice: sugar, fried dough, and freshly ground coffee percolating on the side. Someone had been at the floor with a wicked broom and mop, leaving the tiles to gleam in the late morning light.

A number of customers sat out front at the tables with newspapers, laptops, and phones, enjoying the music and free wi-fi. Rows of doughnuts stood invitingly in the well-lit display. Frank wasn't a connoisseur, but, as far as the doughnuts went, they looked good enough. There were your sprinkles, your chocolate cake, and your regulars. He didn't know if they'd win at the national doughnut bake-off, but who cared? They looked a heck of a lot better than any confection he'd gotten on D block in cell 38.

Ms. Mary pushed his resume to the side with one finger and looked up. "I don't know," she said. "Folks come here for celebration, not to see Ted Bundy standing behind the counter. Doughnuts are a happy product."

It was technically illegal for her to reject him for reasons based solely on his status as an ex-con. But Frank wasn't one of those pissants who was going to push that. Besides, he tended to agree with her: who in their right mind wanted to hire somebody who had already proven they couldn't be trusted?

"Ted Bundy was a friendly good-looking guy," Frank said. "He would have charmed your customers. Charmed you. Only then would he have taken you out back and slit your throat. People aren't always what they seem."

"That's right, but first impressions count. You look more like a bouncer than a baker. Some people are going to come in here and wonder if they took a wrong turn." She motioned vaguely at his arms and the side of his head. "And those tattoos don't help."

Frank decided he liked Ms. Mary and her direct approach. Most of the other employers beat around the bush, made vague excuses, offered drips of false sympathy. There was none of that here.

"Your customers will probably just figure I'm the Pillsbury Dough Boy's leaner, bigger brother."

"The one that went to prison?"

"No, not that one. The one who grew up to cook pretty doughnuts."

"Pillsbury's got a family now?"

"Look," Frank said, "big doesn't need to be scary. You want happy and friendly? I can do that." He turned on his best hundred-megawatt smile. "Who's going to resist that?"

Ms. Mary grunted.

"Come on," he said with a tease.

She shook her head. "Why aren't you applying at the oil rigs, a guy like you?"

"That's a good question. Oil rigs pay well. And they don't seem to have too many problems with my big house fellows. But here's the deal: I just spent a number of years living in the middle of nowhere with a bunch of stinky men. I'd kind of like to get away from that. Move on to better things."

"Like being a doughnut man."

Frank shrugged. "Exactly. You can call me Crème Brûlée."

"Do you even know what a crème brûlée is?"

Frank pretended to think for a moment. "The distant relative of a doughnut?" he offered.

"Lord," she said, but she said it with a smile. A real one. He'd gotten that out of her, which was a start. Hope glimmered. Maybe this time he might be able to avert the inevitable flush.

"Tell you what," she said. "I'll think about it. And I'm only doing that because, if this resume here isn't a bunch of spam, you were once military. And that's worth something. You give me a call next week."

Frank let out a little sigh of disappointment. It was the standard answer. The familiar flush. The rumble of the toilet water filled his ears. Ms. Mary, it appeared, was just like all the rest. He'd call, and she'd say they weren't looking just at the moment, but they'd keep him on file.

Frank nodded and put on a happy face. "I'll call for sure," he said, then pushed his chair back and stood.

"You ever had one of our bear claws?" she asked.

"No ma'am."

"Sally will give you one on the way out."

"I'll pay for it."

"You'll do no such thing," she said. "Sally," she called out to the door, "get Mr. Shaw one of the claws."

Frank walked to the door.

"Don't disappoint me," she said. "You call next week."

He held up his hand like he was taking an oath. "Telemarketer's honor," he said and exited the office.

Sally was wiping the gleaming counter. She stowed her wash cloth, then walked over to the display and retrieved one of the giant claws.

In Frank's wallet was a twenty, a five, and three ones. It was the extent of his bank account at the moment. And it had to cover this thing called food and another thing called gas and a third called cell service. It already wasn't enough for all three. But he wasn't going to take doughnut condolences. Frank didn't believe in pity jobs. Folks either wanted his services and were willing to pay for them, or they didn't. And if they didn't, he didn't want any part of it.

The bear claws were monsters, each as big as his head. He forked over two ones, a nice seven percent of his net worth, thanked Sally, then stepped out into the hot afternoon sun, holding the massive thing in one hand.

He'd never seen a doughnut like it in his life. It could probably feed an African village. He bit in and found it crunchy and sweet on the outside, light and soft with bits of strawberry and apple on the inside. He pulled the claw back and looked at the beast again with new eyes. That was better than good. It was spectacular. The Fourth of July in his mouth. He took another bite and realized he just might have underestimated the quality of Cowboy Donut.

He looked up into the heavens. "Great doughnut, God. Of course, there's this thing called rent." Not that Frank held God responsible.

He walked out to his '71 Nova, trying to live in the moment and savor each chew because he just might have to savor renting a dog kennel if his situation didn't change. His nephew Tony sat on the passenger's side with the windows down, hunched over his laptop, his fingers pattering over the keys.

Tony was seventeen, still waiting for some real facial hair to grow. He dabbled in an assortment of odd non-school sports like parkour, which consisted of a lot of running around places most people left to the cats. Tony was spending a few weeks of summer here because he was like a little brother and begged his mother and promised to give her ground reports on Frank.

Tony heard Frank and looked up. "So," he asked, "was she convinced by your winning ways?"

"She thought I looked like a serial killer."

Tony nodded. "Could have been worse."

"What? The creature from the black lagoon?" He pointed upward. "I was sure I was going to get some help."

"I heard there's some tribe in India that believes God is a big snake. Maybe you need to do some mouse sacrifices or something."

"If God's a snake, he's a mighty big one. It would take more than mice."

"Annoying neighborhood dogs?" Tony offered.

"I'm thinking bigger," Frank said. "Something your size would be perfect."

Tony furtively pattered his fingers over his laptop keyboard. "You know, I do have other solutions."

Frank glanced through the windows of Cowboy Donut at the folks working on the wi-fi. He looked back at Tony. "You didn't."

Tony smiled. "Me? I'm just checking email," he said and folded down the laptop's lid.

Tony called himself a white hat. He'd explained that in the hacker world you had black hats, gray hats, and white hats. Black hats hacked maliciously—to steal and do damage. They included lots of dweebs and a lot of not so dweebish folks like the Russian mafia. They liked to steal identities and credit cards, wipe out bank accounts, destroy corporate computers. White hats, on the other hand, hacked you so you could improve your computer security against the black hats.

Tony said, "Dude, Cowboy Donut is totally exposed. Their wireless is like fishnet. I'm parked on their root drive."

"You're not going inside."

"It's a quick three hundred dollars," Tony said. "I take my laptop in, tell them I think they might be exposed. When they tell me to show my stuff, I get in, freak them out a bit. Then I secure their system. Hold a training session. Boom, a little cash for Yeti, Inc. Three hundred bucks, man. And then I can sport us some real food. No man should have to eat rocks."

They were down to the last jar of peanut butter, the last few tins of sardines, which were high in essential omega-3's. They weren't anywhere close to eating rocks.

"Dude, Yeti is here for you."

Yeti Inc. was the name of the company Tony had set up back home in Los Angeles. He even had a business card. Across the top it asked the question: *Is your system secure enough to block a teenage hacker?* Below that was the name of the company in big letters followed by *Providing White Hat Audits & Cyber Security Training* at the bottom.

Kim, Frank's sister, said Tony actually made money down in L.A. selling his services to mom and pop stores, although he'd almost gone to jail once before he figured out you don't reveal to someone that you hacked into their system, even if you're trying to do them a favor. It's kind of like breaking and entering to peek on the Mrs. while she's in the shower before trying to sell her some door locks. It's both alarming and illegal. Not the best way to start off a hacker-client relationship.

Frank opened the car door and got in. He worked part-time graveyard at Walmart, stocking shelves. "You're not sporting us nothing," he said. "My Wally check is coming this Friday. I'm good till then." Which was a lie. The money wasn't nearly enough. But he wasn't taking charity from his nephew.

"Dude, they're fishnet."

"They'll think it's some kind of con." He inserted the keys in the ignition.

"They won't."

"Ms. Mary will. I would. Big ugly guy just out of prison goes in first to case the place, posing as an interviewee. She'll think I did something, pilfered a password or loaded something when she wasn't looking."

Tony said, "Ms. Mary and the fine folks of Cowboy Donut are naked to anyone who comes along. They're just waiting for someone to steal them blind. You going to do that to them?"

Frank held out the bear claw to Tony. "Here," he said. "Why don't you work that mouth on this?"

Tony took the bear claw. "Okay, Frankie," he said. "A man's gotta follow his conscience, or his lack thereof."

"Look," Frank said, "whether I get the job or don't get the job, we'll come back and let you ride in on your white hat and save them. But not before. There is such a thing as timing."

"Dude, I can't eat another peanut butter and sugar sandwich. Maybe you can borrow out of that jar you keep on the shelf in the kitchen. Just until Friday."

Tony knew he wouldn't. That was blood money, sacred money, and nobody was going to touch that, which was another reason why the Wally check didn't stretch as far as it might. "Man up, soldier. On Friday, we have steaks." They would be old ones that were going to be thrown out by the meat guys, but they'd be steaks nevertheless.

Tony sighed. "I think I'm getting rickets."

"You're definitely getting something," Frank said. He pumped the gas three times, then turned the ignition.

The old Nova roared to life. It roared mostly because it lacked part of its exhaust pipe. There were other things missing as well: knobs, radio, an engine mount. A number of gaskets were leaking. There were dings and tears. But she ran, and that was a start. She'd get a new engine with aluminum heads. Some paint and body work, and she was going to shine up real nice. All she needed was honest work.

Frank backed out of the parking stall and then rumbled onto Dewar Drive. His gas gauge said empty. He usually had about twelve more miles at that point—he knew because he'd run out twice and ended up having to push it. But the gauge had hit empty yesterday, which meant they has less than twelve. He'd need to stop and put in a few shekels' worth soon. The problem was he really didn't have money for gas, so he'd just have to hope they made it home and found something left in the can he used for the lawn mower.

He sighed. "When we get back, I'm going running," he said. He'd never really liked running as a kid. Never liked it when he was in the Army later. But he'd missed it in prison. Almost as much as he'd missed the shine and smell of a woman's hair. Almost as much as fries, coleslaw, and ribs. Sometimes he missed it more than either of them. There were times when he'd wake in his cell, the dream of rucking a pack over hills and through woods still looping about him. There were a number of days where holding the remnants of that sweet dream of running free in the sunlight was all that had kept the blackness away.

And it was running that now kept him focused on the future instead of the bright and happy moments like his excellent interview at Cowboy Donut. The exertion would also clear his mind. Let him think.

There had to be a way out of his non-employment cage. Frank was a man with dreams. He was still in his thirties. He still had the possibility of a long, happy life ahead of him, but he was going to need a lot more cash than Uncle Wally provided for what he was planning.

"I'll run part of the way with you," Tony said, "but you're all crazy with that running crap."

"Fair enough," Frank said.

They cruised back toward the center of town, Frank's worries bearing down on him. "We're not in a nuclear war," Frank said, trying to keep himself positive.

Tony pointed at a police car coming the other way. "And that guy isn't coming for you. That's a positive."

Frank's heart jumped a little at the sight of the patrol car. When it was closer, he saw that Sergeant Lee sat behind the wheel. Rock Springs liked to keep tabs on its felons, and Lee had paid him a friendly welcome visit not long after he'd moved in. Frank waved at Sergeant Lee. Sergeant Lee waved back. No reason not to be on waving terms.

"That is indeed a positive," Frank said. He hung his arm out the window to feel the wind. "And it's a glorious sunny day. An amazing day to be out of a cement box."

"What else could a man want?" Tony asked.

The car chugged. "Gas," Frank said. But then the engine picked right back up where it left off, and they continued on to the house he was renting north of the cemetery in the old section of town. On the way, he and Tony finished off the bear claw and licked their fingers, which he supposed was another positive.

They pulled up to the house. It wasn't much. An old 1950s bungalow that hadn't been updated since the 1970s. It was barely 900 square feet, if that. But Frank thanked the Lord every day for it, orange counter tops and all. Besides, it was only temporary. Frank had himself a five year plan. He'd work like a dog now, save up some cash. He'd get himself through technical school. And along the way he'd accumulate himself some assets. Five years from now Frank was going to be in a different situation entirely.

There was a driveway and stand-alone garage on one end of the house; on the other end, an empty cement RV pad ran all the way into the backyard. Frank backed into the driveway and saw that someone had left something on the front door step. He parked and cut the engine. The car bucked and kicked, fighting to stay alive a bit longer, obviously much preferring to be out on the road. Actually, it dieseled because he couldn't get the blasted timing right. But that too would be fixed. The car and Frank were on this journey together.

He and Tony got out. Tony went for the mailbox at the curb. Frank walked over to the front door. A plate of homemade cookies wrapped up in blue cellophane sat on the stoop. Frank picked the plate up. A business card from Sam Cartwright, the local neighborhood nice guy, had been stapled to it. He tore off the business card, put it in his shirt pocket, and opened the cellophane. Chocolate chip cookies. Last time it had been homemade bread.

"Food," Frank called out to Tony. Another positive. A healthy addition to his cuisine of sardines on toast. "I think that Mormon's trying to make me fat."

"He's just buttering you up for their missionaries," Tony said, crossing the lawn with a handful of what looked like junk mail. "It's like that witch with Hansel and Gretel."

"I'll be sure to look for indications of cannibalism."

"I'm telling you," Tony said.

Frank said, "That Mormon's the one who greased the wheels for me at Walmart."

"And you don't think that's suspicious?" Tony asked. "Who goes making friends with ex-cons? I bet it's all part of some racket."

"Maybe you can penetrate their networks and find out the truth."

"Maybe," Tony agreed.

Frank put his key in the lock and turned, but the door was already unlocked, which was wrong. He always locked both doors to the house.

He swung the door open, took two steps inside, and stopped. Tony pushed past and stopped as well.

A man stood in the entry leading from the kitchen. He was a little under six feet, wearing a black leather vest over a denim shirt. He had a dark goatee and receding hair line, but the hair he did have was a bit long and mussed like he'd been riding in the wind, like he was Mister Born To Be Wild. He held a nine millimeter gun in his hand. A Springfield XD-9 subcompact.

Frank knew the man. Knew him far too well. He also knew that he had the subcompact, not because it was easy to conceal carry. Ed Meese needed the small gun because of the size of his idiot baby girl hands. The Springfield wasn't a bad gun, even the subcompact, but a gun was the last thing that man should be holding. Not with where he'd been.

"Jockstrap," the man said with a wide-mouthed grin. "We just about figured we'd come to the wrong place. You had us worried."

In the kitchen, someone scraped back a chair.

Frank bristled all over. "What are you doing in my house, Ed?"

Ed looked all surprised at Frank's tone. "That's no way to talk to a friend."

"You're not my friend, Ed."

"No gratitude," he sweetly reprimanded. "I saved your life."

"You did."

"Well, Frankie boy, now I'm coming to collect."

2

White Hat

FRANK WASN'T ON parole anymore, but he was on a journey, and the conditions he'd set for himself were similar. And they were clear. The first was that you did not have any contact with other convicted felons. Having contact with someone like Ed would get you a free ticket back to the big house.

It would also probably get you infested with roaches. Maybe give you a flesh-eating skin disease. Ed looked fine on the exterior. He was all smiles and clean teeth and had gone to prison for nothing bigger than a small drug rap, but that small-time criminal bit was a facade.

Spend three minutes with him and you'd know something was a little off. Five minutes and a faint warning would start sounding in the back of your mind. Spend two years sleeping above him, listening to his jabber, smelling his excrement, and there wouldn't be any doubt. Frank had lifted the lid on Ed's soul and found a wriggling tangle of two-headed snakes roiling in a filthy backwater. Frank was all for rehabilitation, but there were some folks who'd gone rotten to the core. Some folks who couldn't be fixed, at least not in this life. There were some folks who simply needed to be culled from the herd.

Frank said, "Here's the deal, Ed. You're going to leave right now, and I'm not going to break your neck."

Ed grinned. "I don't think so."

The person in the kitchen began to walk toward the front room. Each step knocked clearly on the old brown octagonal-patterned linoleum like maybe he was wearing cowboy boots or dress shoes. Something with a hard heel. He stepped into view behind Ed and stopped.

"Jockstrap," Ed said, all pleased with himself, "say hello to Jesus."

Jesus was Hispanic. He was taller than Ed. He was north of two hundred pounds, and most likely pronounced his name as "Hey-SOOS," not "GEE-zus" as Ed did. His face was pock-marked and rippled, like something knobby was growing there. There were tattoos on his arms, a sleeve of them around his neck. The blue gothic script on his neck tagged him as Mara Salvatrucha, MS-13, which meant Frank had not only a felon but also a member of one of the nation's finest upstanding drug gangs in his house. Excellent. The neighbors were bound to love that.

The tattoo on his upper arm and shoulder marked him as a follower of Santa Muerte, Saint Death, the cult saint of the narcos and poor. Frank had seen these tattoos in prison. Some were of a grim reaper. Others were of a dead woman's face, stitched lips, black eyes rimmed with the petals of flowers, a spiderweb on her forehead. This was the classical version, a play on the image of Saint Guadalupe—a skeleton in the robe of a holy order belted with a rope, hands pressed together in prayer. About her was a cloak of stars. Rays of light like sharp yucca leaves ringed her, shining out to indicate her holiness. The original Saint Guadalupe stood in flowers. This one stood in a vine of roses mixed with the skulls of the dead.

Nice. But it wasn't the tattoos that told Frank this situation had gone from orange to red. It was Jesus's eyes. They were flat and lifeless. The spark of remorse and sympathy had been sucked out of them. There was no smile to those eyes. There was nothing human there at all. Jesus was nothing more than a shell of bones and flesh. Frank had plenty of experience with a collection of such shells during his years in the fine Pleasant Valley state prison in Coalinga, California.

"Tony," Frank said, "why don't you go out and mow the lawn."

Tony had read the situation as well. His face showed a bit of alarm, but that quickly started to turn into something else.

"Go on," Frank said. "We're just going to talk."

"Ooh," Ed said as if impressed, "he's got himself a Tony. I didn't think you swung that way, Frank. But I will hand it to you—he's young and sweet. Sweet enough to tempt even me to take a dip from that honey pot."

Frank nodded at door with his chin. "Go," he said to Tony.

Tony went. He glanced up at Frank on the way out. His jaw was set; there were small sparks of anger in his eyes. The kid's mind was whirring; Frank could see that. Tony did not like jerk morons. He did not like being pushed around.

"Just mow the lawn," Frank warned. "Okay?"

"Sure," Tony said and pushed out the door.

A few more years and bit more muscle, and Tony would be exactly the kind of operator you'd want with you behind enemy lines. But not just yet. Not here. Not now. Not with these two.

With Tony outside, Frank turned back to Ed and Jesus. "Who gave you my address?" Frank demanded.

"A little bird," Ed said. "Just making sure I keep tabs on my friends."

More like tabs on those he thought owed him, folks he could exploit. Ed was always talking about keeping score. He probably had a book like a businessman for collections. Problem was, there was no way Ed could have known this address, not unless he had someone inside the California justice system who could have gotten into the records and read it to him. Frank had tried to cut all ties, to break away from old acquaintances and haunts, to change the patterns that would work to suck him back into his old life. Frank had come to Wyoming to start fresh. And here Ed was, like a chigger wanting to dig in.

Ed moved into the front room and motioned nonchalantly with his gun at the couch and chairs. "Sit down; let's talk."

Frank didn't move. "No time to chat. You're on your way out."

"Frank," Ed said, "you're talking to me, your cellie."

Ed stood about three strides away. Not too far if Frank was fast. It had been almost seven years now, but the old skills had been burned into him. No way he'd be as fast or as exact in his moves as he'd once been, but he'd been trained to disarm men like Ed.

Then what? Jesus would be carrying. He'd pull. Or not. Who knew? Maybe Ed was carrying another piece. Or maybe he wasn't. There was a good chance Frank would walk the two of them out at gun point. But there was also a good chance he'd have to put one or both down. That was the truth written in Jesus's lifeless brown eyes.

Officer Lee and his pals would not look kindly upon a dead body and a few pints of blood in the living room. Not kindly at all. Even if it was the result of Frank ridding the world of a bit of filth. "What do you want, Ed?"

Outside, the garage door rattled up. Moments later the mower kicked to life and droned.

"Here's the thing, Frank. Jesus and I have had a big day, getting some old-time religion out west; we talked to some of them Mormon missionaries, picked up an extra wife." He grinned at his own joke. "We're bushed. We just need a place to crash. Maybe a new set of wheels. I saw that junkyard you drove up in. We've got a nice Nissan out back. Let us borrow it."

"You drove hours just to switch me cars? Is that it, Ed?"

"You were on the way. Why not stop in? Besides, we've been going since early yesterday morning. Driving sleepy is as bad as driving drunk. We're trying to be responsible citizens and keep the roads safe. We just need a bed."

"Get a room at a motel."

Ed sighed and dropped the old buddy routine. "Frank, you owe me. You yourself said you owed me. Now it's time to pay up. I'm not asking anything unreasonable."

"You're not staying here. I'm not putting anything on the line. Not for you and especially not Señor Zombie there."

"Okay," Ed said, "but I do need your car. You're going to give me your car."

Jesus had his hand behind his back, up under his untucked shirt. So that's where he carried his piece. Or maybe that's where he carried a knife. Maybe he'd used that knife to saw the heads off of a couple of victims south of the border.

Jesus was giving him the eye.

Frank gave him the eye back. "What? You want this?"

Jesus cocked his head, his expression begging Frank to say one more word, to just give him an excuse to pull his hand out of the back of his pants.

Frank cocked his head and invited Jesus right back. Señor Zombie was big, but not as big as Frank. And there was a bit of a gut on him. He'd looked like one of those brawlers that could take a punch, and from the looks of his nose he'd taken a few. But Frank hadn't been trained to dink around giving punches. He hadn't been trained to brawl. If Jesus wanted to throw down, it would be the last time he did.

The tension ratcheted up, and then Señor Zombie's eyes slid to the side. He shook his head and looked over at Ed. "It's time to blow," he said.

"Give us the keys," Ed said in a hard flat tone. "Jesus is going to move some bags. And we'll be out of your hair."

Frank had heard that tone of voice before. He knew Ed meant business.

Frank didn't have any good options. Their car was dirty, no doubt about that. It was stolen, or they'd been tagged in it, or they were being followed. Or it was something else. It didn't matter—the car was a liability every minute it was around. Which meant Frank was going to have to get rid of it.

But that wouldn't solve his problem because if Ed had Frank's car and something happened, if they pawned the Nova off to someone else who got into trouble, the VIN would go into some cop's computer and a moment later point directly back to him. It would reach across state lines, and the next thing he knew, here'd come Sergeant Lee with his sunny cop pals.

Ed was taking a risk coming here. He was into something. Something that might require leaving no witnesses. Suddenly Frank didn't think it was such a good idea to be in this house with the two of them. It was a lot easier to kill someone behind four walls than outside where some nosey neighbor might see.

Frank said, "Sure, I'll give you the keys. Outside." Then he backed up a step, and before they could say anything, he opened the front door and walked out to the porch.

Ed and Jesus shared a moment of silent communication, and then Ed shrugged. He slipped his gun in his vest and said, "I knew you'd see it my way, buddy." Then he walked out and joined Frank on the porch. Jesus followed.

Ed smelled of cigarettes. Señor Zombie had some kind of rancid medicine breath, the kind that reached out three or four feet to shake your hand. He walked past Frank down the steps and around to the side of the house where the RV pad lay, dragging his bad breath with him.

Ed stayed on the porch, took in a big breath of air. "We're going to use your garage," he said. "Jesus will bring the car around. It will be easier to switch the bags in there."

Frank glanced back into the house and noticed his blood money jar stood on the counter. It was empty.

"You took money out of the jar in my kitchen."

"Jar?" Ed said all innocent. "What are you talking about?"

He should pound Ed right here. One-on-one. Take his gun and deal with Jesus. But Tony was out there.

Ed smiled and moved down the steps and out onto the lawn. "Thinking can get you killed," he said.

"When are you going to bring my car back?"

"Oh, we'll get it back to you tomorrow at the latest."

Right, and there were gold bricks in Frank's basement. "You'd better have it back. And the money better be on the seat. That car and I are on a journey, Ed. Don't mess with my journey."

Some kids a street over squealed with delight. In the distance someone honked a car's horn. Then Frank noticed the lawn mower wasn't running. It hadn't been running for four or five minutes.

Frank looked for Tony, and then Señor Zombie cursed from around the corner of the house and shouted for Ed.

Ed looked at Frank with one of those "what did you do?" looks and then ran toward the corner of the house, his black vest all shiny in the sun. Frank followed. The concrete RV pad on that side of the house ran along a wooden fence between his yard and the next door neighbor's all the way to another fence at the back. Tall junipers grew along that back fence, shading a two-toned silver and gray Nissan that sat below them.

Frank and Tony had driven up from the other direction; they'd pulled into the driveway on the other side of the house, and, therefore, had missed seeing the Nissan. The car was chopped low and had windows dark as cola. Jesus stood at the back end, the trunk high and open, showing nothing inside. "Gone," he said.

"What do you mean *gone*?" Ed asked.

Jesus pulled back his top lip tight with anger. "Gone," he said.

Ed's eyes narrowed, then his face took on a feral look. "I don't hear a lawn mower, Frank. I thought Tony was supposed to be mowing the lawn." He reached into his vest and pulled out his gun.

At that moment, on the other side of the house, the Nova rumbled to life.

Both Ed and Jesus looked at each other and then turned and ran toward the sound. Jesus raced through the backyard; Ed took the front.

But they were too slow. The Nova shot out of the driveway. It bounced out onto the street with a scrape and turned in front of the house with a squeal of rubber. Tony sat in the driver's seat, both hands at the wheel. In the passenger's seat was a woman in her early twenties. She had dark hair. She looked Hispanic. She held her hands up in front of her like she was praying, except her wrists were bound together with a long white zip tie.

Tony floored it. The Nova's engine roared, and the front of the car lifted a bit as the vehicle accelerated. Tony glanced over, saw Frank, and then he was gone, hurtling past the neighbor's lot and down the road.

Not bad acceleration for an old piece of junk. Frank just wished Tony had decided to race in more friendly circumstances.

Ed shouted over the roof for Jesus to get back to the Nissan, then he came at Frank, gun in hand, murder in his eyes. He stopped maybe four feet away and pointed the barrel right at Frank's face.

The hackles raised on the back of Frank's neck. "Put it down," he said.

"You call that boy back here!"

"My phone's inside," Frank lied. "Half the time I don't carry it with me."

"You call him now!" Ed said through clenched teeth.

In the backyard, the higher-pitched Nissan motor raced. Then Jesus and the Nissan came barreling out in reverse, the motor whining. He slammed on the brakes.

"You have no idea!" Ed said. "You stupid pile. That boy just bought himself a plot." Then he ran over to the Nissan, skirted around the back, and slid into the passenger's side.

Jesus was cranked around, looking out the back window. He floored it before Ed could shut his door. The Nissan hit the road with a loud scrape, swung around and stopped. Then Jesus threw it into drive and squealed out after Tony and the Nova, Ed's door still hanging open.

Frank's mind reeled. What in the Sam Hill?

A girl in the trunk?

That Nissan wasn't dirty. And they weren't transporting drugs. It was a ransom. Or a hit. Except if you want to kill someone in Wyoming, there were miles and miles of lonely roads to do it on. No reason to give someone a bus ride in the trunk. Just do it and be done and leave her in the dirt. The vultures and skunks would be on her within twenty-four hours.

Frank pulled out his phone, fumbled for Tony's number.

At the end of the street, the Nova squealed round the corner. It accelerated then squealed again. Tony was coming back along the street behind the house.

There was no use using a phone when a face-to-face would do. So Frank stuffed the phone into his pants pocket and then sprinted into his backyard. He leapt onto a pile of old firewood that had been stacked against the fence and grabbed the top of the wooden slats. The junipers here were too thick to let him hop the fence, but he sprang up anyway, got a toe on the top of the fence and pushed his way through the prickly branches and fell into the neighbor's backyard. He landed sideways and scrambled up.

The neighbors had one of those little annoying white dogs with curly hair and weeping eyes that stained the fur on its face. It came yapping out from its spot in front of the sliding glass door. Frank ignored it. He ran past a kiddie pool, a ball, and some plastic toys that had been left out on the lawn. The neighbor kids were sitting at their kitchen table in swimming suits, watching him through the glass. Frank ran for the front gate, unlatched it, and slammed it behind him, right in front of the yap-dog, which was snarling like the devil himself had just run by. Lucky for Frank he'd had a head start. One more step and the thing might have launched a full-out attack on his ankles.

Frank ran down the driveway and out into the street. The Nova was at the far end of the street, barreling in his direction.

3

Sam

FRANK WAVED, TRYING to get Tony's attention, worrying about some kid riding out into the street or running after a ball because there wouldn't be any stopping. But Tony didn't see Frank and turned at the street half a block down.

Farther back, the Nissan squealed round the corner.

Frank looked around for a projectile. There was nothing but fences and lawns and curb. Never a good-sized stone when you needed one. Nothing but the annoying mutt from the yap patrol that sounded like it was working on an aneurysm. Too bad it didn't have more heft. He would have happily used it to smash Ed's windshield. Then he spotted a row of white bricks across the street. They were standing up at a diagonal, acting as a border between a lawn and flower bed full of puffy orange marigolds. He raced over to the yard, yanked two bricks out, and charged down the street at Ed and Jesus in their Nissan.

He was about half a house away when they reached the corner Tony had taken. Frank hurled the first brick as hard as he could, followed with the second. The bricks arched high. Ed and Jesus squealed around the corner. The first brick sailed completely over the car. The second struck the Nissan in the panel over the rear tire, made a huge clunk, and fell to the ground.

Jesus put on the gas, and the Nissan bolted forward, racing after Tony. So much for bringing bricks to a car fight.

Frank ran out into the middle of the road and watched the Nissan speed down the street. Tony was heading south, probably trying to lose them in the residential streets on the east of the cemetery and then get out to the belt route. But he wasn't going to outrun them, not in that Nova. And where would he go once he got out of the neighborhood?

Tony! What had he been thinking!

Probably exactly what any man with a speck of humanity and courage would when finding a woman locked in a trunk. Especially when she was locked in by two fine pieces of work like Ed Meese and his friend Jesus.

Frank could call the cops, but how long would it take to get his report, call it out, and then get someone to respond? And that's if they even could respond.

Frank grabbed his cell, slid it open, and thumbed down for Tony's number. He hit the green button to dial then started to run, not south after Tony or the Nissan, but north. He held the phone to his ear and began to run down the middle of the road, his tan work boots slapping the asphalt.

Tony needed to go west. He needed to get on Thompson, run along the north side of the cemetery, or go around the south end, then get himself to the sheriff's office on C Street. It was just a few blocks away. He needed to pull right in, horn blaring. Let Ed and the zombie pull in behind him. No sense waiting for the cops when he could go right to them.

Tony's phone rang. Rang again. *Come on, Tony, pick up!*

Frank reached the top of hill on G Street and ran down the other side. The steep hilly streets were like something out of a baby San Francisco. Lines of bouncy tar squiggled across the asphalt like thin black snakes where the road crew had been filling cracks.

G Street was so narrow the drivers had to parallel park their cars with half the car up on the curb to make room for one lane down the middle. The street was in an old residential neighborhood filled with small bungalows and ramblers from a time when a house cost $7,000 dollars. The front yards had small front lawns, some behind chain link. Willows and elms, stunted by the harsh Wyoming climate, grew out over the narrow street. The leaves rustled in the hot wind. Frank ran down past the houses and the cars, the incline letting him stretch his stride and pour on the speed. Tony's phone kept ringing.

A vehicle turned onto the narrow road behind him. He glanced back. It was an old green Suburban with a mismatched door panel. He moved over and waved the driver for help.

The woman behind the wheel gave him an alarmed look, punched the gas, and sped on by.

Frank must have been scowling in the hot sun, must have looked like a mad dog. Problem was he didn't think he could do bunny rabbit at the moment. There was a tower of anger rising up in him. Who did Ed think he was? Frank had a life going here. That girl had a life, although who knew if she was clean or some nasty piece of drug work? More importantly, Tony had a life, bless his freaking white hat head.

Tony's phone went to voicemail.

Frank cursed, cut the call, and dialed again.

He ran past a yard where a Daschund and some other bigger mutt charged the chain link to bark at him. He ran past an old woman digging in a bed of flowers that was looked over by a fat and happy gnome. He ran past a place where the lawn looked like each blade had been tended with a pair of scissors and watered every day and another place that looked like they'd used gasoline on it. He kept running, big old strides thumping the asphalt, his work boots feeling large and loose on his feet.

Up ahead, a dozen kids were squealing at a birthday party out in front of a blue house. They had balloons and a clown with yellow hair. *Clowns?* What kind of parents invited clowns to their kid's party? Clowns had to be one of the scariest things on the planet. Ed probably had clowns at his parties when he was a kid. In fact, Frank was willing to wager that if you did the research, you'd find clowns featuring prominently in every serial killer's history.

Frank ran past the kids and their horror show and turned onto New Hampshire.

Tony's phone was still ringing. "Pick up!" he growled. "Pick the phone up!"

Tony picked up.

"Tony!" Frank said.

"Frank—"

"Shut up and listen. Get to C Street. Lead them to the sheriff's office."

"Sheriff's? Down past the bowling alley?"

The police station was by the bowling alley. The sheriff's office was about half a mile closer. "No, the other end of C."

The phone went quiet. Frank stopped running and stood in the middle of the road. "Are you there?"

"I'm here—"

Now was not the time to give five minutes of directions. "Just get to the cops. Forget the sheriff. Go to the station by the bowling alley. You hear me?"

No response.

"Tony!"

Frank looked down at the phone. The call was gone. He pressed dial again; it rang and went directly to voicemail. He broke the call, dialed again. This time he hit the speaker button then lit out with all the speed he could muster. He came to the end of New Hampshire, turned on Massachusetts. The phone rang and rang. He cut across a vacant lot and field at the back of the Boy and Girl Scout office, and emerged on C Street.

To his left, next to the Scout office, stood the sheriff's office. Frank ran past and turned right toward the police station.

He dialed Tony again, then prayed the Lord to let him make it, let him make it, let him make it, even though Frank didn't know how easily the prayers of an ex-con rose up into the ears of deity. The call went to voicemail. Frank dialed again, the speaker playing the tone, and he continued to hoof it down the middle of C Street, his boots eating up the pavement. It was still residential here, same 1950s and 1960s bungalows, some with green siding, some with rust red, most with white. The sun was hot, shining off of the chrome and windshields of the parked cars with bright little spots of arc light. The phone rang and rang and rang and went to voicemail again. He killed the call. Maybe Tony was trying to get through on his end.

Frank ran a few more blocks and entered the commercial district. He ran past the bowling alley, through the intersection on 2nd, and arrived at the police station. He turned into the narrow parking lot at the back, but Tony and the Nova weren't there. He skirted around front.

Nothing.

On the pole at the station, the flags of the United States and the great state of Wyoming snapped in the wind. Stars and stripes over a buffalo.

The parking in front of the station spanned the whole block. Frank ran through the parked cars to the D Street side, ran around the back corner there. But there was no Tony. No Nova. No Nissan. No nothing.

Had he gone to the sheriff's after all? Frank prepared to run back when the phone rang. Tony's name came up on the screen.

Frank pushed the answer button. "Where are you? You okay?"

"I can't come to the station, Frank."

A chill shot right to Frank's core. "If Ed has you, say the word 'five' into the phone."

"No, Ed's out of the picture right now. It's the girl."

"What do you mean? She got a gun to your head?"

"More like box cutters. To the throat."

"Box cutters?"

"I used them to cut the zip ties on her wrists and ankles."

"Hang up," a woman said behind Tony. She had a Spanish accent.

"We'll be okay, Frank. She just wants to get out of town. She says not to call the cops. She says they're dirty."

"Tell her you'll let her out."

"She doesn't want to get out here."

Who knew what this woman was strung out on? Who knew what she might do? "This isn't happening."

"I think it's happening, Frank."

Frank took the calmest tone he could. He needed to keep Tony focused. "Tell me where you are. Tell me your direction."

"We're on the belt route. I'm going to try to get to I—"

There was a double tone then nothing. Frank looked down at the phone. He knew Tony wouldn't answer if he called back.

I-80. Tony was going to I-80, but was he going to get on at the north, east, or west end of town. And which direction would he go then?

Frank took a calming breath. He needed to get his mind straight. Needed to put it into gear. Needed to start listing his options.

A kidnapped woman had box cutters at his nephew's throat. She didn't want to go to the cops. Maybe she was from some rival organization, a criminal in her own right. Or something else. Didn't matter. Frank was right here at the station. He could walk in and spill the whole story. They'd call it out. They'd share it with the sheriff's office and the Highway Patrol. He could have a dozen eyes on the street, minus those that were otherwise engaged and those too far out to be of any help. He turned to go into the station and then stopped.

He had no doubt the Rock Springs officers were good. But he'd learned long ago that delegating sometimes meant the job didn't get done. If he sequenced it right, he could get all those officer eyes plus his own. All he needed was a vehicle.

He looked at the cars in the parking lot. No way was he going to steal a car here. And he didn't have to. He fetched the business card that had been stapled to the cookies on his doorstep out of his pocket. Didn't Sam, the happy neighborhood Mormon man, work around here?

Frank turned the card over and looked at the address. Sam Cartwright, accountant by day, cookie man by night. He was a few blocks down and across the tracks. Frank punched Sam's number into his phone.

Sam picked up on the second ring. "Good afternoon, this is Sam."

"Sam, this is Frank Shaw—"

"Frank, my man. You're eating those cookies right now, aren't you? You're a puddle of joy on the floor. You're calling to thank me."

"Actually—"

"Dude, that recipe is contraband. Contraband! Half-a-dozen caterers in this town would kill to get that."

"Sam, look, you told me to call if I needed anything. Bro, I got a situation. It's crisis. Condition red."

Sam's voice modulated to a serious tone. "What's going on, Frank?"

"It's a long story. But I need a car." Frank knew how that sounded. "You can drive. I'm not asking to take your car."

"That old Nova finally gave up the ghost?"

"Tony's been abducted."

There was a pause. "What?"

"They're still in the city. I need some help, Sam."

"Holy crap, Frank. Did you call the cops?"

"I'm going to call them, but we need all the eyes and ears possible on this. There are only so many officers in this town. Every minute counts."

"Right," Sam said.

"Can you come?"

Silence. Frank thought he was going to make an excuse, and then Sam said, "Tony's a good kid. You bet your boots I'll come."

"Let me meet you. You in the office or out with a client?"

"I'm at home."

"Okay. I'll be running your way on D Street. Come as quick as you can. Bring something fast. Something tall so we can see is even better."

"I'm heading out the door right now."

Frank shook his head; what kind of people were like that? People that were too naive or had some angle, that's who. Maybe Sam did have a racket going. Maybe he thought Frank had some ex-con criminal connections that might come in handy some day. He was going to be disappointed. But it didn't matter what Sam's scheme was—Sam had wheels, and that's what Frank needed at this particular moment.

Frank ended the call and punched in 9-1-1. He wrestled with what to tell them. Did he go into MS-13? Did he talk about Ed's connections to some drug lord named Rico and his supposed western state operation. Ed had said he was Mr. Logistics for the guy, Mr. Get Her Done. Which could have all been a bunch of blather. Frank decided not to go into all that. Not now. What they needed to know was that Tony had been kidnapped. He started to run, phone ringing in his ear.

The dispatcher picked up. Frank identified himself, told her about the kidnapping, described Tony, the car, and the woman. The dispatcher took the information. Asked him for his contact info. Asked him if he could come in with a picture, or email it. Frank said he was on the street looking for the kidnappers that very moment and wasn't near a computer. Told her Tony had been heading toward I-80. Then he hung up and began to run. Big-booted strides.

His phone rang. It was the dispatcher. He let it ring.

He ran across the intersection on D and 2nd, past the bowling alley on the back side, past the lumber store and into the old residential part of town. He approached the fuel oil dealer with the yard full of oil tanks stacked up next to the fence. Sam should have been here by now. Frank swore Sam had a Mustang. Not tall, but fast. It would do just fine.

Up ahead, tires squealed. A motor raced. The tires squealed again and some soccer mom with serious road rage came around the corner up ahead in her baby blue Mazda minivan.

Come on, Sam. Come on.

And then Frank saw that the soccer mom wasn't a soccer mom. It was Sam, driving like a bat out of Hell.

Sam saw him, flashed his headlights, then hit the brakes hard and pulled over in a rush of debris. He leaned over and opened the passenger door. "Where we headed?"

A minivan? Seriously? But beggars couldn't be choosers. "Dewar and I-80," Frank said and slid in. A box of wet wipes lay at his feet. He picked it up and tossed it into the back seat. Cheerios had spilled out down the center aisle along with a lime green ball and some plastic robot toys. A jumble of other stuff rose from behind the back seat, including some fat PVC pipes.

Sam was in his thirties, medium height and build, clean shaven, tidy shirt, tidy accountant hair. He was a little overweight, not in a fat greasy sloppy way, but in a cuddly, chubby, happy way. Like a good luck charm.

Frank had never seen Sam without a Bluetooth receiver in ear. He was wearing one now. "I-80, out past Walmart," he confirmed to some-one on the phone.

Frank said, "I'll tell you which direction on I-80 when we get there."

"You got it, buddy." Sam looked in his mirrors. A car was coming up behind, but Sam put on his blinker, stepped on the gas, and the Mazda shot out into the road in front of it.

The person behind laid on his horn and slammed on his brakes.

Sam glanced in the mirror. "I put on my blinker, buddy," he said.

"Thanks for coming," Frank said.

"No problem."

The Mazda was small as minivans went, but it accelerated well enough to escape the driver blaring his horn behind. "This thing has a couple of gerbils under the hood."

"Couple?" Sam asked. "It's got a whole village, complete with a town square."

Frank was sitting up so high he was looking through the shaded top of the windshield. He fumbled around for seat controls, but only found a lever to lower the back of the seat.

"The wife's got the pickup," Sam said. "Otherwise, I would have brought that."

"This moves. It's better than roller skates."

"I can get more help."

"What do you mean?"

"I can make some calls."

Who would Sam call? The Mormon pastor? "I don't think the missionaries on their bikes are going to be much help at this point," Frank said.

Sam's eyes widened like a light bulb had just flashed in his head. "The missionaries have a car. I didn't think of them, but I could call them too."

"I already called 911," Frank said. "We're good."

They raced past the fuel oil place, took a hard left, worked their way out onto Blair which ran parallel to the train tracks. The whole time Frank scanned for the Nova.

When they crossed over the tracks onto Dewar, Sam said, "Hey, Honey."

Frank looked over at him.

"Yeah, I've got the van. I'm a little busy now. Mind if I call you back?" There was a pause, then, "Chow," and Sam turned onto Dewar.

Frank decided yet again that phones in the ear were just plain wrong. Who walked around making everyone you passed think you were talking to them?

Sam kept his eyes on the road. "So who did this? Why in the world would they want Tony?"

"It's kind of complicated."

"More complicated than the tax code?"

"Probably not," Frank said, "but I'll give you the details later. Right now I want to focus."

They drove past the ridge of short cliffs and the strip mall. Frank searched the parking lots. They passed pickups and SUVs and an old Honda coming the other way. There was no Tony.

"I figure it's not some random kidnapping," Sam said. "Who kidnaps teenagers in broad daylight?"

"Not too many people around here."

Sam weaved past two vehicles that were slowing for a turn. He said, "A car pulled up to your house after I'd dropped off that plate. Colorado plates. They didn't look much like choir boys, Frank."

"They're not, Sam. Either one would kill you. They had a girl in their trunk. Tony sprang her."

Sam's mouth hung open in surprise. Then he recovered. "So they caught him, and abducted the both of them?"

"No, Tony and the girl made an escape in the Nova."

"So he wasn't abducted?"

"She's holding a box cutter to his throat. She didn't want to go to the cops. Our choir boys are after them."

A car pulled into their lane up ahead, and Sam juked into the lane next to it. "Choir boys, huh? I can do choir boys."

Frank looked over at him. Looked at the toys in the back, the princess DVDs in a case in between the seats. Some unicorn and star stickers clung to the glove box where one of Sam's numerous small kids had undoubtedly put them. Frank had a nose for people. No way Sam had some ulterior ex-con crime connection scheme going. No way. Which meant Sam probably got his ideas about choir boys like Jesus and Ed from TV. He'd probably never seen a real bad guy in his whole life. Never been in a situation where the wrong move meant somebody died. "Well, Sam," Frank said, "then it's good thing you're along. Now we just need to find Tony."

"Roger that," Sam said. He picked up a blue bottle from a holder, took a long drag, then held it out to Frank. "Vitamin water?"

The lip of the bottle glistened with the residue of Sam's sucking lips.

"Thanks, I'm good. You watch the road."

Frank gave this rescue chase 50-50 odds. Then he thought of all that could happen to Tony before he got to the interstate, and those chances started to plummet.

4

Nova

FRANK LOOKED AHEAD at the I-80 interchange. Tony knew the Nova wasn't a freeway car. Not only did it start to shimmy like a hoochie when the speedometer hit sixty-two, but the old engine was tired. You had to be going downhill to even reach that speed.

There was nothing but interstate and high country desert for a hundred miles east of Rock Springs. Everybody drove eighty-five. So if he tried an interstate escape that way, the Nissan would soon catch up without even breaking the legal speed limit. East was no place to run. Frank had to assume Tony would see that.

On the other hand, if he went west, it was only seventeen miles to Green River. Lots of streets. Lots of hiding places. More cops.

Tony had been heading south-east when Frank had last heard him. Probably to get on I-80 at the east end of town. Frank was on the west end.

Frank said, "I want you to go east on I-80. I think he's going to be coming our way. We can get a visual, and I'll call the cops—there's always at least one highway patrol watching the stretch between Green River and Rock Springs." Although that might not be exactly how it played out. The median on the interstate wasn't too bad. If worse came to worse, he'd have Sam cross it. And then what? The mighty minivan against a Nissan and at least two semi-automatics?

"Are you carrying?" Frank asked.

"Carrying?"

"A gun."

"No," Sam said. "I'm really not a big gun guy. The best I've got is a spud gun in the back. It's for the Cub Scouts."

That was splendid news. If this thing went south, Frank would show up to the rumble with vegetables.

Sam shook his head. "All these years laughing at the gun heads, and now I need one. I used to go paintballing all the time."

"It's not a problem," Frank said. Except it was. But you played with the hand you were dealt, even if it was Mr. Mormon in his minivan. Frank would have to count on the Wyoming police to bring the fire power.

The last light before the interstate turned yellow. The car in front of them started to brake. Sam did not. Instead, he put on the gas and maneuvered into the other lane, passing the car, and shooting toward the backside of the braking pickup just ahead.

"Sam!" Frank said. He put a hand on the dash, pushed his foot to the floor, braced for impact.

The pickup was jacked up, its big fat steel bumper just about the right height to come bursting through the windshield to crush chests and heads. Frank watched it zoom toward them.

They were going to die.

But then Sam yanked the Mazda back into the first lane in front of the car and sped through the intersection just as the light turned red.

They both took a breath.

"That was close," Sam said.

"You think?" Frank said, his whole body still on high alert. "Let's not go out of this life just yet."

"I'm with you on that, bro."

"And not in this vehicle. I'm pretty sure Saint Peter will pull our man cards for having bought it in a baby blue minivan with unicorn stickers."

"You get special points in heaven for rainbow unicorns," Sam said. "I didn't know that."

"Sure. You're totally covered in this van."

"I feel so much better now," Frank said.

They raced the last half mile to the interchange, peeled off Dewar and motored hard up the long on-ramp to the interstate. They passed

Walmart. The community college was next, standing proudly in the distance amidst acres of dry blue-gray sagebrush and scorched weeds. Ahead, the freeway rolled out in front of them, and Sam merged onto it.

I-80 was the main artery through Wyoming. The only artery. On any given day anywhere from six to ten thousand semis hauling freight rumbled past Rock Springs. There was a clog of them on the road right now coming up behind. Sam gassed the minivan, then put on his blinker and pulled into the fast lane.

"You watch the road," Frank said. "I'll keep my eyes peeled for the Nova. And no more of that Mario-Andretti-Doctor-Jekyll-Mister-Hyde."

"Are we chasing bad guys or going out on a stroll?"

"We're avoiding getting hit by big hunks of speeding metal, glass, and rubber that weigh a couple tons."

"I had gobs of room back at the light," Sam said. "Things were totally under control."

"I'm just saying."

Frank searched the interstate and side streets and then searched the interstate again in a clockwise pattern. He used his fingers to direct his gaze so he didn't miss anything. Nothing but regular traffic.

Sam said, "I still don't see why the girl put a box cutter to his throat."

"She doesn't know who we are. Ed came to my house. Which means Tony and I are just two more of Ed's upstanding associates."

"Ed's the bad guy?"

"Ed is a soul slimy with rot. I think maybe this is a ransom kidnapping. I think she's illegal, or part of some rival organization. I think that's why she's afraid of the cops."

Sam shook his head. "You read about the kidnappings in Arizona. You don't ever imagine that crap coming here."

"Rock Springs isn't what I'd call a pure town."

"It's not gang land either."

"Don't worry. That crap didn't come here. It was just passing through and ran into a little snag called Tony." Mr. White Hat. The one person who had written Frank faithfully all seven years. The one person who'd never given up hope. Frank had all his letters in a box.

All of them. From the ones when Tony was ten that were mostly drawings of stick figure army men and dinosaurs and sharks, all the way up to the one where the boy had included a bit of poetry he'd written for his high school Language Arts class. It was about playing Call of Duty on his Xbox. Not Robert Frost by any stretch of the imagination, but it was certainly a heck of a lot more fun. Tony was the closest thing he had to a little brother.

Up ahead on the other side of the freeway an older car pulled to the far side of a Schwan's refrigerated food truck.

Frank's heart leapt. "I think I see them," he said.

The Schwan's truck approached then passed on the other side. Frank spun in his seat to see the old car behind it, but it wasn't the Nova. It was a Camero that looked like crap. His heart fell, and he turned back around. "False alarm."

There were three Rock Springs exits on I-80, each about two miles apart. They were coming up on the middle one. A white Lincoln Town Car with Oklahoma license plates started to pass Sam on the right. Frank scanned the streets below, searched the oncoming traffic. The Nova wasn't anywhere. He tracked the frontage road, looked behind him and Sam. He turned back around. They were approaching the overpass for the second exit. He glanced down at Elk Street, which ran underneath the interstate, and froze.

The back end of a two-toned silver and gray car slipped underneath the overpass. Had he seen the brick dent in the panel above the wheel?

Sam and Frank sped onto the overpass. Frank looked out Sam's window to watch for the car as it came out the other side, but two semis blocked his view. He waited. Waited. Come on! Then the semis heading west passed by, and beyond them, down on Elk, the Nissan emerged from underneath the overpass. Frank looked farther up the road, and about a quarter mile in front of the Nissan, racing north past the Flying J truck stop, was the Nova.

"That's them!" Frank yelled. "They're heading north! We've got to exit."

"I already passed the exit," Sam said.

"We've got to exit!"

There was no way they could go off road across the median here—too much oncoming traffic, and even if there wasn't, there was a fence. The big Lincoln Town Car was still in the lane on their right, the off-ramp growing small behind them.

Up head on the right, the on-ramp was coming fast.

"Sam!"

"There's a car."

"Down the on-ramp. It's time for Mr. Hyde."

Sam didn't balk. No panic. No questions. He tapped the brakes, put on his blinker, and jerked over into the right lane. And then he was off onto the shoulder, dust flying behind the van, the tires roaring across the whump whump whump of the rumble strips.

They were going too fast. Furthermore, two cars and an SUV were accelerating up the on-ramp.

"Hold on," Sam said.

Frank braced himself.

Sam slammed on his anti-lock brakes. The van pitched forward. Frank strained to keep from flying into the dash, and realized he should have put his seatbelt on because Sam wasn't having any problem staying in his seat. A ten-pound sack of potatoes slid out from some hiding place in the back, flew up the center aisle of the van, and slammed into the foot of the console.

On their left, two cars rushed past followed by a semi Frank was sure was going to hit them. Then the minivan came to a halt and rocked back just about dead center of the on-ramp. The first two cars coming up saw them and maneuvered quick stops. The last one slowed to a controlled stop.

Sam cranked the wheel, gave the minivan some gas, and turned down the on-ramp. He moved over to the right shoulder and pushed the button to set the hazard lights blinking.

The man in the first car was shocked and angry and gave them the bird with both hands. He was shouting as well, but Sam had the windows rolled up. Sam waved like a friendly neighbor and drove on by. He accelerated down the on-ramp, half on the asphalt, half on the shoulder, the minivan tipping sideways. The second driver was in shock. The third rolled down her window to take a picture of Sam and Frank in the minivan with a cell phone. Maybe to post on Facebook, maybe to send to the cops, maybe both. By that time Sam was moving at a good clip. He waved for the camera and called out a pleasant, "Sorry." He was a road hazard, but a very polite one.

Two more cars entered the on-ramp, but Sam paid them no mind, just drove with speed, his hazards flashing, until they got to the bottom. Then he looked both ways and punched it out onto Elk Street.

Frank said, "I'm impressed, Sam."

"My wife's going to kill me."

"Not when she hears what this is all about." Frank brought up his cell and dialed 911. The dispatcher answered, and Frank said, "I called in earlier about the kidnapping. I've got a visual. They're heading north of I-80 on Elk Street. They're still in the Nova. There's a second car involved. A two-tone silver and gray Nissan Maxima that's been hot-rodded and chopped. Colorado plates. We're following them."

"Please do not try to handle this on your own, Mr. Shaw. Officers are on the way."

"You should know the two men in the Nissan are probably armed."

"I'm going to leave this line open, Mr. Shaw. Again, the officers will be there. We need to keep everyone safe."

"Sure," Frank said.

Sam sped under the overpass and then out the other side. The Nissan was some distance ahead of them, but still visible. They cruised through a green light, past a Best Western on one side and a Taco Time on the other, then a trailer park. Sam accelerated, not wildly, but enough that they began to gain on the Nissan.

"Get a little closer," Frank said. "Then we'll just pace them." The fact of the matter was that the police were indeed much better equipped to deal with this situation than he and Sam. But if the situation made a turn for the worse before they arrived, there was no way Frank was going to stand by and watch. If nothing else, Sam could ram them.

They drove past the last subdivisions on the city's edge and out into the barren landscape. There were no trees out here except at the golf course a few miles off. The rest of the land was nothing but dirt, blasted grass, and stunted gray sagebrush as far as the eye could see. Bluffs rose a few miles to the west. They looked like they'd been made by stacking a fat layer of pale orange dirt on top of a layer of pale tan dirt on top of fat layer of gray. Devoid of almost all vegetation. Most of the hills around Rock Springs were like that—unclothed earth, showing the erosion lines wriggling their way down to beds of dirt and rock.

In the distance, the Nova approached the Yellowstone Road cutoff, but Tony kept going straight. Farther up the road was the DMV and the office for the Highway Patrol, which couldn't be any more perfect. Tony hadn't gone where Frank had thought he would or where he'd been originally directed—maybe the woman with the box cutters had overheard the first directions—but this was probably just as good. The Nissan sped past the cutoff. A half minute later Sam and Frank followed. Elk Street turned into Highway 191.

There wasn't much along the road at this point, just a couple of warehouse buildings sitting a hundred yards off the road and spaced widely apart. The road narrowed into a single lane. Sam passed an old pickup, but farther ahead a gasoline truck in their lane blocked the view of the road beyond.

"Do you see them?" Frank asked.

Sam moved a bit into the empty oncoming lane and then back. "I see them," he said.

A few miles down the road were the offices for the Highway Patrol. "Ha!" Frank said. "I think Tony's got this."

"He's taking them to the Highway Patrol."

"That's my boy."

They rolled past the dead landscape. A few seconds later, he and Sam crested a low rise. In the distance was the Nissan, then the Nova, then the Highway Patrol offices.

The Nova approached the entrance to the office.

Frank waited for the brake lights. Waited for Tony to turn. But

Tony didn't slow. He didn't turn. He rode up to the entrance and then continued right on by.

"They didn't turn," Sam said.

"It's okay; we've got eyes on the target," Frank said. But inside, his stress began to elevate.

The Nissan flew past the entrance.

The Nova came to the fork in the road. Tony stayed on the main fork and headed for the railroad crossing. There weren't any gates blocking the crossing, just railroad crossing lights overhead. The two red lights were blinking in an alternating pattern, the warning clanging. A freight train was approaching from the north. A few cars were waiting in the oncoming lane on the other side of the tracks. On this side, a big yellow Dodge pickup and a tractor were stopped, waiting for the train to pass. The train with its double-stacked engines was almost to the crossing. Tony pulled up behind the tractor, then pulled out into the other lane and gunned it. The train was blasting its horn, maybe only thirty yards from the crossing. Tony sped across the tracks and cut back into the right lane. The Nissan didn't slow or hesitate. It moved into the left lane and shot across the tracks.

"Sam!" Frank said.

Sam accelerated, then immediately braked—they were too far away.

The train engines lumbered across the road in a blast of noise. It stretched back up the valley for quite some distance.

Sam slowed and pulled up behind the tractor. It was a big green deal with an old man enclosed in a glass cab up on top. The old pickup pulled in behind Sam and Frank. It was followed by two other cars.

They were going to be here for a few minutes. Unless they turned around and tried to beat the train to Wyoming Road two miles back. Then they could scoot up around the golf course and join up with Highway 191 about a half a mile past this crossing.

"We've got to get around the golf course," Frank said.

"I'm on it," Sam said. He made a U-turn, then gunned it back the way they'd come. As they accelerated, a police cruiser coming toward the crossing crested the rise with its lights flashing. They sped past the cruiser, and Sam gave the minivan more juice. Off to their right the train moved along the tracks, but they easily pulled ahead.

Frank talked to the dispatcher. "Are you there?"

Silence.

"Hello?" He looked down, but somehow the call had been dropped.

Sam said, "Have you looped in the man?"

"The man?"

Sam pointed up. "The Man," he said.

"The Man's out today."

"He's always in."

"Then he's putting me on voicemail. It appears I'm just not your big hallelujah prayer type, Sam."

"I'll say it."

"Don't you need to watch the road?"

"Fold your arms."

"I'm sure the Lord's apprised of the situation."

"Of course, he is," Sam said. "But it's our job to ask. You don't know what he might do, unless you ask."

"Sam," Frank said. "Focus on the train."

"You want God working with you on this problem, or do you want to go it alone?"

Frank looked at Sam. "You're Conroy all over again."

"Conroy?"

"Sergeant Conroy. Our 18C."

"You doing that military talk thing?"

"18C. Engineer. Builds things, blows them up. Conroy was our all-around Jesus freak. We couldn't fill the latrine bag without him saying a prayer."

"I'm sure you exaggerate."

Frank shook his head. But maybe the Mormon man had a special line. "You got any sacrificial mice?"

"What?"

"Never mind. Say your prayer, but make it quick."

Sam didn't close his eyes, just spoke out at the road. "Father, as thou

Tony needs thy help. We're on the job. If there's anything we [...] [th]inking of, let us know. If thou art willing, help the cops. Help that woman be calm and see things straight. And if there's anything else thou thinkest might shut this thing down—a blown tire, a deer on the road, we would be grateful. In the name of Jesus Christ, amen."

Frank blinked. "I couldn't tell for sure with all that Shakespeare, but did you just pray for road kill?"

"I prayed for creative options."

"Like road kill. With antlers crashing through the windshield."

"It could slow them down."

"Let's hope God doesn't go big and send an elk or some stray cow. You ever see a car slam into three-quarter's ton of beef?"

Up ahead a well-used pickup with a tool box in the bed was making a left hand turn, pulling into their lane. Sam moved into the left lane and shot past the pickup. "Go big or go home is what I say."

"Yeah, go home in a body bag," Frank said. But who knew? Maybe road kill miracles *were* on God's order menu. It wouldn't be any weirder than some of the things recorded in the Bible. The term "holy cow" suddenly popped into Frank's mind and took on whole new dimension.

They covered the two plus miles back to Wyoming road in less than two minutes, turned off, and crossed the tracks. The train was still way back on the line. They raced along the two-lane road, looped a mile or so past the developments of North Rock Springs on the left and the golf course on the right. Sam braked and accelerated to get around a couple of cars, but then they came to the cutoff and raced back toward Highway 191.

The racing around had cost them about five minutes, and the train wasn't as long as Frank had first thought. By the time they got back to 191, all the cars they'd been waiting with had already passed.

"Shoot," Sam cursed.

"We can still hope for the divine road kill," Frank said.

Sam turned onto the highway and sped up. The road ran straight and flat for a number of miles. Up ahead the big green tractor they'd been in line with moseyed along. About a mile beyond the tractor, the police cruiser was pulled off to the side of the road, its lights flashing.

In front of it was the Nova.

Sam passed the tractor. The officer was standing by the Nova calling something in on his radio. Sam slowed then pulled over a few car lengths in front of both cars.

Frank threw open the door and stepped out onto the shoulder of the road. "Officer," Frank called. "I'm Frank Shaw. I'm the one that called this in. Is Tony all right?"

The officer put a hand out telling him to keep his distance for a bit. "Who did you say you were?"

"I'm Frank Shaw. That's my car. Is Tony in your cruiser?"

"Sir, there was nobody in this car when I found it."

Frank blinked. Nobody in the car? He scanned the dry land stretching out all around. There was nothing but small clumps of dry weeds and dirt. The wind buffeted the minivan. Frank approached the Nova. "Did you see the Nissan?"

"There was nobody here," the officer said.

Frank walked up to the driver's side. The keys were still in the car. What did they do, force Tony out at gun point?

"I turned the keys on," the officer said. "The gas gauge reads empty."

The words hit Frank like an anvil. He closed his eyes and rocked back a bit. Empty. Tony had run out of gas. And Ed and Jesus had been right there to pick both of them up.

"There are some ravines and hillocks, but it's pretty flat out here," the officer said. "Someone on foot isn't going to get far. I've called in backup."

"They're not here," Frank said.

"Where do you think they are?"

Frank's phone rang. The display said it was Tony calling. Frank flipped it open and brought it up to his ear. "Tony," he said.

"Tony's doing fine," Ed said, all happiness and slime. "A real hero. But here's the deal, Jockstrap. You send the cops after us, and he's going down. Lots of empty hilly space around here. Lots of roads to nowhere. You understand me?"

Frank looked at Sam. So much for prayer.

Frank watched the officer walk back to his cruiser. "Put Tony out of the car now."

"Naw, I don't think so. And it's not me, Frankie. See, Jesus is not too keen on going back to jail. You send a bunch of Dudley douche bags after him, and he's going to be pissed. He's going to want to take it out on someone. So here's what's going to happen, Frank. You're going to sit tight. In a day or two, we'll give you a call. Tell you where you can find your boy. By then we'll be long gone. Tony will be just fine. In fact, he'll have just the thing to write about when his teacher asks for a paper on his awesome summer vacation."

He wouldn't be fine. Ed might be thinking about keeping Tony alive, but he'd also be thinking other things. Furthermore, situations like this tended to go south real quick. Especially if Tony, Mr. White Hat, gave them any idea that he just might go to the authorities once they let him out.

"Here's something else to think about," Ed said. "A little bit more motivation to keep your end of the deal. Your sister Kim is a good-looking woman, Frank. I remember the pictures. I know where Kim lives. I was hoping to meet her some day. The interesting thing—Jesus has some associates who live rather close to her. In fact, he's calling them now. If the cops come after us, well, I'm just saying."

"Ed, you don't want to go there."

"We don't have to go there. That's the beauty of the whole thing. I'm not out to get you, Frank. You'd do the same if you were in my situation. It's just a little insurance to keep Jesus from getting twitchy."

Ed had always taken too much interest in Frank's affairs. Frank thought of the family photos sent to him while in prison. Photos of Kim and Tony. He thought of Tony's letters. And Ed had always been right there.

Ed said, "You can call the dogs off now, or you can call them off later. Either way you're going to have to make up a story, say you were mistaken. But if you do it now, there's less chance that two fine folks will get hurt."

Frank should have disarmed Ed back in the house and taken his chances then. He'd been playing it safe, playing defense. But you couldn't do things like that with guys like Ed. Frank had no doubt Ed knew where Kim lived. If he'd been able to ferret out Frank's unlisted location, he'd been able to ferret out hers. Frank had no doubt Jesus had people who would take her. And if they took her, there was no guarantee she'd come back. It's one thing to kidnap an illegal who the government doesn't know about and who wants to fly under the radar. You could let them go and trust they wouldn't go to the authorities. Kidnap someone else, and things became a lot trickier.

But it wasn't going to get to that. Not even close. Ed had picked the wrong man to mess with.

"Here's what's going to happen, Ed. You're going to put Tony on the phone every hour on the hour. Each time you do, that will buy you one more hour of time that I don't go to the police. You miss, then you've got the police, the FBI, the DEA, whoever I can round up. And you'll have me. Because I kept tabs on my cellies as well."

"No can do. Parts of Wyoming don't have cell service. We'll call tonight around five, right around dinner time."

"Every hour, Ed, starting right now. Put him on."

"Big brother wants to talk," Ed said like he'd turned his head away from the phone. "And just so you don't get clever, I've got you on speaker."

There was a moment of silence, and then Tony came on. "Frank."

"You injured?"

"No, I'm good."

"If Ed or that twelver he's with touches you, they'll answer to me. You got that?"

"Yeah," Tony said.

Ed came back on loud and clear. "See? He's still breathing. We'll talk again at five. You sic someone on us, someone close to you goes down. It's a simple transaction, Frank. Now, I'm missing the fine sights of this scenic sagebrush highway."

The called ended with a double tone.

There was a moron at Tony's high school who liked to harass Tony and his friends. He'd gotten a twelve on his ACT, and he'd been trying. Tony and his buds had used that to coin the term twelver. But it meant more than "stupid bully." Tony and his dweebish friends had hacked into the twelver's phone. Then his school login. Then his home. Every time he caused them trouble, he got a little anonymous love back.

Ed and Jesus were about to learn that principle. But it wasn't going to be anonymous. Not by a long shot.

The officer retrieved something from his car and began to walk back. Frank shook his head, spread his arms like he was embarrassed all to heck. "Officer, oh man," he said with regret, "I'm afraid I put everyone through a fire drill. I'm so sorry."

The officer tilted his head, waited.

"I just got a call from Tony. It's all a dumb teenage gag. On me. L-O-L."

"You know we have to follow up."

"I know, I know," Frank said. "I just feel so stupid. We had a talk about abductions last night. Tony was rolling his eyes the whole time. I guess he thought it would be funny to give me a heart attack."

Frank shook his head, tried to play the part. The officer nodded, but Frank didn't know if he bought it or not.

The officer said, "Let's push this car off the road. You have a gas can?"

"I'll get one. We'll be back in a minute, and I'll get it out of here."

The officer nodded. "You sure he's okay?"

Frank waved his concern away. "Yes. In fact, I'm going to bring the little jerk in to the station, if that's okay. I think it would do him good to sweat a bit."

The officer cracked a smiled. "We can do that."

Sam got out of the minivan, and the three of them pushed the Nova well off the road. The officer went back to his cruiser and picked up his radio. Sam and Frank got back into the Mazda.

"What's going on?" Sam asked.

"Just go back and pull into the first gas station you see."

Sam started the Mazda, put it in gear, and made a U-turn onto the highway. They headed south. Frank waved at the officer as they passed.

"So it was all a joke?"

"It was no joke, Sam."

"But you sent the cop away."

"I keep the cops out, and Ed promises not to hurt Tony, and to keep his hands off my sister."

"You sure this isn't a bluff?"

"You know that good little man that sits inside your soul, prompting you to do what's right? Ed killed his off a long time ago. Then he pickled his eyes and put them in a jar on his shelf. Ed looks like a human being, but he's one of those pod people. He'd take my sister, your sister, your dog. He'd take his own children, if he's spawned any, and cut them up into pieces. He'd do whatever it took. Because to him and his kind, humans are ants."

"So we're going to just sit tight?"

"I figure we have forty-eight hours. We don't get to Tony by then, we might not ever get him back."

5

Killer App

FRANK PULLED OUT his phone and looked at the time. 2:33 p.m. He dialed Kim. It rang five times and went to voicemail. "Doesn't anybody answer their phones anymore?" he asked.

"Text her," Sam said. "She's probably in a meeting."

Frank opened a message, punched in "call me asap!" and sent the text. He couldn't believe this was happening. Tony had begged to come up and visit Frank. Kim had finally relented, issuing all sorts of rules and regulations to go along with it. Now he'd let her down, and put the creature called Ed Meese on her trail.

Good night! What a mess.

They sped back across the railroad crossing, back past the Highway Patrol station, back the two plus miles to the outskirts of town. Sam pulled into the first gas station they saw. Frank ran in and purchased a red two gallon plastic gas can. Then he went out, placed it on the cement in front of a pump, and started to fill it.

The officer at the scene passed the station. Frank waved all happy like. He topped the can off and screwed on the lid. He was now down to just a few bucks in his wallet. He checked his phone, but Kim had not texted him back.

Frank got back into the minivan with his gas can, and Sam drove him back up to the car. Frank poured the gas in. Just as he was screwing the lid back on, his phone rang. It was Kim.

He put as much go-lucky-calm-so-good-to-hear-you in his voice that it sounded like he might be in Disneyland. "Miss Black," he said.

"How's the chief tooth fairy today?" Kim was the top dog dental hygienist at an office in North Hollywood.

"Fine, Frank," she said with noise in the background. "I just finished a cleaning; we're headed to lunch."

"Late lunch," he said.

"But worth it," she said. "We're going to this amazing new bistro. So what's the emergency? Tony isn't into any trouble, is he?"

"Naw," Frank said. The fact was that Kim didn't need to know just yet what was going on. She'd stress nigh unto death. She'd call the cops. What mother wouldn't? But Frank was fairly confident he could wrap this up in the next three or four hours. "There are some guys in the neighborhood who invited him over this evening. I just wanted to keep tabs on him. You said you had this way to track his phone?"

"Yeah," she said. "It's this great little killer app."

"How can I get that setup on my phone?"

"No setup necessary. You just go to a website and use my login and password."

"You trust me with the keys to the kingdom?"

"No, I don't. But I'm hoping you prove me wrong."

"Can I make his phone ring?"

"Yes."

"Can I make the phone take pictures?"

"No, we didn't get that. By the way, my phone's on it too. Don't get any funny ideas. I don't need my phone ringing in the middle of a cleaning."

"I won't mess with your phone," he said. "At least not right off."

She groaned. "Why do I always ignore my better judgment?"

"Let me get myself something to write with," Frank said. He climbed into the Nova and opened the dash compartment. He fetched out a pen and the envelope with the receipt of his last Big-O Tire purchase in it. He put his phone on speaker. "Okay, I'm ready."

Kim gave him the website and login information. Frank told her to hold on as he tested it. He logged into the website, saw a button labeled "Phone," another labeled "iPad," and one more that said "Nurse Ratchet."

"I'm guessing you're Nurse Ratchet," he said.

"You like that? How about you help him come up with a different nickname? Something like Saint Kim for putting up with both you and him."

"I'll do my best," Frank said. There were little dots next to each button. The two for the phone and Nurse Ratchet were green. Underneath it said they'd been found. The dot for the iPad was red. Apparently, the app couldn't find a device that was off, which made sense. He tapped the button for phone. A moment later a Google street map opened on the phone's screen that showed an area north of Rock Springs. A little round pink push pin said, "Tony's Phone." The pin marked a position about fifteen miles north on 191, heading in the direction of Farson.

Ha! Got you, Ed.

"Slick," Frank said.

"We should actually put you on the account," she said. "I'll get that other app for you. It will not only tell me where you are, but will show me what's on your screen, log your calls. Heck it will even silently take a picture when the phone's open so you can see who is using it. It's all very Big Brother."

Frank thought about that feature. Recordings of Ed's face and calls would make a huge splash with the prosecution. "And you didn't load that on Tony's phone?"

"Are you kidding? Spy on Tony? He'd figure it out in a minute and then reroute it so I was always looking at someone on their phone in Bangladesh."

"Too bad," Frank said.

"You know, I was a bit hesitant to let him go visit. But he says he sure is enjoying himself. Don't let him down."

Yeah, Frank thought. He said, "Kim, you're talking to Frank version 3.0. I'm not going back. That life is over. I'm the picture of the model citizen."

"Hey," she said like she was admitting a mistake, "a mother worries."

Frank paused. He figured he'd better give her the other part of this straight. "On an unrelated topic, I don't want you to worry. But I have reason to believe one of my cell mates, who is now out, has your address."

"Why would he have my address?"

"Because he's a freak."

"I delisted my information when you went in."

"I know. I don't think anything's going to happen. I just want to remind you that you need to be living in yellow. None of that oblivious white crap."

"I live in L.A. I'm always in condition yellow."

"Okay, just stay that way."

"What's going on, Frank?"

"Just keeping you safe."

There was a pause, then, "Prison's going to be with you a long time, isn't it?"

"It's not something you forget."

"It's not the same outside. Not everyone has got a shank in his pocket."

"But some do, Sis. Some do. And you don't want to be the one in one hundred."

"I won't be, Frank."

"One of these days you need to get out of California so you can carry."

He heard people in the background on her end.

"I'm not weaponless," she said. "And now we're about to go in and face some awesome roast beef. I'll make sure we clear the room of hostiles before we sit down to eat. I'll call you later."

"Be safe," he said and ended the call. Then he brought the phone tracking site back up and refreshed it. Tony's marker had moved farther north.

Sam walked over and looked down at the phone. "What's next, Chief?"

Frank looked up at him. "You go back to work, Sam. You've been a big help. But you don't want to be involved in this."

"I'm already involved."

"This is not your thing, Sam."

"You can drive off, but I'll just follow you. My Mazda will kick that Nova's butt any day. And you've seen my mad driving skills."

"No," Frank said.

"Sorry, dude. You don't have a choice."

"Sam—"

"Frank, your nephew has been kidnapped. Nobody comes into my neighborhood and does that. Not to my friends. Not to my neighbors. Not to anybody."

Frank nodded. "So now you're going to go all Tonto?"

"Actually, I'm the one driving. You're the one riding shotgun. So if anyone's going to be Tonto, it's you."

"Right, and what about your work?"

Sam blinked, then looked like his intelligence had just been insulted. "Work? Hello, your nephew? Maybe we should go after him."

Despite his happy chubby bear demeanor, it appeared Sam was not one of those guys who would look the other way. "Okay then. Let's park this. They won't recognize the Mazda, and, despite the unicorns, you're correct—it's going to be faster than the Nova."

"Of course, it is. It's like the family version of the Bat Mobile."

"Right," Frank said. "And it comes with weapons too. We can pelt our foes with that nuclear Bat Diaper I saw rolling around in the back."

* * *

Frank and Sam rolled north on 191. Then they turned west and rose up out of the valley over the western ridge and headed north-north-west. All about them, for miles and miles, was stubby, gray, water-starved sagebrush. The landscape was napped with it. Not a single tree to break the view. No houses, no barns, no telephone poles, nothing but a barbed wire fence running a number of yards off on each side of the road, looking much too puny to contain so much land. Every now and again an anemic dirt road would run off the highway, across a cattle guard or through a closed barbed-wire fence, and disappear in the distance.

A dead and broken deer lay off the shoulder of the road. A mob of crows pecked at the carcass, pulling bits off as a snack.

"Road kill," Frank said.

"Too old," Sam replied.

Frank tried to refresh the tracking page. The display showed the working circle. The last position of the pin showed Tony was stopped a few miles ahead, probably about halfway between Rock Springs and Eden. He'd been at that location for some time.

Sam raced along the highway. When they were about to the spot, Frank told him to slow down. Sam did, but the Nissan was nowhere to be seen.

A knot of worry began to churn in Frank's gut. He looked down at the tracker, looked back out at the barren land. The tracker said Tony should be right on the road.

Sam pulled the van over to the shoulder. "Maybe it's off a little," Sam said. "I have a buddy who had a GPS once that was always taking him miles from his destination."

"How's it going to get mixed up?" Frank asked. "There's only one road." The sagebrush was scrubby, but it was tall enough that if you dragged a body a hundred yards off the road, well away from the fence, nobody would find it. Nobody but the ants, the buzzards and crows, and the windy Wyoming sun. A body could disappear out there for years, until it was nothing but a few weeds growing up between bleached and dried ribs. Frank had run across enough partial skeletons of deer and cattle on his long jogs to know that.

Frank's worry began to rise.

"You want to get out and look around?"

"Go another hundred yards," Frank said, "and then we'll turn around."

What was he going to tell Kim? This just couldn't be happening. A small white rage began to build in him.

Sam moved forward slowly. Frank looked down at the tracker, trying to refresh it. The page hung and hung. Then his connection dropped. He had no signal.

"Sam, you have cell service?"

Sam pulled out his phone, opened it up. "Nothing."

Relief washed through Frank. It blew a huge hole in the dark mountain of despair that had been poised to crush him. "This was his last known position. All this time the stupid connection was trying to update."

"You want to search one of those side roads?"

"No," Frank said. "Just get on down the highway."

Sam looked up at the ceiling of the van. "Lord," he said.

Frank couldn't tell if he was stating a request, gratitude, or giving a status update.

Sam pulled back onto the road and accelerated to about eighty. A few miles farther they met and passed a pickup pulling a horse trailer coming the other way. A few miles past that Frank got service again. He logged back into the tracking webpage, clicked on Tony's phone, and opened the map. Tony was up ahead about eight miles, moving on one of the streets in the town of Eden.

And that's where this would end. When Tony was safe, Ed was going to learn the meaning of tragic miscalculation.

6

Eden

FRANK AND SAM drove into the Eden, Wyoming valley, which was not, alas, a lush garden for naked folks and fruit trees. It probably didn't get more than seven inches of rain each year. However, there was one spot of green in the middle of the valley.

Back in the 1800s, thousands of pioneers had rolled through here as they made their way along both the Oregon and Mormon trails. The Pony Express had built a station here. But it wasn't until a man named Farson financed a big project back in 1907 to irrigate from the Big Sandy and Little Sandy rivers that snaked through the valley that anyone really stayed. The rivers weren't wide and deep; they were smaller shallow things, and calling it "Eden" was all part of Farson's PR. Still, the result was two little ranching communities about four miles apart, one named Farson and the other Eden, with a combined population of 628 souls. The land was green for a few miles around each community. Beyond that, it was all miles and miles of high plains desert, sagebrush, and wind.

Frank had been up here a couple of times, the last time with Tony, to stop at the Farson Mercantile, the "Home of the Big Cone," which served monstrous ice cream cones—the extra large was five scoops, each as big as a softball. But the locator said Tony hadn't gone for Farson ice creams. It said he was stopped in Eden.

Frank zoomed the map in and went to satellite view. They were at a home, surrounded by fields, about two miles off the highway that ran straight through the community. There was no Google street view for these roads, which meant he and Sam would have to drive by to get eyes on the situation.

Frank unbuckled and moved into the back seat of the minivan, behind the tinted windows. They rolled down the highway. He told Sam to turn at an intersection next to an old clapboard shack that was painted light blue.

"Eden Bar" was painted in red letters above the shack's doorway. It was still early afternoon, but there were a handful of cars out front, parked in the shade of the tall cottonwood trees. It appeared the old Biblical Edenites weren't the only ones to fall for forbidden fruits.

Frank wondered who Ed or Jesus would know up here. Or had they just stopped at the first house that seemed empty? The folks who lived in these little towns rarely locked their doors. They rarely took the keys out of their cars. If it were Frank, he'd be wanting to ditch the Nissan as soon as possible, and this place would be easy pickings.

Ed turned onto a country dirt road with fields of thick hay on both sides. He slowed to keep the dust down, but it was so dry a large cloud billowed up behind him anyway. The strong afternoon wind blew crossways, carrying the dust right off the road and into the fields. The ranchers had begun mowing one of the fields, and the hay lay in wind-rows drying until it had just the right moisture content to bale.

Sam drove toward the house where the locator said Tony's phone was. It was a single story manufactured home with cream siding. A number of tall elms lined the property. A wooden pine-rail fence ran along the front. An open gate made from fat lodge poles had been erected over the driveway. The poles were about fifteen feet tall. Black bears carved out of wood climbed the poles on either side. One little cub lay across the top pole with his paw reaching down like he was swatting at whatever might roll through that gate. In the driveway, a well-used pickup with mud spattered all along the bottom half sat out front along with three minivans of different makes and colors, but there was no Nissan.

Frank checked to make sure he had service. The phone showed full bars.

They drove past the house. No Nissan on this side either. There was a barn out back; its front door was rolled up, revealing a red tractor inside along with some barrels along one wall, probably full of oil.

Sam said, "I don't see anything."

"Pull off to the side of the road," Frank said.

Sam slowed and pulled over. The small dust cloud following them blew into the field. A trampoline stood on the lawn on this side of the house. It was tied down with rope to four long rebar poles that had been pounded into the ground. Two girls were jumping on the tramp, the big wind blowing their clothes tight against their bodies, streaming their long hair out almost straight out behind them. They were laughing, squealing in the wind. A little boy in nothing but a diaper stood next to the tramp with a popsicle held high, trying to keep it away from a calico dog that looked like an Australian Shepherd. The Australians, Great Pyrenees, and Border Collies were the main work dogs of a good portion of operations Frank had seen in the area.

The girls squealed again as a big gust of wind blew into them. The wind picked up a scrap of paper from the lawn and whipped it out above the field across the road.

Frank refreshed the locator. Tony had to be inside. Maybe that's why the kids were outside on the tramp.

Frank said, "Sam, how do you feel about doing some recon?"

"What do you mean?"

"We've got to get eyes in that house. Turn around and park in front. I want you to go knock. If the kids talk to you, tell them you need to speak to their mom or dad. Say you're looking for the reservoir. No, better yet—tell them you heard there's a cutoff through Opal to Kemmerer. Ask for directions. Maybe ask to use their phone. If you see Tony, act like he's part of the furniture. I need to know what the backside of the house looks like as well. Places we could enter. I'm going to slump down in the back. If Ed looks out, he can't see me. Not just yet."

Sam nodded.

"You up to this?"

Sam blew out a breath to screw up his determination. "Piece of cake, my man. I'm just asking for directions."

Frank positioned himself low, behind one of the middle seats. He refreshed the phone display. It said Tony was right there. "Let's do it. Roll down your window so I can hear."

Sam rolled down his window, then made a U-turn and parked in front of the house.

Frank said, "That ear thing makes you look like you belong on Star Trek; you might want to take it out so you're not so memorable."

"Take me to your leader, Baby," Sam said and made the Spock split-finger signal. But he popped the thing out of his ear and put it in his front shirt pocket and then opened the door.

The girls watched him get out. The dog barked a bit, but then the little boy walked past the dog, and the dog figured it had bigger fish to fry and went for the popsicle again. Sam walked to the front porch, bounced up the steps, then gave the door a solid knock. A gust of wind rocked the van.

A man in his thirties opened the door. He was balding but had a longish goatee growing on his chin. He had a classic farmer's tan—fish belly white from the forehead up, dark as cinnamon on his face, neck, and arms. He wore a T-shirt tucked into a pair of jeans. Sam talked. The man nodded, then he held the door wide and invited Sam in.

Frank watched the barn, the girls. A profusion of white and pink petunias grew along the front of the house. The lawn was well-maintained with clean lines marking its edges. There was a big decorative five-point star hung next to the front door; it was painted dark and looked like it was made out of tin. There was a craft sign with happy faces on the front door that said "Welcome." There were bird feeders, all cutesy looking, a flag pole with an American flag snapping in the wind. Frank looked back at the girls who looked like they were having the time of their lives.

Something here wasn't right.

A few moments later Sam came back out and walked down the steps. The man closed the door behind him. Sam moseyed over to where the girls were.

The van window was down so Frank could hear. Sam said, "We were supposed to meet some friends out here. Have you seen a white and silver car? Real low to the ground. Super dark windows?"

The oldest girl shook her head.

Sam made some comment about the tramp, then walked back to the van. He said through the open driver's window, "They're not here."

"Tell me what you saw."

"Four mothers upstairs. A couple of babies. Some kids down the hall. The ladies were doing some stamping craft party. Everyone was all happy and chatty."

"Was there a basement?"

"Yeah. I heard some yelling, but it sounded like a bunch of boys."

"I can make Tony's phone ring. Go on back and knock again."

"Frank, I'm telling you—it's a stamping party. Just a bunch of moms."

"It was just a bunch of moms in a house in Yemen sipping tea. Moms and babies and a guy who had taken one hostage in the back. You'd be surprised what a bunch of moms can hide."

"Frank—"

"Just do it. We'll never see these people again."

"You won't, but I might," Sam said. "We've got clients all over."

"Sam."

"All right," he said, then turned around and walked back.

If Ed and Jesus were in there, it was going to be a nightmare. nine millimeter bullets didn't stop for drywall. They didn't stop very well for plywood either. There'd be potential for all sorts of collateral damage and hostages.

Sam bounced back up the porch steps and knocked on the door again. A woman opened the door this time. One of the moms.

At that moment the husband with the goatee and farmer's tan rolled up the garage door from the inside. He'd put on some knee-high field boots like he was going out to work. There was nothing in the garage but shelving and normal garage stuff. A tidy garage with sleeping bags up on one shelf all in a row and tools on a peg board on another wall.

Frank brought up the page showing Tony's phone, iPhone, and Nurse Ratchet. He tapped the button on the page to make the phone ring. Reveal yourself, Ed. Reveal yourself.

Sam turned, looked at the muddy pickup. He walked down the steps and over to the bed of the truck. Then he reached in, pulled something out, and held it up for Frank to see.

A phone.

Frank moved out of the back seat, slid open the side minivan door, and got out.

The farmer walked out of the garage. "Is that yours?" he asked Sam.

Frank strode over, took the phone from Sam. It was Tony's all right.

Frank looked at the farmer. Looked for any signs of unease.

"Who are you guys?" the farmer asked suspiciously.

"I'm trying to find my nephew. This is his phone. It was in the bed of your truck."

Frank was pushing six foot three. He'd worked out all he could in prison. His tattoos and build probably didn't look so friendly right now.

The farmer shrugged.

There was something about this guy that Frank didn't like. His eyes were moving weird. Little jumps back and forth. "I need to see your basement," Frank said.

The man hesitated.

"Two minutes, and I'm out of your hair."

He was going to balk. Frank could see his face hardening to it. A natural reaction to a strange request. A natural reaction when you had something to hide.

The farmer's T-shirt was tucked in. Frank had seen him from the front. Seen him from behind. He wasn't carrying anything in the waistband. He doubted he had anything in those rubber work boots either. That left his pockets. They were tight against his thighs.

Frank walked past the farmer.

Maybe he was overreacting. Maybe not. But he'd learned long ago that you cleared the area you're supposed to clear. You took nothing for granted.

The mom standing at the door backed up, concern and a bit of fear crossing her face. She was a pretty brunette, medium hair kept back with a yellow plastic hair band. She wore two of those paper thin woman tee-shirts, a yellow one slipped over another that was white. She wore knee-length tan shorts and open sandals. Her toenails were painted shiny pink. She looked like she was going to close the door, but Frank said, "I've got it," then pushed past her into the house.

There were kids in the kitchen. Kids down the hall. Three girls were playing with little plastic horses in the front room. Frank strode past them. He cleared the bathroom and three bedrooms upstairs, including closets and shower. He found another group of kids playing some card game. Found a little boy sitting on the toilet, his feet dangling off the floor. It was a freaking kid zoo.

Frank walked back to the front room and into the kitchen past three other women sitting at the table and headed to the stairs leading down to the basement.

He was down the stairs in less than two seconds. The basement smelled of concrete. A bunch of boys grouped around a two-player electronic basketball game shooting basketballs the size of grapefruits at small hoops. It was like what you might find at a fun park, only smaller. They didn't even notice he was there. There was another bathroom, storage room, a boy's room with clothes in a heap. No Ed. No Tony.

Ed had planted that idiot phone in the back of that pickup. And Frank had fallen for it hook, line, and slimy sinker. The enormity of his mistake punched him between the eyes.

Ed was now somewhere in a forty-five minute radius from Rock Springs. Going Wyoming speeds, seventy-five to eighty miles per hour, that could mean Ed was a 100, maybe a 120 miles from Frank's current position.

Frank sighed heavily. The boys finally noticed him and looked at him like he might be the plumber. Frank bounded back up the stairs, taking three at a time. He turned into the kitchen and pulled up short.

The children were all herded into the back of the kitchen away from the stairs and table that still held the stamping crafts. The mothers stood in front of them. The yellow-shirted mom, the lady of the house, the one with the sandaled feet and cute hair band, stood in front of all the rest just where the counter came out in an L shape. She was carrying a big Smith & Wesson revolver, pointing the .45 caliber barrel right at him. It looked like a cannon from this side. It was huge in her mommy grip. It was a gun to drop a bear.

In his career, Frank had shot close to a million rounds on various guns. His team had employed a Caspian 1911 as their personal firearm—a fine .45. And so a good portion of those million rounds was with, not that Smith & Wesson revolver, but something close enough. He could feel the heft of the gun in her hand, imagine the kick, the deafening bang, and the pungent smell of smokeless powder. His nostrils flared at memory. The cupboard next to her stood open, which is probably where she kept the gun. Smart woman to keep a kitchen gun. If you were going to spend a lot of time there, you ought to have something close.

She had a good two-handed stance, the barrel lined up with her dominant eye, pointing, not at his head, but his chest. No one-eyed squinting. No hysteria. This was a woman well acquainted with firearms. And she'd know her rights too—know she'd be well within them to blow five or six inches right out of the back of an ugly intruder like him.

Frank put his hands up. "Ma'am, I'm going to walk out this back door. I know I gave you a fright. I just had to be sure he wasn't holding you hostage."

"Get out of my house."

"Yes, Ma'am," Frank said. He sidled over to the door and grabbed the knob. "I'll walk right to our vehicle, and then we're gone."

The woman's finger was on the trigger. She was breathing hard. One sudden move on Frank's part, and she'd put him down.

Frank turned the handle and opened the door. "Please accept my apologies," he said. Then he turned his back on her—knowing how easy it was to accidentally pull a trigger when a tsunami of adrenaline was washing through you—pushed open the storm door against the wind and walked out and down the steps to the lawn. The hair on the back of his neck raised up: he knew she had that gun trained on him still, knew she was thinking about those kids on the tramp and the big intruder out there with them, knew a bullet was coming. Frank didn't look back, didn't want to startle her. The wind buffeted him. He marched past a rainbow-colored wind ornament spinning at high speed and then turned the corner around the garage.

Maybe Kim had been right. Maybe he still carried too much of the distrust of prison with him. But what else could he have done? Call the cops? And all the while, if Ed had been down there, every second would have given the juices in his sociopathic brain time to come up with a plan.

Frank strode past the garage. The whole incident had taken probably no more than a minute, but the husband, with the farmer's tan and rangy goatee, was clearly angry now. He had his cell phone out and was dialing. He probably wished he had been carrying something in his knee-high gumboot.

Frank said, "I'm leaving now."

"Who the hell do you think you are?" the farmer said.

"Where's the sheriff's office?" Frank asked.

The man looked Frank up and down, aggression and fury building in him. But Frank was a big guy, and the man knew it. "Straight down the main road toward Farson. Now get off my land."

"You tell them I'm coming," Frank said.

Then he and Sam got back into the minivan. This time Frank sat up front in the passenger's seat. "Drive straight to the main drag," Frank said.

"Holy crap," Sam said.

"We don't have much time," Frank said.

Sam cranked the ignition. "You going to bring the cops in?"

"No."

"I think you raised some heart rates back there."

"Which is why we need to get the heck out of Dodge. Somehow, I don't think the local sheriff is going to look kindly on an ex-con breaking and entering on a hundred kids and four stamping moms."

7

Pinto

SAM PUT THE van in drive and pressed the gas.

"We need to get a map," Frank said. "I think my brilliant plan just screwed the pooch."

Sam pulled out onto the road and headed back toward the main road and the Eden Bar, dust kicking up behind them. Frank popped open the glove compartment. "You got a map in here?"

"I'm not going to flee the police, Frank."

"I'm not asking you to flee. Just proactively evade." Frank flipped through the things in the glove box. Lip balm, a pen, envelopes, owner's manual, a pacifier that was nowhere close to sanitary.

"There's an atlas in the pocket behind your seat."

Frank reached around behind him and pulled the atlas out of the wide pocket. It was an oversized thing with a picture of a black road running up a hill of yellow wheat on the cover. He flipped it open to Wyoming. Then he took the pen and envelope out of the glove compartment. He positioned the corner of the envelope on the mileage scale up at the top of the map and marked off seventy miles on the envelope, slid it, then marked 140. He put the corner of the envelope on Eden, and using the envelope as a compass, drew a light circle 140 miles out.

And the circle showed him just about how hopeless this now was. By the time he and Sam got back to Rock Springs, if they made it that far, Ed could already be in Colorado, most of the way to Utah, or just pulling into Rawlins, Wyoming. If he'd actually come in this direction, he'd be well on his way to Jackson Hole.

The van rumbled down the dirt road toward the main drag and bar. Behind them, the house grew small in the distance.

Frank looked down at the map again. What was the math? How fast would they need to go if Ed was already eighty or a hundred miles ahead? "I need to make a decision. Pull in behind that bar so nobody can see us."

"I don't think we want to do that."

"You're not fleeing the authorities, just pulling into a parking lot."

"There's a sheriff's pickup in that parking lot."

Frank looked up. A white pickup with lights on top rested peacefully in the shade of the trees.

"I don't think anyone's in it," Sam said.

Frank squinted. He didn't think anyone was there either. Nor was it parked like it was waiting for them. The dirt road he and Sam were on continued on the far side of the main drag. There was a house and a metal barn about a hundred yards down that road. "Go straight across," Frank said. "Park it behind that metal barn."

Sam pulled up to the main road. The Eden Bar and the sheriff's truck both stood off to his right. There wasn't anyone in the pickup, but if anyone came out, the first thing they'd see was him and Sam sitting at the stop sign. Sam looked both ways. There were no vehicles coming. Then he gave the van some gas and drove across the road.

Frank turned around and watched the bar. Just as they got to the other side, the door to the bar opened. A deputy in a nice tan uniform walked out. Another man wearing a dirty baseball cap followed him. The deputy put on his dark pilot sunglasses.

Frank's heart began to beat like a drum. They were going to get detained, taken to the sheriff's office, have to make some report. And then he never would catch Ed.

Sam rumbled onto the dirt road, dust billowing up behind. The deputy walked round the corner, talking to the man in the baseball cap. They shook hands, and the deputy walked to his pickup. Sam continued down the road. The deputy got into his truck. In just a few seconds he'd check in. Or his box would squawk. Breaking and entering would be a big deal in a community so small the town didn't even have one stop light. Sam's evasion might be over before it even began.

The deputy picked up his radio. Sam put on his blinker and turned left into the gravel driveway, the stones crunching under the wheels. A blink later the minivan slipped behind the metal barn.

Frank's mouth was dry.

"You think he saw us?" Sam asked.

"I don't know."

"What are we going to do?"

"We're going to figure this out." The deputy was going to come, or he wasn't. That was out of Frank's control. The farm house itself was dark, but a couple of dogs sat up by the porch. A wide gravel yard ran from the house to the street. It was big enough to turn tractors around on it, but there were no vehicles parked anywhere.

Frank set the map up on the dash. "Where's Ed, Sam?"

"He had Colorado plates," Sam said.

Frank nodded. "Colorado's home, at least for one of them. That is, if that car wasn't stolen."

He thought back to the conversation. Ed had said they'd been in Utah, picking up an extra wife. At the time, Frank thought he was making a stupid joke. But he could have been talking about the girl he had in his trunk. And if they'd come from Colorado, then maybe they were on their way back. If all that was true, then they'd be heading east on I-80. Or maybe they were heading south for Craig, Colorado to take the back way into Denver.

Or maybe that was all just a pile of crap.

Sam said, "You think that deputy saw us?" He was looking out his window through a gap between the metal barn and the last remnants of a stack of round ton hay bales. A slice of the intersection was barely visible through the gap.

"Maybe he's calling in backup," Frank said.

Sam ran his hand down his face. "Oh, brother."

Just then, back on the main road, the deputy's truck accelerated hard, the engine roaring, lights flashing on top. It turned down the road to the house with the cute mom with her .45 and all her stamping friends.

"We don't have much time," Frank said. "Two minutes. Three. By then every deputy they've got up here will be buzzing the roads like hornets. We need to get ahead of them."

"We going east, back to Rock Springs?"

Frank looked down at the map. "That's the problem. There are a couple of routes into Colorado, all more than a hundred miles apart. If I was still working for Uncle Sam, we'd get some eyes in the sky. Satellite, choppers. But we've got squat."

"Maybe I've got some guys."

"What kind of guys?"

"From a ward I used to live in."

"Ward? Like a mental hospital?" Holy cow, this was a total cluster.

"A *Mormon* ward," Sam explained, "is a church congregation."

More with the church ladies and missionaries. Frank shook his head. "No disrespect, but we need more than a bicycle brigade and a bake-off."

"How about an airplane?"

Frank looked at him.

Sam looked back like he was dealing with someone who, the Lord love them, had a somewhat pointy head.

"Talk," Frank said.

"Brother Korea. Just outside of Lander. He's got himself a Cessna, takes people around, spots lost cattle, whatever."

Frank looked down at the map. Highway 191 and State Road 28 crossed each other like a big X in Farson. 191 led up to Jackson Hole or back to Rock Springs. 28 led north-east to Lander, about fifty or sixty miles from their current position. It was not at all on their route, but they could cover a lot of ground in a plane, even in a small Cessna. "Make the call," Frank said.

"You got it." Sam put the van in drive and began to turn around on the gravel. Then he made the hands-free call.

Frank's hopes began to rise a bit. "So this Korea, does he have a cookie racket too?"

"Actually," Sam said, "Brother Korea has a very nice snickerdoodle."

Mormons were just too weird. "Is this like part of your religion?"

"Dude, what do you think those temples are? They're big bakeries."

"No, they're not."

Sam smiled. "The Holy Order of Cookies. We wear baker's hats."

"No, you don't."

"Actually, we do."

Sam was such a liar, except he didn't look like he was lying. "Whatever," Frank said. "Let's just get on the road. If I recall, there was a deputy and flashing lights."

Sam exited the gravel drive and turned north on the dirt road, away from the bar. A moment later the person he called picked up. Sam put him on speaker. A deep, but faraway tinny voice said, "Cartwright, you mad man. How you doing?"

"I've got a massive cow in the mud, Pinto. You at home?"

"What's going on?"

"I'm about fifty minutes out; I'll tell you when we get there, but we're going to need your plane."

"Yolanda's not doing so well," Korea said. "But don't you worry about that. You just get your bookkeeping kiester up here."

"I'll call you when we get close," Sam said. He turned to Frank. "Looks like it's a go."

"Who's Yolanda?"

"His plane."

"If we get up there and have to turn around—"

"He'll have it fixed."

"Falling out of the sky can kind of put a damper on your day."

"We won't fall out of the sky. Cessnas can glide."

Frank pulled out his phone and brought up the phone locator. The push pin showed their current location on Google Maps. Frank zoomed in. The roads of Eden appeared in a rough grid. But there was a river between them and State Road 28 that led to Lander. They could go back to the main drag and then on to the center of Farson, but that was too risky, too out in the open.

Frank dragged the map and saw their escape. "Follow the road we're on to the end of the line and then turn left," he said. "We're going to get on a Ryepatch Road and skirt right around Farson. It will take us over the river and dump us out on 28."

"Right," Sam said, but he was checking his mirrors, looking out over the fields for the deputy, ignoring the road. The van started to veer toward the shoulder and the ditch beyond.

"Sam!" Frank said.

Sam snapped his attention back to the road and pulled them back from the shoulder.

"You keep your eyes on the road. I'll scout for our boys in brown."

Sam focused on the road.

They passed a half-dozen fields and houses. Some with big pivots to irrigate them, others with long wheeled or hand lines. Frank scanned the horizon.

"I've got binoculars in the back," Sam said. "Nothing spectacular. I got to help the older scouts with their bird study merit badge."

Frank clambered into the back and dug past the spud gun and the other crap that was there. The binoculars were all nice and tidy in a case. He flipped the case open and pulled them out. They were a dull pine green set of bird watchers, straight roof prism design with 7x32 magnification and objective diameter. Nothing like the target acquisition glasses he used in the good old days, but it was not like he was going to be doing any sniping.

He climbed back to the front seat. "These aren't so bad," he said and brought them up to his eyes. "A lot better than squinting."

He scanned the main road as well as in front of them across the river. No deputy, just regular cars, houses, and some horses in a pasture.

The road they were on met up with Ryepatch and then wound around a barren ridge, and crossed the river, which was so low you could see all the rocks along the bottom. About two miles later, they drove through an opening in the barbed wire fence and dumped out onto State Road 28.

There was nothing out here. The irrigation hadn't come this far, which meant the land was flat and dry. The trees of Farson were small in the distance. Frank looked through the glasses. Nothing was on the road.

"Time to get hopping," he said.

Sam pulled out onto the road and accelerated. "One of the deputies could be ahead of us. It's not like there are a lot of roads around here to patrol."

"We do the best we can," Frank said. He'd spent years of his life learning how to hide from men who wanted to kill him. If Frank could get thirty yards off the road, he could blend in just fine. The problem was the land here was miles and miles of flat pan. He might be able to hide, but the van could not. It would be visible forever. They were like sitting ducks.

Sam got up to seventy-five, then eighty. The miles of dry land flew past on either side of them, the road running straight as far as the eye could see. The Wind River mountain range rose in the distance on their left.

Frank picked up Tony's phone. Maybe Tony had taken a picture. Maybe he'd left a note. Frank slid it open. The screen lit up, and an electronic note did indeed appear. It was yellow, like a Post-it, with blue script. It said, "Strike one, Jockstrap. Hope you enjoyed the ride :)"

Frank clenched his teeth and closed his eyes. *Tony. Dude, I'm so sorry.* But he was going to make it right.

"You okay?" Sam asked.

"Fine," Frank replied.

Sam made calls to a client, his office, and his wife. Frank checked the roads ahead and behind. Some time later they came to the end of the broad flat pan of the valley, and the land began to gently rise as they approached the tip of the big mountain range. A few minutes after that, they entered the softly rolling foothills at the outer edge of the range. Cedars, aspen, and pines grew in the distance on the slopes. The road ran on. Visibility stretched in all directions for miles.

He checked his phone. It was 3:45 p.m., well past the time he should have received a call from Tony. Obviously, Ed wasn't going to call on the hour. Not a good sign.

Frank dialed Kim. The phone rang and went to voicemail. He told her to call him. Then he sent her another text.

They continued on and the landscape became greener. The road no longer ran straight, but bent through the gentle hills. They passed two separate herds of pronghorn antelope out in the sagebrush, grazing on whatever small bits of grass they might find there. Frank liked the pronghorns. They had exotic horns and coloring—tan backs, white bellies, and an interesting series of white and black bands on their necks and faces.

But pronghorns didn't just look pretty; there was nothing that could touch them. Pronghorns ran faster than anything on land except the cheetah. And while the cheetah could run up to seventy mph, it could only maintain that for a few hundred yards before it had to stop and pant in the grass. Pronghorns on the other hand, could sprint almost as fast, sixty-two mph, but then they could kick it into travel gear and cruise at thirty or forty mph for mile after mile. These bad boys evolved to outrun Pleistocene mega-predators like the dire wolves, giant bears, and the extinct American cats. They'd not only outrun their old predators, they'd outlived them, which, when you thought about it, should make them into some kind of herbivore gods. A testament to peaceful grass munchers everywhere. Of course, some predators you couldn't outrun. Some predators just needed to be removed from the face of the earth. Frank was thinking about pod people like Ed.

They came around a bend, and about two miles ahead an RV moseyed along. It had mountain bicycles on the back. It didn't take Sam long to catch up to it. He put on his blinker and pulled up along side. A sunglassed grandma was at the wheel. Frank lifted the binoculars and looked down the long road.

About a half a mile ahead, an SUV was pulled off to the shoulder in the other lane, pointed their way. It was white. It looked like it had a light rack on the roof.

Frank's blood began pumping. "Good night," he said.

"What?" Sam asked. Then he saw the SUV.

It was too late for them to pull off to the side of the road. Frank threw himself to the floor between the front seats and crawled to the middle aisle.

"Is it a cop?" Frank asked.

"Oh, boy," Sam said.

A second passed, then another. Plenty of time to travel that distance at the speed they were going.

Sam started to laugh.

"What?" Frank asked.

"Department of transportation," Sam said.

Relief washed through Frank, but he stayed where he was.

About two minutes later Sam said, "I think you can get up."

Frank popped his head up and looked back at an empty road. "How much farther until we get to this Korea guy?"

"He's just this side of Lander. I give it about ten minutes."

Frank stayed in the middle seat and scanned the road. They skirted round the tip of the Wind Rivers and found a lot more green on this side. There were a lot more hills and bends too. And every corner they went around, every rise they topped, his heart thumped, waiting to see a cop. Periodically, he looked behind, knowing he was going to see flashing red and blue.

They entered irrigated country. Instead of sagebrush, fields of late-season meadow grass ran up to the hills, hundreds of acres of them, all ready to be cut. Farm houses dotted the valley. Sam kept trying to make a call. At last he got service and his phone dialed.

A few rings later, Korea picked up.

"Just passed the Wamsley's place," Sam said.

A tinny voice replied, "We're in the shed."

"And Yolanda?" Sam asked.

"She's under the knife," Korea said. "I hope you've said your prayers today."

"Tell me she'll fly."

Korea just laughed and ended the call.

Sam looked over at Frank. "We'll be fine. Really."

They were going to go up in a plane held together with bubble gum and baling wire.

Off to their right, a farm boy rode a four-wheeler over a field of mown meadow hay. Two scruffy black and white border collies chased after him; they were stretched out, running at a full gallop, looking like they were having the time of their lives. "When I get reincarnated," Frank said, "I want to come back as a farm dog."

"We're not going to need reincarnation."

"I'm just putting in my order," Frank said.

About a minute later they came to a dirt road that shot off from the state route and led to a house and cluster of barns and other buildings about a half a mile off the road. Sam slowed and turned onto the road.

The ranch looked like most of those in Wyoming. Wide fields to grow hay and alfalfa for winter feed. Some corrals and a barn. Not too many animals—the cattle would still be up in their summer range. There were two large sheds—one for tractors and other vehicles. Another was clearly a small airplane shed made out of corrugated tin and fiberglass. Beyond the buildings stood a pole with an orange wind sock flapping in the wind.

They drove into the yard, scattering some chickens and two peacocks. They passed a small stack of old hay bales, a hay wagon with tires that looked like they belonged on an old Ford pickup. The house was an old red brick thing with huge wooden butterflies decorating the gable. A dog rose up from the yard to come greet them.

The wind sock stood at the end of a dirt runway that had been leveled in the middle of the sagebrush. It was covered with bits of small desert grass and scrubby weeds. Sam drove round to the airplane shed. The door was open, the airplane inside. It was an old Cessna 182, with the wing on top and fixed landing gear underneath. One of the wheels was missing its cover. The plane was white with a yellow cowling from the prop to the windshield and a brown stripe running the length of the fuselage—the colors for the University of Wyoming Cowboys.

Standing in front of the plane were two men, riveting a sheet of aluminum onto the wing.

The men were in their early forties. The skinny scraggly one wore a cowboy hat and looked like he'd been baking about a hundred years in the sun. The big guy looked like he might have killed a few people in his day. He wore bib overalls and boots. His goatee was a grungy mess. There was a tattoo on one meaty arm. What was it with Mormons and ex-cons?

"Did he just get out of supermax?" Frank asked.

"Who?"

"Jimmy Hoffa."

"He's a teddy bear."

"Right," Frank said.

Sam parked the van and they both got out. The Mafia hit man with the rivet gun finished and inspected his work. The skinny piece of leather shrugged, clearly not knowing if their wing repair would hold.

"So where's Korea?" Frank asked.

"Right there," Sam said. "Brother Korea's the big one. The other one is Brother Young."

"Those two are Mormons?"

"Card carrying."

"I didn't think Mormons came in that variety."

"What kind of varieties did you think there were?"

"I figured you had your basic cookie-baking type and then the guys wearing suits on bicycles."

"Well, now you can add the Brother Korea and Brother Young types to your collection."

Frank grunted.

"You can't judge a book by its cover," Sam said.

A few hours ago Frank had been trying to convince Ms. Mary of Cowboy Donut of that very thing. Now he wasn't too sure. Either way, he supposed the Church authorities were happy these two were way up here in Lander where they were out of the public eye. See them come knocking on your door with a Bible, and you'd be liable to get your gun.

"He doesn't look too Asian," Frank said.

"Why would he be Asian?"

"Well, I thought Korea . . ."

"No, not Korea, the country. It's Pinto Correia, with a C. Correia," he said, rolling his r's. "He's Portuguese."

"Italian mafia Portuguese?"

"His family are all dairy farmers in California."

"At least that's what he told you." This guy was surely some mobster in the witness protection program.

"I helped him with his genealogy. His people came from the Azores islands."

"Right," Frank said. He was sure the Marshalls had done a real bang up job on this guy's backstory.

He looked down at his phone. No call or text from Kim, nothing from Tony. It was 4:07 p.m., about an hour and a half since he'd gotten the call from Ed. That was ninety minutes of travel time for Ed. The circle was widening. Ed could be 120 miles from Rock Springs in any direction. Three times 120 squared—what was that? He brought up his phone, did the math. 45,000 square miles, give or take. Every minute widened that radius by another mile or so. Another hour and the circle would encompass—he did a little more math—an additional 80,000 square miles.

They needed to get in the air. Any longer and this was going to be searching for a hair in a haystack. Frank said, "Tony's waiting. Whatever kind of Mormon thing you got going up here, as long as that plane flies and these two don't carry garrotes, I'm good. Let's go talk to yonder brethren."

Frank and Sam walked toward the airplane shed. A big golden retriever trotted out from behind the house and barked. Sam called out to him by name, and Henry the dog switched to happy tail-wagging shimmy mode. "Come on," Sam said, and the dog ran up to him for an old friend pet and scratch.

"You'd think you're some long lost uncle," Correia said.

Sam gave Henry one last pat, then stood. "Pinto," he said and held up his hand for a homey hand shake.

But the supermax guy was a hugger. As was the baked cowboy. There were back slaps and man hugs all around. A real love fest. Then Sam introduced Frank.

Yonder brethren were cordial and shook hands. And Frank swore he'd met this Pinto fella in a bar somewhere as a bouncer.

Pinto turned to Sam. "So what's with the 911?"

Sam filled them in on the details, running through them like he might a balance sheet, not missing a thing. Henry stood the whole time with the men, nosing a hand every now and again for some happy scratching. When Sam finished, Pinto said to Frank, "Where's your sister?"

Frank held up his phone. "Not responding."

"You sure you don't want to call the cops?"

"Oh, I'll call them. But not just yet. Dimes to doughnuts Ed has already convinced Tony he has his mother. So if I sic the cops on them, the girl won't say anything because she's illegal, and Tony, thinking his mom's life is on the line, will swear up and down he and Ed are long-time friends, and that he and I had an argument or it's a misunderstanding or whatever. And then what's the cop going to do?"

"They've got protocol for suspected kidnappings."

"They're going to let him go. And Ed will know we called the cops and begin to think about liabilities and all those lonely Wyoming roads stretching out miles and miles into nowhere. No, Ed and I need a little one-on-one."

"How do you know they haven't switched cars?" Heber asked.

"If they steal a car, somebody reports it. Then the cops *would* be looking for them for sure. That doesn't reduce their risk."

Pinto nodded. "So let's say we do find them. What then? Buzzing around in the air won't do you one lick of good. We'll just follow them until the plane runs out of gas."

"I know," Frank said. "This operation requires someone on the ground."

"I can drive," Sam volunteered.

"Naw," Pinto said. "Two sets of eyes are better than one. You and Frank both know what you're looking for. You both should be in the plane." He looked over at Heber.

Heber nodded. "It's way too windy for this cowboy's stomach anyway. You guys go up in Pinto's tin can; I'll bring up the rear."

"Use the minivan," Sam said.

Heber said, "This is going to cost you a plate of those pink frosted cookies."

"I'll throw in some sprinkles," Sam said.

Heber's weathered face cracked a smile. "Now you're talking."

Was Sam slipping something weird into the cookies? Is that what was going on? Like narcotics on postage stamps, except the Mormons were putting it in the cookies? Frank said, "I think a support vehicle is a good idea. But Heber's going to fall behind. Way behind."

"Depends on where we find them," Pinto said, "*if* we find them."

"Even if Heber's right there," Frank said, "I don't want you guys getting involved."

"So what are you going to do? Parachute in and cling to the roof of the car? This ain't James Bond."

"Of course not. So we spot them and fly on ahead. You drop me off, and I take it from there. No reason for you to be involved past that point."

Pinto nodded. "That could work." The other two seemed to agree. "Of course, if these guys are as bad as you say they are, you going to need a gun."

Frank shook his head. "I don't have a gun. Can't. One of those rights I forfeited when I decided to join the felon club."

"You got a stick?"

"I'll figure something out," Frank said.

"One mind, any weapon, is that it?" Pinto asked.

Frank shrugged. "Basically."

"Yeah," Pinto said, clearly not buying it. In fact, Frank was picking up a bit of general wariness and suspicion from Pinto about the whole situation. He was obviously still assessing whether or not he could trust this ex-con Sam had dragged up to his front door.

Pinto looked over at Heber. Heber shrugged. Something was decided between the two of them without any words being spoken, and then Pinto said, "You need anything?"

"I'm good to go," Heber said and patted his pocket.

Pinto nodded. "I'm not. Wait here a minute."

He walked over to his garage, opened the small swinging door beside the main rolling door, and walked inside. A few moments later he came back out, holding two extra semi-automatic magazines, and shut the door behind him. He slipped the magazines into one of his copious bib overall pockets. Frank looked to see where Pinto's holster was, but whatever he was carrying, it was well hidden under the yards of fabric required to cover the big man.

When he returned, Frank said, "Sam's got a pair of binoculars in the van. We're going to need another pair."

"Already have one in the plane."

"Then let me get Sam's atlas."

"Already on it," Sam said. He hurried back to the van and fetched the binoculars and the atlas.

Frank looked at the time on his phone. 4:16. Another nine minutes had ticked by. He looked at Pinto and Heber. "Burning daylight."

"Roger that," Pinto said.

Sam handed his keys and a credit card to Heber. "For gas," he said.

Heber took the keys and card.

"I appreciate your help in this matter," Frank said.

"Well, we haven't done anything yet," Pinto said. "We'll see if you're thankful come nightfall."

"Okay," Sam said.

"All right," Heber said.

"Ladies," Pinto said, "let's see if Yolanda's in the mood to fly."

8

Yolanda

PINTO MOTIONED AT the Cessna and said, "Each of you take a strut."

The Cessna 182 had one wing that crossed over the top. Under each side of the wing, a strut connected to the fuselage. Frank took one strut, Heber the other. There were words painted on the cowling behind the propeller in a cursive script; they said, "Reach For the Sky."

Frank thought they could be motivational. Or they could be referring to a good old-fashioned Western holdup.

Pinto went to the front and lifted up the end of a red tow bar. It looked like the long skinny version one of those old push mowers, except instead of holding rolling blades, its two-fingered claw held the nose gear just above the wheel covering. Pinto threw a lever to lock the claw in place, then grabbed the handle with both hands and leaned back.

Yolanda moved forward. Frank and Heber helped a little, pushing on the struts, but Pinto did all the work. He pulled the plane out onto the wide gravel drive and faced her toward the dirt runway past the house and barns, then threw the tow bar in the plane behind the back seat. Pinto pointed at Sam. "You ride shotgun. Frank, why don't you sit in the back, a bit kitty-corner to even us out."

Frank went around to the passenger's side door and noticed the section of aluminum Pinto and Heber had been riveting on when he'd first rolled into the yard. Gum and baling wire. "What happened here?" he said.

"Buzzard," Pinto said. "Should have seen him. He was a big old boy.

A gust brought him right up into me." Pinto shook his head. "What kind of idiot hits a buzzard?"

"Is it going to hold?"

"I certainly hope so," he said.

Frank pictured the wing coming off and them falling from the sky, but he climbed into the back seat anyway. Pinto took his position behind the wheel in a seat that was adjusted lower than the passenger's seat and scooted farther back to accommodate the man's height. When he settled in, the leg of his overall hitched up a bit to reveal a portion of an ankle holster. So Pinto was a leg man. Or maybe that was just the backup. You could hide a whole lot of ordinance in those overalls.

Sam took the seat in front of Frank. Then there was a flurry of action, and Henry jumped in, climbed over Sam, and took a sitting position in the back seat next to Frank.

Frank looked over at Henry. Henry looked back. He was sitting prim and polite. But then he couldn't contain his excitement. He grinned, shivered with joyful expectation, and thumped a happy tail. All that was probably Woofish for "dude, we're in a plane!" Then Henry quieted again and focused forward like he was just one of the guys.

"We taking the dog?" Frank asked.

"No reason to leave him here to be bored," Pinto said. "He usually sits up front."

"Okay," Frank said. He'd known about teams that had K-9s attached. Heck, there'd been a Belgian Malinois named Cairo with the SEALs that had dropped in on Osama Bin Laden at his Pakistani compound. Cairo had gone in completely suited up: protective vest, Doggles (goggles for canines), and an ear piece. Henry didn't look like one of those serious dogs with mad warrior skills. He looked more like a party dog. Like if they went down, he'd do it saying "duuuude" in his own happy dialect.

Outside the plane, Heber gave them a two-fingered wave and headed for the van. Up front, Pinto checked his controls. The plane was immaculate inside. It smelled clean and pretty, almost as if a woman had been in here. Up front, a toy fairy with lacy wings hung from the ceiling. She was dressed in a green leaf outfit with the top of an acorn for a hat.

"Nice fairy," Frank said.

"Isn't she," Pinto replied.

Frank could not figure this man out. Affixed to the wall above the passenger's door was a small framed photo of a pretty woman. She was Black. She had a fine smile and luminous eyes. Maybe Pinto hung the fairy for her. Maybe it was her fairy to begin with. Or maybe Pinto just had a weird side.

Pinto's checklist was laminated and inserted into a holder that kept it right in front of him. He primed the engine with three pumps, turned his beacon on, then turned the ignition. The motor kicked to life. Sounded like a lower pitched lawn mower. He radioed out a call and fiddled with a few more knobs and ran up the rpms. "Here we go," he said.

Behind them, Heber started up the van and rolled out of the yard.

Pinto pushed in the throttle, the whine of the propeller climbed, and the plane started to move through the yard toward the dirt and weed runway. The wind was blowing the grass out in the fields, rolling it like waves. The windsock flapped, showing the wind was coming from the west.

"We've got about fifteen knots," Pinto said. "This should be fun."

"Fun?" Frank asked. "As in a wing falling off kind of fun?"

Pinto just smiled.

Frank began to suspect this was going to be a rough ride.

The plane bumped along. A gust shook them as the plane rushed across the fields and between the buildings. Pinto gave the plane more throttle. A few seconds later he was lined up with the runway, and gave it yet more gas. The little plane shot forward. Henry gave a woof.

They bumped down the dirt runway, the plane picking up speed. Another gust raced across the open land. It slammed into the plane, lifting it up in a nice little hop and setting it right back down. All of which demonstrated why you wore seat belts in these contraptions. No seat belts and that wind would have introduced his head to the ceiling.

The plane continued to pick up speed. Frank wondered momentarily what Pinto would do if they got too close to the end of the runway. But he didn't need to worry. The plane began to lighten. A moment later there was one more bump, and then Pinto was pulling back on the wheel, and they were rising above the fields in a sliding float. Pinto pulled back a bit more and the Cessna began to climb at a fairly steep angle.

The houses and cars below them grew small, toy-like. The land stretched out until Frank could see Lander and the ranches beyond making their small quilts of green and brown patches in the middle of the sagebrush.

Another gust hit them. The tone of the propeller changed; the plane dropped a bit and then shot up like a roller coaster.

"Hoo!" Pinto said. "Put your hands in the air!"

Frank shook his head. Pilot humor.

They climbed into the wind for about another minute or two, the plane hopping and sliding every now and again, then Pinto leveled it off. The view of the Wind River mountains and the surrounding land was spectacular. Frank spotted Eden close to the southern horizon.

Henry looked out his window and let out a happy bark.

"Okay, Kemosabe," Pinto said. "What's our target? We've got about six hours of gas."

Frank opened the road atlas on his lap. It was now 4:30 p.m. Ed had a two-hour head start. He made the calculations assuming Ed had taken the interstate, which meant he could be as far as 160 miles out. That was all the way to Elk Mountain if he went east. If he'd gone west, he'd be in Salt Lake City.

But Frank had already figured he was going east, mostly likely to Colorado because of the plates. There were three main ways into Colorado from Rock Springs. The first was Highway 191, which ran straight south into Utah. After sixty or seventy miles you came to Vernal; Ed could head east from there through Dinosaur on Highway 40. That route would take you right though mountains in eastern Utah and the Rockies west of Denver. That was a lot of mountain.

The second route was to head east a piece on I-80, turn south to run through Baggs to Craig, Colorado, and then hook up with Highway 40 there. That one avoided the mountains on the first leg, but took you right into the same twisting and climbing in the Colorado piece.

Something about all that mountain driving snagged in Frank's mind. Why had Ed wanted to switch cars?

At first Frank thought it was because the car was dirty and the authorities were after him. Ed was trying to go to ground. But the presence of the kidnapped girl changed that.

The cops *might* be after him, but that didn't feel right. If she was from a rival gang, then maybe her boys would be after Ed, but Ed had picked her up way out in Utah, not Colorado. Any of her homies would be way off their turf. Ed had to be bringing her back.

So why ask for a trade?

Maybe Ed had wanted to drop in, maybe make sure his info on Frank was good. But Frank didn't think so. Maybe Ed had car troubles; something wrong with the radiator. Could be something else. But Ed couldn't stop in and get it fixed, not with a girl tied up in the trunk.

The riskiest time guarding precious cargo was during transport. Which was why a sizeable portion of America's gold was in Fort Knox— a fort. not in a bunch of vans driving around the countryside. It was why they kept felons locked down in another type of fort. There were too many uncontrolled variables when you were out on the road. And a kidnappee would only make things more risky. They'd drug her and keep her sedated so she was less likely to call out or make sounds. They had probably drugged Tony as well. But even with a drugged prisoner, things could go wrong. Tony had proven that when he'd walked by and sprung the girl. So Ed would want to be on the road as little as possible. And if his car did have troubles, he certainly didn't want to be going up and down mountainous roads.

No, Ed was not going down to Highway 40. He was simply trying to get his cargo to its destination as quickly as possible.

I-80 stretched to the east, the quickest way to Colorado. Ed would be heading to Cheyenne and then straight down to Fort Collins and on to Denver, or whatever the destination was.

"How fast will this thing fly?"

"You've got ground speed and air speed," Pinto said, "which are two different things. When you're in the air, the plane's like a boat in a river. If the boat can go twenty miles per hour, and the river is moving ten miles per hour with it, then the boat can go thirty, but maybe only ten if it's going against the current."

"We're heading east," Frank said.

"That would be with the wind," Pinto said, "which means we can probably do 190 easy. Maybe 200, depending."

Frank nodded. "You have a pencil?"

"In the pocket behind Sam's seat."

Frank fished in the pocket and came up with an old thing featuring an exceedingly dull point. Ed wouldn't be going faster than the normal traffic because he wouldn't want to attract attention. Wyoming cops loved pulling over out-of-staters. So Ed would probably cruise with the slower vehicles. In fact, 80 mph was probably too generous. Frank figured Ed had, maximum, a 160 mile head start, and that was if his gas tank was full and they didn't need to make any stops and nothing broke down. Frank did a bit of math on the edge of the atlas. "We'll catch up in a little less than two hours," he said.

He measured the distance on the map. "I think we can get ahead of them if we shoot straight for Cheyenne. We'll work back from there."

"Roger," Pinto said, dipped one side of the plane, and banked a soft turn.

"How far up are we?" Sam asked.

"About 5,000 feet."

Behind them the tall peaks of the Wind Rivers rose into the sky. In front of them lay a line of small brown hills that didn't rise nearly high enough to get the water the Wind Rivers did. Or maybe the Wind Rivers forced all the water out of clouds that passed over them, leaving nothing for the country beyond. A cloud shadow.

Pinto took a course that followed Highway 287 below, which ran between two lines of mostly barren hills stretching out roughly in the direction of Cheyenne. The hills were about four miles apart. A river squiggled its way between them, parts of it flashing like a mirror in the sun. The land was green for about a quarter mile on either side of the river, irrigated by a patchwork of ranches. Beyond that, the sage desert stretched forever.

Most of Wyoming was like that—farms here and there clustering thinly along the scarce small rivers that were probably what people back East would call creeks. Roads like a thin spiderweb connecting it all. Every ten, twenty, sometimes forty miles along one of those lines was a small town, sometimes nothing more than a couple of houses. Sometimes it was a mine or a natural gas plant. Tiny dots and threads of civilization in miles and miles and miles of huge, open, very often treeless, landscape.

Frank knew he probably wouldn't be back to make his graveyard shift at Walmart. So he made a few calls and finally got someone to cover. The dispatcher back in Rock Springs called to follow up on his missing person report, but Frank told her what he told the officer and then set up a time the next day to bring Tony in as he told the officer he would. When he hung up from the last call, he was on the edge of nausea. The wind was pretty strong, and all the jarring was working on him. He used to have an iron gut, but something had happened in prison. He took in some big breaths and focused his vision on a wisp of cloud a few miles in front of them. It was now about ten to five. Ed *should* be calling soon. Unless he'd changed his mind, which Ed was wont to do.

There'd been an old guy in the prison. He was doing four years for battery with a deadly weapon. He'd taken a bowling ball to a big tough-guy neighbor who kept throwing dog doo in his yard. Nailed him as he went out to his car one morning. Ed had chummed up to the old guy and then turned on a dime. First he'd demanded the guy's spot in the yard. Then he'd demanded soap. Food. He took socks, crayons. Whatever the guy had. He just kept pushing and pushing until one day old Bowling Ball had enough. He came at Ed, and Ed shanked him with a poker made from wire. It had been fast, and the guards hadn't seen.

The code inside requires you keep your mouth shut, so Frank

played like he hadn't seen a thing. Which meant he had to listen to Ed glory in his big showdown. On and on about the goading and the attack. On and on about the fine feel of the wire as it broke through the skin and muscle. On and on, trying to get Frank to talk about the details of his own kills in the service, until Frank had told him that if he didn't want to look like a friggin' idiot, he'd stop crowing about throwing down on some old grandpa.

That had shut Ed up, for a while. It had also changed his demeanor, awakened some animosity that lurked in the corners of his eyes. Frank had never trusted Ed. He trusted him less after that. It was quite possible that Ed might have determined right then he was going to pay Frank back for the insult. Sooner or later, he was going to make Frank eat his words.

Sam started to get sick. Pinto handed him some chewing gum and a bag. Then he offered a piece of gum to Frank.

It was some minty thing. Frank took the piece and said, "Who's the lady above the door?"

Pinto looked over at the portrait of the handsome Black woman. "That's my north star."

Frank unwrapped the gum and popped the stick in his mouth. "Yolanda?"

"No, Yolanda was a woman my wife Kerry knew when we were first married. She was always getting away, going off to see Yolanda, going to bake a cake with Yolanda, going on a walk with Yolanda. Those two were joined at the hip. So I got me my own Yolanda." He patted the plane.

When Pinto didn't go on, Sam said, "Kerry died a couple years back from cancer."

"She'd just turned forty," Pinto said.

"Sorry to hear that."

"She loved to fly," Pinto said. "Said it put everything in perspective. Made you look to the stars. Made you realize there was a lot more to this universe than the thin layer humans inhabited."

Getting some altitude certainly gave you something; right now the jerky flight was making Frank sick, but he nodded. He imagined Pinto and his wife had taken a number of rides in this plane—all decked out with fairies and lace. Maybe with Henry sitting in back like he was now.

Pinto said, "Sometimes, I swear she still takes a ride now and again."

Frank didn't know much about spirits and the next life. From what the pastors said, folks seemed to be constantly sucked up into the light or down into the other place. Like a tug-o-war between two huge vacuum cleaners. The earth ought to be a tidy place. But maybe a few souls got caught in the cracks and crannies. Maybe the vacuums didn't reach everywhere. Frank knew he'd be motivated to find cover if Hell's vacuum was coming after him.

"You married?" Pinto asked.

"No," Frank said. "Mine didn't quite work out."

Which was an understatement. It had started well enough. He had met Blanca one summer in Colombia. He was there teaching Colombian soldiers assigned to fight the cartels. She was broken down on the side of the road in a bad part of town. He and the other guys had stopped, helped get her on her way. Then she'd come back to the base to say thanks with empanadas. Frank had been struck the first time he saw her—quick-witted, smart, fun. Gorgeous Colombian skin and eyes. She worked for a bank, managing their ATMs.

They saw each other multiple times. He sent her flowers, a necklace with a jade pendant, and Maduritos, these sweet plantain chips she loved. And then he had to leave. He told her on the patio of a restaurant, the mariachis playing in the background and red macaws squawking in the trees, that he was going to come for her. But Uncle Sam had other plans. So he paid a coyote to bring her over the border. He married her in Texas at the side of the sea.

The first years were good. But he'd had to ship out a lot. She was alone and didn't speak the language. He thought she was doing well. But the back-to-back military tours took their toll. He loved the service. Hated turning his back on his team, but there was no way things were going to work between him and her if something didn't change. And so he left the Special Forces when his enlistment ended.

But it was too little, too late. By the time he came home, Blanca was already halfway out the door. He said hello and her gorgeous hair and quick-witted smile walked right out of his life.

A few weeks later, he made the dumbest decision of his life and got involved with Simon Haas, an acquaintance who was making big bucks in the private sector using the skills he'd learned on Uncle Sam's dime. And he was doing it for clients that you didn't ask questions about.

It had been good money, but it had also been dumb money. Almost nineteen months after Frank took off his camo, he found himself putting on another uniform—one that was Day-Glo orange. The consequences of his decision smashed through his idiot life like a tornado.

Tony and Kim had been there for him. But now the consequences of those actions years ago were reaching out again to take them.

Pinto said, "Kerry was one hell of a woman."

"You can say that again," Sam said.

Frank thought of Blanca, Kim, and Tony. He sighed with frustration.

Pinto said, "She was a little bit of fire and a bit of banana cream pie."

They flew on in silence for a bit, and then Pinto looked over at Sam. "Have we said a prayer?"

Sam nodded.

Frank said, "Sam's two and O. I think he's hooked up to the wrong answering service."

Pinto said, "You praying to your Excel spreadsheets again?"

"I've repented of that," Sam said with a grin.

Pinto said, "If anyone's hooked up, it's Sam."

"Well, then maybe I'm the one dragging us down. Because God's not been answering my calls."

"Maybe you're not going about it right," Pinto said. "I once read this book that claimed to have the secret to life. The secret to getting anything you desired. Basically it said that God, the Universe, whatever you want to call it—it was this big vibrating genie. That was the secret, hidden for ages, now come to light. And all you had to do was vibrate your wishes out, and the Universe would respond. Things would suddenly pop out of the woodwork to help you. You vibrate a new TV, and suddenly there's a coupon in the mail. You vibrate a better job, and suddenly your uncle's mailman knows about one. Ask, and you shall receive. Vibrate, and the Universe will open the way."

"Tony's with a psychopath, and you're telling me the answer is to vibrate?"

Pinto said, "It all seemed true. God's like this big vending machine in the sky, but one that doesn't work all the time. I mean I've prayed. Sometimes the candy bar falls; sometimes it doesn't."

Frank had to admit it sometimes felt that way. Right now the machine wasn't doing anything but eating his quarters.

"But then I saw the flaw. Say you buy yourself a big yellow truck. What happens? Suddenly there ain't nothing but big yellow trucks on the road, and you wonder where they all came from. But the thing is: they were there all along. What's changed is your focus. What you paid attention to in the first place.

"If you have a problem and start thinking on it, you're primed to notice solutions. And as you discuss it with others, you prime them to notice too. That isn't some galactic genie. That's just what happens when you've got a limited working memory that forces you to choose what to pay attention to. Same thing happens a lot of times when people pray. You're praying, and so you're paying attention. And so you can see the solutions that were there all along plus others that arise which you would have missed. It's not a vending machine or a genie. It's all big yella trucks."

"You're saying I shouldn't be waiting for help. There is no God. Prayer's just a way to get focused."

"I didn't say there wasn't a God."

"You're going to jinx the little connection I have with the upstairs brass."

"I'm not saying not to pray. I'm saying it's easy to think every little thing has some divine origin. I'm saying you've got to have the right expectations. Sooner or later, unless you're living on the moon, it's going to rain, right? But you've got some farmer out there praying, and all he can see is that he prayed, and then it rained sometime later. And there's no thinking about cause and effect. Did his prayer change the weather? Who knows? But to him it's shazam—an answer! That, my friend, is your classic post hoc ergo propter hoc."

"Cut the Greek, Aristotle."

"It's Latin," Pinto said. "It means coincidental correlation, false cause. The two events just happened to occur one after the other. There's no relationship whatsoever."

This guy wasn't in witness protection. He was some farmer-philosopher combo transplanted from weird-land California.

"But you can't always say there isn't a relationship," Sam said. "It's not always easy to separate out cause and effect. Sometimes when there are too many factors, or the effects take too long to show up, you can just as easily miss a causal relationship. Some folks used to believe smoking tobacco was healthy. The cancer effect happened too long after the cause for them to see the relationship. And sometimes it didn't happen at all."

"But they figured that one out with science," Pinto said.

"Sure," Sam agreed. "But there are some things science can't test. Variables you can't control. Things we can't even detect and measure. And if you can't measure and control, you can't do science.

"The physicists claim there's this stuff called dark matter and dark energy out there. They theorize that it makes up ninety-five percent of the universe. Another four percent is invisible atoms. So ninety-nine percent of everything is stuff they cannot see, feel, hear, or detect in any way. They don't know what it is. They don't really know if it's even there. The only reason they say it's there is because they can't get their equations to work without it. But they're just doing some big-brain guessing. And their equations are changing.

"The universe holds far more mysteries than we can begin to unravel at this point, including the technology of God. You can talk to somebody thousands of miles away with a radio or satellite; I'm sure God's got his own science. I'm a hundred percent sure he's got the technology to hear and respond."

Pinto said, "I never said God couldn't help. I only said you need to have the right expectations. Not get your panties in a wad if things aren't happening all television style."

The plane droned on. The little fairy with the acorn hat slowly swung to the plane's vibration.

"All I know," Frank said, "is that I need to get Tony back. And my assets are two hicks—no offense, big guy—a cookie man, and this plane." He looked up. "And you, God, if you want to play, which would be first class."

Sam smiled. "The petition has been made."

Frank said, "Let's just hope it hasn't been filed with some divine desk jockey."

Henry had been looking at the men like he was trying to follow what they were saying. Frank gave him a scratch on the head. "You think it went to a desk jockey?"

Henry shimmied.

Frank shook his head. Typical Golden Retriever.

At that moment Tony's phone blooped. Frank pulled it out of his pocket and saw an anonymous text. It said, "Jockstrap, this is God."

"Is it Kim?" Sam asked.

"We vibrated," Frank said, "and brought back the devil Ed Meese." Then he texted, "I am two minutes away from calling the cops."

A moment passed, and then the phone blooped a reply: "Not a nice way to talk to your maker."

"One minute forty-five and counting," Frank texted.

He got down to one minute nine before Tony's phone rang. Frank tapped Talk and said, "Put him on."

Ed laughed, a big belly buster, like he was laughing so hard he might fall over, like his eyes were all squinting up with laffy tears. "You followed that phone," Ed said and laughed some more. "You followed that phone! Priceless."

"You now have forty-five seconds."

Ed regained some control. "Come on, Frank. You've got to admit it's funny. Mr. Green Beret Army hunter chases the phone. Did you do some recon?"

"Thirty-nine seconds, Ed."

"You're no fun, Frank. No fun at all." Then he must have held the phone out for Tony to speak because his voice came through as from a distance. "Say something to Uncle Frank."

"Tony?" Frank asked.

"I'm here."

"Location?"

Ed's voice came up close to the phone. "Uh-uh," he scolded. "None of that. No reason to keep Tony around if he's just going to blab our whereabouts. You want me to get rid of him? Is that what you want, Frank?"

Frank's anger rose up in him, but he kept control. "Put him back on."

Ed's voice was far away again. "Go on, my minutes are ticking."

Frank said, "They touch you?"

"I'm okay," Tony said.

Ed chimed in, "He's got a mouth on him, but he's learning real good, aren't you? I'll have him trained here soon enough. Maybe you'll rent him to me."

Frank said, "Meese, you're digging your own grave."

Ed's voice was close now. "None of this would have happened if you had just lent us your car."

"Just like a con—everything is everyone else's fault."

"Then Tony here went all Lone Ranger, saving the damsel in distress. My hands are tied. The boy's got to learn: this is what happens when you stick your fingers in somebody else's pie."

"I'm sure he's learned his lesson."

"Naw," Ed said. "You can see it in his eyes—he wants payback. The material just hasn't quite sunk in. Sometimes people are slow. But we'll call you around ten. Just a few more hours and this will all be over."

"Ed—," Frank said, but Ed hung up the phone.

Frank looked at the phone, his anger running through him like ice. A few more hours gave Ed a total of nine on the road. Plenty of time to slip the net, to be so far away Frank couldn't catch him. But it was the tone in Ed's voice that chilled him. If Tony pissed those two off, if he threatened them, if they thought he would go to the authorities later, Ed would slip a bullet in his head and not look back.

They'd have Frank to deal with then. Except they knew he had nothing. Frank hadn't kept tabs on any of his cell mates. He'd tried to forget every last detail about them. And even if he could track down these two pieces of trash, it would be too late. Because Tony would be gone. Dragged to the side like road kill. And no amount of vengeance would bring him back.

Frank was not going to lose that boy. "This plane go any faster?"

"She's topped out."

"But we have the wind," Sam said.

Pinto asked, "What did this Meese jerk say?"

Frank related the details of the call, and then Pinto said, "If we were in California, I'd be calling a couple of my brothers right now."

"Ha," Frank said. "I knew you were in WITSEC."

But Pinto was right: they needed more assets. Frank asked, "What about Henry? Can he put on a ferocious guard dog show?" A ferocious show of intent, even if Henry did nothing but bark, could put Ed and Jesus on their heels. There was something about a mouth full of sharp canines that tended to psychologically deter someone from contemplating stupid acts.

"You'd be a bit hard pressed," Pinto said. "He does the big happy slobber, and he fetches, mostly sticks and frisbees. That's the extent of his current skill set."

"Maybe we can convince him Ed is a big frisbee," Frank said.

Henry knew they were talking about him. He woofed and thumped his tail.

They flew on, the hills passing below them, the wind bumping the airplane every now and again. Frank thought of old Bowling Ball back in prison. He thought of the stories Ed told of his other victims. Then he used the rest of the time to think of ways he might break Ed's neck.

* * *

About an hour and forty-five minutes after they took off, they flew over the last mountain range in southeastern Wyoming. The beginning of the great American plains rolled out before them toward Nebraska. A string of huge windmills rotated a few miles ahead of them. Beyond the windmills, Cheyenne rose from the landscape like a big oasis.

Frank had a bit of a headache to go along with his low grade nausea.

"We're going to have to go south or skirt around," Pinto said.

"We got gas troubles?" Frank asked.

Pinto pointed up ahead. "No, that's Warren Air Force base."

"We don't need to go that far," Frank said. "I figure we drop down to I-80 and then follow it back."

"You feel good about your calculations?"

He'd gone over them about twenty times in the last hour, and there were a hundred variables that could throw everything off. The fact was the more he thought about them, the less sure he became. "It's a bit late if I'm wrong," he said.

"Roger that," Pinto said. He radioed into Cheyenne Regional. They cleared him and gave him a code, which he punched into his transponder so they could easily track him on their radar. Then he banked a gentle turn and headed south for the interstate. The fields below stretched to the east. From here on out things just got greener and greener. Another hundred miles and it would be nothing but wheat, corn, and soybeans.

Pinto kept close to the mountains. They passed the Air Force base on their left, and then the interstate came into view, the semis and cars racing east and west.

"Why does he call you Jockstrap?" Sam asked.

"I found God down in Pleasant Valley. I'd always believed, but prison makes you focus. For the first time in my life I started actually reading wisdom books—the Bible, some Buddhist meditations, books on the afterlife. Ed thought it was funny. Thought it was all a show for the parole board, which for many it is. He started calling me Preacher Shaw. Then he landed on 'Jockstrap' because I gave others such fine spiritual support."

"You want me to shoot this Ed fellow?" Pinto asked.

"I just need you to fly."

Pinto took the plane across the cars and turned so they were flying parallel to the interstate. That way both Frank and Sam could get eyes on the road. Pinto slowed the plane way down. The pitch of the motor dropped. "We're at 500 feet," Pinto said. "This is as low as I can legally go unless I'm landing."

Frank picked up his glasses, found the interstate in them. He could make out the faces of the people in the cars. "This will be just fine," he said.

9

Crosswind

THE CARS AND SEMIS raced along the interstate. The motion of the plane and looking through the binoculars made Frank's stomach heave. He chewed his gum that had long ago lost its flavor and took in measured breaths to steady his gut and kept searching, but there was no Ed, no Jesus.

There was everything else. A bored male driver. A woman driver with kids in the back watching TV. A woman reading a book and a man spitting something out the window, probably shells from sunflower seeds. There were two adult men in one car singing and rocking out to some tune. There were Fords, Chevys, Toyotas, Hondas. There was some Ferrari-looking thing all black and low like it belonged to Batman. But there was no two-tone Nissan.

Cars and trucks spaced in between semis. Semis spaced in between trucks and cars, all of them barreling down toward Cheyenne.

Pinto kept the plane steady, and they followed the road back to the foot of the mountain range, and then up along the ridge. They left the controlled airspace around Cheyenne. A few minutes later they entered the airspace controlled by Laramie Regional and reported in the same transponder code. They followed the interstate up to the summit and the Lincoln Monument rest stop. Someone had thought it would be a good idea to refresh weary travelers with the sight of Abraham Lincoln's head—it was bronze, set stylishly atop a thirty-five-foot granite base of stones, and about the size of a FedEx truck. Every day hundreds of weary travelers came chugging up the hill, and there was Lincoln looking down at them like a beacon, reminding them that this was still the blessed U. S. of A., even in the middle of nowhere Wyoming.

But Frank wasn't thinking about Lincoln. The rest stop had a parking lot and bathrooms. No reason for Ed and Jesus to stop, unless maybe their car was overheating after the steep climb up from Laramie and needed to cool off.

Frank told Sam to keep his eyes on the road while he searched the parking lot. In the last twenty minutes Frank had seen a number of silver cars. A number of gray cars. He'd seen a few two-toned cars of various colors. But not the Nissan.

Except what was that on the third row with dark cola glass?

He looked closer, but it was some Volkswagen outfit.

He cursed under his breath. Pinto asked if they needed to circle, but he told him to go on. The thought began to tickle the back of his mind that maybe his assumptions had been all wrong. Maybe they should have started farther east. They flew past Lincoln and followed the freeway which dropped into a canyon that ran down the other side of the mountain toward Laramie.

Sam trained his glasses on the road ahead; Frank searched the stretch that was alongside the plane. Henry looked out his window as well; at what, Frank had no idea. But then Henry started to whine.

"I believe Henry has got to go," Pinto said.

"Can he hold it?"

"I guess we'll find out."

The wind was pretty rough on this side, and the plane bounced around. By the time they reached the bottom, Frank was truly sick. "I should have taken a Dramamine," he said.

"I wondered about that," Pinto said.

"He's not the only one," Sam said, looking a little green.

"Pantywaists," Pinto said. Then he fished around up by his seat and produced two more barf bags just in case and handed them out.

"At this low altitude, we're going to need to stay clear of the airport," Pinto said. "But I think we'll be okay following the road."

"They should be well beyond this point," Frank said. Well beyond. And then he realized they had another problem. The interstate through Laramie had four exits into the city. Each exit had its collection of motels, gas stations, restaurants, and truck stops. They were going to have to check the parking lots of each one of them.

"Lord," Frank said. "I think I'm going to go blind."

But he and Sam split up the work. One of them kept an eye on the interstate while the other checked all the parking lots and on-ramps. Frank figured this is where they'd miss them. And by the time they came to the last exit, he was sure they had slipped past or were already behind them when they'd first turned in Cheyenne. And that was if they'd even come this way at all.

His heart began to sink. If they'd gone west, they could be in Nevada by now. South, deep into Colorado. He couldn't imagine they'd gone north, unless Jesus had some drug distribution route that took him to Jackson Hole.

Frank began to search the parking lots of the businesses around this last exit. There was a Wendy's, a couple of gas stations, a Best Western, and some store on one side. He made sure to search in lines so he didn't skip, but the Nissan wasn't there. He flipped to the other side. There were two hotels with mostly empty parking lots. More importantly there was no Nissan in either of them. The last spot was a big truck stop with two buildings and what looked liked four acres of parking lot. It was huge. There were more than a dozen semis in the lot out back, and it didn't even begin to fill the area. There were rows of parking for cars out front.

Frank searched the rows. It took him so long he made Pinto circle round. But in the end, there was no Nissan.

He sat back and sighed in frustration. It was now 7:01 p.m. Four and a half hours since Tony had been taken. There was no way Ed was going this slow. And he'd seemed smug enough when he'd called last, so Ed wasn't broken down somewhere on the side of the road. Frank had missed him. Or he was tooling along hundreds of miles from here in another direction.

Frank dialed Kim. No answer. He texted her: "you're freaking me out! call now." No reply. He dialed her home phone and went to voicemail.

"What do you want me to do?" Pinto asked. "We're getting close to the halfway mark. I'm going to have to turn back or set Yolanda down and get some fuel."

Option A, Frank just let Ed play out his game. But that girl had talked to Tony, which meant Tony knew things he shouldn't. And even if he didn't know things, Ed was involved. Option B, Frank called the cops. But with Kim not responding, he didn't know she was safe. And Ed would want payback. If Frank sent him to jail again, Ed would most assuredly exact payback. And that payback would not be focused on Frank's person. Ed would go after the kid; he'd go after Kim. So for Frank to pull this off, Ed needed to know that when he screwed with Frank, he was bringing a mountain down on top of himself.

But Frank had nothing. It's hard to pound a guy like an avalanche when you don't know where he is. Frank brought up the keypad on his phone to dial 911.

Sam said, "I think I see them."

The words shot through Frank. He leaned forward. "Where?"

Sam was looking through his glasses and pointed beyond the truck stop. "About two miles west of Laramie coming our way. They're drafting behind that McDonalds semi."

Frank followed the interstate west, saw the McDonalds semi, saw it was a Nissan with his naked eye. He found the car in his binoculars. The windows were too dark to see in the back, but sitting in the front were Ed and his personal zombie Jesus.

"Thank you vibrating genie!" Frank said.

"Post hoc," Pinto said.

"How do you know God didn't smite that car?" Sam asked.

"I don't care if it was Buddah or the University of Wyoming Cowboy. We've got our target." Then Frank looked up. "Unless, of course, you *were* involved. Don't want to give any offense."

The Nissan sped below.

Frank started to get anxious. "Turn the plane around," he said.

Pinto executed a banking turn.

Frank kept his eyes on the car. It rolled up to the outskirts of Laramie, exited the freeway, and headed for the huge truck stop. "I need to get on the ground," Frank said.

"The airport's right there," Pinto said.

"No, by the time you call in and get down and then back up to spot for me, we'll lose them. I need to get down here; while they're in the truck stop. This is it." Frank scanned the area for a suitable spot. "Look, there's a road just a few hundred yards west."

"Maybe Heber can catch them," Pinto said. He pulled out his phone and dialed a number. A moment later, he said, "Where are you?"

He and Heber exchanged their locations, and then he hung up. "Heber's just past Elk Mountain. He's about an hour away."

"Not good enough," Frank said.

"Is it even legal to land?" Sam asked.

"There's no FAA rule against using roads," Pinto said. "As far as they're concerned, you can land a plane anywhere. The great State of Wyoming hasn't banned it either. But I don't know if the controlling municipality has passed any laws. But legality isn't the problem. The problem is that road. It's one thing to land on a country road used mostly by jack rabbits out in the bush. It's quite another to land on one close to town. You've got to watch for cars and power lines. A roadside sign can easily wreck a wing."

"I don't see any signs," Frank said. "And there's only one car way down by the interstate."

"You feeling this wind?" Pinto asked. "The road runs north-south. The crosswind will blow us to Hell and back."

"Pinto," Frank said. He had to get down. He'd been in enough situations to know that you took your opportunities when they presented themselves. A bird in the hand was always better than two hundred in the bush. "I know you don't know me. But I'm begging your big old Portuguese heart."

Pinto sighed heavily.

"I believe the cow is in the mud," Sam said.

"Yeah, yeah," Pinto said and licked his lips. "And we're going to sink into the mire with her. Right into a big old friggin' eight foot deep manure lagoon."

There was a beat of silence.

Then Pinto said, "Aw, hell. Here goes nothing. You two might just be picking me up in jail. That is if they aren't picking us all up in pieces off that road."

He turned the plane in a big circle to get it lined up with the road.

"How much space do you need to land this thing?" Frank asked.

"About 1,400 feet."

"That's a quarter of a mile."

"The man can do math," Pinto said.

"That road is at least two miles long. You've got plenty of room."

"Oh, do I?" Pinto said dryly. "Good thing I've got you navigating."

Sam was looking back at the interstate with his binoculars. "They're just pulling into the truck stop."

Frank looked down at the road. The one car was heading away. "We're good," he said. "The road's clear."

Pinto finished his turn, dropped altitude. Dropped more. They flew over the fields west of the road.

"That's a dirt road," Pinto said. "You know what happens if we hit a rut or pot hole?"

"We bounce a bit?" Frank offered.

"If it catches the tire, we slam our nose into the ground and go tumbling."

They dropped closer, maybe two hundred feet. Then a hundred. The wind was pushing them east, pushing them closer to the road, buffeting the plane. They passed over a group of black cattle in a green field, dropped lower.

Henry must have seen the cattle. He woofed excitedly.

"Yeah," Frank said. "Cows."

They flew over the tops of a line of cottonwood trees. They were close enough to the ground that Frank could make out the barbed-wire fences. They passed over the roof of one of the few houses along this road. A couple of kids were digging in a sandbox. Their little hand shovels glinted in the late afternoon sun.

They dropped lower. Fifty feet. "This is going to be tight."

A gust of wind slammed into them and blew them to the side of the road.

"That's got to be twenty knots," Pinto said. "Which means this method ain't going to work." Pinto turned the wheel a bit, moved the foot controls. The tail of the plane suddenly spun around, and they roared down the road sideways, Frank looking out his window like he was in the driver's seat. They dropped lower, twenty feet now. They were almost there.

"Uh, Pinto," Sam said, "we're kind of sideways."

"You think?"

"Shouldn't we be turned the other way?"

"Not in this wind," Pinto said.

That's when the car pulled out onto the road. It was a beat-up brown Ford, all boxy corners in a 1980s style. It had been parked beneath a tree. Easy to miss in the late afternoon shade. One second the road was clear. The next the car was right there. A teen was driving it, white earbuds in his ears. The car accelerated, kicking up dust.

"Hell's bells!" Pinto shouted.

The plane roared up behind the car. There were stickers all over the bumper, the trunk, the back windshield. One said "Big Hairy Deal" in block letters. The plane and car were both kicking up a storm of dust.

The kid at the wheel looked into his rearview mirror. He saw the plane. His eyes went round as eggs. Not every day you get rear-ended by a plane.

"Get out of the way!" Frank yelled.

They were going to crash into the car. They'd hit it with the landing gear, which would tip the wing on Frank's side down, and then they were going to roll, and the propeller was going to cut into the driver's side. They were all going down in a mess of tin and airplane gas. Maybe a nice ball of fire.

Frank thought about Tony and Kim. And Ed, the evil genie.

Then the car's brake lights lit up. Frank braced himself, but the landing gear did not hit the back of the car. Instead, the plane roared, what must have been no more than five centimeters, above the roof of the car, leaving the freaked-out driver in a thundercloud of dust.

They flew maybe another fifty feet, about six feet off the ground, and then Pinto spun the plane straight and dropped it onto the road with a solid thump. They jostled about, and then they were bumping and roaring down the road.

"Thank you, Lord," Sam said.

"Unbelievable," Frank said.

Pinto shook his head. "Shaw, you're officially on my dead man's list." He idled the engine and put on the brakes, and after another hundred feet the plane came to a stop.

They were all still breathing hard.

They looked at each other, and then Pinto began to laugh. "Now that's a landing, boys."

"I'm off your death list then?" Frank asked.

"Don't get your hopes up."

"That was definitely a new technique," Frank said.

"That's an old technique," Pinto said. "It's called crabbing into the wind."

"It's called crazy," Sam said. "I think I'm going to need a diaper."

Pinto said, "You get out of here and waylay that S.O.B. If I'm going to have the locals on my tail, it had better damn well be worth my while."

Frank clapped Pinto on his big shoulder. "I owe you, man. I owe both of you."

"That doesn't even begin to describe it," Pinto said. "Now get."

Sam opened his door and climbed out. Frank piled out after him, happy to have dirt under his feet. Henry jumped out, ran to the side of the road, and lifted his leg to take a leak in the grass. He finished and raced back into the plane.

Sam got back in behind him, shut the door, and Pinto cranked the motor back up. The plane rolled forward, then Aristotle and the Lone

Ranger drove down the road like they were taking a Sunday drive, the dust kicking up behind them into the wind. Henry sat in the back watching Frank. He woofed a couple of times like, "Dude, I'm still in a plane!"

Frank turned around. The kid in the car was still parked down the road, probably hyperventilating. A car ride would be quicker than running, but Frank wasn't going to ask the kid for a ride.

Across the fields, about half a mile away, stood the truck stop with the semis and cars clustered about it. The buildings were white. A huge sign towered over them. Frank descended the shoulder of the road, jumped the barbed-wire fence that ran along the side, and sprinted out into a field that was about calf-high with the beginnings of a second crop of hay.

It had taken them maybe three minutes to land. It would take Frank another three to cross this field to the truck stop. He prayed Ed was standing at the back of a long line to the crapper.

10

Truck Stop

TO THE UNTRAINED EYE, fields of hay looked peaceful, pastoral. And some might be, but not in Wyoming. Frank had found that those fields the farmers irrigated were actually gauntlets. Mosquitoes thrived in the moist cover. And so when any idiot thought it would be a dandy idea to prance through one, the swarms of Hell rose up to suck every last pint out of the man. Or at least try to infect him with malaria or West Nile. In some places where they flood irrigated, the mosquitoes swarmed above the field in columns and sheets as big as Winnebagos, whining with mad blood-fury.

You hoped for a wind. Because the little buggers would be swept away when they rose to devour you. Frank had a wind. He took this as a good sign and ran through the field of meadow grass. He came to the end, hopped another barbed wire fence, and ran into another field of dark green alfalfa. Halfway through, he realized he didn't know exactly where Ed had parked, so he called Sam.

Sam picked up, the roar of the Cessna in the background, but then Frank spotted the Nissan. There was a gray car parked way out in the southwest corner of the massive parking lot, away from everything else. The hood was up. A moment later Jesus appeared from behind the hood, his back to the car and the field, holding his hand to his ear. He was on the phone.

Bingo.

Frank hung up. So it *was* engine troubles. Which meant Ed was probably inside trying to get a part or fluid. Or maybe just getting something to eat.

And where was Tony? No way Ed would take him into the truck stop. So Tony had to be in the car behind those cola windows. Unless Ed had already taken care of him, which was an option that had to be considered and might explain why Ed was so late getting to this point. Maybe the car troubles were secondary.

Frank didn't want to contemplate that. He'd go in with the assumption Tony was there. And if he wasn't, then this little hostage rescue mission was going to take on an entirely different flavor.

He was standing in plain sight of anyone in the parking lot. He needed to get to the edge of the field, to the road that fronted the entrance to the truck stop. There were cottonwoods all along the road that would provide good cover. He could get within twenty feet of the Nissan going that way. Frank was about to move when Jesus turned around, sunglasses on the top of his head, still talking on the phone. He looked right at Frank.

Frank's heart banged. He wanted to hit the deck; instead, he bent over and dug up a handful of dirt. He brought it up to his nose and crumbled it in his fingers. He had no idea if ranchers ever smelled their dirt, but he was pretty sure Jesus didn't know that either.

He threw the dirt down and walked a few more paces, ignoring Jesus. The mind often saw what it expected to see. He bent down, grabbed another handful of dirt and smelled it. He turned his back to Jesus, put his hands on his hips like he was surveying the field. Then he pulled out his phone, acted like he was calling someone and began to gesticulate. He walked slowly through the alfalfa straight toward the cottonwoods. He told himself he was a farmer, concerned with his field. He was boring, unremarkable, nothing to look at.

He just kept walking, talking to nobody on his phone, looking down at the ground. He desperately wanted to see what Jesus was doing, but controlled himself. Only when he was almost to the fence did he glance back.

Jesus had moved. He was now standing in front of the hood, looking down at the motor, still holding his phone to his ear.

Frank pressed down the top strand of barbed-wire and swung one leg over. Still holding it down, he swung the other leg over. Then he slipped between two huge old cottonwoods onto the shoulder of the road. The trees broke the wind, and a number of mosquitoes came at him. It was summer; Frank had shaved his head. He swatted the buggers away from his neck and exposed scalp and wished he had more hair.

He watched the Nissan through the trees. He watched for Ed. There was a lot of deadfall here, but none of it looked useful. The branches were either too thick, or too old and rotted, or much too small. He thought about picking up a stone, but there weren't any visible in the tall grass. So it was just him, with the gifts Mother Nature had given him. He was going to need to get in close.

He walked the final fifty yards and approached the corner where the field ended and the parking lot began. Jesus had lit up a cigarette. He was leaning against the side of the car, facing the truck stop, his phone still up to his ear.

Only a fat tree and a few yards of blacktop stood between Frank and the car. The wind was making a racket through the branches of the trees, which would mask his approach.

The hood was up, blocking most of the view inside the car. He looked past the car at the front doors of the truck stop. Ed wasn't there. He wasn't in the parking lot. This was about as good as it was going to get.

When you practiced raids, you quickly learned that the times you employ speed, surprise, and shock action work out a lot better than the times you don't. Especially in hostage situations. Surprise was easy to blow on the approach. You needed noise discipline. You needed to walk quietly, avoid obstacles, and keep out of view.

The wind gusted through the trees which cast shadows over this part of the parking lot. There were some small twigs on the ground between him and the car. There was dirt and grit that would grind under foot. He looked around the parking lot to see if there was anyone watching; way down the strip of lawn at the other end of the parking lot an extremely fat motorist in shorts, sandals, and socks was letting his tiny dog sniff about the lawn. The man was looking the other way.

Frank moved out, walking until the raised hood blocked Jesus's view of his approach. Then he slipped across the sidewalk and over a strip of lawn that bordered the whole stop. He kept the raised hood between him and Jesus. He stepped over the curb and onto the asphalt. The wind gusted again, masking the grating of the grit under his feet. He crossed the last few yards to the front of the car. The engine was filthy. The yellow caps to the windshield wiper and brake fluids and the yellow handles to oil and transmission fluid were dark brown.

Frank walked around the open hood to the side where Jesus leaned up against the car. He was still on the phone, taking a drag on his cigarette. Frank took another step, and Jesus glanced over. Then his eyes widened in alarm. He reached for the gun in the waistband behind his back, but Frank was already on him.

He grabbed Jesus's gun hand with both of his and twisted it up and around into his back. Jesus automatically faced into the car. Jesus struggled, but Frank grabbed him by the hair and banged his face into the car. He banged it again hard for good measure. He kept Jesus's arm twisted up behind his back with one hand. With the other Frank slid the gun at Jesus's waistband out of its holster and into his own pocket. It was a nice nine millimeter semi-automatic.

Frank's adrenaline and rage kicked in high gear. He banged Jesus's head into the car a third time, and blood began to run down the man's nose. You wanted controlled aggression in a fight, but Frank didn't know if he was going to be able to control this.

He yanked Jesus back and marched him around to the front of the car, away from the eyes at the truck stop. But Jesus still had one free arm. He reached into his pants on that side and came out with a tactical knife. The double-edged spear point blade shot forward out of the housing and locked in place.

"Not smart," Frank said and swept the man's feet out from under him. Jesus slammed into the car and slid down by the front passenger's wheel. Frank fell upon him, put one knee into the man's back, then banged the knife out of his hand. It was a Benchmade. Said so right on that razor sharp four inch steel blade. Four inches is about a long as a big man's index finger. Plenty of length to slash, plenty to strike vital organs in a thrust. He kicked the knife away. "Those knives are only for law enforcement and the military," Frank said. "I don't think I saw your badge."

"You're dead," Jesus slurred.

"Don't give me ideas," Frank said and pressed on the back of Jesus's neck with all his weight. He looked back across the parking lot toward the front of the truck stop. There was nothing going on. Out along the curbing, the fat motorist had missed the whole thing and was watching his dog.

Frank turned back to Jesus, and searched him for more weapons. There was nothing in his waistband or pockets, nothing around his ankles.

He thought a moment about finishing Jesus right there. Frank had not been trained as a cop. He'd been trained to kill. And killing Jesus would have been the smart thing to do. If interrogated, he could say it was in self defense. He could say he'd feared for his life and the life of his nephew in the car. Jesus was a dirt bag. A judge and jury would certainly take that into consideration. Of course, to them Frank was a dirt bag as well. But Frank wasn't going to kill Jesus.

It would have been nice if he'd thought to bring some rope or wire—something to tie up this moron. But he'd have to make do with what he had, so he undid Jesus's black leather belt and pulled it off his pants. It was a real looker, all studded with bits of chrome. Frank cinched it up tight around the man's wrists, retrieved Jesus's knife, and made a nice hole and buckled it tight. Then he wrapped the rest of the belt round and round the wrists and tied it so there was nothing for Jesus to grab onto.

Frank felt his back prickle, and he twisted round. Ed was standing about five yards away, pointing his Springfield subcompact right at him. On the ground next to him, stood a blue radiator fluid container. The container was all wet, but not with coolant. It was wet with water, and Frank realized Ed hadn't been in the truck stop; he'd been around back or out among the semis getting water.

Frank cursed.

Ed said, "I wouldn't be making any sudden moves if I were you."

Frank was in an awkward position, but action was always faster than reaction. Two or three steps and he'd be ten feet away and running. Ten feet might not seem like a lot of space, but they'd done studies on New York cops, which had been repeated elsewhere. They'd counted the number of bullets shot versus the number of hits in real-life shootouts. Here were guys that repeatedly practiced their marksmanship, but put them in a high stress situation, and they had a hard time hitting more than twenty-five percent of the time. And that was within a range of six feet.

Ed wasn't a cop. Frank would be surprised if Ed practiced at all. Frank would put some distance between him and Ed, and then he'd turn and train Jesus's gun on him. And then they'd see what was what.

Frank had years of training, multiple tours, numerous missions. He'd lost some of his edge, but Ed was nothing more than a psychopath. There was nothing in his muscle memory except evil. And now he was going to go down.

Frank said, "Ed, your hair looks like crap. Looks like someone's been at it with a leaf mulcher."

"What?"

Now, Frank thought.

But at that moment a white panel van shot past the back end of the car and slammed on its brakes, cutting off Frank's escape. The side door slid open. Inside was a Hispanic guy in his early twenties. His hair had been moussed up. His arms sported a number of tats. He knelt on one leg. In his hands was a twelve gauge shot gun with a short eighteen inch barrel. A riot gun. Perfect for crowd control, for home defense, and backing up your fellow crack-brained vato in parking lots. He pointed it at Frank. The driver opened his door and jumped out as did another man riding in the passenger's seat.

Frank could try to draw Jesus's piece in his pocket, but he wouldn't be quick enough. Not with three of them. Not with him kneeling all awkward over Jesus.

Ed said, "What am I going to do with you, Frank? You're like a freaking bad penny. Showing up here. How the hell?"

"Just give me Tony, and I'm out of your hair."

Ed motioned at Jesus who was trying to squirm out of his bonds. "You've gone and complicated things, Frank. You're going to get into the van; we'll talk on the road."

"We're not going anywhere."

Ed motioned with his head, and the driver and third man walked around to the other side of the Nissan and opened the rear door. They pulled Tony out, who was awake, but groggy, and helped him into the van. His wrists were zip-tied. Then they went back for the girl, who was zip-tied as well. Somebody must have got a bulk deal on those restraints.

Frank glanced around the parking lot. If anybody had been watching, it would have made a real spectacle. But nobody was looking. The Nissan was way out in the corner of the lot, in the shade. And anyone looking this way from the truck stop would have the sun in their eyes.

Ed said, "You're starting to piss me off, Frank. Now get in the van."

Ed's eyes were flat and lifeless. He was ready to kill.

Frank said, "I'll get in the van. Then we're going to talk about things you don't do to your ex-cellie."

Ed said, "Lie face down on the ground and put your hands behind your back."

If Frank started shouting, nobody would hear over the wind. Not clearly. They wouldn't know what was going on. And Ed still had Tony.

Frank had blown it. He should have done a 360 recon round the whole place, but then he probably would have missed his opportunity. Frustration bunched up inside him, but there was nothing for him to do. He'd lost this round, so Frank lay down on the ground and put his hands behind his back. Made nice big fists side to side, gave himself lots of room.

The driver obviously knew Frank's fist trick because he turned Frank's hands so they were facing each other and only then bound them up with a sturdy cuff zip-tie. He searched Frank and took his phone and Jesus's gun. Then he stepped back.

Ed hid his gun in his vest pocket, but kept it pointed at Frank. No reason to flash it in public for all the truck stop patrons to see.

Frank walked over and climbed into the van, the guy with the shotgun tracing him the whole way. The back of this van was mostly bare like a delivery truck. A piece of filthy carpet had been thrown on the floor, and someone had made a solid bench out of particle board to go over the wheel well along one side. The bench was bolted to the floor. One end of a long cable used for locking bicycles up was bolted at one end. Frank wondered what it was for.

Tony and the girl sat on the carpet. Shotgun motioned Frank toward the bench. Then the driver came up and slid the bicycle cable between Frank's bound arms, then through the bound arms of Tony and the girl. Then he padlocked it to the bolt on the far end. The mystery of the cable was solved. They must be transporting a lot of people to go to the trouble of pounding together a bench and rigging a line. And that presented another mystery.

"Worried someone might steal me and ride off?" Frank asked.

"Yeah," Ed said. "This place is lousy with thieves."

The others helped Jesus onto the floor of the van. His nose was off kilter, and there was blood all over his face. He was having a hard time keeping his eyes open, but that's what happens when your face meets a hard object.

"I'm going to kill him," Jesus snarled.

"Not here," Ed said.

Jesus gently felt his nose, then groaned and jerked his hand away. Ed climbed into the driver's seat and closed his door. Shotgun moved into the passenger's seat. The original driver got out, and he and his original passenger closed the side door. This van had obviously been called in for a switch.

Frank was kneeling in front of the bench, his arms behind him. He wasn't going to ride this way. He wasn't the slender steel of seven years ago. He had a lot more muscle on him now, but he'd made sure to stay limber. He lay on his side and brought his tied hands down below his thighs and then, with a bit of a struggle, slid his legs through and sat up on the bench with his hands in front of him like a regular Harry Houdini.

Frank looked at the cables and bench. They were worn, well-used. How many people had they transported in this van? And to what destination? He looked for blood and saw a dozen blotches of various sizes on the filthy carpet that could have been blood, but could have also been the drippings of someone's cheeseburger.

Frank said, "You ordered a replacement vehicle, and they brought you this? You need to rent from a different car company."

Ed said, "You're a funny man, Frank. Unfortunately, you're not too bright."

"All I want is Tony."

"I heard you the first twenty times," Ed said. "I don't need a rerun. So just chill, and think about your future. One that's most likely going to feature you getting well acquainted with Jesus."

11

Precious Cargo

FRANK GOT HIMSELF comfortable on the particle board bench. Then Ed pulled out of the truck stop and turned onto the road. They passed the fat motorist and his dog; the man was still oblivious. A few moments later, Ed made a right and accelerated up the on-ramp to the interstate heading east.

Jesus lay on his back behind the front seats and gingerly felt his nose. He said, "It's broken."

Shotgun looked down at his face. "You look like a bulldog, man."

Jesus cursed, something in Spanish. "We're getting it looked at," he said.

"Sure," Ed said. "But we lock down everything first." He looked in the rearview mirror.

Frank ignored Ed and turned to Tony. "I didn't know Yeti Inc. had expanded its services."

Tony shrugged and looked down. He was completely strung out. Heavy-lidded eyes he could barely keep open.

"What did you give him?" Frank asked.

"Bugs Bunny vitamins," Ed replied. "They're chock full of B."

Frank turned back to Tony. "You're going to be all right."

Tony didn't respond.

Frank nudged him with his foot. "Look at me."

Tony looked up through slits.

"I told you I'd find you. We're going to be all right."

Tony gave a half nod. His lids fell. "Dude."

"You lie down," Frank said. "It will all work through your system."

"Hey," Tony said, but the rest was mumbled. Then he lay down on the carpet.

Frank looked at the girl. Early twenties. Smooth brown skin. Jeans and a green button-up blouse that had come untucked. She wore work boots. What kind of girl wore work boots? And those weren't designer jeans either. They looked like they belonged on a man. Her dark hair hung down loosely to her shoulders and covered part of her face. What it didn't cover revealed recent bruising. There was a scrape on her cheek. One lip was cut and swollen like she'd taken a fist or elbow to the mouth. She was out, sleeping like a baby on the filthy carpet next to Tony, her zip-tied wrists all angry and red like she'd been working at her bonds.

From Frank's position it appeared she'd been abducted, beaten, thrown in a trunk, probably beaten again. She had not had a very good recent twenty-four hours.

He wondered how much these dirt bags were asking for her. Was she some drug dealer's daughter? Or the daughter of an illegal who was now a prosperous businessman? Someone who could pay a hefty ransom. Or maybe this was blackmail—maybe her daddy was a politician, maybe someone in her family was chosen to testify in some court. Or maybe this was payback.

Frank shook his head. There was a whole shadow world out there where people were killed and kidnapped; they lived and died and worked for dirt, unseen, in the shadows, and only the tip of the iceberg ever came to the attention of the police. They lived on U.S. soil, but the suburban-apple-pie-fourth-of-July Americans rarely saw them. When they did, it was like the fleeting sighting of a mountain goat up in the rocks as you raced past at seventy mph.

Frank looked around the back of the van. He looked for anything—a screw, a pencil, a piece of wood. There was nothing. Up behind the passenger's seat sat a clear plastic tub with handles that came up and locked on the sides. It was full of what looked like black socks.

Frank twisted his wrists: the zip tie was good and tight. They'd done a bang-up job on him, or at least that's what they thought.

He assessed the space between him and Shotgun. Jesus was lying still in his own miserable world. Ed was driving. Frank could probably make it to Shotgun before he brought his weapon around. One blow to his face, maybe to his eyes, and Frank could break his skinny, but finely decorated neck.

But what would the cost be? Shotgun would likely have his finger on the trigger. He would discharge the shotgun with the barrel pointing somewhere in the direction of the back of the van before he said goodbye. It would make one hell of a sound in this little space. Make them all half deaf and put a ringing in their ears that would take hours to fade.

The shot from such a gun might blow a nice hole in the side of the van and then go on to hit any car that might be in the next lane. It might blow a hole in the floor. It might hit Jesus. But it also just might hit Tony or the girl.

A bullet from a handgun punched a relatively small hole through the body. In the right spot it could kill immediately. But more likely it would zip on through the target, and you'd have to wait for enough blood to spill out before the heart failed to pump the life-giving juice to the brain. Only then would your man be truly incapacitated. It was all about blood pressure and springing leaks.

A shotgun, on the other hand, turned everything in its path to ground beef. At six feet, even with that short barrel, the spread pattern would still be just a few inches wide. Maybe as wide as the bottom of a Coke can. If it was loaded with double-aught buck shot, then nine pellets, each about as big in diameter as Lincoln's head on a penny, would fill that space. It was like getting shot with nine .22 rifles all at once. Except these pellets were .33 caliber, a little bigger, a little heavier than the bullets from a .22. They would blast into Tony at more than 1,000 feet per second, chew up anything in their path, and blow out the other side, leaving nothing but carnage in their wake. A wound that big, taken in the torso, was not something you survived, which was why people who got hit that close with a shotgun rarely made it to the hospital.

Frank put aside his plan to break Shotgun's neck and sat tight, watching as Ed followed the interstate through Laramie, home of the University of Wyoming Cowboys. Frank hoped Pinto and Sam hadn't run into any trouble. Of course, with the plane painted in University of Wyoming colors, they could say they were Cowboys coming for an early tail gate. Surely the locals would welcome them with a beer and open arms.

The interstate led into the canyon, then up into the mountains. The sun was setting, lighting up the whole hillside in glorious color. Ed kept his speed right around the legal limit. A highway patrol vehicle shot down the canyon on the other side of the interstate, but by the time Frank spotted it, it was too late to have made enough of a ruckus to attraction his attention.

Frank watched the road and what he could see of the light show out the front, running scenarios through his mind. He could go for them when they unloaded; he could take a dump on the floor and see if that didn't goad Shotgun to come back; he could go for Shotgun's weapon, and not Shotgun himself. They reached the summit and the massive monument with Lincoln's head on top appeared off to the left, a blaze of glory in the fading light, and then Lincoln was behind them.

Shotgun turned around and opened the plastic tub full of black socks. Except they weren't socks. They were hoods. He threw three of them at Frank. "Two for them. One for you, dick head. Put them on." He pointed his shotgun at them.

Shotgun was a skinny thing, a bit twitchy and drawn out. His teeth were bad, which could mean he hadn't learned how to brush as a lad or that something more industrial was eating them, something manufactured in great quantities in Mexico and shipped north. Nothing like red phosphorus, Drano, and battery acid to give a man that winning smile.

"I get carsick," Frank said. "You want me to barf all over the back?"

"I think we just kill the big one," Shotgun said.

Ed looked into the rearview mirror. "It's up to you, Jockstrap. You can make this easy. Or you can dig yourself a hole. Where these boys come from, a dead body doesn't mean a thing."

Frank nodded. A hole was being dug, but it wasn't his. "Are these your boys?" Frank asked.

Ed didn't reply.

Frank looked at Shotgun. "Is Ed the jefe?"

Shotgun pointed at Jesus. "You laid out the jefe's son, verga. Estúpido como un perro." As stupid as a dog.

"But I sure am good looking," Frank said.

"Put on the hood," Ed said.

"Tell me who I'm dealing with."

"You just prettied up one of the Goroza family," Ed said.

Frank had never heard of them.

"Estúpido como un perro," Shotgun said again.

Frank knelt on the nasty carpet, pulled Tony a bit closer, then picked up a hood and slid it over his head. He wondered who the Gorozas were and the size of their operation.

"Get it on real good," Shotgun said.

Frank pulled it down, but made sure the material was pulled as far away from Tony's face as possible. He did the same for the girl.

"Now you, dick wad," Shotgun said.

"How long did you spend coming up with that one? The effort must have been tremendous."

"Shaw," Ed warned.

Frank sat back on the bench and pulled the hood over his head. It was good thick cotton, but it had been used and smelled faintly of rancid hair oil and something else minty that had probably been lip balm. He wondered what woman had worn this last. Frank found he could see out the bottom, so he studied his feet.

Ed turned on the radio to some Mexican station, then searched until he found something classical. Some guy with a heavy voice came on and said they were going to listen to Claude Debussy. Then the piano music started.

The light in the van diminished, indicating the sun was finally setting. Frank figured it was past eight o'clock. Ed and Shotgun talked in low tones. They argued about the radio station and getting food, then rode on in silence.

About thirty minutes later, the van started to slow, and then the blinker began to click-clack and they exited the freeway. Frank concentrated on the movement. They didn't want him to know where they were going, but he could feel his way well enough. They didn't make a big cloverleaf turn to go north, nor did they make a gentle bending turn. This wasn't the interchange between I-80 and I-25. It was just a regular exit before or after that. But he'd heard an increase in traffic five minutes earlier, which meant they were probably somewhere east of the big interchange in Cheyenne, but not too far east.

They drove down a slope and stopped. Then they turned right. South. They traveled straight for a while, stopping now and again at what had to be traffic lights, because he could hear the cars to the side and behind stop and speed up. They went south for quite some time, then turned east onto a dirt road.

It was night, made even blacker by the hood. They rumbled along for a while over the dirt road, made a few more turns, and then Ed rolled onto gravel, let the van idle for a second, then shut the engine off.

Ed and Shotgun got out and slid open the side door. Cool night air rushed in. Frank listened hard. No dogs. No cars. Nothing but the night air breathing with crickets. They were out in the middle of nowhere. Out in the Colorado plains. Out in old Arapaho land.

Jesus got out. Then the back doors opened.

Frank reached up to remove his hood, but Shotgun slapped his head. "Keep your hood on, dick chew."

"Please stop," Frank said. "I don't know if I can bear up underneath this devastating verbal onslaught."

They opened the padlock holding the bicycle cable, and Ed said, "You're going to get out the back. And you're not going to do anything stupid, because I don't want to have to kill you, Frank. Or your fine piece of Tony."

Not here in the van, but Ed could very well want to kill him as soon as he stepped out and moved to a better spot.

"Get up," Shotgun said.

The girl got up and exited the van, crunching on the gravel. Tony followed. Frank came last. It was pitch dark outside. No city glow, no street lights, nothing but a bit of moonlight.

"This way," Ed said.

Frank shuffled blindly forward, the gravel crunching under his feet. "Tony, you feeling better?"

"I can keep my eyes open," Tony said.

"Nothing to worry about here," Frank said.

"That's right," Ed said up ahead of them in his best imitation of a friendly snake. "You're all going to be fine. Just a little catch and release."

Except that isn't what this was. Frank knew it. Ed knew it.

A screen door squeaked open; the handle of a regular door turned. Someone pushed on Frank's shoulder to change his direction, and then he walked up some steps into a dark house and onto some linoleum. It stunk like someone had been cooking fish.

"Hey, qué hubo?" How's it going, a new male voice said. So the house had occupants, but they probably kept the lights out just to make sure nobody saw what they brought in.

"Primo," Shotgun replied. "We got the puta."

"This way, people," Ed said. "You're going downstairs."

They walked around a corner, still in the dark, and then someone flipped a switch and a light went on. Not much, but he didn't need much for it to make a big difference. Frank could see the stairs out of the bottom of his hood. They were narrow stairs, covered in old linoleum, going down into an old basement.

He didn't like this, but he followed the girl and Tony down the creaking stairs. It smelled of old cement and must. There was a whiff of old urine overlaid with something floral.

Someone put a black nylon restraint belt around Frank's waist, the kind used to transport prisoners. The kind that had a metal loop in the front to which hand cuffs were attached.

Who said convicts couldn't learn from their betters?

They backed him up to a home-made 2x4 and plywood bench, knocked him off balance, and sat him down. He was going to protest, but Shotgun pressed the barrel of his weapon hard into Frank's face and shoved his head against the wall. And then they broke out the zip ties again, looping one through the zip tie on Frank's wrists, down through the loop on his restraint belt, and finally through a wide half-moon hole someone had cut out of the front of the bench. They'd run a long length of rebar all along the underside of the seat right at the front. This new zip tie was attached to that. But they didn't stop. Two more zip ties came out, one to tie each ankle to one of the many bench legs. When they were done, they stood back.

Frank tried to move, but they'd done a solid job, and he began to wonder if maybe he should have done something on the way in.

They zip tied Tony and the girl next to him. Then Shotgun ripped the hood off Frank's head.

Jesus stood in front of Frank, his hand in a work glove, all wound up for an angry haymaker. He really did look like a bulldog. An ugly zombie bulldog. But hey, it's not like Frank had been trying to make him look pretty. If Jesus had wanted to look good, he should have kidnapped the nephew of a hair dresser. Or a plastic surgeon.

Jesus swung. Frank tried to move out of the way, but there's only so much you can do when you're tied to a bench that's nailed into a concrete floor and wall, and Jesus connected. Frank turned his face and shed some of the power of the blow, but it wasn't nearly enough. His head whipped to the side, and if he hadn't been tied to the bench, he would have fallen off.

Jesus definitely had an arm. A couple more of those, and Frank was not going to sleep so well. Jesus pulled back for another blow, but his effort had sprung a leak in his nose. A line of thick red blood ran out of his nose and dripped onto the floor.

The side of Frank's face was stinging from the previous blow; it was going to swell up real nice. He braced himself, figured he'd duck forward this time.

Jesus smiled a terrible smile, his face bruised and bleeding.

Shotgun said, "Vato, you want to get that on the night shift, man. You don't want to be walking into the hospital during the day and having to wait in some line."

"Wait too long," Frank added, "and they'll have to break it again. Too many breaks, and it's just not going to heal right. That's only going to compound your problems with the ladies."

"Shut up," Jesus snarled.

"This dick fart isn't going anywhere," Shotgun said.

Jesus glared then flashed some gang sign at him instead, the meaning of which was lost on Frank, but which probably meant he'd cut off Frank's head, drink his blood, and then eat his brains, the brains of all his children, his dog, his goldfish, whatever.

Jesus pointed at Frank with a vigorous and showy snap. "You and me, pendejo. You and me!" Then he turned and climbed up the stairs, leaving Shotgun behind.

Shotgun was pretty pleased with his skinny self. He smiled, showing a set of black and brown things that used to be teeth. Definitely a tweaker. "Buenas noches," he said.

"You really need to see a dentist," Frank replied.

Shotgun flipped him a slow bird, then turned and walked back up the stairs.

Now that was a gang sign Frank could understand.

He wanted to touch the throbbing side of his head, but of course, the zip ties prevented that. He thought about Jesus's little theatrical ambush. If your goal was damage, you didn't punch someone in the side of the head. It's the hardest part of the body. There were plenty of other areas that were softer and would cause more pain. Which meant his first assessment of Jesus had been correct. He was a brawler.

Frank looked at Tony and the girl.

"You okay?" Tony asked.

Frank said, "I might have lost a few years of my life looking at the little one's teeth, but I think I will survive. I hope you don't have to go to the bathroom."

"Oh, man," Tony said. "Why did you even have to mention it?"

Frank noticed the urine smell was stronger here by the bench. If one of them did the deed, he or she wouldn't be the first.

"Don't think about it," Frank said, and then he caught the stare of the girl. She wasn't looking at him; she was looking with dismay at something past him. Frank turned.

This was the basement of a small, old house, much like his 1950s bungalow in Rock Springs. They were in the main open area. One naked light bulb illuminated the room that seemed to stretch the length of the house. There were two small windows, both boarded up with plywood that had been driven right into the cement of the foundation. There was an old water heater and furnace. There was a door standing open to a tiny bathroom that looked like it didn't have more than a toilet and sink in it. The toilet bowl itself was stained brown.

But none of this is what dismayed their female companion. What dismayed her were the girls sitting on two filthy mattresses thrown on the floor in the shadows at the other end. Four were in their early teens. The fifth looked more like she was ten. She was holding a worn teddy bear, wearing pink pajamas. They were all Hispanic. Anywhere else, and you might think they were having a sleepover. But it was a little difficult when there were no movies, games, or party snacks and everyone was locked in, prison style, with Ed and Jesus upstairs.

"Hello, girls," Frank said.

Then a boy moved out from behind the others. He looked about as old as the girl with the teddy bear. He had a bruise on his face.

They said nothing. The giggly girlyness of youth that should have shone in the girl's eyes was so long gone it wasn't even a memory. The boy's face was a stone.

Frank had seen such eyes before. He'd seen them in Colombia. Seen them in Afghanistan. These were eyes that had seen fifty years of hard labor. Like maybe someone had taken their dreams by the hair and cut their throats.

"Who are you?" Frank asked.

The oldest girl gave a warning glance to the younger ones. "We are homeschooled," she said with a thick accent.

"Jesus is teaching you math and biology?"

"Yes," the oldest girl said.

She was a terrible liar.

Special Forces operators were required to learn a language. Frank had learned Spanish, forgotten much of it serving in Afghanistan, then learned a different type in prison. He wasn't fluent, but he knew enough.

He said, "Dios no quisiera que vivieras con lobos."

"What are you saying?" Tony asked.

"That God never wanted them to live with wolves."

A few of the other girls looked at Frank with fear. Like something bad might happen if the oldest girl didn't play this right.

"We are fine," the oldest girl said. "We are homeschooled."

Then somebody flipped the switch upstairs, and the light went out.

12

Locks

THE ROOM WENT black. As Frank's eyes adjusted, a wan light appeared on the other side of the room. It was cast on the floor by the tiny furnace pilot flame. Upstairs, Jesus and Shotgun talked about the hospital and urgent care. A few minutes later the back screen door banged shut. Then a vehicle started outside and pulled out. A chair scraped back, someone walked to the sink, turned it on, turned it off, then walked to another part of the house. Someone turned on a TV and tuned into a Spanish station. Someone else laughed.

Frank spoke into the darkness, "Are they having you work in the fields or in the houses?"

"Señor," the oldest girl said. "We are homeschooled."

They weren't. Not by a long shot. They were being transported. Out to the fields in California or the orchards in Washington. Or maybe to some fine buyers who needed someone to wash dishes in the back of their restaurant.

Six kids. What was the going rate for a little slave these days? $800 to $1,200 bucks? They could sell them to individuals, but they'd more likely sell them to a subcontractor that would bid out harvesting services. He'd show up with his crews, including some children like these, and they'd pick the apples and strawberries that the rest of America ate. The contractor might pay them a pittance, tell them they were working off their fee, but it would never work out that way.

There was a long-shot that Jesus was actually transporting these kids to uncles and aunts who had paid for a coyote to bring them over.

Maybe even a parent or grandparent who'd preceded them into the land of plenty. But coyote services usually stopped close to the border. And willing kids didn't need to be locked up in the back of a van with a bicycle chain.

"Someone has these kids trained," Frank said. And he hated Ed and Jesus even more.

"Dude, what are we going to do?" Tony asked.

"That all depends," Frank said. This whole time the woman Tony had freed had not spoken a word.

Frank said, "Señorita, you mind telling me why Ed had you in his trunk?"

Silence.

"Do you know where we are?"

No response.

"Habla Inglés?"

"She speaks English," Tony said.

"Well, buddy, here's what I think. We're in a stash house. Those girls over there are being sold up the river. Literally. The one you freed, best bet is they picked her up in Utah. But what's in Utah? Maybe there's a small business owner they're trying to extort. Someone undocumented who doesn't have his paperwork in order. She's his daughter. What would they ask? Fifty thousand, a hundred? Is that what this is, Señorita?"

Nothing.

"She wouldn't tell me nothing," Tony said. "Then Ed drugged us. He kept calling her his pot of gold."

Frank said to the woman, "We're in this together. I personally hate Ed; so the more we work together, the better our chances of getting out of here."

"Right," she said.

She obviously didn't believe him. Didn't trust him at all.

"At least tell me your name. I'm Frank Shaw. Frank Moses Shaw, actually. The Moses came from my Dad's grandfather, a wild west preacher who is said to have shot a number of criminals in his time."

No response.

She was not a happy camper. But then, if Frank had been beaten and stuffed in a trunk, he might not be Mr. Customer Service either. "I'm not the one that put you in the trunk."

"Does that matter?"

All she knew was that Frank knew Ed; in her mind they could be buddies. It was the old guilt by association. "I'm not involved with Ed. I only know Ed because the great State of California assigned us to be cell mates for a while. That's my crime; what's yours?"

"Talking," she said.

Frank waited, but she didn't say more. "We're going to get out," he said. "The question is whether I take you and those kids with me."

"You're just going to break your bands?"

"More or less."

Tony said, "He was a Green Beret. Those morons upstairs don't have an idea."

"There are five of them."

"They'll need ten more to make it fair."

Frank smiled ruefully. If only. One unarmed guy against four or five with guns only worked out in the movies. But he appreciated a little hero worship now and again; besides, the oldest girl needed to believe, or she just might rat him out instead. And Tony needed to believe as well.

Frank said, "In a couple of hours they'll all be asleep."

"Should be a piece of cake then," she said.

This woman had some definite trust issues. Furthermore, she should be scared. Worried. Something. Kidnapped daughters of businessmen don't act like this. Something else was going on here.

Frank said, "Look, I don't know what's between you and them, but I'm fairly certain that the Jesus upstairs isn't the forgiving type. I suspect this Jesus wants to saw my head off with the serrated edge of a steak knife. You were asleep at the time, but I'm the one that re-arranged his face. I'm not too keen on losing my head or any other body part; that's where I'm coming from."

"Then it sounds like you'd better get busy," she said.

"Thanks for the helpful advice," Frank said. Why didn't she want to talk? Why does anyone not want to talk? Because you think it won't get you anywhere. Or you think it might make matters worse.

"You think I'm a plant, don't you," Frank said.

No response.

"You've got something they want."

Silence.

That was the only reason to keep her alive. But what she had wasn't the riddle Frank needed to solve at the moment. He assessed his situation. Jesus was gone to get his nose fixed. Probably took Shotgun with him. That meant there were three men above.

Three was better than five.

The bench he was now zip-tied to appeared to have been built by the same guy who built the bench in the van. The guy had put some thought into it. He'd been a regular Leonardo. Except he hadn't thought out all the things the Gorozas might attach to this thing. They hadn't thought, for example, of Frank. If you're going to engineer, you really need to build things to go above and beyond the regular expected use.

He began to work the mouth of the zip tie binding him to the bench around so he could get at it. These weren't landscaping ties. They were bigger and built for human restraint. Perfect for scared girls. Perfect for your run-of-the-mill guy.

Frank said, "Jesus has an MS-13 tattoo. The Gorozas are into something big, aren't they? Meth? Cocaine?"

"You would know," the woman said.

So she did think he was in cahoots.

Frank slid the locking mechanism of the zip tie around in front of his hands. With a finger he bent the loose end of the tie around his wrists and began to shim it into the lock of the zip tie binding him to the bench. It took some jiggering, and it was tight, but he soon had the end of the one zip tie inside the lock housing of the other, creating a barrier between the teeth of the tie and the lock. He pushed it in a bit further. With the strip between the teeth and the housing, there was no lock holding the tie tight. Frank quietly slid open the tie binding him to the bench.

He stood up, used his teeth to slide the zip tie around his wrists so the lock was facing up. He grabbed the loose end with his teeth and pulled the zip tie as tight as it would go. Then he raised his hands above his head and brought them down hard against his gut, shooting his elbows out like chicken wings. The tie held. He adjusted the lock so it was in the center between his wrists, tightened it, raised his arms again. This time when he came down, the plastic lock broke, making a tiny snap.

"Dude," Tony said.

"Shush," Frank said. The fact was that the Stockholm syndrome was real. It didn't happen all the time, but it happened enough. Just ask a veteran cop who has answered his or her fair share of domestic dispute calls. Ignore the wife and focus on her wife-beating husband, and you just might find a knife in your back. These girls were young. He didn't want to think about the abuse they'd already suffered. They might be shot up with cocaine or heroin or meth. The last thing he needed was for one of them, in a poor twisted mechanism of self-defense, to warn their captors. It was called operational security.

Same went for the woman. She might be a Goroza herself. Maybe she'd fallen out of favor with the family. Maybe she was a dealer who'd stolen drugs. Maybe she was a meth head and by tomorrow morning would be ready to sell him out for her next hit. The only one he trusted here was Tony.

He bent over and used the end of the now worthless zip tie to shim the two that held his ankles. It was pitch black in the room, so he had to feel his way. When he finished, he sat back in the darkness. It was very dark down here. But it wasn't quiet; the sound of the TV came right through the floor boards. That was a good thing. He leaned close to Tony and spoke in his ear. "Snap your fingers, and keep snapping them until I say stop."

Tony began to snap. It was a good masking sound and added to the TV soundtrack.

Tony said, "How—"

"Shush," Frank replied. "Ancient Chinese secret. Now listen. In about an hour I'm going to get up. Do not trust anyone. If one of the kids or our mystery woman asks about me, you say I'm right here sleeping. Clear?"

"Clear," Tony said.

"You can stop snapping," Frank said.

Tony stopped.

"You want to sleep?" Frank asked. "Just lean on my shoulder."

"I'm not tired," Tony said.

"Then tell me about your ride with Ed."

Tony related their abduction and drugging with Benadryl. He described a snippet of one phone conversation he'd heard where Ed told the people on the other line that she'd be ready. But for what Tony couldn't guess. And she didn't fill in any blanks.

When Tony ran out of things to say, Frank told him a couple of humorous stories from his days in the service. He wanted to keep Tony's mind off of the situation. He also wanted some baseline of noise.

About an hour and a half later, he asked Tony to sing.

"Dude," Tony said.

"Keep it low, nothing that will wake anyone above."

Tony began to sing, "You are my sunshine, my only sunshine. You make me ha-pee when skies are gray."

That was not quite what he'd expected. Frank said, "Is this what you and your buddies listen to? No wonder you haven't got a woman."

"It's all I could think of. It's what Mom used to sing to me when I was little."

Kim. Holy cow, if she knew what was happening . . .

Frank said, "Sing away, Romeo. Maybe next you can favor us with a medley from *Blue's Clues*."

"I'm the map," Tony said. Then he started back up again.

Frank stood ever so slowly in the pitch black. He felt forward with one foot, and when he was sure he wasn't going to step on anything, he slowly moved away from the bench.

He moved like he was in extreme slow-motion, like he was some kind of tree sloth. Like a chameleon stalking prey, one ancient leg at a time. It took him ten minutes to get to the stairs. Tony finished "You Are My Sunshine" and began with "The Ants Go Marching One By One Hurrah."

Frank used the edges of the steps. He used the hand rail. On the third step he creaked, but the rest of the stairs were solid. By the twelfth chorus of ants Frank was at the door. He'd seen through the crack at the bottom of the door on his way up. The light was off in the kitchen, which is where this door led. The TV was in the other room.

It was still running, but it had been some time since Frank had heard any conversation or footsteps from above.

He grabbed the doorknob. It twisted. It hadn't been locked! This might end up being easier than he thought.

He set himself and prepared to open the door as slowly as he'd crept up here. He pushed, but the door didn't budge. He pushed harder, but it wasn't moving. He felt along the door and about six inches above the knob ran across a circular metal plate. The back end of a dead bolt. One without a key slot.

He paused. Dead-bolted doors weren't impossible. A lot were installed improperly. They needed at least an inch long mortise into the door frame to allow the bolt to lock. If the bolt wasn't fully extended and locked, you could slip a putty knife in and push the bolt back. Frank didn't have a putty knife, and he hadn't seen any tools down in that basement. He could try to kick or ram it in, but he was in no kind of good position to do that. His first attempt would wake the house. If it took more than one try, he'd open the door to find the men upstairs waiting with their guns.

No key hole to pick. No putty knife. No good angle of attack.

He could wait right here until morning. The moment they opened the door he could rush them. But there was a good chance they'd bottle up, and he wouldn't get the door fully open. If it was him alone, he might risk it. But he couldn't risk getting shot and leaving Tony downstairs to their devices. He needed something with a lot better odds.

He immediately thought of the bathroom he'd seen and got an idea.

Tony finished the seventeenth chorus of marching ants and started up with "Ninety-Nine Bottles of Beer on the Wall." Frank was pretty sure Kim hadn't sung that one to him.

He did his tree sloth crawl back down the stairs. He carefully felt his way across the darkness of the basement to the bathroom. He quietly and painstakingly felt around the counter and then in the drawers by the sink until he found what he was looking for.

The fact was that the human body was soft. Eye material was soft. And just about anything could be made into a shank strong enough to penetrate. He'd seen a great variety in Pleasant Valley—melted plastic coffee lids, a long screw, the nub of a pencil. Anything that could be fashioned into a hard, sharp point. He wrapped his fingers around a standard-sized toothbrush, then slipped it in his pocket.

In the main room, Tony was down to thirty-five beers.

Frank exited the bathroom as slowly as he'd entered and slow-walked back toward the bench. About ten feet away, his toe struck an aluminum can. Frank froze, but the can rolled and rolled. The loudest sound in the world.

It finally came to a stop. He paused, waited, and just as he was about to resume his journey, the older girl turned on a small LED flashlight, the kind you might find on a key chain, and shined it across the room. It wasn't much light, but it was more than enough. She found Frank in a second and lit him up for everyone to see.

So much for operational security.

The girl looked at him for a moment more, then turned off the light. Tony had stopped singing when Frank kicked the damn can. There was nothing now but the TV.

Frank walked over to the wall, felt his way to the bench, and sat down.

"Dude," Tony said.

Frank didn't know the woman or the girl. He didn't trust either of them. There are a lot of things you'd do to curry favor with your captors. Narking on the big ugly guy who had broken free of his restraints was a no-brainer.

The woman and girl were both silent as the grave.

Probably wondering what he truly was. Was Frank a victim like them?

If so, they could score points with the men upstairs by giving him up. Was he a plant sent to cozy up and get the woman to talk? If so, she might say something as soon as someone came down to show she knew their bluff. Or did Ed and Jesus have these kids terrified, telling them they'd send people to test their loyalty? They might think Frank was just such a test and decide the way to pass was to reveal he'd been walking about.

Hell's bells.

Nothing to do about that now. He was just going to have to improvise.

"I'm going to take first watch," Frank said to Tony. "Get some shut-eye."

Tony said, "I can't believe the cops didn't respond. How do we drive hours on Wyoming roads and not run into one single officer?"

"I put them off your trail," Frank said.

"Why?"

"What would you have told any cop that pulled you over when Ed told you he knew where your mother lived and had friends in the area?"

A beat passed.

"He knows where we live?"

"You willing to risk that he doesn't?"

"That twelver. If I'd had a gun . . ."

Which is why Frank wasn't going to free Tony from his bonds any time soon. The last thing he needed was Tony popping up into the fray.

"What are we going to do?" Tony asked. "You've got to get me out of these ties."

"We're going to sit," Frank said. "We're going to be good little prisoners."

Tony sighed.

"Get some rest; you're going to need it."

It took Tony a while to calm down, but he eventually succumbed to sleep.

A moment later Frank pulled the toothbrush out of his pocket, took the end, and began to slowly grind the handle on the rough concrete wall.

It was around two a.m. when he finished. He felt the end of the toothbrush, which came to a nice hard point. It wasn't going to win any wars, but it just might turn the odds of a fist fight. Outside, a vehicle drove into the yard. Someone crunched over the gravel to the back door. The screen door opened. Slammed. Two people stomped around upstairs, got something out of the fridge then went to another part of the house. Everything fell quiet again except for the TV that was running an infomercial.

Frank reattached the zip ties around his ankles, except did them up backward, which meant they wouldn't hold at all against any amount of pressure. He did up his wrists the same way and used the tie he'd broken to look like he was still fastened to the bench. Then he set his internal clock for three hours, two REM cycles, and made himself as comfortable as possible and fell asleep.

13

Bang Bang

FRANK WOKE UP sometime before his two cycles had ended. Tony was slumped against him. The woman looked like she was sleeping too. Then he realized the basement was not as dark as it had been before. He looked up at the boarded windows; there was no daylight coming in around the edges. He looked around.

Over in the corner, the older girl was on her knees, rocking back and forth, speaking with a hushed voice. She had turned her little flashlight on and placed it on the cement floor so it shone upon what looked liked a small greeting card that had been set against the wall.

Frank peered closer.

The image on the card was of a person. No, not of a person—a skeleton clothed in a robe of stars with roses and skulls at her feet.

Santísima Muerte, the Most Holy Saint Death, whom Jesus had tattooed on his shoulder, with that vine of skulls and roses curling up beneath her feet. The saint to whom those in drug trafficking, kid-napping, and crime set up shrines and made offerings, rubbing their candles over their limbs and face and hair and then setting them alight at her feet. Of course, Frank had been told that many in both police and military in Mexico were counted among the faithful as well and asked for blessings on their weapons and ammunition. The Catholic church had officially denounced her, calling it all a devil-worshipping cult. But it's hard to argue with the narco prosperity. To those who believed, Santa Muerte was a powerful saint, able to grant favors no other saint could.

The girl picked up a book of matches and tore one off. She held it between the strike strip and front flap and pulled. The little flame burned into the darkness.

One of the little girls said, "No creo que nos puede oír." I don't think she can hear us.

"Why would she listen?" The little boy asked in Spanish. "We don't have candles or wine. We don't even have apples. We have nothing to offer."

"Shush," the older girl said. She held the little flame in front of the card and rocked. "Doña Bella," she said in hushed tones. "You are beautiful and kind. We believe in your powers. We have no candles. We have no cigarettes to light and share with you. Please do not forget us, sweet mother. Please help little Rosa to heal. Do not forget us, please."

By this time the match had burned down close to her fingers. She laid the remnant on the cement floor at the foot of the card and waved the smoke of the match toward the image on the card.

"She helps the Gorozas," the little boy whispered. "She's not going to help us."

"Do not let her hear you say such things," the older girl reprimanded.

The flame flickered and then burned out.

One of the little girls sniffled.

"It's okay," the older girl said in soothing tones.

"It still hurts," the littlest girl whispered.

"I think he might be too injured to ask for you tomorrow," the older girl whispered. "Did you see his face? He went to the hospital. Maybe he'll be in too much pain to want to touch you. Even if he takes Viagra."

Viagra?

A small point of rage filled Frank's heart. Was that Jesus's game—a transportation racket with a continual supply of victims to prey upon en route?

The little girl sniffled again.

Frank's mind went back to a warlord they'd made contact with in Colombia. A man who their contacts had said could lead them to one of the carnales, one of the cartel big shots. His mind went back to tin hut at the edge of a camp in the Colombian jungle. The warlord had led them to the hut; he'd removed the chains that held the door closed, then pulled the door back. Sunlight had streamed in to illuminate five little girls huddled on the dirt floor. "Pick one, Gringo," he had said with a smile. "They are fresh. No disease. I think you'll like the one there with the big eyes."

Frank and the other Special Forces men with him had turned down his offer. But they did not forget him. A week later a cartel hit squad came in and decimated the place. They'd received a strange anonymous tip that the warlord had been working with the Gringos.

"It won't be forever," the older girl said. "We only have to work off our debt. And then you can be an American."

"I don't want to be an American," the little girl said in the darkness. "I just want to go home."

"It's only for a little while," the older girl said.

"I can never go back home," the little boy said. "Not now. If my father found out, he would kill me. The other boys would stone me like a diseased dog."

The cold rage inside Frank rose and settled along his jaw. It ran down his neck, across his shoulders, and wrapped his chest. It wrapped him from head to toe.

He shifted his position, and the bench squeaked.

The children froze, their faces full of alarm.

"Qué onda?" Frank asked. What's going on?

The alarm gave way to fear.

A beat passed. Then another. Finally, the older girl replied in an even tone, "Sometimes, Rosa, she has nightmares."

"She's hurt?"

None of them moved.

"She's fine," the older girl said.

They didn't know who he was. And every trafficker who had anything to do with them would have told them they couldn't trust anyone. They would have told them that other prisoners, the police—they'd all be in cahoots with the captors. And if they were clean, the traffickers would have told them the good cops would figure the kids were in cahoots with the traffickers. Either way, they'd sell them out, kill them, or worse.

Frank said, "I had dreams as well, niños." The image of Jesus and that little girl in her pink pajamas rose in his mind and made his blood boil. "I believe Santa Muerte has spoken to me."

He settled back against the wall. Santa Muerte had spoken loud and clear.

The woman at the end of the bench was awake and watching. She gave Frank a fierce look he couldn't read.

"What's your name?" Frank asked.

She said, "You can call me Carmen."

But it wasn't. That was clear. Why would she give him a false name?

Plenty of reasons, but finding out why wasn't the mission. Frank looked down at Tony. Tony was the mission. But how could he leave these children?

* * *

It was sometime after seven a.m. when the first folks upstairs began to move about—Ed and one other guy from the sound of their footsteps and voices. They turned on the TV, ate something, ran the kitchen sink, then left the house. Moments later a vehicle started and drove away. Another hour went by, and then someone else got up, went to the bathroom, ran the sink. The water whooshed down the pipes in the basement. Others awoke. Someone else made a phone call. Someone else started up the microwave. It dinged loud and clear as a bell.

Frank checked his zip ties, picked up the one supposedly securing him to the bench and re-attached it. He rolled his shoulders and arched his back for a stretch.

By this time Tony was awake. He said he had to pee something mighty. Frank told him to hold it. Tony groaned as a few of the girls used the bathroom and got drinks of water straight from the tap at the sink.

Things settled down for a while, and then someone approached the door at the top of the stairs and worked the lock. It slid open with a loud click. The one naked light bulb in the ceiling flipped on. The door to the basement swung open.

"Buenas días," Shotgun said.

He came down first, holding his weapon. He was bright-eyed. Bug-eyed, actually. He was definitely riding something in his veins. Not very smart of them to use what they sold, especially not meth. The best drug organizations had a bit more discipline. Maybe a little weed and coke now and again, but never meth.

Jesus came next, his face all bandaged up. The bruising around his eyes was nice and purple. Behind him came a third man Frank hadn't seen before. He too was Hispanic. A real stumpy guy full of hard muscle. He wore a white tank top shirt with a pair of dark sunglasses hanging from the scoop of the neckline. He wore a gold bracelet and khaki pants. His dark hair was short and tidy.

Frank looked over at the older girl. He glanced at the woman at the end of the bench. If they were going to give him up, now was probably the time. Shotgun was about ten feet away. If Frank was fast, he might be able to get to him before he got his gun up. But by then Jesus and Stumpy would have pulled their weapons.

Jesus said, "Take her upstairs. I'll have some of that after I finish down here."

Stumpy walked over to the kids on the mattresses. They all looked up at him with apprehension, but the little one hung her head, her face blank.

Stumpy snapped his fingers and pointed at her.

She looked at Frank, her face flat, her eyes full of death.

Stumpy turned, Mr. Sunglasses, and walked toward the stairs. The little girl rose and followed, a slight child in pink pajamas, brightly colored elastics holding her dark hair in two braids that had come a bit loose during the night. Stumpy's steps were heavy on the stairs. The light tap of her step could barely be heard.

When she got to the top, she stopped. "Por favor," she said. Please.

Stumpy raised his hand as if to strike her. "Shut up. You have debts. Go wipe yourself down with the lotion and get ready."

The two of them moved into another room up above, his big steps following her little ones.

Shotgun turned to Frank, "Sleep well, dick job?"

Frank said, "No, I had nightmares about your teeth."

Shotgun smiled.

"Agh," Frank groaned. "Of course, you aren't half as ugly as Jesus. I think his mother must have been one of those donkeys they use in the Tijuana sex shows."

"You are not very smart, are you," Jesus said and pulled on his leather gloves.

"No, I'm real dumb," Frank said. "But I know you're going to let me out of here. I want to talk to Ed."

"Ed went out," Jesus said.

Frank had to make the sale, so he widened his eyes just a bit.

"That's right," Jesus said and pulled his Benchmade knife out of his pocket. He flipped the lever, and the four-inch, razor-sharp spear blade shot out and locked into place.

Frank decided a charge with the toothbrush really wasn't the right tactic in this situation. The old maxim that no plan survives contact with the enemy had been proven true yet again. There was another maxim that said: when in stress, men don't rise to the occasion—they fall back to their level of training. He wondered what level of training Shotgun and Jesus had.

Frank put some worry in his voice. "Look man. What's between me and you isn't personal. It was business. You had my boy."

Jesus smiled. He transferred the knife to his left hand and approached.

"Dude," Frank said. "What are you doing?"

"You're going to pay me."

"I got a little stash at home. We can work this out; just calm down."

"You're going to pay me in blood." He raised the blade in his left hand up and across to his other shoulder for a backward stroke. It was a good powerful move. One more step and he'd bring the knife down in a slashing arc across Frank's face. It would cut deep, slicing open his cheek, maybe slashing an eye. If Jesus hit it just right, that scalpel blade just might slice right through Frank's nose, cleave it right in two, which wasn't going to help Frank with the women folk at all.

Jesus took that last step, his eyes full of satisfaction.

"Dude!" Frank yelled, then lunged forward and up. The zip ties holding Frank released him like he was Superman.

Jesus flinched back; his eyes went wide.

Frank grabbed the forearm with the knife. With the other hand he struck Jesus in the groin once, twice. Then Frank slammed his big fist with all his power right into Jesus's bandaged face.

Jesus cried out, stumbled back, but Frank kept a hold of that knife arm and stepped into him, as close as any couple on Dancing with the Stars. They did a half rumba for two steps.

Shotgun raised his weapon, a little uncertain, but Frank turned Jesus so that he was between them. Then he reached around behind and grabbed the nine millimeter out of Jesus's waistband. It felt heavy, fully loaded. He brought it up. It was a Glock 19. No safety.

Shotgun saw what was going to happen, but he was too slow.

Frank had shot hundreds of thousands of rounds. The pistol was like another part of him. A long lost part. It felt good in his hand. It felt right. He'd missed the feel of a couple of pounds of steel in his hand. Or polymer, which this was. He pulled the trigger twice. A loud bang-bang hammered the air in the room.

Shotgun stumbled back, two holes blooming blood on his chest. He fell to the concrete floor, the shotgun smacking into the concrete.

Frank slammed Jesus in the side of the head with the butt of his pistol, still heavy with rounds. Then he hooked his leg behind him and shoved him over it, tripping him and sending him reeling to the floor. Frank shot him in the chest.

Shotgun groaned. He rolled over on his side and brought the shotgun around.

Frank still had men upstairs; he didn't want to waste another round.

Instead, he strode over, kicked Shotgun in the jaw, then reached down and took the weapon from him.

"Frank!" Tony yelled.

Frank turned. Jesus was getting up, blood staining his shirt, murder in his eyes. He tossed his knife to the floor and pulled another pistol out of his front pocket. Two points to Jesus for carrying a spare. But he was still going to lose this game.

Frank raised the shotgun with his right hand, took one step to the left so the girls weren't directly in the line of fire and pulled the trigger. The shotgun boomed and just about kicked right out of his hand. The buckshot took Jesus in a glancing blow to the lower side of his gut. A number of pellets struck the wall and sent chips of concrete flying.

Jesus raised his pistol.

Frank pumped the gun. The spent red shell ejected out in an arc. Frank slid in the new shell and this time took better aim. The shotgun banged again, so loud in this concrete place that the sound felt like it had shattered bones in his ear. It blasted its payload into the center of Jesus's chest. Nine pellets of lead, a couple probably churning right through him,

The air filled with smoke and the smell of burned gunpowder. Frank's ears rang. Surely everyone down here was now deaf. He turned to make sure Shotgun wasn't rising again, and found him on his back gasping. Frank looked at Tony for any sign he'd been hit by rogue pellets. "You okay?" Frank shouted.

"Okay," Tony shouted, sounding far away.

Frank walked over to where Jesus's knife lay, picked it up, then went back and cut Tony loose. Tony's hands were red, almost blue from the lack of circulation. Frank handed Tony the knife. "Free yourself and the woman." Then Frank shoved the semi-automatic into his pocket and crossed the floor with the shotgun in both hands to the base of the stairs.

He slid the shotgun's pump back, sending a spent and smoking red shotgun shell flying, and racked another shell into the chamber. This was a Remington 870. Eighteen-inch barrel. Used for more than half a century by the police, the military, hunters, and home-owners who were unwilling to take breaking and entering lying down. Frank had carried the military version in a number of close combat situations. Like the military's M870, this one was all black, made from synthetic materials. However, this model didn't have the extended magazine tube, so instead of being able to hold seven rounds, this gun could hold five—four in the magazine tube and one in the chamber. He assumed he had one more round after this. But if Frank's assumption was wrong, it could get him killed. He didn't have time to check.

He arrived at the base of the stairs, knowing Stumpy was sure to come running, and began to climb. He raised the shotgun firmly to his shoulder, aimed at the open doorway at the top of the linoleum stairs. There was no use listening for Stumpy because the only thing Frank could really hear was a steady ringing in his ears.

A moment later someone came round the corner with a semi-automatic pistol in his hand. But it wasn't Stumpy. It was a fourth man.

Frank pulled the trigger, blasted into the man's torso. Two pellets over-penetrated and slammed into the half open door behind him, splintering the cheap wood.

The man dropped his pistol and fell back. The pistol thudded once, tumbled, and lay heavily on one of the upper stairs. The man stumbled out of sight, but he didn't go far because Frank could hear him shouting in pain around the corner.

Frank pumped the shotgun, expelling the red shell, and slammed one more into the chamber and continued to climb. He figured he had one more shell. He kept the muzzle of the gun and his eyes on the open stairway door above and climbed to the last step before the top.

The back door beyond the landing at the top of the stairs had a small window in it. There was a wall on his left. On his right, the house opened into the kitchen, which is where the fourth man lay now, shouting something in Spanish.

Stumpy wasn't running to the fourth man's aid. Stumpy would be waiting for Frank to pop his head out of the stairwell so it could be blown off.

Frank moved to the left side of the stairs, as far from the corner leading into the kitchen as possible, which wasn't much. He began an angular search, shotgun up, ready to fire. It was like sliding along the perimeter of a circle, revealing the room beyond a slice at a time.

There were cupboards, counter, a sink. He saw the edge of a kitchen table at the far end, saw blood all over the floor, and the fourth man on his knees with his back to the stairway, groaning.

Frank reached the top of the stairway. The area right past the corner was the fatal funnel where most people would be aiming to shoot an approaching threat. Frank stepped into it, then out, still swinging round the perimeter of his circle, his shotgun up, aiming directly in front of him.

Stumpy was standing in the wide entry leading from the far end of the kitchen into a living room. He held an FN P90 in one hand like a pistol, pointing it in Frank's direction.

The P90 was a compact submachine gun that looked more like a kitchen gadget with a can opener than a gun. It utilized a fifty-round box magazine that slid in flat on top instead of sticking out the bottom. It shot the 5.7 millimeter round, the one designed to pierce body armor, the one the narcos called the Mata Policía, the cop killer.

Frank dropped to one knee.

Stumpy let loose with the P90. On full-auto, the P90 can shoot 900 rounds per minute. Fifteen per second. The muzzle lit up. The bullets flew. The rounds came out so quickly it sounded like a monster hailstorm on a tin roof.

The bullets whistled past like angry insects, blowing into the wall behind Frank, into the stairway door, into the cupboards a foot away. They marched up the wall and into the ceiling. Then the gun clicked.

Drywall dust and splinters fell into Frank's hair. He brought the shotgun round. Stumpy's eyes went wide, and he dashed for the entryway. Frank fired, but Stumpy was a fast little man, and the shotgun blast blew past him and into the wall of the far room in a pattern the size of a large musk melon.

Frank rose and pumped the shotgun. A spent red shell flew out, but there wasn't another to take its place. Frank tossed the shotgun onto the counter and pulled out the Glock he'd taken from Jesus.

Around the corner in the other room, Stumpy dropped something to the carpet then snicked in a new magazine. Stumpy obviously realized his mistake in trying to Rambo the P90 with one hand.

The morning light was coming in the big front room window, casting shadows. A somewhat short man-shaped shadow moved on the floor by the entryway where Stumpy had disappeared, then stopped. The shadow showed the distinct, if distorted, shape of someone holding something like a gun out in front of him. Frank figured Stumpy was standing a few feet away from the wall and a few feet back from the corner of the wide entryway between the kitchen and living room. He was waiting for Frank to make another circle and expose himself. If Frank was a betting man, he'd lay odds on the fact that Stumpy had taken the P90 off full-auto so he didn't spray his ammo all over creation again.

So now it was a nine millimeter Glock against a waiting submachine gun, but Frank wasn't willing to enter that fight. He gauged where he thought Stumpy was standing, and then he brought up the semi-automatic and fired five times into the wall on the other side of the kitchen that stood between him and Stumpy. It was a quick bang, bang, bang, bang, bang in a line about two feet long. Neat little holes appeared in the wall. Little puffs of drywall dust followed. More importantly, Stumpy cried out on the other side.

Frank rushed around the perimeter of another circle, giving the corner of the entryway as wide a berth as possible. He had a two-handed grip, the gun up and ready. He'd only gone halfway around when Stumpy came into view. His face was screwed up in pain and rage. Bright red blood was spreading out and staining his white shirt just below his ribs. Stumpy looked down at it, then raised his gun to fire right back through the wall at where Frank had been, but he must have caught Frank's movement because he whipped his head around. His eyes went wide. He snarled and swung the submachine gun toward Frank.

Frank sent two more bullets Stumpy's way, right into the center mass. He hadn't even had to think. His hands worked of their own accord.

Stumpy fell back, pulling the trigger of the deadly can opener as he fell. There was one bang, and a bullet blasted into the wall, but Stumpy had indeed taken it off full-auto, and so there were no more strays. Just the thump of the gun as Stumpy hit the floor.

Frank proceeded forward, gun up, expecting another shooter to pop out of one of the doors.

Stumpy writhed, looked up at Frank with extreme pain and dismay in his eyes. Knowing the girls and Tony were below, and that a nine millimeter bullet at this range had a chance of sailing right out the back of someone's skull, Frank bent over and put the killing shot sideways through Stumpy's head.

It was never pretty to see someone die. Back in the day, when he'd taken men from a distance, he had gloried in it. He'd talked about his targets like some might talk about targets in a video game. But then he'd been involved in some close work. He'd seen how some people mutilate their kills, and the glory and game had quickly faded.

Frank stood. A Glock 19 had a standard fifteen round capacity. Frank had shot nine rounds, but it didn't feel like he had six rounds left. It felt like he had maybe two. So he picked up Stumpy's P90 loaded with a brand new magazine minus one and moved to clear the rest of this floor. There were two bedrooms, a bathroom, and three closets. He cleared them all and found little Rosa hiding behind a dresser in one of the rooms. She was still in her pajamas. More importantly, she hadn't been hit by any of the loose bullets flying through the house.

He smiled as gently as he could. "Es bueno," he said. It's good. "You're going to be okay."

She looked up at him with eyes that belonged on a woman that was seventy years old.

He motioned for her to stay where she was, then went to the big pane front window, looked outside, and saw nothing but flat farm fields that stretched all the way to the horizon. He opened the front door of the house, walked out and cleared the front yard. Then he walked back inside past Stumpy to the kitchen and stepped past the fourth man who lay on the floor. The pool of blood was large; he hadn't died quickly, and his heart had continued to pump his life out onto the floor.

Frank walked to the back door, opened it, and stood out on the porch. There was a patio table with a faded umbrella to keep the sun off those who sat in its shade. Beyond it, ringing the gravel yard was a metal barn painted red, some old chicken coops, and a few other small buildings that looked like they hadn't been used in about a hundred years. There was nobody out there. No vehicle. Nothing but an empty yard sitting in the slant light of the morning sun.

"Tony!" Frank yelled. "It's clear. Bring them up."

Frank went back to get the little girl. In the corner of the living room was a shrine to Santa Muerte. There was a little table. Upon it stood a two-foot-tall statuette of the skeleton saint. She wore an ornate dress made out of purple fabric. Black hair flowed out from underneath the cowl of her robe. It looked like the kind of hair you might see on a doll, although he didn't think Mattel was going to be producing a Saint Death Barbie any time soon. Not with those red ruby eyes. And he doubted Ken would find her getup anything but village kitsch. She held a doll-sized scythe in one hand and a doll-sized set of scales in the other. Arrayed in front of her were half-a-dozen black and gold candles. Another was blue. They were burning, flickering away, carrying the prayers of those that had set them there into her ears. Standing beside the candles was an open glass next to a bottle of mescal, an apple, and an ash tray holding a smoking cigarette.

The girl was crouching behind the dresser where he'd left her. "We're going to get you out of here," he said. "Come on. Es bueno," he repeated.

Maybe she spoke some English. Or maybe she read his body language; either way, she rose and followed him out.

Tony came up with the fourth's man's semi-automatic in his hand. Carmen and the children followed behind looking like they'd seen ghosts. They spilled into the kitchen, their tired, haggard eyes wide at the sight of another dead body and the dark pool of blood on the floor.

"I don't know when Ed's coming back," Frank said. "But we need to be gone before he does."

They needed to be *long* gone because the land was flat without a tree or bush to hide behind, and the visibility, with the sun high in the bright blue sky, stretched all the way to the horizon. If there wasn't anything in that barn, they'd have to go on foot, and Ed would spot them a mile away.

14

Stolen Assets

FRANK'S EARS WERE ringing. He pointed to Tony and shouted because the boy's ears were probably ringing as well. "Watch the front of the house."

Carmen was telling the girls something, but he could barely hear what she was saying. Smoke and the smell of burnt gunpowder filled the kitchen and living room. The iron tang of blood filled his nostrils. A memory of a house in the woods in Honduras flashed in his mind. It too had been an operation with a lot of gun smoke, a lot of burnt powder, and a lot of blood. An operation with a small old stove just like this one.

Frank pointed at Carmen. "Watch the back."

Ed had taken Frank's phone, which wasn't an issue except it had Kim's number. Frank went back down into the basement, P90 in hand, and searched the pockets of the two dead bodies, going slowly and carefully because you never knew when someone using hard drugs might be carrying a dirty needle.

He didn't find any needles, but he did find a Leatherman multi-tool on Shotgun. It was the modern day rural version of the Swiss Army knife and had everything from pliers to a small saw. But there was no phone. Nothing but lint and a gum wrapper in the rest of Shotgun's pockets. Jesus was cleaned out as well. You'd think that between the two of them they would have been carrying something more than a Leatherman.

He climbed back up the stairs, and found Carmen ransacking the drawers and cupboards in the kitchen. She was hunting methodically, dumping food and plates and knives and forks on the ground, tossing the place like a pro.

"What are you looking for?" he asked.

"Records, phones, anything," she said.

"Are you a cop?"

"Do I look like a cop?" she said and moved to a new drawer dumping its contents on the floor and kicking through it. The fourth man and his pool of blood lay less than two feet away.

Frank hadn't seen a landline in the house. "I'm looking for a red phone," he said. He knew he was speaking too loudly, but his ears were still ringing.

She dug into her pocket and pulled out a black iPhone. A number of bills folded in half and held by a gold clip tumbled out of her pocket and fell to the floor. Ben Franklin's face stared up at them. The fold was thick. He wondered how many more hundreds were in there. She held the phone up.

"You get that off Jesus?"

"He didn't seem to need to it," she said.

Frank motioned at the fourth man. "You search him?"

"Not yet," she said and retrieved the fallen clip of cash.

"Keep an eye out for a red phone," he said loudly.

She nodded and went back to a drawer. Inside sat a yellow box of rat poison with fat black lettering on it.

Frank searched the fourth man and found nothing. He searched Stumpy and found a wallet with fifty bucks cash, a comb, and a package of chewing gum to help the man keep his breath minty fresh. The Glock and the first magazine used in the P90 were lying on the floor. Frank picked them up and quickly moved through the rest of the house.

He didn't find his phone, which meant Ed must have it. Not a good thing. Ed would have looked through his contacts. He would have found Kim's number. It was one of the few contacts Frank had. And then Ed would have smiled.

A sick feeling took hold of Frank. If Ed got her on the phone, he could make all sorts of threats. Extort Kim into any number of things by telling her he had Tony and now Frank and was going to kill or torture both of them. He growled with frustration.

He went back into the kitchen. Cereal boxes, plastic plates, plastic bowls, cans of beans, salt, and other crap littered the floor. He said, "Let me use that phone."

Carmen nodded and pulled the iPhone back out, but when he went to unlock it, it asked him for a password. Of course it had to be locked. "Tony!" he called.

A moment later Tony walked through the entryway from the living room. Frank held the phone out to him. "Hack this thing."

Tony took it, slid his finger across the display to unlock it. Turned it over. "The older ones were a cinch."

"We need to call your mother."

"I'm working on it," Tony said.

Carmen opened a cupboard with boxes of ammo and gun cleaning equipment inside. There were at least four guns in this house: the semi the fourth man had dropped on the stairs which Tony had picked up, the Glock Frank had taken from Jesus, the shotgun, and the P90. The shotgun was a fine gun, but it only held five rounds. Furthermore, it was a close range weapon, and he didn't intend to be storming any houses with it. But he didn't want to leave it for Ed to use when he got back.

Frank cycled the shotgun's slide a couple of times to be sure the receiver and magazine truly were empty. Then he removed the barrel nut at the end of the magazine tube and slid the barrel from the gun. The magazine spring popped out. He tossed the stock into the yard, the receiver to the front room, and dropped the barrel behind the fridge. It clanged when it hit the floor. He left the spring in the blood and mess Carmen was making.

In the cupboard, he found a box of 5.7 millimeter rounds and another for a nine millimeter. He tossed the box of 9s to Tony and kept the other. He also found two fine orange ear plugs, which had been in who knew how many ears. He took one and stuffed it in his right ear. He put the other in his pocket.

The girls were crying. "Tell them they're going to be okay," Frank said to Carmen. "We're getting out of here right now. Today they're going to be free."

He crossed over to the back door and walked out into the sun of midmorning. The air smelled cool and fresh. The area behind the house had been paved with brick cobbles, forming a nice patio. The table with the umbrella sat on those cobbles. Beyond that the yard and driveway were covered with gravel. If this had been a regular farm, the traffic on the graveled area would have crushed any weeds that had tried to grow. And what the traffic didn't get, the owners would blast with judicious squirts of Roundup. But this wasn't a normal farm, and the weeds dotted the pale gravel like mold spots on white cheese.

Off to the right stood the red metal barn. It had a big garage door on its narrow side and a regular man door just around the corner. On the opposite side of the yard stood three old sagging chicken coops that were as gray as cheap newspaper. Next to them stood a white propane tank, looking like a shiny nine-foot long capsule of Tylenol.

Beyond the coops, the graveled yard, and barn stood some old farm equipment including a rusted tractor that looked fifty years old. Beyond that were fields of hay, shining nice and green in the sunlight, stretching out for as far as the eye could see. And with this flat land, that was pretty far. In the far distance, a few blocky houses rose up from the fields. They looked odd, like something from Mars.

Frank walked down the back steps. A carton of empty Corona bottles sat on the brick cobblestones by the table with the umbrella. Tony came behind him, followed by the children. But they stopped when they reached the bottom of the porch. Two of them were crying, pleading with Carmen, refusing to move forward.

"What's going on?" Frank asked.

"They say the Gorozas have promised to kill their families if they try to run away without paying their debts. They have connections in Mexico. The Gorozas told them one telephone call is all it takes."

The oldest girl was adamant. "No," she said. "We will pay our debts."

The little boy's face was even more bruised out here in the sunlight. The littlest girl was still in her pajamas. Frank couldn't promise them the Gorozas wouldn't kill their families. He couldn't promise them that the U.S. authorities wouldn't deport them right back into the arms of those who had sold them into slavery here. But who had to tell the authorities?

There were plenty of folks living here illegally. It wasn't the best life. As an illegal you always ran the risk of being preyed upon. Anyone could threaten to rat you out to ICE. if you didn't do what they told you to. Likewise, there was little recourse if someone committed a crime against you. You had no protection. That's why MS-13 originally started. In the 1980s Salvadoran immigrants were being bullied and preyed upon by more established Mexican and Black L.A. gangs. So those immigrants took matters into their own hands to protect themselves in their little district in L.A. But MS-13, like all gangs and criminal organizations, carried the seeds of its own host of cancers and mutated into the very thing it fought.

The law of the criminal order was not exactly designed to promote life, liberty, and the pursuit of happiness. But these girls didn't have to join a gang. There were other ways. The life of an illegal wasn't the best. But it wasn't the worst, especially if they found a place in a decent community.

Frank said, "Tell them I'll take responsibility. Tell them the Gorozas will think I stole them, and so they'll come after me, not them. Tell them they can't stay here anyway because the Federales are going to come to this place."

Carmen relayed the message, and it seemed to stress them out even more. She gave Frank a look like she was contemplating something, and then she turned to the children and said in Spanish, "It's me the Gorozas want. I'm the one they were hunting."

"You're the Matanarcos?" the little boy said.

"I will take you to safety," Carmen said.

"They will kill our families," the older girl said.

"They will not," Carmen said. "Come with me."

The children hesitated, clearly held back by the older girl's worries. But then the little boy stepped forward and took her hand. The littlest girl was next. And then the rest followed, tears and worry and all, trusting Carmen.

"Matanarcos?" Frank asked her. The narco killer. What was that all about?

Carmen looked at his gun, looked back at him warily. She had a gun in her hand, the spare Jesus had pulled on him in the basement. "We'd better split up."

"You're not going to get far without a vehicle," Frank said. Then he turned to Tony. "Keep an eye on the road out front. Holler if you see anything."

Tony's face was a bit ashen. "What are we going to do?"

Frank set the extra ammo and P90 at Tony's feet. "I'm going to see if the fine owners of this establishment have provided us a ride."

There had been hooks with two sets of keys hanging on them inside the back door of the house. Frank ran up the back steps and fetched the two sets of keys and came back out. Then he walked over to the barn. None of the keys worked on the big rolling barn door. He walked to the man door on the side that was made of metal and had a dead bolt.

He tried every key on both chains again, but none of them worked. He looked around on the ground. No mat, rock, or bucket. Nothing but weeds growing up the sides of the barn. Then he reached up and felt along the lip of the top of the door frame and brushed something. Bingo. He grabbed the key and brought it down. It was a dull bronze with a round head. He fit it into the dead bolt, and gave it a turn. The deadbolt slid open. He fit the same key into the lock in the door knob and opened that as well.

He stepped into the barn, found the light switch just to the side of the door and flipped it. Nothing. Then he found the box that controlled the door. He pressed one of the square buttons. The hum of a motor up above started, and then the big barn door began to rattle up.

The morning light streamed into the barn. The front half of the barn floor was covered with cement; the back half was covered with gravel.

The barn door continued to rattle and hum, letting more light in. Frank had thought maybe there might be another car here or a motorcycle or a four-wheeler. This was a farm, after all. Heck, they could make an escape on a tractor if it came to it. But there were no wheeled vehicles. There were some shelves with tools lying on them and a big white enclosed trailer with a dual axle just a little back of center. The trailer was about twenty-five feet long with a V-shaped front. A round plate on the front of the V said "Wells Cargo." Down below, a hitch extended from the front to hook to a pickup or other truck.

Frank had seen plenty of these back in Rock Springs. He smiled. He just might get lucky. Or he might find it full of contraband.

The trailer had three doors. The back end swung down like a draw bridge to make a ramp, as did one half of the front's V wedge. Between the two, just above the wheels, was a man-sized door.

Frank walked over. The back and front doors were held tight with two bars about a foot long on either side. To let down the front or back doors, you had to swing back the bars. Each door had a bar on either side. And each bar was secured with a padlock. But the man door on the side was not secured in the same way. It had a simple handle that could be locked, one that was flush with the side of the trailer like what you might find on an RV or camper. Frank tried the keys. None of them fit.

There was a pry bar hanging on a pegboard on the wall. Frank fetched it. The RV lock and handle was a rectangle of metal set in the door. Frank jammed the teeth of the pry bar into an edge between metal and the door. It took some muscle, but he worked the sharp end of the pry bar through to the other side of the door. Then he slammed the pry bar forward. The metal block popped out about a quarter of an inch. He slide the pry bar up a bit more, slammed it again. This time the whole side of the block moved. He pushed and pulled and finally popped the whole unit out of the door. He tossed it to the garage floor.

Frank reached in through the hole and pulled the door open. He must have been living right because snuggled inside the trailer were three Polaris snowmobiles. A lot of folks thought snowmobiles were just for the snow, but they would be mistaken. They worked just fine on hard earth. In fact, people raced them on grass. And that's exactly what stretched out for miles all around Frank's troupe of escapees.

A snowmobile had a track like a tank that was made of rubber with stiff, paddle-like studs to give it traction, except instead of being built for war, the snowmobile's track was built for high-performance and speed. Depending on the surface, a snowmobile could quickly reach speeds of sixty to seventy miles per hour. But even if he and the others had to go half that speed so the children didn't fall off, that was still a heck of a lot faster than his crew could go on foot.

Two of the snow machines were red; one was blue. The red ones looked like aggressive insects. Their seats were short, just enough for one person; however, the flat aluminum chassis the seat rested on stretched out behind another couple of feet. It was long to make it easier to climb steep inclines. But it was also good for loading gear when going on a mountain tour. Perfect for loading a bundle of kids. The blue snowmobile was a two-seater, complete with heated passenger grips that rose up on either side of the back seat. Three helmets with face shields hung on the wall.

The Gorozas obviously liked their snow. Or maybe they'd stolen the machines and were storing them here until they could find a fence. Frank hopped onto one of the red insectile machines and unscrewed the gas cap. He rocked the snowmobile a bit. The dark contents sloshed and blinked in the wan light.

On the wall just inside the side-entry door hung a key ring with four small keys of the type used for padlocks. Someone had slipped colored rubber covers over the round key heads. Two were black and two were green. Frank took the keys outside to the front of the trailer and tried them on the padlocks holding the front door. The green ones opened the locks. He tossed the padlocks to the ground, unlatched the bars, and swung them out of the way. The door was fairly heavy, but it would have to be somewhat sturdy to bear the weight of a snowmobile and its passenger. He guided the door partway down, then let the top edge drop with a thump and crunch onto the gravel floor. It made a nice ramp, built out of wood with five long, black traction blocks running across the length at spaced intervals to keep the snow machine from just sliding down.

Tony called in from outside. "I see a dust trail! It's coming our way. Can't tell if it's a car or truck."

"How far?"

"I don't know," Tony said. "It's a ways out there. The dust trail is two or three miles out. Could be going anywhere."

"Keep an eye on it," Frank called back.

These were higher-end models that didn't have a pull cord start like a lawn mower. These had keys, which were in the keyholes. Frank pulled up the red kill switch knob on the right grip and turned the key. The snowmobile coughed a few times, then started right up, spitting out exhaust. He softly pressed the accelerator lever on the right grip with his thumb, and the snowmobile moved forward. He drove it down the ramp, across the garage floor, then out into the yard. He left it idling and went back for the second. It too started up after a few coughs, and he drove it down the ramp and out onto the sunlit gravel.

The dust trail in the distance was closer now. It was made by two vehicles. The one in the lead was a pickup he didn't recognize. The other, eating the pickup's dust, was a white panel van, just like the one that had brought him here. Frank figured they were two, maybe three minutes out. He yelled for Tony and Carmen to come over, then ran back for the third machine.

The blue two-passenger took a little longer to start than the others. When he finally got it going, he gave it a bit too much gas and almost careened off the ramp, but he righted it, made his way down the ramp, through the barn, and out into the yard.

The three machines idled, rumbling with the pitch of dirt bikes. Frank spoke to the oldest girl. "Three of you behind Tony; the other two behind Carmen." He didn't want anyone behind him because he might have to run some interference.

Carmen looked down at the snowmobile with a bit of apprehension.

Frank pointed at the speedometer. "Keep it under forty miles per hour."

"I've never driven one," Carmen said.

Frank feathered the accelerator and the snowmobile moved forward a couple of feet. "Just push this lever to make it go." He gripped the brake on the left handle bar. "This is your brake." He shoved the kill switch down, and the engine cut out. "Pull the knob up, then turn the key to start it. You're going out into the field. Right through that gate at the back of the property. You keep going until you get to that house way out there. The one with the trees all around it. We'll go from there." The house looked small in the distance. At least five miles away.

He glanced back toward the vehicles. The truck and van were coming fast. "Get going," he said. "And tell the girls to keep their feet on the running board well away from the track."

Tony moved to his machine and helped two of the kids up onto the chassis behind the seat.

Frank picked up the P90. He had the Glock in his pants. They weren't nearly enough for a shootout. So he walked back to the house. By the time he reached the back door, Tony and Carmen were loaded.

The oldest girl sat behind Tony. The two youngest sat behind her on the flat aluminum chassis. The little one in the pink pajamas was the caboose. She was clutching the girl in front of her, arms wrapped around her torso, feet in her lap. Tears still stained their faces; one looked back at the oncoming vehicles, probably thinking this very act would kill her parents.

Tony gave his machine some gas, the pitch in the motor changed, and he rolled out, the two steering skis slipping over the gravel. Carmen gave hers a bit too much gas. The snowmobile shot forward. She and the children behind her all jerked back. She braked and they jerked forward. She tried again. It still wasn't smooth, but it was better this time, and she followed Tony to the fence and gate at the far side of the yard.

Beyond the house, the trucks were coming fast. Frank turned around and opened the back door.

15

Rusty Shooter

THE OLD STOVE in the kitchen was a gas stove, preferred by chefs everywhere. Much better control for cooking. Much better for other things as well. The candles to Santa Muerte burned in the next room and would have provided an ironic ignition, but propane was denser than air, which meant the gas would spread out like water until it found the stairway leading into the basement. Then it would flow down and pool there.

Frank wanted a big pool of gas. He figured the propane would have to rise about six inches before it reached the level of the furnace pilot light. He figured a six inch pool that was about 900 square feet would do. He turned the knobs on all four burners to full. The gas hissed loudly, a nice heavy flow. The stinking odorant filled his nostrils.

He remembered the extra magazine for the P90 that Stumpy had dropped in the living room. He retrieved it, then walked back through the kitchen and the stinking propane to the back door. He secured it and walked down the steps, the screen door banging behind him.

The trucks were still coming, sending up huge trails of dust.

If things worked out, Frank would send up his own smoke signal for help. If not, he'd just have to trust his guns out there in the fields where he'd be a sitting duck.

Frank walked over to his snowmobile, which was still obediently idling. He made sure the Glock was secured in the back of his waistband. He wedged the submachine gun between his legs, placed the extra empty magazine in the small storage compartment, then pressed the throttle with his thumb. The motor revved up, the track studs bit in, crunching the gravel, and the snowmobile moved forward.

A lot of places held annual snowmobile drag races on short grass. He didn't know how these machines would run out in the tall grass of the field, but it seemed Tony and Carmen were doing fine. They had already opened the gate and were out in the field, cutting a path through the grass. The whine of their motors carried across the flat field as clear as a bell.

Frank drove across the yard and through the gate at the back of the property, then stopped. The two trucks on the dirt road made their last turn to the house and accelerated hard down the dirt road, the dust billowing up behind. They were a couple hundred yards away. The land was too flat for them not to have spotted the two snowmobiles trekking away from the house. Not unless they were stoned out of their minds.

Frank got off his machine, walked out to the end of the open gate, then walked the gate back to the fence and latched it closed. Forcing Ed to open the gate would add precious seconds onto their lead, and he wanted Tony and Carmen as far ahead as possible. They were already more than a hundred yards ahead of him. He straddled his seat, secured the P90 again, and pressed the accelerator hard with his thumb.

The engine whined, the studs bit in, and the snowmobile jumped forward into the thigh-high grass that slid by on either side with a hiss. Pale butterflies danced about the meadow along with bees and other bugs. The machine accelerated. The ride on the grass and hard ground was bumpy, but he pressed the accelerator down a little more. The snowmobile lunged forward, picking up speed. He hit some random grasshopper with the front of his machine, and it bounced up over the small windshield and smacked into his cheek. One of its hard spiny legs poked him, leaving a sting behind.

The field was huge, at least a mile deep, maybe more. A field made for the capacity of modern machinery. Next to it, separated by a barbed-wire fence, was another deep field. Frank looked back. The big yellow pickup rolled into the driveway and sped past the house and barn to the gate. The van emerged from the dust on the road a few seconds later and pulled in behind.

The snowmobile was doing just fine in this grass. But he suspected the yellow pickup would do better. Tony and Carmen were probably going thirty. Fast enough, but not so fast the children would bounce off. However, thirty would be nothing for the pickup. Its big wheels and suspension were made to go off-road, and the terrain here was fairly smooth, all the hard edges leveled from years of plowing and harrowing. The pickup would easily catch up.

Frank turned his snowmobile in a wide arc until he was crossways to the house. The big yellow pickup stopped at the gate. Ed got out.

Frank got off the Polaris and left it idling. He knelt behind it, alongside the track. He fetched the second ear plug out of his pocket and stuffed it in his ear. Then he snugged the P90 into his shoulder and rested his elbow on the seat to stabilize his aim.

The gadget-looking P90 was an animal between a handgun and a rifle. An average hand gun had a barrel that was around four inches in length. The M16, the standard Army issue rifle, had a barrel length of twenty inches. The P90 Frank held in his hand had a barrel just over ten inches, but it was pulled back in a bullpup configuration, which brought the action and magazine behind the trigger and alongside the shooter's face, putting part of the gun in the stock. This meant the P90 was only twenty inches long, about the length from the end of a man's middle finger to his elbow—a compact and deadly little thing, designed for tight spaces, designed to be easy to stash and operate in the cab of a car, a cockpit, or in a hallway. It was also designed to be shot from the left or right side without any adjustment; all the spent casings were ejected downward, not to the side.

The maximum effective range of a hand gun on a point target—the range where an average shooter could hit a human-sized target 50% of the time and cause a casualty—depended a lot on the ammo, the gun, the weather conditions, and the shooter. But on average, it was around fifty meters. The maximum effective range of the M16 was about 550 meters. The P90 Frank held had an effective range of 200 meters, about the length of two football fields.

The gate was a ways back, closer to the two footballs fields away, but Frank wasn't an average shooter. At least, he hadn't been in the years before his time living in concrete. He was looking at maybe a tenth of a mile, 170 yards. Maybe less. And while skills degraded without use, the pickup was a large target.

Ed opened the gate and swung it wide.

Frank couldn't let them in. There was just too much room in this field. He took a breath, let it out, used the red dot of the reflex sights to acquire his target. Then he squeezed the trigger. There was a bang and the gun kicked. A moment later the bullet thwacked against wood. He thought he saw it hit the ancient chicken coop, which meant these sights were way off or prison had indeed put some rust on his skills. Or maybe this particular gun just wasn't reliable at this range.

Ed spun around at the noise and drew his handgun. At 170 yards, he was as likely to hit a stray cow as he was to hit what he could see of Frank sticking above the grass.

Frank adjusted his aim and squeezed the trigger again. Another bang and kick. This time the bullet smacked through the windshield, not of the truck, but of the van about five feet on the other side. Half the windshield turned white, then disappeared.

Ed yelled and waved his arms at the men with him. The driver of the pickup put his vehicle in reverse and punched it hard. The tires spun gravel all over, and he shot back past the van. The side door of the van rolled open and three guys piled out. Two of them had handguns, but the third had something much larger. The two with handguns ran behind one of the old weathered coops. One of the guys was wearing a gray and white baseball cap. The other had big hair. The third had an assault rifle and took cover behind the old rusting tractor. The driver of the van got out holding the side of his face. Ed barked at him, and the man climbed back in and backed up the van in a big J to move it out of the way.

Frank adjusted his aim, put Ed right in his sights, and squeezed again. Ed jumped, but where that third shot had gone, Frank had no idea. It probably buzzed right by Ed and continued on past the barn and house and was right now sailing over the fields. He was shooting like some friggin' Gomer in his first day of boot camp. Back in the day, Ed would be on his back by now. Frank sighed. He wasn't going to nail anything with this current setup unless he got closer.

Ed popped back up and ran to the pickup.

The guys behind the coops opened up. Their muzzles flashed. The guns banged. The bullets zinged past Frank, yards off target, but still close enough they might get lucky if they put enough lead into the air. The third man behind the big back wheel of the rusted tractor took his shot. The muzzle of his rifle flashed with a smart crack. The bullet whistled past Frank, maybe only a foot or so away, and sent a surge of adrenaline that made the hair on the back of Frank's whole body stand up and dance.

The Gorozas weren't employing a gang of idiot punks who were still in puberty; it appeared Tractor Man had received some training.

Tractor Man's muzzle flashed again and the snowmobile's windshield shattered. Frank flinched. His heart stopped a beat.

Tractor Man definitely had some training.

Frank swung his aim away from Ed.

Tractor Man stood behind the wheel of the tractor, using the top to brace his arm, exhibiting a great deal of shooting sense.

Frank abandoned the red dot of the reflex sight and lined up the backup iron sights on the hollow of Tractor Man's neck, which was the center of the portion of Tractor Man that was visible, and squeezed the trigger. A moment later the bullet made a metallic smack into the big steel disc of the tractor tire very close to the target. Tractor Man flinched, but he did not duck down.

Frank used the iron sights again, raised his aim a bit more, and squeezed the trigger. Another bang, another metallic clang.

Tractor Man fired again, but he was off. Those last two shots had probably gotten the man's heart pounding, and he was now finding it a bit more difficult to aim.

Frank let loose another round. Didn't hit, but it was close enough that Tractor Man ducked down. Frank lined himself up and waited for the man to show himself again. The other two men by the coops were still cracking the air with their pistols, the bullets singing all about him.

Frank risked a glance back at Tony and Carmen. They should have been a mile away by now, but they weren't. They were stopped in the field. Tony and the girls with him were off his snow machine. Carmen was sitting on hers, waiting for the little boy to shoehorn himself on. There was a girl in front of Carmen on the seat. Two behind, one on either side, looking like they were standing with one foot on the running board and the other on the flat chassis that extended behind. The little boy was struggling, then Tony helped him get his leg up into the lap of the girl in front of him, then Carmen gave her snowmobile some gas and moved forward. The kids lurched a bit, but stayed on.

What where they doing?

Frank turned around, saw Tractor Man slowly rising up and positioning his gun.

Frank fired at him. There was another thwank of metal on metal, which irritated Frank to no end. He should have had that shot. Frank adjusted his aim up just a bit and squeezed the trigger again. The compact P90 banged and kicked. A moment later a piece of the rubber close to Tractor Man flew up. He stumbled back a few steps like maybe he'd been struck by something and fell to the ground.

Frank glanced back at Tony and Carmen. Carmen was now moving east, across the field toward the fence, not south as they'd been traveling at first. Tony was still back with the other snowmobile. It was obviously having some kind of engine trouble, which illustrated the problem with stolen goods—you never knew what you were going to get.

Frank turned back to the house. Ed and his driver were in the pickup, pedal to the metal, backing out. The driver cranked the wheel and spun the front end around. Then he put it in drive and floored it. The wheels spun, kicking up dust and gravel, and they fish-tailed out the driveway.

Tractor Man had moved from his last position out of sight. The two by the coops were slowing down, taking their time. One bullet hissed through the tall grass only a few feet away.

Then the pickup exited onto the dirt road and accelerated past the house. Ed didn't scare that easily. Where were they going?

Another gun cracked, and the bullet sang right above his head. Frank needed to even up the odds of this fight. He needed to get in the game. No more pot shots. He slid back onto his snowmobile all hunched over, then pressed the throttle lever. The engine revved up to a whine and he shot forward through the tall grass. The guys by the coop started shooting wildly again, crack, crack, crack, probably thinking this was their last chance. Then they emptied their magazines and the guns fell silent.

Frank made a wide arc toward the shooters, kind of like a fat C, then quickly slid off and positioned himself behind the Polaris. He was now about seventy yards out, positioned so any overshot would fly away from the direction Carmen and Tony were traveling.

The driver of the van had been hunkered down this whole time. Now he ran to the back door of the house, all bent over to make himself a small target. He was probably going for ammo. Probably wondering where Jesus and the others were.

Frank raised the P90, looked for Tractor Man, but couldn't see him. So he aimed at the coop, waiting for the two guys to show themselves.

There was a loud crack and a bullet struck the passenger's seat. Another crack, and another bullet slammed into the chassis a little closer.

Tractor Man had taken up a new position between the seat of the tractor and engine. The tractor seat and engine blocked him in. It was like he was shooting from a bunker.

Frank swiveled his gun, took aim, his elbow on the seat again. His heart was racing, his breath coming quicker, his arms itching to move with adrenaline. Frank exhaled, tried to relax, squeezed the trigger. There was a bang and kick, then a metallic clang from the tractor. He took in a breath, exhaled again.

Then Big Hair and Baseball Cap by the coop opened up. The guns cracked, the bullets whistled by much too closely. One hissed into the grass to his left. Another thudded into the seat.

Frank ducked down. Holy hell, maybe seventy yards was too close.

The guys by the coop rushed the fence, taking up position behind some old metal barrels. Past the house, the big yellow pickup suddenly appeared in the field adjacent to this one. A flanking maneuver? Trying to get behind him?

Frank needed to soldier up. This was turning into a complete cluster.

The guys by the coop opened up again as did Tractor Man. The muzzles flashed. The bullets whistled over head and buzzed through the grass. They were keying in on the snowmobile.

Frank dove away from the Polaris, rolled, and came up again.

The man who had run to the house opened the back door and shouted something. He must have seen the dead man on the kitchen floor. He must have smelled the propane.

He turned, but it was too late. There was a dull thump then the doorway behind him flashed bright yellow. The propane had finally filled the basement to the level of the pilot light. The flash was followed by a horrendous thunderclap and one half of the house exploding in a massive ball of flame. The sound and shockwave slammed into Frank like a sledgehammer. It rang him like a gong. Every hair follicle on his body stood on end.

The fire rose up in a tall, fat pillar of flame, smoke, and debris, and then the cloud began to roll in on itself. Chunks of wood and drywall and siding fluttered up into the sky. A huge chunk of roof spun like a UFO, sailing out in a huge arc.

Frank couldn't feel his heart. It was like the blast had emptied him right out. The driver of the van wasn't anywhere to be seen. The men by the barrels were on the ground. Tractor Man had disappeared.

The flames and smoke rolled up in a small mushroom cloud.

Now that was a bomb!

A moment later Tractor Man rose. He put a hand out on the tractor to brace himself and gawk at the spectacle, obviously forgetting Frank was behind him in the field.

Frank exhaled. Found Tractor Man with his iron sights. Calmed himself. Squeezed. There was a bang he barely heard. A moment later the bullet slammed into Tractor Man's back, about where his left shoulder blade would be. The lead blew a hole out the front and spun him around. His rifle went flying, and he dropped like a stone.

Frank turned to the coop boys. The two coops had been blown over. It appeared Big Hair was trapped under some of the debris. Frank pivoted to find the guy with the gray and white baseball cap with his sights, but the man took off running toward the field where Ed had gone.

Frank took two shots and missed both times. Then he remembered Ed was on his flank somewhere. He turned.

Ed was way down the adjacent field. His brake lights were on. He'd obviously heard the explosion and stopped, but the brake lights went off, the motor revved, and the pickup shot forward. Way down where Tony was, it looked like there was a gate in the barbed-wire fence linking the field Frank was in to the one where Ed was. Carmen and the children had already ridden through the gate into Ed's field. They were moving at their steady slow pace, the children all stacked on and clinging to each other. The pickup was gaining on them.

Tony, who must have fixed his snowmobile problem, was racing toward the gate to try to cut Ed off. Tony pulled out his semi-automatic.

How far down were they? Three-quarters of a mile? Ed was racing through the field. Tony was flying, his motor whining. No way Frank was going to catch up before those two collided.

Hell-a-mighty.

An aluminum window frame fell out of the sky and thumped into the grass not three feet away from Frank. He started and looked up. Chunks of debris, some of them trailing smoke, dotted the sky above him. They began to thud into the grass all around him. The big piece of roof that looked like a UFO was starting to fall as well, but it was way up there and on the other side of the burning house, twisting slowly in the sky, headed for someone else's field.

Frank jumped onto his seat, wedged the P90 between his legs. "God," he said. "Now would be a really good time to step in."

16

Dirt

FRANK DUCKED LOW and pushed the throttle, hoping he didn't get conked on the head by the kitchen stove or a can of beans. A length of 2x4 that had been split to a point came sailing from the heavens and staked the ground up ahead on his left. A spoon smacked into the plastic shroud covering the snowmobile's engine. He knew a set of knives would be next. Frank jammed the throttle forward, and he and the snowmobile raced away from the death by bungalow falling from the sky.

In the distance, Tony shot through the gate, gunned his machine out into the field, then stopped hard, placing himself between the racing yellow pickup and the snowmobile with Carmen and the children farther down the field. He stepped off his snowmobile and raised his semi-automatic and began firing.

The pickup did not slow down. Instead, the driver gunned it.

Tony emptied his gun. Brave as he might be, the fact was he was too far away, much too far for an inexperienced shooter—it appeared every shot had missed.

Tony looked down at the gun, looked up at the pickup still racing toward him.

"Get behind the machine!" Frank yelled.

But Tony didn't hear or listen. Instead, he ran out in front of the oncoming truck, took a few running steps, then hurled the pistol at the vehicle.

The gun arced over the grass and bounced off the corner of the windshield on the passenger's side. The glass cracked. The driver swerved and slowed.

Then Tony realized he was standing out in the middle of the field with nothing between him and the men in the truck. He turned and ran, high-stepping it through the tall grass toward the fence.

Ed gesticulated, and the driver punched the gas and sped after Tony.

Frank had his throttle pressed all the way down. His speedometer said he was going sixty. He was flying through the meadow grass, but it wasn't going to be enough.

Tony looked back, stumbled, regained his footing.

The pickup roared behind. The passenger's side door flew open.

Tony tried to juke right; the pickup corrected. He tried to juke left, but the pickup was on him. Tony's eyes were wide with desperation. Frank could see it all the way from where he was.

Ed struck Tony with the passenger side door and knocked him flat into the grass.

The driver jammed on the brakes.

Tony tried to rise, but Ed jumped out the open door. He struck Tony in the face with the side of a gun. Tony reeled back, and then Ed grabbed him by the arm and nape of his neck. He opened the back door of the king cab and shoved Tony in.

Frank sped toward the gate.

Ed stepped up on the running board and turned to look directly at Frank. He brought up his index finger and pointed it under his chin then flicked his finger away. To Ed and his associates in prison, that meant you had just shot yourself in the head. Then he climbed inside and slammed the door.

The driver floored it. He didn't go after the girls. He cut a tight left turn, then straightened up and headed back toward the dirt road. The pickup's motor roared, the exhaust pipes rumbled, the big knobby tires threw grass into the air.

In the distance at the other end of the field, Carmen and the girls continued south at a steady pace.

Tony had kept them safe. The dumb kid. He'd delayed Ed and the others just enough for Frank to get there. Otherwise, Ed surely would have sped down the field and caught Carmen and the children. There was a gate at the far end. Ed would have loaded them in and driven through and left Frank behind.

Now it was time for Frank to return the favor. He slowed down to make it through the open gate, then shot through it into the next field and gunned his machine. The motor whined. The grass slapped the cowling. A moment later he passed Tony's snowmobile and headed after Ed.

Up ahead the truck slowed to pick up the guy with the gray and white baseball cap who'd been taking pot shots at Frank from behind the chicken coops. The guy jumped in with Tony, and the pickup took off again. But the delay allowed Frank to narrow the gap between him and the truck.

The truck hit something in the field and bounced violently into the air, daylight showing under the fat round axles. It slammed down, jostled, and continued on. Frank moved to the side to miss whatever was hiding in the grass. A moment later he passed by and saw they'd hit a ditch. Then the truck was at the gate. They braked hard, turned left, and floored it up onto the dirt road.

Frank kept the snowmobile at full speed and reached the gate only a few seconds behind. He pulled his brake hard and fish-tailed out onto the dirt road. Then he jammed the thumb throttle all the way forward. The motor whined again. The studs of the track bit in.

The grass in the field had been deep. He suspected the track hadn't been a hundred percent efficient, which meant the speedometer had overstated his speed. But this dirt road was an entirely different matter. The pickup might be able to go faster out on a freeway, but this wasn't a freeway. It was an uneven dirt road with plenty of turns, which meant the race went to the one with the fastest acceleration.

He shot forward, the springs and shocks of the steering skis bouncing over the hard dirt. In front of him, the yellow pickup kicked up dust and gravel. When it neared the first T in the road, its brake lights lit up, but it took the corner a little too fast and almost flew off the other side. The driver braked hard, skidded to a stop, and went part-way off the road. He gunned it back up on the road, but he'd lost quite a bit of his lead. He was about to lose more.

This dirt road was built up above the level of the fields and so the shoulders dropped off a number of feet on either side to a strip that ran in front of the barbed-wire fences. In this section, the drop-off was probably five feet or more.

The dust was heavy in the air, but the T in the road was clear enough to see. Frank slowed, but not nearly as much as the pickup had, and dropped onto the slope of the shoulder. When he reached the T, he dropped out of sight, cutting the corner, using the banked curve of the shoulder like someone on a high-speed race track. After banking the turn, he came flying up out of the barrow pit having made the turn. The snowmobile caught air and slammed down just about the middle of the road with a clunk and skid. He punched it again; the paddles bit in, and the snowmobile raced forward. One of his ear plugs fell out, and the sounds that had been muffled came in loud and clear.

The pickup wasn't too far ahead of him now, and he was gaining on it. Dust billowed up behind the big tires. Bits of gravel and rock flew past. Frank squinted and ducked low behind his shot-out windshield. Dirt coated his teeth and the inside of his mouth. It was stinging his eyes, making it so he almost couldn't see.

He moved to the left, to the driver's side of the road, and suddenly was out of the dust plume. The shoulder dropped steeply away to a thick growth of cattails. Up ahead the fields gave way to some kind of marsh.

The driver saw him in the mirror. Ed opened the slider in the back window and stuck his pistol out. He fired twice. Missed twice.

Beyond the pickup, two men on four-wheelers were coming this way, gazing toward the house and what must now be a spectacular column of smoke. A dog sat up behind one of them. The men saw the truck and snowmobile racing toward them and moved over to hug the shoulder.

Frank steered the snowmobile back behind the pickup. A few moments later he flew past the men and the barking dog. Then he moved back out of the dust plume and gunned the throttle.

The snowmobile was jerking and bouncing over the hard dirt, but he pulled closer to the truck. Close enough to shoot. He grabbed the P90 with his left hand, kept the throttle down, and took aim at the rear tire on the driver's side. He squeezed, banged, missed. Squeezed again, banged, hit the rear bumper. Squeezed again, banged, hit the tire. A piece of rubber flew up and off, but the tire didn't burst. He must have only knocked off a bit of the fat tread. He prepared to take another shot.

Then the driver jerked over in front of Frank and braked hard. The wheels locked and skidded over the dirt. The brake lights shone through the dust.

Frank turned the wheel, trying not to wrench it because if he did, he'd tumble, and tumbling at almost eighty miles per hour into the steel bumper of a pickup was not a good way to extend your days upon the land.

He shot past the pickup, an inch from scraping the sidewall, and had one hundredth of a second to see he was headed for the side of the road where the shoulder dropped away to the marsh. One hundredth of a second later he shot out over the edge of the road, airborne, the engine whining into an even higher pitch because there was nothing holding the track back.

You can fly quite a distance in just one or two seconds at eighty miles per hour. Frank soared over the cattails and the barbed-wire fence that was half submerged in the water. He released the submachine gun, grabbed the steering handles with both hands, and pulled with all his might. He stood, pressed down on the running boards, trying to move his weight to the back, desperately trying to keep the snowmobile from nose diving.

A moment later, and more than forty yards from the road, he hit the brackish water at an angle with the flat of the track. The four hundred pound Polaris didn't quite skip, but it didn't sink. It kind of bounced and surge forward like a huge rock.

Frank crammed the throttle lever forward and heaved up on the front of the snowmobile. The motor whined; the track spun with the speed of 120 horses; the studs bit into the water like a high-performance version of a paddle boat, and Frank shot forward.

A mound of firm ground rose forty or fifty yards away. A sturdy black cow stood on it munching grass, swishing its tail, looking up to see what has just splashed into the marsh. Frank headed for the cow.

The cow took a couple of chews on its cud, trying to figure out what in the world was on the water. Then it realized the thing was coming its way and splashed into the water, sprinting for another hummock.

Frank rode up on the firm land all covered in grass and small prickly thistle-like plants and took stock. The water drained from the snowmobile as well as his pants and boots.

Out on the road, Ed and his driver were barreling along, dust flying up behind. But beyond the pickup, that road made a ninety degree left hand turn around this marsh. If Frank took the diagonal across the marsh, he could cut them off. On the far side of the water was an open spot in the fence where it looked like someone had been making repairs, probably those two on the four-wheelers with their dog.

Frank gunned his engine and stood in a slight crouch, his feet firm on the jagged teeth of the running board. The snowmobile shot forward, off the firm ground, onto the soggy ground and swamp grass, and then out to the open water. He kept the nose high and throttle on full. The Polaris paddled across the thick water toward the gap in the fence.

He wasn't going anywhere near eighty, but he was going fast enough. He plowed through a swarming mass of gnats with his face and ended up eating a few through his nose. He gave another couple of cows standing a ways down something to gawk at and discuss around the local salt lick.

Ed and his man approached the corner in the pickup and slowed. It was going to be close.

Frank scared up a handful of ducks that beat away with thick velocity, and then he plowed through a mass of cattails and bumped up onto firm ground.

Ed and the big yellow pickup turned the corner and accelerated.

Frank punched it. He grabbed for the P90, then remembered he had dropped it when he'd first flown off on the road. It was now resting someplace in the muck at the bottom of the marsh. He reached around to pull the Glock out of his waistband and felt nothing. He reached farther. But it was gone. Long gone. In the marsh, in the field back by the house, along the road—no telling where.

The pickup was coming fast. Frank looked around for a weapon. Up ahead was the portion of fence that the two men had been repairing. A small two-wheeled trailer rested off the side of the road. The ends of a couple dozen six-foot green fencing posts stuck out of it. These weren't made out of wood, but steel, the cross-section shaped like a T with a single row of tabs running its length that looked like they belonged on the back of an alligator. The tabs were designed to hold metal wire clips that fastened lines of barbed wire to the post.

Frank raced for the small trailer, slowed just enough to grab one of the posts, then took off for the road. A moment later he rolled up the shoulder and onto the hard dirt and faced the pickup down at the other end.

Frank adjusted his grip on the post. About six inches from the bottom of the post was a metal plate in the shape of a tall chevron. When the post was pounded into the ground, the points of the chevron pointed up, resisting any pressure that would pull the post out of the ground. Frank raised the post in his left hand like a spear, the chevron plate pointing forward like a blade, and gunned it. Rocks and dust spat out from the track behind him.

The American Indians had met with plenty of success throwing lances from horseback in these parts. And what was the snowmobile if not a replacement for the horse?

Nobody was taking Tony. Not this time.

Frank shot forward, but kept the post down at his side, hidden.

Down at the other end, Ed's driver gunned his much bigger horse. The motor growled, and the front of the pickup raised up a bit with the acceleration.

17

Threefer

THE DISTANCE BETWEEN the two vehicles shrank rapidly. The Polaris was going a little over forty miles per hour. The truck was doing more than that. Maybe sixty. Which meant the combined force of any impact would be around 100 miles per hour. The post felt like it was eight or nine pounds. The big yellow truck with its big black tires had to weigh two tons. If he had a pencil and paper, Frank could work out the velocity, maybe the force per square inch on the tip of his steel lance. But you didn't need paper to know that an eight pound shaft striking a king cab pickup at 100 mph was going to do some damage, especially where Frank was going to put it.

The Polaris bumped and rattled as it flew over the ruts in the dirt road. Ed popped out of the passenger's side window and took a pot shot that flew who knew where. He took another that whistled by exceedingly close.

They were close enough that Frank could see Tony sitting up in the back seat. The driver hunched up over his steering wheel and grinned.

Tony got down.

Smart boy.

The truck was closing fast, the grill looking huge, coming right at him. Frank lined himself just to the driver's side of center. They probably weren't going to try to run him over. You hit a 400-pound snowmobile at these speeds and you were going to have some problems. On the other hand, this was Ed and his druggie friends. Maybe they didn't think much about velocities. Maybe all they saw was road kill.

The words of Sam's road kill prayer sounded in his mind. Good Lord, Frank thought, let's hope the desk jockeys didn't get that order mixed up.

Ed's gun banged; the muzzle flashed again, and the bullet struck the snowmobile's engine shroud. *That's right, Ed. Use up as much ammo as possible now. That will be less for me to deal with later.*

The truck was closing fast, seconds from impact.

The driver's eyes went all narrow and mean. He moved slightly to the side. He was clearly smart enough to know that hitting a snowmobile at these speeds straight on wouldn't work, but clipping one with the pickup's thick steel bumper just might do the trick.

Now was the time.

Frank rose up on the running boards. He brought the lance aloft with his left hand, right hand steering and keeping the throttle pressed down. He cocked the lance back.

The driver's eyes went wide.

Frank yelled and hurled the post as straight as he could at the center of the windshield.

The driver, as expected, jerked the pickup to avoid the shaft, but he was too close, which meant he moved the truck and his child-molesting, narco grin directly into the lance's path.

"Ya-ta-hey," Frank said.

Then he realized he'd cut it too close. He leaned, tried to move the Polaris out of the path of the hurtling pickup, but they were going to impact. Frank lunged to the side, away from the Polaris and truck.

The pickup hit the side of the snowmobile with a crash and crunch. Something struck Frank's boot and spun him in the air. He flew down the road, over the edge, then slammed into the slanted shoulder at somewhere close to forty miles per hour. He bounced, tumbled, figured he would die from a blow to his head, then saw the barbed-wire fence and knew it would be decapitation.

It was neither. He crashed to a stop in a scrubby stand of wild rose bush.

Behind him the big Polaris flipped and rolled, caught air again.

It was coming right at him. If it hit him, he was dead. But the Polaris crashed to the ground five feet away, rolled once end over end past Frank, then slammed into the dirt on its side.

Frank was dazed. He was disoriented. But he climbed to his feet. His rib cage and part of one forearm was burning road rash. His elbow pinged. And his leg had a hitch in it. He looked down. A stick as thick as a pencil and nine inches long poked straight out of his shin.

Frank turned toward the pickup.

The truck was stopped, pointing across the road. The steel post stuck straight out of windshield. "Moron," Frank said and began to shamble toward the truck. He'd make sure Ed and the driver were securely out of this picture, and then he'd fetch Tony. With every limping step, his wet pants and boots squished with water.

The side of the truck's bumper and part of the panel were smashed in where it had hit the Polaris. Had Frank not flung himself to the side with his mighty catlike reflexes, that fender would have been the spot of his demise. He would have definitely made one hell of a bug splat.

Frank hoped Ed was in shock. He hoped a piece of windshield glass had skewered him in the eye.

But the driver, who'd just been sitting there, moved. He turned and looked at Frank. Frank's heart sank a bit—the post hadn't skewered him. It appeared to have missed and gone right between him and Ed.

Frank hurried his shamble.

The driver saw Frank and went all white-eyed.

Frank's leg was starting to throb, but he pushed himself to run. If he could just get close enough to jump up on the running board.

The driver shouted something unintelligible, then put the truck in gear and punched it. The tires spun. If the driver cranked the wheel one way, he'd have no problem running Frank down. No problem at all.

But the driver cranked the wheel the other way.

Fight or flight, and he'd chosen to flee. After all, he didn't know Frank had lost his guns. The motor roared, and the pickup bumped back out onto the road.

"No!" Frank shouted. He half ran, half shambled forward, but the pickup roared away and left him to choke on its dust.

Cowards. *Cowards!*

He turned and shamble-loped back to the Polaris and righted it. The windshield was gone. The shroud was in pieces, revealing the motor underneath. Frank straddled it and found the handlebar was bent. He turned the ignition. Nothing. He pulled the kill switch up, turned the key again. This time the motor turned over, coughed, and started.

He was going to chase their worthless hides out onto the freeway if he had to. He was going to chase them down and rid the world of their scum.

Frank pressed the throttle and the motor revved, the studs of the track bit in. He raced up onto the road, gave it more throttle, but something wasn't right. The back end bumped and kicked, and then the Polaris ground to a stop.

Frank looked down. The track had come completely off. The wheels that kept the track in motion—the whole back end of the chassis— were all bent to hell. This fine horse wasn't going anywhere.

The pickup accelerated along the dirt road, Tony inside.

Desperation rushed through him. He needed to call 911. How far could they get in a pickup with a post sticking out of the windshield? The cops would spot them a mile off.

He looked around. The closest house looked like it was five miles away. To the north, the direction the pickup was moving, there was nothing but fields. To the south, the remains of the Goroza's stash house burned, the flames leaping a hundred feet high, a huge pillar of black smoke rising into the sky. That was going to draw some attention. Fire, police. But it was going to take some time for them to get out here in the middle of nowhere. And the more time Ed had, the easier it was going to be for him to ditch the pickup and find a better ride.

Frank saw the two guys on four-wheelers with their dog. They were moving slowly on the road, gawking at the fire. Surely they had phones. If he could get to them, he could sic the cops on Ed.

He began to run in his soaked boots, but pain shot up his leg. He remembered the stick and stopped. He reached down and yanked it out. A length about a long as his pinky finger came out of his leg all covered in blood.

Gah! He cast the stick aside. Then he took off his shirt, removed his undershirt, which was bloody from the road rash all along his rib cage, and tied it tightly around the wound with a double knot. He checked himself for any other injuries and found none. Then he picked up his shirt and began to hobble-run back down the road. He yelled, hoping the sound might carry, and waved his arms.

He thought one of the men spotted him, but they didn't stop. Didn't turn. And who would turn to help the guy with the P90 who'd been chasing a pickup truck? The men looked from the house to Frank, and then something spooked them, and they high-tailed it out of there. Maybe the propane tank was still standing, waiting like a time bomb. Regardless, they did not come for Frank.

Frank's leg was killing him. No way he was going to run five miles on it to get to the next house. He was going to have trouble just walking. Frank took another step. The pain shot up his leg. He could do pain. His choice was the burning house or the neighbors five miles away. The burning house would draw people to it. The neighbors— who even knew if they were home?

Both gave Ed too much time. He glanced back north. Ed's pickup was gone. Frank blinked and performed a pattern search of the horizon. Nothing.

"Lord," he prayed.

To the south, the house burned, smoke piling into the sky. From the marsh, a column of gnats moved over to give him a sniff. Out across the water the cows swished their tails and chewed grass. A large flock of black birds wheeled into the field next to him. In the distance, something made a high-pitched whine.

Frank's whole body was lit up now: his leg, elbow, and ribs all throbbed. He began walking toward the burning house, hoping every second to see the flashing lights of an emergency vehicle on the horizon. He knew Ed's people were going to be pissed, knew they were going to take out their anger on Tony, knew this whole situation was now out of control.

He walked another twenty yards. The house continued to burn. The smoke continued to rise. But there were no flashing lights. The volume of the high-pitched whine grew louder. Frank turned, looked around. There was nothing on the road. No motorbike, no four-wheeler, no cars.

In the field, the flock of black birds rose up in a undulating cloud that flew one way, then suddenly changed direction and sped another way. When the black mass cleared away, it revealed a plane flying toward him maybe two hundred feet off the ground.

It was a Cessna.

It had a yellow cowling and a brown stripe down the side.

He watched it come, watched it buzz past, and Frank swore he saw Henry looking out the back window.

There was no freaking way.

The plane banked and turned, then came back around.

Two men sat up front. The big man on the pilot's side was definitely Pinto.

Freaking way.

Frank waved both his arms, yelled.

A moment later he heard the distant sound of a car horn. From the northeast, a vehicle was coming, kicking up a trail of dust. It wasn't Ed's yellow pickup. It wasn't an emergency vehicle with flashing lights. It was a Mazda mini-van. Baby blue, shining in the sun.

Frank looked up into the heavens. Looked back down at the van. Looked back up. "Is this some post hoc joke?"

Silence.

Maybe it *was* all intermediaries, and the desk jockeys *were* in charge. Maybe God had servants assigned to watch various regions. Maybe he gave the hosts of Heaven jobs, because who would want a bunch of sycophantic folks in robes singing at you day and night? Unless it was Michelangelo's vision of heaven, and then it would be a bunch of sycophantic naked people doing the singing. But even that would get old.

"Thanks for moving my number up," Frank said. "I assume you realize things have just hit the fan?"

The heavens did not reply.

The plane circled around once more, then flew off toward the burning house. Frank began to hobble toward the mini-van.

About two minutes later the mini-van turned onto his stretch of road. He watched it grow larger, watched the trail of dust kick up and blow away in the slight breeze. When it got closer, he could see Sam at the wheel. Sam gave the horn a couple of happy toots, then a few moments later rolled up and stopped to let him in. The cloud of dust that had been following the van blew over Frank.

Frank opened the passenger's door. "Sam."

"I've got him," Sam said for his Bluetooth's ear. Then he turned to Frank. "You look like crap."

Frank climbed into the car. The van still had all the junk that it had before—spilled Cheerios, a sack of potatoes, and all the PVC Cub Scout mess in the back.

Sam said, "Where's Tony?"

"You talking to Pinto?"

"Yeah."

"Tell him to go north-west of us. Tell him to look for a bright yellow pickup with a fence post sticking out the windshield."

Sam looked at him with puzzlement.

"Just tell him."

Sam repeated the message, then said, "Who's in the truck?"

"Ed. He's still got Tony."

"Aw, crap," Sam said. He relayed the info to Pinto, then turned to Frank. "Dude, we were looking all over."

"Tell me you have Tony's phone."

"Yeah," Sam said. He dug down into the pink diaper bag between the seats and came up with it. "You left it on the back seat."

Frank took the phone. "Hang on," he said. He scrolled through the log of calls and found the number he was looking for and pressed the dial button. The phone on the other end rang once, twice, three times. Frank was thinking maybe Ed wasn't going to answer; maybe the fencing post had given him pause, but then someone picked up.

"Frankie," Ed said in an angry voice.

"Let the boy out now."

"You just dug yourself a grave, Jockstrap. You dug it deep."

"I'm going to put your head in a meat grinder, Ed. You let him out."

"Forget the house. Forget the foot soldiers. Frank, you just killed Jesus Goroza. Do you know what that means?"

"Self-defense."

"You just took this to a whole other level. You just sent a missile into Red Square."

"That's right. *I* sent it. Not Tony. So put him out."

Above Frank the Cessna buzzed to the north-west.

"You put me in a bad position, Frank. I don't know that you're going to get Tony. I'll call you back."

"Ed."

Nothing.

"Ed!"

Ed hung up.

Frank dialed again, and it went to voicemail.

He turned to Sam. "Tell Pinto the pickup was heading west, right along that road up there, about a mile out."

Sam relayed the message.

The Cessna was high up over the area. High enough to get a mighty good view. There was no way Ed would be able to hide the pickup.

A few moments later Sam said, "Pinto says there are a couple of pickups, but none are yellow."

"It's got to be there," Frank said. "He was just there ten minutes ago. Tell him to look farther north and west."

Sam relayed the message.

Frank said, "Turn this thing around. We need to follow Ed. We want to go out along that road you passed about a half a mile back."

Sam slowed to a stop and made a three point turn. Then they headed back the way he'd come. They traveled the half mile and came to the intersection where a road shot west of the one they were on.

"Turn here," Frank said.

Sam turned onto the road and accelerated. "Where now?"

"Just keep going."

They drove maybe another mile, and then Sam said, "They found a yellow pickup. Its windshield is all busted. It's sitting in the shade of some trees. But there isn't anybody inside."

"What?"

"Pinto's going to fly lower to get a better look, but he says there isn't anybody in it."

"Anyone on foot? Any houses nearby?"

Sam relayed the questions. A moment later he said, "No. Closest house is a few miles away and there isn't anybody anywhere. Just some farmer moving some sprinkler pipe."

Frank was pretty sure that farmer hadn't walked out there. Ed must have taken his truck or car. Frank's heart sank. They needed to cordon the place off. Set a perimeter. He dialed 9 then 1. He was about to dial the other 1 when the phone rang.

It was a number Frank didn't recognize. He moved to press the cancel button, then stopped and pressed answer instead.

Ed's voice came through, but it was in the background. He was yelling at someone. Someone else shouted in Spanish, but Ed talked over him.

What was this—a butt dial? Someone else in Ed's car?

Then it hit him. It was Tony.

That was Jesus's phone. Tony had hacked it. But why call Frank? He should have called 911. Then Frank remembered their conversation in the basement.

Tony had called Frank instead. And now Frank had that number in his phone.

What was he going to do with a number?

He could do everything with a number. Bring the authorities in, and they could locate that phone. Triangulate it. The phone company didn't even need GPS.

Then Ed's voice came in loud and clear. "What is that? What are you doing! You little—"

The call ended.

A moment later, Tony's phone buzzed again and Ed's number came up on the screen.

Frank thumbed the answer button. "You're a dead man, Ed. This is your last warning."

"Here's the deal, Jockstrap."

"The cops are going to find that pickup," Frank said. "They going to trace it back to the Gorozas. Then they're going to have a lot on their hands. And they'll blame that on you."

"The cops will trace it, all right," Ed said. "And the registration will lead them to some old couple, or some kid that died five years ago somewhere in Arizona or Mississippi. Same with names on the house. The Gorozas aren't stupid."

Frank covered the microphone on the phone and said to Sam, "Tell them to look for any vehicles heading west from the pickup."

Ed continued, "We caught your boy making a call. Now I wonder why he'd do that? You ready for another goose chase?"

So much for triangulation. Frank had to hand it to Tony; he was trying.

Ed said, "They want the girls. They want that whore we were bringing back to them. And they want you, Frank. You've suddenly become popular."

"Geez, maybe I'll run for mayor."

"Give us the threefer, and we set Tony free."

That lie was about as big as they came.

Frank thought about Carmen. He said, "Maybe I'll just take the woman myself."

"That would not be wise."

"The Matanarcos; I bet she's worth a pretty penny to the right people."

A pause. "You do not want to jump my claim."

Claim, like he'd found gold in a stream. But Carmen wasn't a victim. Victims had nervous breakdowns and freaked out with fear. Carmen was all business. She was some kind of operator. Which meant this wasn't a ransom. There was a bounty on Carmen's head, and Ed was bringing her back to collect the money.

But upon what kind of person did a cartel put, not a hit, but a bounty?

Someone they wanted to torture before she died. Someone from whom they wanted to wring information. Or someone they wanted to rescue.

Was Ed going all noble on him?

Naw, you didn't beat the people you rescued, zip-tie 'em, and throw them into the trunk of your car.

Bottom line: Carmen, which Frank knew wasn't her real name, was someone who had eluded those who sought her. She might be a sicaria herself. A hired killer. One that had perpetrated a few too many hits on the Gorozas or someone friendly to them.

"Looks to me like you need a new partner," Frank said just to see what information he might shake loose. "Team up. And we can split the reward."

"Right," Ed said, but Frank knew his twisted brain was turning, trying to scheme a way to use this to his advantage. However, he must have come up with dead ends because he said, "The reward for you, Jockstrap, is a Tony that hasn't been mutilated in some awful fashion. Don't lose your focus."

"You just bought your grave."

"Keep your phone charged. You don't want to miss the next call. And just so you know, this phone I'm using now, it's going out the window. The next call will be coming from a different device."

Frank listened in the background of Ed's call for anything that might help him with his location, but Ed hung up.

Frank looked over at Sam. "They find anything?"

"Nothing."

Frank closed his eyes and pinched the bridge of his nose. These people were ugly, tiny-eyed eels.

They wanted him, did they? They wanted to play tough?

They had no idea how tough Frank could play.

The only problem was they currently held all the cards. They had all the aces and kings. They had the deck stacked.

18

Sugar Beets

FRANK SAID, "I need Pinto to circle round to the burning house. He'll see a track through the field going south. He's looking for a bunch of children piled on a snowmobile like circus clowns."

Sam relayed the message. A moment later the Cessna wheeled in the sky and headed south. Sam asked, "I assume we're going to follow?"

"That's right," Frank said. "We need to turn Silver here around." He also needed to make a call. He opened Tony's phone and brought up his contacts. He found Nurse Ratchet and dialed the number. It rang and rang, and then Kim answered. "Hey, baby."

Finally. "Don't you ever answer your phone?" Frank asked.

"Frank?"

"You need to listen to me, Kim. You need to get out of L.A. You need to do it now. Do not go home. Do not go to your office. You just head out."

A beat passed.

"Kim?"

"What's going on, Frank?"

"I told you what was going on. You're in danger. And now it's worse. I'm tracking Ed right now, but I think he's going to be sending someone your way."

Her voice took an angry edge. "And Tony?"

"Tony's okay."

"Put him on."

Frank took a breath. He could hear people talking in the background around her. "He's not here right now."

"Frank."

"He's fine, Kim. But you need to get out of Dodge."

She sighed. "You're a wrecking ball. Do you know that?"

He thought of Tony's face in the back of that truck. "Oh, I'm well aware of the burdens I bring. Look, I'm going to take care of it. I'll explain it all later. Right now you need to move."

"I've got work."

"Tell them you just got a goiter. No client's going to want to see you with Voldemort's head growing out of your neck."

She sighed again in annoyance.

"Don't you have a friend up in San Jose?"

"Yeah."

"Then tonight's girl's night out. If you leave now, you just might be there in time for the late show."

"You're lying to me, Frank. I know when you lie. For example, I know you are in Colorado, not Rock Springs. At least, that's where Tony's phone is. What are you doing in Colorado?"

"Kim, you're getting side-tracked. Ed has made a threat, which I will handle. But until I have him wrapped up, I need you in a safe place. The most important thing you can do for Tony right now is put yourself beyond Ed's reach."

Frank cringed at his last sentence.

"What does Tony have to do with this? Sweet Lord, something *has* happened to him. I knew it. Frank!"

He could see her in his mind's eye. Worry, anger, alarm all rising up in her face.

"I'm not going to San Jose, brother. I'm coming to Rock Springs. And when I do, we're going to sit down and have ourselves a come-to-Jesus."

Rock Springs was actually . . . a perfect place. At least for now. "The spare key is under a rock in the back corner of the yard. Actually, I'm pretty sure the house is unlocked."

"Frank."

He could hear the worry in her voice. "Tony's fine, Kim. But you cannot go to your place in L.A." He slowed down, put as much everything's-fine-we're-having-a-picnic-with-strawberry-cake in his voice as he could muster. "Love you. You're the best sister ever. We'll have a big barbeque when you arrive. Maybe you can bite the head off a rattler."

"Oh, I'm going to bite somebody's head. That's for sure."

"Gotta run," Frank said and ended the call.

Frank put the phone down. That had gone swimmingly. When this was all said and done, she would probably drive a steak knife through his heart. But, hey, what was family for?

He sat back and knocked his elbow. The pain shot up his arm. In fact, the pain in his arm, leg, and ribs pounded with each heart beat. "Do you have any Tylenol?" he asked Sam.

Sam fished around in his diaper bag and came up with a bottle of pink pain killer for kids. It was three-fourths full. "This is all kiddie potency," Sam said. "I'd just chug the whole thing."

Frank took the bottle from him, pressed down and screwed off the child protection lid, and drank the thick sickly-sweet medicine. "Bubble gum," he said. "Yum."

Sam turned the van around and headed back toward the Gorozas.

Frank punched up the maps app on Tony's phone. Then he tapped and scrolled until he was looking at their current position and the lonely country roads that crisscrossed the area. "You're going to take a right at the T."

"You got it, Tonto."

"I don't know that I want to be Tonto. Wasn't someone always beating the snot out of him?"

"It's a hard job, but you're our man, Frank."

"Thor then."

"Thor has lots of blond wavy hair. I'd say you are a little hair challenged at the moment."

"Whatever," Frank said and tried to swallow the last of the medicine. But it wasn't going down. Sam had replaced his bottle of vitamin water. Frank pointed at it. "Do you mind?"

"Help yourself."

Frank took the water and washed the medicine down. Then he put the bottle back.

He said, "How did you find me?"

"We saw your abduction," Sam said. "Watched it through the field glasses. But we didn't have a handy field for takeoff. There was no way Pinto was going to do that particular road again. Heber was still a ways out. About forty-five minutes later and a tense chat with some cops, we finally found a road. By then you were long gone. So we headed the way we'd seen you go. We picked you up again just this side of Cheyenne, but then night fell and we mixed you up with another truck. By the time we figured out our mistake, it was too dark. So we camped out. Pinto put it down at an airport nearby and then we all went to some cockroach motel. We got up this morning before dawn and went back to the point where we'd gotten confused and started looking around, Pinto and Heber up in the plane. We were just about to give up when that house exploded. Buddy, that was one heck of a beacon."

"Hey, I figured we were out on the plains; it was perfect for Indian smoke signals."

"What was that? Arapaho for 'holy crap'?"

"Something like that."

By this time Sam had turned the corner around the marsh and started heading for the spot where Frank first flew off the road. From this angle Frank realized that had been one fine piece of snowmobile flight. But it hadn't been enough. He would have had very few options indeed if Sam hadn't shown up.

"Why?" Frank asked.

"Why what?"

"You three spent the night. I'm just some white trash ex-con that moved into your neighborhood. You don't know me from Adam."

"I know enough."

"No, you don't." Frank shook his head. It was the super-trusting people like Sam, who ended up being exploited. Or maybe it was Frank that was going to be exploited. Who knew what those Mormons were really up to?

Sam said, "I know that this is about Tony, whom I do not see in this van. Or out in the fields."

"Tony thinks you're involved in some kind of racket."

"The bail-out-your-neighbor racket?"

"The schmoozing ex-cons racket. Like maybe you're trying to make contacts. Like maybe you've got some plan."

Sam still looked confused.

"Like you're running a con, like the cookie man business is all a front."

"A cookie con?" he asked. Half of his face turned up in one of those bemused oh-this-is-rich smiles.

"Hey," Frank said, "you'd be surprised at the originality I met in prison."

"A cookie con," Sam said again. The hilarity was bubbling up in him. He scrunched up his eyes and started to shake with a dry laugh. A moment later the van filled with a full-bodied clean-cut chubby mirth.

"It's not that funny."

Sam wiped a tear from his eye. Then he started up again.

"Watch the road." Frank shook his head. "What did you do? OD on vitamin B?"

They came to the turnoff where Frank had banked the inside of the corner, but instead of turning to go to the Goroza's marshmallow roast, they'd keep going straight.

Sam pitched his voice low. "We're taking over the sprinkles trade. Gonna clean house. You in or not, Homie?"

"Laugh it up. You've got to admit it's odd."

"Helping a friend isn't odd."

"I'm not a friend. I'm an acquaintance. And it *is* odd. Especially when considering my former status."

Sam let the last bit of mirth run its course, then got control of himself. "Dude, you called me. I didn't call you."

"That's the point."

"Frank, you keep forgetting I'm a fraud dog. I talk to a lot of people. I hear a lot of truth. I hear a lot of lies. I don't have a badge that says Special Agent Cartwright, but I'm getting pretty good at sniffing out the BS."

"Yeah?"

"Yeah. And my manure meter says you're like a three on a scale of ten. A little bit of a mess, but an honest one."

"So says the cookie man."

"Many people fear the cookie man."

Frank looked him up and down. Mr. chubby good-luck charm. "Right."

"It's true," he shrugged. "I'm like the Dirty Harry of accounting. And now you're going to tell me what's going on. And you're not going to feed me some line like you did your sister."

"Oh?"

"Do not anger the cookie man," Sam said.

Sam had saved his frying bacon twice now. And there really wasn't any reason not to brief him, so Frank told him everything that had happened from the time he ran across the field to the truck stop to the moment Pinto buzzed by in the plane. By this time the Goroza's house was a couple miles behind them. The blaze had been joined by the flashing lights of two cop cars. About a mile out, a fire truck was also making its way to the house.

When Frank finished, Sam shook his head. "You've gotten yourself involved with some real pieces of work."

"I might use different adjectives."

"That little girl is nine years old?"

"Best guess. She might be younger. Trauma like she's going through tends to age you."

"*Nine years old*," Sam repeated and narrowed his eyes. "My oldest daughter is nine years old." His face turned hard. It appeared the Cookie Man was now officially in the Dirty Harry mode.

They followed the road into a dale, the tires rumbling over the gravel. Then the blue light on Sam's phone blinked, indicating he had a call. Sam said. "You find them?"

A beat passed.

"Roger that," he said and turned to Frank. "We're going to turn up here. The girls are hiding behind some shed at the corner of a field."

Frank looked at Sam. He said, "Thanks for coming after me. I owe you."

Sam took on a fake mafia Godfather accent. "One a deez a days, and that day may a never come, we're gonna aska you to do a service. Until then, accept this as a gift." Then his face turned hard again.

"Ha," Frank said. "I knew it was a racket."

Sam did not smile.

Frank thought, indebted to the Mormon mafia. It could be worse. What favor could they possibly ask?

* * *

Sam drove them down a long road between two fields of sugar beets. A shed stood in one field a little distance from the dirt road.

Frank said, "Don't let them see us just yet."

Sam slowed the van and stopped before they came alongside the shed. He said, "We're not taking these kids anywhere."

"No."

"You're not trying to capture the woman?"

"We're just going to talk," Frank said. "Right now I'm operating on low information. I might as well have none, and that is no way to conduct an operation. We need to figure out what's going on."

Sam nodded then the two of them got out and walked forward of the van. The leaves of sugar beets in the field and surrounding the shed were probably knee-high; the late morning wind had picked up and was blowing through the greens, rippling the whole field. Frank and Sam came parallel with the shed in the field and looked down its side.

In its shade, squatting among the beet leaves so their heads looked like so many cabbages, were the children.

They saw Frank, saw Sam. Their eyes were alert and full of apprehension. Frank waved at them. They did not wave back. They didn't move. He looked around for Carmen and didn't see her.

Beyond the children in the distance, the smoke from the burning house still rose in a black pillar into the sky. Down around the house, the lights of the emergency vehicles flashed.

"Slaves," Sam said and shook his head. "This is unreal. Who does this?"

Frank climbed over the low barbed-wire fence, found a row, and limp-walked along it into the thick field of beets. He leg ached the whole way.

Sam came behind. "It's okay," he called out. "We're going to help."

When they were about twenty-five yards out, the oldest girl whispered something to the others, and they rose like they were going to bolt. The snow machine Carmen had been driving wasn't anywhere to be seen. "We're going to get you out of here," Frank called to them.

"We've got our own people."

Frank turned. Carmen stood just inside the fence. Where had she come from?

"You should leave," she said.

"We're not leaving you here," Frank said.

Carmen shouted something in Spanish at the girls, and they began to move out into the field away from Frank.

"We don't need your help," Carmen said.

"I need yours," he said. "They took Tony."

She stopped. He saw her run the calculations in her mind. Saw her come to the wrong conclusion.

"No," he said. "I don't want you as a bargaining chip."

"Corre!" she shouted. Run!

"Stop!" Frank said, but Carmen was already high-tailing it back to the road. The girls ran into the field, away from him and Sam.

Frank took off after Carmen through the beets in a lame lope, the leaves dragging on his boots, his gimpy leg hurting with every stride, his ribs burning.

"The woman or the children?" Sam asked.

"The woman," Frank said.

Sam began to run after him.

Carmen was fast. She flew back down the little bit of row, climbed over the fence, then ran up onto the road.

Frank hustled down the row next to the one she'd been on. He finally reached the fence, climbed over, and took off after her. He poured on as much speed as he could, his feet crunching the grit on the road, but it wasn't going to be enough. She turned, saw him, and put on some of her own speed and pulled ahead. "Holy smokes, woman," he called. "I just need to talk."

She lengthened her stride.

Behind him, Sam was only just now climbing over the fence. Gimp and the Cookie Man were not going to get this job done.

Frank gritted his teeth at the pain, took in deep breaths, and tried for more speed, but he wasn't going to catch her. This was going to be a long game, and his leg put him at a distinct disadvantage. He hoped she was a sprinter who'd been laying off the exercise for a couple of years and would start blowing hard after another twenty yards. He hoped she didn't run marathons.

Carmen crossed over to the other side of the road. She was running in the opposite direction from the children. Leading him away. Showing no sign of slacking.

Back where they'd entered the field, the van started. Frank kept loping along, watching Carmen's fine braid bounce with each stride of her athletic-looking backside, watching her pull away.

A few moments later Sam pulled up alongside, the van's wheels crunching on the road. The driver's window was down. "Hey, Tonto," Sam said, "you want a ride?"

Sam had opened the sliding side door. Frank veered over and jumped in. Sam accelerated, and Frank moved over to the passenger side.

Up ahead, Carmen looked back. Sam sped up and almost caught her. But she abandoned the road, ran down the shoulder to the field on the other side.

Sam slammed on the brakes. Frank rolled open the door on the passenger's side and sprang out. Carmen climbed over the fence and ran into another vast field of sugar beets.

Frank scrambled down the slope, grabbed a post and did and awkward one-legged hop over the barbed-wire. It wasn't pretty, but it got the job done. She wasn't too far ahead. Furthermore, the beet greens were bigger in proportion to her frame. They slowed her down more than they did Frank. There were also some rough chunks of dirt down these rows. She had smaller feet that would be tripped up by gouged ground. He had big boots to simply mash over it. He put on a burst of speed. She tried to juke him, but he swatted at her shoulder. "Carmen," he said.

She twisted away from his grasp. He lunged, tripped, caught her pant leg on the way down, and the two of them fell into the crop.

She struggled away.

Frank shoved himself up. "Carmen," he said.

She rose, knife in hand.

"Carmen, it's not what you think."

"You're not going to trade me in for Tony. You're not going to trade those children."

"I wasn't planning on it."

She backed away, stepped into the row behind her. "You're all the same."

Frank held his hands out wide. "I am *not* going to trade you."

"He's your blood. Of course, you'll trade me." She took another step back, knife ready, looking like she just might know how to handle that thing. You had to be really good to kill someone with one knife stroke. You didn't have to be quite as good to stab. Or slash. And that knife's blade was razor sharp.

But a gun would be better. She'd been holding Jesus's spare gun back at the house. Why didn't she pull that instead?

Sam jogged into the field.

Carmen said, "I will kill whoever touches me."

Frank motioned for Sam to keep back. "Let's not crowd her."

"I will not be traded."

"Carmen, I am not going to rely on the word of men who rape little girls. Ed and the Gorozas are not going to make any kind of trade.

I killed Jesus. They must retaliate. An eye for an eye. Nothing but my death with satisfy them. So even if I bring you and the children and a suitcase filled with five million dollars, they're still not going to trade. They'll take you and the children and the suitcase, and then they'll kill Tony. They'll slaughter him right in front of me. And then they'll kill me. So there is not going to be a trade."

"Then what do you want?"

"I want Tony."

"I can't give him to you."

"Right now they hold all the cards. The only way out is to get ourselves a card. A big card. I need to leverage their leverage."

She shook her head, took a step back.

Frank took a step forward.

"I'm not your leverage."

Sam crossed over a few rows to head her off.

"All I need from you is information," Frank said. "You've obviously had some dealings with the Gorozas. Give me a leg up, and I'm out of your hair."

"Step back," she said.

"You gave that gun to those kids, didn't you?" Frank asked.

She took another step back.

Frank did not follow. She was protecting the children. "Who are you?" he asked.

"None of your concern."

"Who runs the organization? If I'm going to track Tony, I need a name."

Carmen took another step back. "Flor," she said.

"Flor who?"

"Goroza."

"A woman runs this thing?"

"She's the mother of the Jesus you killed."

They were definitely going to want payback. Which made it even more critical that Frank get information now. Every minute counted.

"There's a high chance Tony is not going to live through the night.

I could have left you in that house. Tony could have left you in the trunk of that car. I helped you. Now help me."

"You were saving your own skin, and we happened to be in the neighborhood."

Frank could disarm her. He could tie her up and force her to speak. Maybe. If he caught her again. He said, "You're not a cop."

"Oh?"

"No. If you were a cop, you would have continued to the nearest house and made a call. You would not have stashed those kids in a bunch of beet leaves. And you're not from a rival organization either, because if you were, you would not have given those kids your gun. You'd want the gun to keep control of the kids because you'd be planning on selling those kids up-river or bringing them back as a prize. You'd want to show off how you'd outwitted those Goroza morons. And yet there's a bounty on your head."

"Ha," she said. "And now you show yourself."

Frank shook his head. "I only learned about the bounty after we escaped that house, and Ed took Tony and told me he wanted you and the girls in exchange."

Her hand gripped the knife harder.

"Carmen," he said. "I told you there is not going to be an exchange. I'm not that kind of a guy. But even if I were, it does me no good."

"You want the bounty for yourself then."

"I don't even know what the bounty is. I want my nephew back. He's the one that wrote to me while I was in prison. He's the one that drew dinosaur pictures that I put on my wall. He's the one who had faith I could beat my own dumb decisions. I will not let him down now, which is why I'm going to go into the lion's den and pull him out. But if that's going to be more than a suicide job, I need some data."

Carmen looked from Sam back to Frank again.

"I know what you are," Frank said. "We can help each other out."

"I don't think so."

"You're not a drug dealer. You're a tough operator, but you don't have the right tattoos. You don't have the look. I saw your face when you saw those children. You were angry. You were full of righteous indignation. You knew exactly what they were. I'll tell you why the Gorozas have a bounty on you, Matanarcos—you've been messing with their operations. You're a vigilante, an *abolicionista*. You've been helping free the Goroza's merchandise."

She smiled ruefully. "You're a clever man. But still way off."

No, he was much closer than way off. He could see it in her face. "Work with me. I cut the head off the snake, and that's one less snake you have to deal with."

"They will kill you."

"Maybe," he said.

A beat passed.

"Carmen."

Another pause.

"Show me I can trust you," she said.

"Sam," Frank said.

"What are we doing?" Sam asked.

"Can I have your phone?"

Sam pulled his phone out of his pocket, tossed it to Frank. Frank caught it then thumbed the icon for the keyboard and typed in Tony's phone number. Then he thumbed dial. A moment later, Tony's phone rang in Frank's pocket. Frank disconnected the call. He held Sam's phone up. "My number is now in the call log. We do not have much time. But we're going to walk away. Give you space. I hope you decide to help save some lives. All you've got to do is push the call button."

He slipped Sam's phone into the center of a cluster of beet leaves. It looked like something in a spring basket. Like something for a TV commercial. "Do not let them kill an innocent boy, Carmen."

"You're giving her my phone?" Sam asked.

"Lending it. Is that okay?" Frank asked.

Sam looked at his phone: a man parting with his best friend, making the sacrifice. "The password is cocoa puffs," he finally said. "One word, lower case." Then he spelled it out for her.

"Be nice to Sam's phone," Frank said to Carmen. Then he signaled to Sam, and they both turned their backs on her and the phone in the beet leaves and walked to the edge of the field. They climbed over the fence and up the shoulder to the van.

"What's the range of your Bluetooth?" Frank asked.

"Not very far," Sam said.

"We'll get it back," Frank said and opened the passenger door.

Back in the field, Carmen hadn't moved. She was still watching them.

Frank got in and closed the door. Sam walked around and got in on the driver's side.

"Drive a couple hundred yards down the road," Frank said.

"You know we can track her? I set up that GPS service on my phone when we were looking for you. Figured better safe than sorry."

"I don't think we'll need to track her."

"Let's hope you are right."

Sam put the van in gear, turned it around, then headed away from Carmen and the girls.

To the north, the fire truck had gone to work on the house. A long cloud of thick smoke smeared the sky, but the fire was dying down, the smoke thinning. All about the house, the lights of the emergency vehicles flashed. Soon the cops would start canvassing the houses within view of the fire, asking if anyone had seen anything. He was sure those two guys on four-wheelers were already there, giving a full report.

They drove past the shed where the children had been waiting. They were nowhere to be seen.

A few hundred yards later, Sam said, "You want me to stop?"

"Keep going."

They came to the intersection at the end of the road, and Sam turned south.

"You think she's going to call?" Sam asked.

Frank pulled Tony's phone out of his pocket and held it in his lap. Would he call if he were in her shoes? He gave it a forty percent chance. "She'll call," he said.

19

Instructions

FRANK HELD THE phone as Sam drove south along the road. One mile. Two. Five.

Carmen did not call.

They came to an intersection that led to a gas station. Frank had Sam pull over. Bison grazed in the field next to them. They waited and watched the bison, which didn't do anything spectacular except chew grass.

Fifteen minutes later Carmen still hadn't called.

"Maybe you should call her," Sam said.

"She's going to call," Frank said.

At that moment the phone rang. But it wasn't a call originating from Sam's phone. Frank thumbed an answer.

"Jockstrap," Ed said. "You picked up on the first ring. Good boy."

Frank said, "You need to think about your future because if Tony doesn't come back to me, I'm going to hunt you down. I'm not going to rest. Your end will not be pretty."

"Let's not get nasty, Frank. You don't want to scuttle this deal in a pout."

"Last chance, Ed."

Ed chuckled. "You got a pen and a piece of paper? You're going to want to write this down."

Frank asked Sam for paper and pen.

"Who you with there, Frank? Did you get all stupid on me and call the cops?"

"I'm with the Lone Ranger."

"You get all stupid, and our deal goes south. You listening to me?"

Frank didn't think he could bear to hear one more word from Ed.

Sam fished around in his pink diaper bag and came up with a pen that had some crud on it. Then he fished around and found an envelope.

Frank said, "Talk."

"Four a.m. tomorrow morning you're going to be waiting at the truck stop on the west side of the freeway in the fine little town of Hudson, Colorado. You're going to have the children and that whore with you. You'll receive a call."

"And?"

"That's it, Frank. See how easy this is going to be?"

"Yeah."

"T-T-F-N," Ed said. Then he hung up.

Frank googled Hudson on his phone. It was a small little place north and east of the Denver metropolitan area. It was right at the edge of nothing. Miles and miles of open farms. It would be very hard to hide a police tail out there.

Frank figured he knew how it would play out. They would call, tell him to move along to a second spot. They would watch as he moved to see if he was alone. Not many people out at four a.m. Not even out there in the rise-and-shine countryside. If they saw he was alone, they'd give him another destination, and tell him to drop the children off at some lonely spot. They would watch from afar. Then they'd direct him to another location to make an exchange—the woman for Tony. Except Tony wouldn't be part of the deal. Frank would be driving to the location of his grave.

Or maybe they would do the whole deal in one place. They'd have him drive to some barn out in the middle of nowhere. They'd have him line the girls and Carmen up. They'd send Tony over, and then, with everyone in one spot, they'd gun all of them down.

The fact was that they weren't planning a trade. They were planning a killing. And those were two entirely different types of operations. If Frank were planning it, he would send a backhoe out this evening to dig a nice deep pit. Have the guy wear a uniform from the gas company. Have him dig a hole big enough for ten bodies. It would be a piece of cake.

"So?" Sam asked.

Frank told him what Ed had said and showed him Hudson on the map.

"You need to call the cops."

"Think it through. The Gorozas are using false identities. We don't know where Tony is. So they show up, hassle the Gorozas, find nothing, and go home. Or they put up some surveillance, find nothing, and go home. Either way, Tony's buried in a hasty, but deep grave out in the middle of someplace nobody will ever find."

"What about the FBI? You have Ed's old phone number. They could look through the Goroza's phone records; link the two. Tie it all together."

"That's TV magic. Things don't work all lickety-split in the real world. But let's say they did. Ed's using pre-paid cell phones. Probably paying cash. Which means it tracks to a dead end. He knows phones can be traced. He's the one that sent us off to Eden. But even if they catch him, the Feds can't prove anything without a body."

"DNA in his vehicle. Fingerprints."

"I'm sure Ed's watched CSI too."

"You sure he's that smart?"

"What I'm sure of is that I can't take chances. Some cons are as dumb as rocks. Some are mean. Some are crazy. And some will do calculus on top of your head. Ed isn't one of those you want to underestimate."

"So what are you going to do?"

Frank looked down at the phone. He had a name. Not much to go on.

If his guess about Carmen was correct, then she wasn't operating on her own. She'd be part of an organization. She wouldn't have called them on Sam's phone because then the call would be captured in his log. So she'd go down the road and made a call with a stranger's phone. Or find a public phone somewhere else. She could still be en route to make that call. Or she could have decided to get out while she had the chance. That would be the smart move. What was the life of one boy when hundreds or thousands of others were on the line?

He sighed. "Looks like we're going to have to go to plan F."

"The FBI can put a drone in the sky," Sam said.

"This is an operation that smuggles drugs and slaves. I think they know that." Frank exited the app and put the phone in his front shirt pocket. "I'm going to have to go in loaded for bear."

"You're going to round up those girls like he asked?"

"No."

"Frank, I'm not comfortable with this."

Frank wasn't either, but he didn't see how he could increase his odds. If he called this in, it would be his word, the word of an ex-con who had just killed some guys and committed arson, against that of the Gorozas. A classic he said, she said. No body, no witnesses. Just the off chance that they might find some hair off of Tony's head in that pickup, which they could match against what? Nothing. They'd have to get DNA back in Rock Springs and it would take a week and even then they wouldn't be positive it was Tony's because they hadn't taken anything from him.

He needed firepower. He needed that P90.

"You think she left the phone in the field?" Sam asked. "It's got a lot of information on it."

"I know," Frank said. "Let's go back and see if she did. Then I need you to take me to that big pond."

They went back to the beet field, walked out to where they'd talked to Carmen. They pushed back the plants and looked about. The phone was gone.

What did that mean?

"Dang it," said Sam.

"I'm sorry," Frank said. He was sorry for a lot of things. Most of all to Tony and Kim. He just hoped he wasn't sorry for more things by this time tomorrow.

"Nothing to be sorry about," Sam said. "It's a phone."

They got back into the van. Sam turned it around. In the distance the fire was out. The smoke had changed from black to gray.

Maybe Frank should go to plan G and call the Feds, but he knew in his heart where that would lead.

Tony's phone rang. It startled him and he fumbled it out of his shirt pocket. It rang again. It was Sam's number.

Frank pressed the icon to answer the call. "Carmen?" he asked.

"The girls are safe," Carmen said. "Now you and I can talk."

* * *

She was waiting for them on an empty stretch of farm road, one of the prettiest hitchhikers he'd ever seen. Sam pulled up next to her and stopped. Frank turned around and pushed back the minivan's sliding door.

Carmen did not get in. She said, "If I feel uncomfortable at any moment, you will stop and let me out."

"Okay," Frank said.

"You will not give my name to the police or even mention I'm involved."

"We can keep that quiet."

She looked at Sam.

"I have more secrets packed away in this brain than both of you combined." He held up three fingers. "Scout's honor."

She said, "I gave your phone to the girls. The quickest ride I could arrange for them is going to take a little while. I didn't want them to be cut off."

"No better use for a phone," Sam said, although Frank was sure his phone separation anxiety had just ticked up a notch.

"We'll make sure you get it back," she said.

"Get in," Frank said.

Carmen climbed into the back seat and slid the door shut. She said, "I'm dying of thirst. I've had exactly two bottles of water since they took me."

Sam gave her the rest of the vitamin water, then fished around in his pink diaper bag and came up with a small, half-empty bottle of orange Gatorade. "This ought to wet your whistle."

She didn't even bat an eye. She took both from him, screwed off the lid to the Gatorade, chugged it, then went to work on the vitamin water. When she finished, she said, "Do you have anymore?"

Sam shook his head.

"Looks like we need to get you something to eat and drink," Frank said. "That will give us a table and a place to get together a plan. We can kill two birds with one stone. Of course, I don't have much money."

"The Gorozas will pick up the tab," Carmen said.

Frank remembered the wad of loot she had. He said, "Let's head back to the interstate, and see if we can't find the lady a place to dine."

Sam said, "You still need to go swimming in that pond?"

"I am indeed going to have to take a plunge," Frank said. They were going to need a gun. They were going to need Pinto's eyes in the sky and his binoculars. They were going to need a couple of other things. And they were going to have to be quick because there weren't nearly enough hours to pull a thing like this off between now and four a.m.

20

Carmen

SAM HEADED DOWN the same stretch of road for the fourth time. Frank turned around in his seat and said to Carmen, "Where does this Flor Goroza operate? Where's headquarters?"

"They have a business at the south end of the Denver area. H.C. and Sons."

"What is it?"

"I don't know."

"You don't know?"

"I've only recently come in contact with the Gorozas."

"And yet they have a bounty on your head?" How could that be? What had she done? "Carmen, I need information. I need all the data you have. I proved my intentions. I need you to trust me."

"I don't trust anyone completely," she said. "But I'll tell you what I know. The Gorozas are part of a trafficking ring. It's like a web. I tickled one end of the web and awoke all the spiders."

"How big is this web?"

"It stretches from Mexico, up through Colorado, and on to Seattle. Parts in Arizona. Parts in Texas. I think there's someone up in Chicago."

"You tingled all those webs?"

"Probably."

Frank said, "We need to know what we've gotten into here."

Carmen glanced out the window at the fields. In the distance by the Goroza's half a house, the lights of the emergency vehicles flashed. She said, "What do you think they do with those children?"

"Sell them to agricultural and construction contractors. To temp agencies."

She shook her head. "No. These are assets with an ROI. They generate a lot of money. Fifty-thousand, a hundred thousand each. Easily. They move them every five or six weeks. Keep them on a circuit. A few months around Denver. Then up to Seattle."

"What are you talking about?"

"I'm talking about high-volume, low price. I'm talking about little houses in residential neighborhoods. Or maybe a mobile home behind a rural bar. They'll put two or three of these kids in each. They're usually a little older. But you have to have young ones in stock because they command a high price for the right customer. And the customers come. A girl might have to service five people a day or forty. Thirty or forty bucks for fifteen minutes with one of those kids. The little ones go for more. They can charge seventy or eighty for that. They can deliver them right to your door."

Sam said, "Sex? They're selling them for sex?"

"This isn't a pimp operation," Carmen said. "It's not some massage parlor. This is big business. You're in, you're out. Next customer please. In restaurants you measure table turns. Here it's bed turns and utilization rates."

Frank shook his head. The little boy had thrown him off, but he should have seen it. He did the math. Forty men at fifteen minutes each—the girl would have to suffer for ten hours. And then she'd have to get up and do it again the next day. And all the while her owners were making thirty bucks a pop. "$1,200 dollars on a busy day. $8,400 per week. $400,000 per year. Or maybe they only did that level of business sometimes. Maybe each only made them $200,000 per year. Three or four houses, two or three in a house, and you're clearing close to two million a year."

"They're doing that much business?" Sam asked. "Surely someone would notice."

"Think about it," Carmen said. "These are repeat customers. A guy comes back two or three times a month. Maybe more. You don't need a huge clientele. And they're not selling to just anybody. There are no advertisements in papers or on websites. No hooking on the street. You don't see this. They hand out tarjetas, little business cards in Spanish, at bus stops, parks and other places for phony products. Only to Hispanic men. If the johns are illegal, that's even better. So the card advertises for 'Gorditas 24x7,' or house-call manicures, or men's cologne. The Goroza's have one card that says 'Mi Casa, Su Casa,' the other says 'Botas Y Tejanas.' It's all in Spanish. If you're looking to buy, you know what it means. If not, it's just some dumb card."

Frank knew the first phrase: mi casa, su casa. My home is your home. But the second didn't make any sense. "Boots and Texans?" Frank asked. That couldn't be right.

"Exactly," Carmen said. "There's a number on the card. You call the number. They ask you questions to make sure you're not a cop, not a Gringo, just some Pedro wanting some action. Then they tell you how to approach the house. Some of these places get a lot of men."

Frank shook his head: what had they fought for in the Civil War? He bet none of those old plantation owners had made anything on their slaves like the modern ones made on these girls—two million on twelve to fifteen kids.

Carmen said, "Some get sick, and they're thrown out. You can get a new girl sometimes for less than a thousand dollars. And some try to run. But most don't because the padrotes inform her if she does, they will kill her family back in Mexico. After all, they know where they live. Or they tell the girl they will kill her themselves. Or their agents in the American police will kill her when she runs to them."

"The cops here are not like the cops in Mexico," Frank said.

"Are you sure?" she asked.

Frank shrugged. There were dirty cops in America just like anywhere else. There just weren't the numbers. "So what did you do to wake the whole web?"

"You really don't know? Ed didn't tell you?"

"If I knew, would I be talking to you?"

Carmen took in a breath and let it out. "We free who we can. We steal what we can from the traffickers to fund our operations. One night things went wrong, and we killed a major player. Trafficking is often only part of the business."

"But they want you for more than that," Frank said.

"He had a lot of money with him. A lot of money."

"Taking it back to Mexico?"

"I don't know."

Frank nodded. He'd been guarding just such a man when things went south for him. "More than a million?"

"Yes," she said.

Sam whistled. "Holy crap. Those are killing amounts. You're going up against the whole organization."

"The Gorozas are a smaller operation. The bounty went out. They just happened to be the ones that found the prize."

"You said 'we'. What about the rest?"

"They are all missing or dead. I'm the last one."

No one spoke. The van fell silent except for the wheels crunching along the dirt road.

Frank now knew why she'd called. She obviously cared about the children. She probably felt for Tony. But this was a woman who wanted payback.

About a mile ahead at the intersection that led to the Gorozas, a cop stood on the road, his car was behind him, lights flashing, blocking traffic to the Goroza's house.

"What do we do?" Sam asked.

"You act like anybody would when you just saw a house explode. We'll slow down. Ask him what's going on."

The van fell silent.

Frank said, "You were one of those that made it out."

"No," Carmen said. "I was never in."

"You don't just start raiding folks like the Gorozas."

"No, you don't. They come to you. Like the woman in a neighboring village who brought another woman to see my mother. My mother made tortillas in the market in a village in southern Mexico. My father only showed up once or twice a year. Sometimes he was drunk. Sometimes he just wanted money. We had very little. And then this woman comes. And she says they need workers in America. She says she told the bosses at her American company that nobody worked harder than Mexicans from small towns. She said she's already taken some boys and men up to work in their factories. But now she needed some girls to clean their homes."

Sam reached the end of the road by the beet field and turned back toward the Gorozas and the marsh.

"She had a nice car. She had pretty clothes. She smelled like flowers. Not like perfume hiding days of sweat, but like flowers. She asked us all sorts of questions. Then the woman showed us pictures she had in a nice folder. Pictures of girls working in a mansion. Pictures of men and boys at a factory. Pictures of kids who looked just like us at a McDonalds in America. They were all smiling. My older sister was fourteen. She and my mama discussed it. It would be far away. The woman said this is how she had herself become an American. She showed pictures of her house and husband."

"The perfect life."

"My mother was hesitant. Then the woman opened her wallet and showed her two thousand pesos. That's only about $140 dollars. But in Mexico, in my village, that was more than a month's pay for some people with a full-time job. She said that would be my sister's advance. But she would have to work that and the cost of her transportation off when she got to America. The woman did not push. She said to think about it. It had to be the right choice. She needed five girls. She already had three. There were only two slots left. She was going to go see some other girls who were interested. She thought she'd have the others by the next morning."

"And that was that," Frank said.

"The woman walked out of our little corrugated tin hut, but before she got into her car, my mother ran after her. My older sister went with the woman that day. I was heartbroken. I was scared. I was excited. We might all go to America! I gave my sister my favorite bracelet. She told me she would write. We hugged. She cried when she hugged my mama, but she was very brave and got into the car, and drove away with the woman. My mother and I stood and watched her go. She turned once in the back seat and waved. We waved back, my mother holding the fat fold of pesos. A few moments later the car turned onto another street. The last I saw of my sister was the back of her head in that car."

"What was her name?" Sam asked.

"Reyna. My sister's name was Reyna."

"I'm so sorry," Sam said. His voice was thick. He looked stricken.

"The woman had all her teeth," Carmen said. "They were so white."

"Did you find your sister?"

"We received two letters from my sister the next year with fifty pesos included. But the hand writing was not my sister's. And then the letters stopped. My mother asked the woman in the neighboring village about Reyna. She asked her about the woman. She said Reyna had shamed us all and ran away in America and not worked off her debt. But I knew Reyna was not like that."

Frank waited.

"So that next year I came north. I was barely a teenager. The letters were stamped with the name of the town where they'd been dropped in the mail—Las Vegas, New Mexico. It can be hard for a little girl in America, but an old Anglo woman and her husband took pity. We found my sister's bones in Texas. My bracelet was still on her arm."

Frank thought about her. He thought about that little girl that Jesus had been raping. He thought about that little boy. Those two should be in school, learning about animals and prepositions. The others should be in a middle school somewhere in seventh grade or eighth grade, worrying about getting on the school bus and if the lunch ladies were going to serve rice with weird gravy.

He thought about the girls he'd been offered in that tin hut in Colombia. Fourteen girls stolen in raids and abducted off roads. Little sisters and daughters used up and then tossed into the trash like empty bottles when they got sick or contracted AIDS or something else from one of the men and the signs started to show.

Ed's sins were piling up. Frank hadn't wanted to be involved in this. But Ed had pulled him in. Sow the wind, Ed, reap the whirlwind, buddy.

"Men are animals," Carmen said.

"Some are," Frank said. "And some are a lot worse."

21

Gun

IN THE ARMY, Frank's company had been briefed about human trafficking, which was not just the transportation of slaves, but also included the buying, selling, and owning. Special Forces worked in places and with people for whom trafficking was no big deal, and so they had to be prepared for it.

As he recalled, the U.S. State Department thought there were somewhere around twelve million people in slavery around the world. Everything from forced labor on fishing boats to forced marriages to child soldiers. The analysts estimated more than half a million women and children were bought, sold, and transported across international borders as sex slaves each year.

More than half a million per year.

The trade in Asia and other parts of the world was huge, but it didn't all occur in far-off places. Thousands of women and children were brought to the U.S. each year. Thousands coming to the land of freedom and opportunity only to find it a land of shackles. A place to be infected with some disease at the hands of people whose chest cavities were missing their hearts.

Where did they go when they were used up and broken? How many escaped? How many died?

And these were the people who had Tony.

He took some deep breaths to calm himself. He needed to see straight. Needed his vision to clear. He could not risk letting his thinking get mucked up with too much anger.

They approached the police officer, and Sam slowed the vehicle. Frank took another breath, then rolled his window down and put on his concerned citizen face. "Officer," he called, "what happened?"

"House fire," the officer said.

"We heard a huge boom."

The officer looked in at Carmen in the back. "It appears they had a propane leak."

"Oh, my," Frank said. There were two ambulances along with a couple of fire trucks down the road. Ahead on the road was a tractor. "Anyone hurt?"

"We're still checking on that."

Four dead bodies in the house, two out in the yard. Surely those on the scene had seen the gunshot wounds on the guys outside. The officer was playing it down. He was also giving them all a hard look, probably knowing that perpetrators sometimes come back around and pose as bystanders, but he must not have seen what he was looking for because he waved them on. "We need to keep things moving here."

"Right," Frank said. "We'll get out of the way."

Sam's pulse was beating in his temple. In his nervousness, he gave the van too much gas, and they almost peeled out.

The cop looked after them.

"You trying to get us caught?" Frank asked.

"My foot slipped."

"It's all right, Sam. We're going to be okay."

Ahead, a tractor was coming their way. Probably another local gawker. They moved over and passed it. The marsh was about a half a mile away. Frank said, "See that black bird sitting on that post?"

"Yeah."

"That's where we're going to stop."

"That cop is just right there."

"He's far enough away. And we don't have time to come back."

Frank thought about Carmen's story. The whole time she'd been talking, he'd been watching and listening for any indication she was feeding him a line. For seven years he'd been surrounded with some of the best liars humanity had produced. As far as he could tell, she was straight up.

Sam approached the post with black bird on it and slowed the van.

There stood the cattails Frank had soared over. There stood the half-submerged barbed-wire fence. Out in the marsh stood the rise of land where Frank had scared the cow. "Here," Frank said.

Sam eased off the side of the road and stopped.

The blackbird, which had a patch of bright red feathers on its shoulders, took off and flew over the water. Frank had seen blackbirds like that before. Those patches always made him think of army sergeants back in the days of Napoleon when soldiers wore bright colors. It made him think of sergeants now and wish he had a few more soldiers on this operation. He said, "You two need to stand watch outside. Get out a map and pretend to look at it. Maybe do some stretches like you're taking a break."

Hopefully, this wouldn't take long. Hopefully, they wouldn't attract too much of his attention. This was not going to be an easy search. But he didn't have a choice. He knew Pinto had some guns, but he wasn't going to ask for those. If something happened, and he lost one, he didn't want Pinto getting hit with the collateral damage.

Frank opened the door and stood on the shoulder, which ran straight down into the mucky water and the cattails festooned with spiderwebs and bugs.

Sam and Carmen got out as well and stood in front of him, looking at Sam's road atlas. Two lost travelers.

Frank stripped down to his black Hanes underwear. He placed his boots, folded shirt, and pants on the shoulder. He looked at the wound in his leg. It was a nice bloody puncture that, despite the yummy kiddy medicine, still burned like a mother.

"Here we go," he said.

Sam looked him up and down. "You don't want to take that leg in there."

"It will be all right."

"Look at that water."

Frank looked back down at the mucky water, guaranteed to be teeming with all manner of bacterial life.

"I have a little first aid kit," Sam said. "Band-aides, gauze, some nifty ointment."

"You have any duct tape?"

"I think so."

Sam opened the back of the van, fished around a bit, and came up with a white plastic container with a red cross on it and a roll of pink duct tape.

"Pink?" Frank asked.

"It's my wife's roll."

"You buy his and hers?" Frank asked.

"It's a girly color," Sam said, "yet still retains its mannish strength."

Frank reached into the diaper bag between the front seats and grabbed a few wet wipes. He cleaned his wound, dried it with a tissue. Then he opened the first aid box and applied a smear of the antibacterial ointment. He stuck a piece of gauze on top, then said to Sam, "Hand me that sissy tape."

Sam handed it to him, and Frank ripped off a piece of tape about six inches long and pressed it down right over the top of the gauze. He smoothed the sides out around his shin and calf, pressing down the hair. He applied two more strips crosswise to make sure the seal along the edges was good and tight. It did indeed feel like the mannish version, which meant it was going to rip out a fine swath of hairs when he yanked it off.

Frank stood on the track made by the Polaris when he left the edge. He said, "Come here. I want you directing me."

Sam walked over and stood next to him.

"See those three reeds sticking up about seventy yards out?"

"Yeah."

"You need to keep me on a line between this spot and them."

"Okay."

He stood right behind Sam, put his head next to his, then pointed over his shoulder at about where he figured he'd landed. "I'm thinking of that spot there. You see it?"

Sam held his own hand out and spanned the distance. "Got it."

"Whistle or honk the horn if that cop comes."

"Enjoy the leaches and snakes."

"Thanks," Frank said. He swatted at a couple of mosquitoes that were already coming in for lunch and climbed down the slope, the gravel poking into his bare feet. He stepped into the warmish, brackish, thigh-high water at the edge of the cattails and sank a good six inches into the squishy mud at the bottom. He brushed aside a big spiderweb between two cattail stalks and made for the fence.

The barbed wire was rusted all to hell, great for tetanus, but it was also fairly loose. He pressed the top strand down and climbed over. A few more strides, and he was out of the cattails, wading in the open water, which was getting deeper with each step.

Gnats and mosquitoes danced on the surface of the water. Some beetle-looking thing struggled along. Frank continued out into the deeper, colder water, his feet sucking into the mud, striking the occasional sharp edge of a rock or stray stick. The cold water rose to the tops of his thighs, then crotch, then belly, and then came to his chest. A couple of mosquitoes gathered about his head and shoulders, and he swatted at them. He glanced back to make sure he was still in line, and Sam waved him over to the right a bit.

He stubbed his toe on a large jagged stone, climbed over it, and went to where he figured he ought to be. He looked back at Sam who gave him the thumbs up. Frank found a reed that he would use to fix his position and bent the top. Then he started to walk a circular pattern around that reed, sweeping back and forth through the muck with his foot because the water was too murky for him to simply dive down and look for it. He found rocks, some rope, something sharp. A number of mosquitoes made off with some of his blood.

Out on the road, Sam and Carmen kept up their tourist act. Frank continued to work. Twenty minutes later he had searched a sizeable radius around the reed and was beginning to wonder if he'd been sloppy. Then he looked at the hummock, and realized he was too far out. He backed up, found another reed, and started his search pattern again.

His fourth time around the new position his ankle struck something hard sticking up out of the mud.

Oh, please, Lord.

He felt it with his toes, found the barrel, the magazine, the odd grip, the trigger. Bingo. Frank dove under, grabbed the P90 with his hands, and came back up with it.

He held it up and inspected it. Everything looked good. Just needed a bit of cleaning.

He folded the stock in and began to swim back. When he was about halfway to shore, Sam whistled hard. He whistled again. Then he pointed discretely, not back toward the intersection, but farther on down the road, across the water. Frank stopped and looked back. Another cop car was coming down the road about where Frank had lanced the windshield of the pickup. If they'd been watching him closely, they might have caught a glimpse of the gun in his hand.

Frank pretended to swat at a mosquito on his chest, and kept wading toward the cattails at the edge of the water, making sure to keep the P90 below the surface.

The cop car drove along the water, made the L turn, and started coming toward Sam and the minivan, the tires rumbling over the gravel, the dust kicking up behind.

Frank kept himself low in the water, even as it got shallower, until he was crabbing along in a squat.

The cop car slowed, rolled up to Sam and Carmen, then simply passed by. Frank waved. The cop waved back. Obviously, he had bigger fish to fry than stopping and talking to some idiot who thought it might be nice to take a swim in the duck and cow poop pond.

He reached the edge of the cattails. "Am I clear?"

Sam looked down the road. "There's a truck coming. You have about sixty seconds before it gets here."

Frank pushed back through the path he'd made in the cattails and climbed over the fence. "Throw me my pants," he said.

Sam picked up his pants and tossed them out. They landed in the cattails a few feet away. Frank grabbed them and rolled the P90 up in them. To anyone, even if they were standing right next to him, his pants would appear to be nothing more than a pair of pants.

He climbed out of the water and up the gravel-studded shoulder to the dirt road and caught a slight breeze that cooled his wet body. Two grinning teens were in the oncoming pickup. The driver did not slow, but rumbled by, trailing a big dust cloud that rolled over Frank and the others as the pickup passed. The dust clung to Frank's wet body and hair.

The boys hooted as they went by.

Frank saluted them. Good one, lads. Nice rural humor.

He wiped himself down with his shirt, and then they all hopped into the van, Frank in his black Hanes, Sam and Carmen more conventionally dressed. Sam pulled out before the dust cloud from the pickup had finished dispersing.

Frank pulled his pants on and said, "Up ahead, past that corner, you'll see the wreckage of the snowmobile I was riding. We'll see if the extra magazine is still in the stow compartment."

Frank finished dressing and found the magazine just where he'd put it. If he could fill both magazines, he'd have a hundred rounds. Much better than a poke in the eye with a sharp stick.

"Where now, boss?" Sam asked.

"Food. With wi-fi."

22

Carrots

THE FOOD WAS salads because Big Tomato was the first place they found with internet service advertised. It was a quick, serve-yourself, be-green, organic-grown, no-hormones, flax-seed-and-alfalfa soup and salad joint that looked like it was manned by a couple of hippies who had escaped from Boulder. The one guy greeted them like they were coming to Disneyland. He was probably so happy because they were growing fine organic bud somewhere out back. This was Colorado, after all. Land of the Libertarians. But they were clean, happy hippies. Guys in their forties who looked like they had learned there was more to life than getting stoned. There were things like showers and socks. And cash.

The place was well lit and decorated. The items in the buffet were numerous and fresh. There were some mega fiber brownies, but Frank passed over those for the tiny sweet corn muffins he loved. They paid the feed fee, piled chow on their plates, and settled into a booth at the back.

Frank consumed his plate full of mini muffins like it might be his last, which was a distinct possibility. Where he was headed, there were only two paths: death or prison. He didn't think they had cute corn muffins in the hot place. They certainly didn't have in any prison.

He might have a slim chance at another road. One that allowed him to go back to being the hard-working Walmart guy who was going to beat the odds and keep his carcass out of the slammer. But hoping for that at this point was like pinning your hopes on the possibility that a gold brick was going to fall out of the sky and thud into the ground at your feet.

Carmen went to eating her three plates of food like someone might approach digging a ditch—no talking, just methodical shoveling. Sam picked at his food in a pensive mode. Frank decided to multi-task. He opened the internet on Tony's phone and googled "Goroza Colorado."

He found nothing.

He googled "Colorado Jesus Goroza."

Nothing again.

He googled "H.C. and Sons Colorado." This time he got a hit. A few seconds later he was looking at a street view of a long building with tall cement walls in the south-western end of Denver. One end of the building was a loading dock with bays for at least twelve semis. In the middle of the building were a couple of small windows for what Frank assumed were offices. The other end of the building had a couple of windows high up in the cement wall. The building ended with a link to a railroad spur. This was a manufacturing plant of some sort.

Frank clicked in and read the details. It was not a manufacturing plant. It was a bakery that specialized in frostings, fondants, and frozen cookie pucks. He could buy five gallon buckets of frosting base. He could buy scones. He could buy bags of strawberry filling.

He showed Carmen the information. "You sure it was H.C. and Sons?"

Her mouth was full of food. She held a chicken drumstick in one hand, a roll slathered with honey-butter in the other. "Pretty sure," she said around her food.

Frank couldn't conduct any type of operation on pretty-sures and maybes. He googled the name of the company with "Goroza." Nothing. He went back to the company's site, found a telephone number and called it.

A woman answered, told him it was H.C. and Sons. Asked him how she could help.

Frank said, "This is Clarence Thomas from Findlay Foods. I'd like to speak with Flor."

"Ms. Goroza doesn't come in much. I don't think she's here."

"What about her son?"

"Hector?"

"Yes," Frank said.

"He's in a meeting. Can I take your information?"

"Naw, it's Flor I really need. But you've been helpful. By the way, they still living at that place in Aurora?"

There was a pause. Come on, he thought, give it up.

"No," she said a bit suspiciously, "I don't think they were ever in Aurora."

"Hum," Frank said like he was surprised and waited. He waited an uncomfortably long time. Usually that's all it took, but this woman did not offer up Flor's real place of residence.

"Sir, are you still there?" She sounded like she was on the verge of interrogating him.

Frank said, "Sorry, I accidentally put my phone on mute. I'll try to catch her at home." He said good-bye and hung up.

"Well?" Sam asked.

"There's a Flor and Hector at H.C. and Sons. And the receptionist is a little cagey."

"Drugs, slaves, and snack cakes?" Sam asked. "Are we sure these bad guys didn't just steal those names?"

Frank thought about how Ed spoke Jesus's name. Like it was some joke. It could have been funny to him because it was biblical. It could have been funny because it was also a stolen identity. "We're not sure of anything," Frank said. "But it's what we've got."

And what they had were a lot of truck bays. He looked back at the Google photo. "Look at that bakery. Look at all those trucks. With twelve plus bays for semis, that bakery is putting a lot of product on the road. A lot of trucks going and coming all over the place. I'm seeing lots of transportation."

"That's what factories do," Sam said. "They make stuff and ship it out."

"Which is perfect, isn't it?" Frank asked.

"What are you talking about?"

"The Gorozas. You move drugs, slaves, weapons—who cares? It's all the same. These folks are in the business of transportation. And they've got shipments coming and going all day long."

Sam sat back, took a thoughtful bite of some kind of lettuce that looked like a weed.

Frank said, "How hard would it be to hide a couple kilos of meth in a five-gallon bucket of frosting? A couple kilos, cut and packaged into the tiny amount you need for a hit, that's worth a couple hundred thousand dollars on the retail end. How many frosting buckets do you have to have?"

Sam looked up, did the math in his head. "Put one in every ten, twenty, fifty trucks, and depending on your schedule, you're moving millions of dollars every quarter." He brought his gaze back down from accountant land. "And who is going to suspect the snack cake man? Nobody's going to look twice. It's just another semi or white delivery van on the road."

Frank turned to Carmen. "Do you have any other information about the Gorozas?"

"I know they're part of the ring," she said.

"Then we need to get down there pronto. We need more data. But we can't show up looking like this."

Frank felt someone behind him and turned. A little boy was standing up in the booth behind Frank watching them. His face was all sober like he understood ever word and was mulling it over. He was eating a baby carrot, munching it open-mouthed. In his little fist, he held the other half of the carrot. At the other side of the table, the boy's older sister was hovering over a piece of pizza, watching Frank suspiciously. The mother was probably up getting food.

The little boy reached into a pocket and brought out little plastic robot car thing. He showed it to Frank, then set it between them on the back of the bench like it held the key to everything.

"Nice," Frank said.

The little boy kept munching, then held his half-eaten carrot out to Frank. Tony had done that when he was a crumb cruncher—always trying to pawn his vegetables off.

The boy's little hand was greasy with some sauce, wet with a bit of slobber. Frank figured why not? He dipped down and sucked the carrot right out of the boy's hand and munched it with a bit of fanfare.

Half the boy's mouth curled up in delight. He picked up another carrot from his plate and held it out. Frank sucked that one. It was like he was in a time warp, back at Kim's house when Tony was just a kid.

Frank fetched one of his last two mini corn muffins. He held it out for the boy. "Try this," he said.

The boy took it, looked at it.

"It's tasty," Frank said.

But the little guy wasn't biting. Frank pointed to his older sister sitting on the other side of the table. "Maybe your sister wants it."

The boy held it back out to Frank.

Frank took his muffin back. The boy went for more carrots. This time he came back with a handful, but instead of offering them to Frank, he took one and put it up his left nostril. It hung there like a tiny orange tusk.

Frank had shown Tony that move. He could see the scene clearly, Tony sitting on the kitchen table at Kim's house, a UFC fight on TV in the background, some kid flying a kite outside.

A knot formed in Frank's chest.

At that moment the mother returned.

"Mom," the sister said, "he's doing the booger vampire again."

"Darius," the mother scolded. "Take that out." She looked at Frank. Looked a little worried. "Darius, turn around and leave the people alone."

"This one's going to be a handful," Frank said, and that knot tightened.

The mother gave him a civil smile that said plenty.

"Bye, bye, Darius," he said and turned around so the mom wouldn't worry about the hard-looking man with the tattoos.

"Booger sticks," Sam said. "A perennial favorite."

"Part of a balanced breakfast," Frank said.

The mother and the children went on with their meal. Frank thought for a moment about the mothers in Mexico, in El Salvador, in Honduras. Poor women sending their girls off to what they hoped would be a better life in the land of plenty. He thought about those girls in the basement of that house. He thought about that little boy with his carrots. He thought about Tony.

Outside the sun was still high in the sky, but he knew that was deceiving. They had miles to go, promises to keep. He looked at the stacks of dishes on the table, most of them from Carmen. "It's time to roll. Next stop is Wally World."

23

Gear

WHEN THEY PULLED into the Walmart parking lot, Sam said, "I'm a little shaky on what we're doing. What's the plan?"

"We're going after the queen of spades."

Sam licked his lips. He was having second thoughts.

"Carmen," Frank said. "You're sure Flor runs this outfit?"

"I am positive."

"Before four a.m. tomorrow morning we need to have Flor in our possession. At the very least we need to have a gun to her head."

"You're going to take down the boss?" Sam asked.

"You got a better plan?"

Sam just blinked at him. "Don't you need troops for this?"

"Not always," Frank said. The facts were this was a hail-Mary at best. When did hostage exchanges ever go well? And why would a bunch of drug runners care about some old woman, even if she was a wife or mother? But Frank couldn't think of anything else at the moment. He needed a card. He needed a big one. And this crap plan was the only thing he had up his sleeve.

Sam looked dubious.

"You don't need to come, buddy. Right now you and Carmen and our men in the sky are all the troops I have. But this isn't your problem. I don't want to make it your problem. I can do this on my own."

Sam nodded, looked out across the parking lot in thought. "There are little kids being raped and enslaved. Another boy who's been kidnapped and who will likely be killed."

"You can just drive."

"Isn't that aiding and abetting?"

"Technically," Frank agreed.

Sam blew out a breath. It was one thing to help a guy chase down kidnappers; it was something entirely different to go on the offensive and start committing felonies.

Sam thought for a moment, then said, "A man went down from Jerusalem to Jericho."

It took Frank a moment to understand the reference. "You sure?" he said. "You've got a wife and kids."

"I do," Sam said.

A beat passed. Then Sam's faced hardened into resolve. "The Queen of Spades it is."

Frank nodded. "I don't need you guys to go in; you're support."

"I'd be happy to go in," Carmen said.

Beautiful and tough as nails. "I'm sure you would, but let's figure out the details first."

"So why Walmart?" Sam asked. "What are we getting?"

Frank had a list. He sent Carmen to Girl's Fashion and Sam to Electronics and Stationary. Meanwhile, he picked up a workman's color of duct tape over by Paint. In Outdoors, it was bear spray, high-lumen LED flashlights, and some gun cleaning items. Gloves in Garden. A sledge hammer, a crowbar, a huge wrench, and a tool belt and toolbox to make it official in Home Repair. Then he went to the optical department to see if they had any zero prescription demo glasses they were sending back. They did. He selected a pair with a thick black plastic frame. He met Sam and Carmen at the front of the store by the cash registers.

Sam held a clipboard and the boxes for two BlueTooth ear pieces. He shrugged. "We're going to need good communication."

"We're going to need some night vision as well," Frank said.

"I don't know where we might get that."

"I had one of the guys check. They have a good monocular at a Walmart on the way to the bakery. Not the best, but better than nothing. They're holding it for us."

"And how much is that?"

"A little under $200."

"You're expensive," Sam said. "You know that?"

"What are we up to? Like three hundred bucks?"

"With the gas for the van and plane, hotel, meals etc., I think the tab is now up to around four hundred twelve twenty-five. Plus I'm taking vacation time."

"You're sure you're not off a few cents?"

"We can go over it. I've kept all the receipts."

"Bean counter," Frank said.

"Criminal," Sam replied.

Carmen had the girl's belt Frank had asked for, plus a toothbrush and little tube of toothpaste.

"That wasn't on the list," Frank said.

"It's been two days," Carmen said.

"Add the hygiene items," Sam said. "Frank can use them when you're done." He turned to Frank. "I suppose me funding your adventure will qualify as aiding and abetting, won't it?"

"Probably."

He sighed. "My wife is going to kill me."

"Maybe the Gorozas will take care of that for her," Frank said.

"Thanks," Sam said. "You're a real confidence builder."

They checked out. The Mormon cookie man, the vigilante girl, and Frank. Then they got back into the minivan and headed south. They picked up the monocular. Then they stopped at a Hilton Express hotel. They slipped into the business center when the gal at the counter went into the back room, and had Sam man a computer. Frank directed him to find the name of the big Colorado natural gas utility. A few clicks later they were at the Xcel Energy website. Frank then directed Sam to copy the image of the logo and slap it on some official looking document notifying homeowners of a survey in their area. He asked Sam to create another document with a number of rows divided into two columns—one for the name and address of the house and the other for "official notes." Then he had Sam print out half-a-dozen copies of each.

Frank slipped these documents into the clipboard, and the trio exited. They waved at the gal at the counter, then walked down a hallway and exited out the back.

The last stop was a feed store, which they found on Tony's GPS. They bypassed the cat food and pesticides and headed directly for the work clothing section. They purchased outfits for both Sam and Frank. The outfits consisted of baby blue, button-up work shirts made from sturdy material and matching caps. Together with the tool belts and clipboard they'd gotten at Walmart it made a complete ensemble. Sam and Frank suited up in the store's bathroom and came out looking like they maybe could belong to some utility company. Or backup singers for the Village People. They certainly belonged to something—no two men would walk around by choice looking like twinners.

They proudly walked out to the van in their stiff new shirts.

"Sam," Frank said, "you left your tag in."

Sam raised his arms to find it, but Carmen was quicker. She reached up and snapped the plastic thread. Then they got into the van and headed for the bakery.

On the way, Frank grabbed Sam's diaper bag, found three diapers, and laid them on the floor. He took the P90, released the magazine and pulled it out. He made sure there weren't any rounds in the chamber. Then he pulled off the barrel and receiver, slid out the bolt, removed the butt pad off the back of the gun, and removed the hammer pack.

He laid all the pieces on the diapers then opened the bottle of solvent, enjoying the smell of the familiar tang. He dropped a bit onto the rod brush and passed it through the barrel to get it working. Then he took one of Sam's Huggies wipes and cleaned as much swamp crap off the various parts as he could. He broke out some Q-tips to get the crannies. Then he finished the cleaning by shoving a few patches through the barrel.

With the gun clean, he lubed the parts with a few drops of oil and a Q-tip. He put the gun back together and performed the function check. Then he went to work on the magazines. He took the rounds out of the one, removed the bottom and spring, and wiped it all down.

Disassembled the second and wiped it. The feel of the gun, the smells—it calmed him, filled his mind with good memories. He'd worked with some of the finest people on this planet. He was working with a few more now, even if they were less skilled.

He put the magazines back together and reloaded both of them. The last step was to take the girl's belt he'd had Carmen get and make a sling for the P90 so he could hang it about his neck and work hands-free.

The stripping, cleaning, and reassembly had taken a little under fifteen minutes. He now turned to the current operation.

In a proper raid, he'd have five or six guys. He'd have two or three snipers providing cover and surveillance. He'd have a number of men creating a perimeter to prevent surprises coming in from outside. He'd have more intel. But you played the hand you were dealt.

"Carmen," Frank said, "your job is going to be surveillance. You watch the area; you look for any approaching danger. You're the eyes in the back of my head. Sam, you're the driver. Your job is to stay with the van and drive, not get all heroic."

"What about Pinto and Heber?" Sam asked.

"Tell them to fly home. They don't need to be dragged into this quagmire."

"I don't think you know Pinto and Heber."

"I'm going in alone."

"They're not going to fly home."

Frank sighed. "Then have them fly a pattern high above the property. We can use the eyes in the sky. Once I've seen it up close, I'll make the final plan." There wasn't going to be much to it. It was a simple recon. One man in, look around, get out. Unless life happened. And life always happened.

Tony's phone rang.

Frank looked down. It was Sam's number, the phone Carmen had given to the children. He put the call on speaker so Carmen could hear. "Hello?" he said.

"Jockstrap."

Frank's mind missed a beat.

"Frankie?"

Sam slowed the vehicle. Carmen looked down at the phone like it was some creature that had crawled out of Hell.

"Did you pick up that whore?"

"How did you get that phone?" Frank asked.

"You were supposed to pick up the children, Frank."

"I was on my way."

"It wasn't too hard to figure out where they took the snowmobile. Wasn't too hard to find them."

Frank's heart sank. Why hadn't he secured them? Why hadn't he done that first!

Ed said, "I'm trying to work a deal, for you, buddy. But I think you're trying to stiff me. Are you trying to stiff me, Frank?"

"That never crossed my mind, Ed."

"So now I've got one part of the threefer myself. Did you get the whore?"

Frank looked at Carmen, who was looking at him with venom, and put his fingers to his lips. "Yeah, I got her."

"This phone has a lot of contacts in Rock Springs. Has your number, Frank. Who's Sam Cartwright? He your friend?"

"I borrowed his phone."

"He helping you?"

"No. He's back in Wyoming."

"I see his wife's number. I see pictures of kids. I see all sorts of things. Put me on speaker."

He waited a second. "You're on."

"Hey, Mr. Cartwright," Ed said over the speaker. "You got yourself a fine wife. Couple of kids."

Sam sat up erect and rigid in the driver's seat.

"You make sure Frank keeps his part of the bargain. You bring that woman in. Do you hear me?"

Sam said nothing. Carmen's eyes flamed with anger.

"Answer me, Sam."

Frank shook his head.

"Or should I call your wife and confirm your location?"

Sam looked at Frank. Ed was going to find out anyway. He motioned for Sam to go ahead.

"Yeah," Sam said.

"Nice phone," Ed said. "I'll see you two tomorrow." Then he ended the call.

Frank put Tony's phone down.

Carmen moved from the front seat to the back like she was going to pick up the phone. Frank moved aside, but she moved past him. And then in a whirl, she was behind him, Jesus's scalpel-sharp knife at his throat.

"I'm not going anywhere."

"I'm not working with Ed," Frank said.

"Liar," she said. "It was all a ruse. All of it!" She pressed the knife closer and a sting raced across Frank's neck.

"You and Ed can go to hell!"

He felt her bunch, felt her prepare to cut his throat.

Frank grabbed her arm. She struggled, but then he twisted around, grabbed her smaller hand in his, and twisted more until she cried out in pain and dropped the knife.

She stabbed at his eye with the fingers of her free hand and connected. The world flashed white and pain in his eye shot through his brain, but he held on. He reached out, felt her hair, grabbed it tight.

He blinked but could hardly keep his eye open to see.

Sam braked hard and moved to the side of the road. The deceleration shifted her closer.

She thrashed like a wild beast. Struck him in the face. Tried to dig out his other eye.

He grabbed her arm, prepared to head-butt her face, but he didn't want to break her nose. So he twisted and brought her down hard in the aisle between the captain chair seating, slammed her to the floor on top of the P90.

She cried out, kicked at him.

"Carmen!" he yelled. "Stop! I'm not going to turn you in!"

She tried to bite his hand.

"Carmen!" he yelled, then rolled her over so she was face down and knelt on her back.

She yelled and struggled. But he was too heavy and the spaced too confined.

"Carmen," he said.

"I won't talk!"

"I don't want to know your secrets!"

"You have no soul," she said. "You're vermin."

He put pressure on her arm. She cried out.

"Carmen, if I wanted the bounty on you, I would have tied you up. You would be in the back bound hand and foot with Sam's lady pink duct tape. But I, don't, want, you. I don't want the frigging bounty. We could have taken you in the beet field and then rounded up those children. But we didn't. Because we don't want that. We are *not* working with Ed."

She took in a couple of ragged breaths. Then the tension in her body lessened.

"I'm going to let you up. Just calm down. We're going to work through this."

Her voice was full of grief and hatred. "They're going to beat those children. They will kill one of them as an example. It will probably be the boy."

"We're going to stop that," Frank said.

He waited a moment.

"I'm going to let you up. The gun's underneath you; you could pick it up and shoot me dead. But I'm going to show you I trust you. That you have nothing to fear from me."

He released his hold and got off her.

Carmen brought her hands around and just lay on the floor.

Frank eased back into the seat behind Sam.

"They killed everyone else," she said. "Hunted them, tortured them to find out where the money was, then murdered them."

He supposed she was talking about the members of her organization.

"But none of them knew."

She shook her head and closed her eyes.

"You can have your vengeance," Frank said.

"That's what you think I want?" She slid the gun out from underneath her and pushed it away. Then she got up on her hands and knees. "If I wanted nothing more than vengeance, we would have just killed them. We would have killed the Santos and the Menedez and Romeros and Morenos. We would have set up with high-powered rifles and shot to our heart's content. Killed the peons and the padrotes and everyone in between. But that would have done nothing. We needed to raise the cost permanently; make it less profitable; make it higher risk. And we needed to free as many as we could in the process. My sister died, but at least I came for her. How many have no one coming for them? We couldn't simply move to the other side of the road and walk on."

She pushed herself up and sat in the seat behind the front passenger's. Her hair had come most of the way out of its braid and hung about her head in a loopy mess.

Frank picked up her knife and held it out to her handle first. She was a soldier. Tough-beautiful. A fighter. He had met tough women before, but Carmen was at a whole other level.

"Take the knife," he said.

She reached out and grabbed it.

"We're going to do this thing," he said.

"Right," she said.

They had to do this thing.

Sam had parked them on the side of the road, the traffic on the interstate racing past. Frank looked up at him. "Let's move out."

Sam turned around, checked his mirrors, then he pushed the gas. The van accelerated down the parking lane, the rumble strips thumping under the tires.

Sam said, "That man has my phone. He knows about my family."

"I'm sorry," Frank said. Ed was like kudzu. He was like bacteria.

Sam's face was stone.

Frank got an awful feeling, a terrible premonition. "Cartwright, I don't want you getting all heroic. You leave this to me and keep your head down. You're not the point of the spear. You're support. Do you hear me?"

"Oh, I hear you," Sam said, his tone pointing out that hearing and agreeing were not the same thing.

"I should have stayed with them," Carmen said.

"Should-haves aren't going to do us any good," Frank said. "What we have now is the mission. We need to stay focused."

He picked up Tony's phone from the floor and noticed the clock. All these stops had taken a chunk of time. The minutes were running by like water. An operation like this needed careful planning and intel, and the plain fact was they didn't have nearly enough.

24

H.C. and Sons

FRANK SAT WITH Sam and Carmen in the minivan in the parking lot of a wholesale plumbing store across the wide road from H.C. and Sons. He set Sam's binoculars down. The bakery with its high cement walls looked as industrial up close as it had in the Google map—one more industry in the industrial part of town. They'd driven the streets around the place, zoomed in with Google satellite view. This was going to be a front door operation.

"Time for the chicken to cross the road," Frank said. "We need a warm body to trade or an address where we can find one."

"You want me to go to the parking lot."

"The cameras mounted on the roof will pick you up. I don't want you recorded on anyone's tape. I don't want them coming out to see who's squatting in their parking lot. So stay here. Watch my back. Let me know when something happens out front." He tapped the Bluetooth piece in his ear.

Frank put on his workman's cap, got out of the minivan, and walked to the edge of the big road. Traffic zoomed by in waves. When there was a large enough break, he jogged across. On the other side his phone rang, and he answered the call without pulling his phone out of his pocket.

"We're conferenced in," Sam said via the Bluetooth.

"Pinto?"

The noise of a lawn mower came on. "Here," Pinto said.

Frank looked up, shaded his eyes from the late afternoon sun, and spotted him up in the sky.

"I'm going to put it back on mute," Pinto said and the lawn mower cut out.

Frank walked down the drive and crossed the lawn. He avoided the front entrance and headed straight for the truck bays. Right to the blue door he'd watched men come and go through the last fifteen minutes. He walked past a truck that said White Transportation. "Going in," Frank said then walked up to the door, opened it, and stepped inside to a wide loading area.

There was a guy at a desk close up to the wall. Fat yellow lines had been painted on the floor around his area. Beyond him was a wide cement floor and then aisles of pallet racks seven levels high, all stacked with bags and boxes and buckets filled with various forms of sugary death.

Frank whistled. "This ain't your mother's bakery."

The guy at the desk looked up.

Frank said, "I'm with the truck that just came in. I got to take a leak."

The guy looked him up and down then pointed at a path on the shining cement floor. "Stay between the yellow lines. It's right around the corner."

"Thanks," Frank said. He followed the yellow brick road of safety that was provided to keep men safe from the forklifts. It led him over to the wall. Frank followed it to the corner and glanced back. The guy was heads down, a testament to the miracles a little uniform can perform. Frank turned the corner. The towering storage aisles stretched out into the distance. Up ahead on the right was the door to the bathroom. Frank walked to the bathroom, opened the door, and went in. A moment later he walked right back out and proceeded down the hallway to the center of the plant where the offices were.

He walked past a woman wearing a white smock and hair hat. Up ahead he saw a number of smocks hanging from pegs on the wall. When he passed, he helped himself to one of the bigger smocks as well as a disposable hair hat from a cardboard box and continued on. It took about two seconds to shove his workman's hat into a back pocket and don the smock and hair hat. The name patch on the smock said Shawn Wykstra. The hat was nothing more than a thin white bag with an elastic around the edge—oh how Chef Boyardee had fallen.

Some distance ahead stood the entrance to the factory proper. Through the double door windows, Frank could see folks in white smocks and white bag hats working along a production line. Frank didn't go to the production area. Instead, he turned into a hallway that looked like it led to the front entrance. A number of pictures hung on the walls. There were pictures of frosting and scones and strawberry filling, pictures of three stellar employees who looked like they needed to get out and see the sun a bit more, and a picture of what looked like a Christmas party. On the opposite wall hung three framed portraits. On one side was José, on the other was Hector, and right in the middle was a woman named Flor.

Flor and José looked like they were in their late fifties. Flor had short hair. She was wearing a pink blouse and too much makeup on a face that had sagged. It was the face of a grandmother, but there were no kindly wrinkles at the corners of her eyes. It was a hard face. Not anything at all that you'd put on TV to sell snack cakes.

José was dried up, like he'd smoked too many cigarettes. Hector was younger, in his late thirties. A good-looking guy. A ladies' man.

Frank walked down the hallway toward the front and found more bathrooms, a closet, a stairway, the reception area, and two small offices. One said Phil Dean on the door plate, and another said Sales. These weren't the digs of a big shot. Those would be upstairs with the window views.

Frank took the stairs. It opened onto a space with a number of low-walled cubicles, the kind where everyone can see everyone else, head and shoulders. There were three women working in the cubicles. They all glanced at him.

Behind the cubicles were three offices lined up side by side. They all had big glass windows facing the office areas with blinds.

Frank walked up to the first woman and said, "Is Hector in his office?"

She looked at his name patch, looked back up at him with a quizzical look on her face. She turned to the other women. "Did Hector come back?"

The women shrugged.

"We all just returned from the meeting in quality," she explained. Her eyes fell back to his name patch. Rose again to his face, her curiosity sharpened.

"I'll check," he said and walked on by. He hoped this would be his lucky day. He hoped in this card game a Hector might be just as good as a Flor. And if there wasn't any Hector sitting in one of the offices, maybe there was an address.

"Who are you?" one of the others asked as he walked past.

"Sam Alito," he said. "Shawn lent me his smock." Two of the offices were smaller. One had a long spread. Frank headed for it and was rewarded when he saw Hector's name on the closed door.

Frank walked right up, grabbed the handle, and shoved. But the door was locked. He wrenched the handle again, but it was a good lock.

"Hector," he called like a long lost buddy.

"Who did you say you were again?" one of the gals asked.

"Doctor Alito," Frank said.

There was a thin slit between the window frame and the edge of the blinds. Frank leaned in close and cupped his hand around his eyes so he could see in. It was dark. He looked at the door. It was seated in a steel frame. It was going to be a bugger to bust down. It would be easier to break the glass. And then what? He'd search, hoping to find an address, and one of these women would call security, and they'd corner him on the stairs.

Frank turned around. The women were all looking at him.

"This is a bit of an emergency," Frank said. "I have his results back. He's going to want to know this."

The older gal shrugged.

"I don't think we want to wait with this. I'm going to need his home address."

The younger woman glanced at the older gal, but the older gal was playing it cool. She said, "Check with the front desk. They can ring him."

"I already tried that. You're his secretary, aren't you?"

"Yes," she said.

"We don't have much time," he said.

"I never made a doctor's appointment for Hector."

"Some things men want to keep discrete. I shouldn't have said anything, but I need the address."

Frank waited. He was playing a doctor. And doctors usually got their way.

She furrowed her brow but took out a piece of paper and a razor sharp pencil.

Footsteps sounded on the stairs. They were heavy footsteps. A man's footsteps.

The older gal scratched out 7-4-3.

A heavyset white guy appeared on the stairs. "There you are," he said. "I think you've got my smock."

Frank looked down. The older secretary had scratched 743 Lu.

They peered across the cubicles at Frank. "Yeah," he said. "That's mine. Who are you?"

"Doctor Alito," Frank said. He looked down at the older gal.

She'd stopped writing. The pencil was still in her hand, poised above the paper.

The youngest gal said, "He said you lent it to him."

"No," the guy said confused.

The women in the back had been careful not to draw attention to herself. She'd been quietly watching the whole scene, which was why Frank almost missed her hand movement. She slowly reached one finger out and pushed a button on her phone and then held perfectly still.

Odds were she'd just called security.

The older woman put her pencil down. She said, "I think he's still here. It's such a big place. The receptionist can page him."

"We checked all over downstairs. Someone said he'd left, but I thought I'd come up here. He needs this information."

The old gal looked at him, and then decided to call his bluff. "I'm really not supposed to," she said. "Talk to the receptionist."

"A man's life is on the line, and I get the run around from his employees. He's going to hear about this."

The women did not budge.

He'd been seconds away. He looked at the gal in the back who'd been silently watching him the whole time. He figured he had less than two minutes before the cavalry arrived.

"If he comes back," Frank said. "You tell him to call me."

"Sure," the old gal said.

Frank walked passed Shawn. "I'll leave it hanging on the hook."

"You're supposed to have an escort," Shawn said.

"It's an emergency," Frank said and crossed to the stairs. He headed down before Shawn could reply. On the way he removed the smock and hat.

At the bottom, he checked the hallway to make sure it was clear. Across from him hung the three framed photographs. He pulled all three off the wall, frames and all, stacked them up, and wrapped them in Shawn's smock.

He heard the static of a personal radio out in the warehouse. Heard someone running in his direction.

Frank saw the women's bathroom for the office folks, pushed the door open and stepped inside. Someone with petite white sneakers was utilizing one of the stalls. Frank said, "Sorry, I've just got to fix the door. It will only be a moment."

"Okay?" the woman said.

Moments later he heard the sound of running footsteps turn into the hallway. Two people. One of them clomped up the stairs in heavy boots. The other ran past the bathroom to the front of the building.

Frank counted to four then walked out of the women's bathroom. At the one end of the hallway, the door to the reception area was closing. He figured the man who had run there would be back in about ten seconds. Frank turned the opposite direction and walked toward the warehouse, smock and photographs under his arm.

Sam's voice came on the line. "Are you okay?"

"It's a bust," Frank said.

"Do we need to come get you?"

"The last thing we need is for our vehicle to be tagged. Just stay put."

He did not turn back and go the way he'd come. Instead he walked out into the aisles of pallet racks, into forklift land, and made a quick turn to put a wall of stock between him and those who had been called to take care of the intruder.

The lane was clear all the way to the end. He could hear a forklift a few rows away, grabbing stock. Frank took long quick strides down the row back toward the loading docks and the blue door. As he walked he pulled the photographs out of the smock. He threw Shawn's smock into one of the stock bays, then proceeded to tear the backs off the frames and remove the photographs. He left the three frames lying on boxes of butter flavoring. The large photographs he folded up and stuffed into the big front pocket of his pants.

He was about halfway down the long row when a forklift drove through the intersection about thirty yards ahead of Frank. There was one guy driving the lift and another guy hanging on the side. The guy hanging on the side was wearing a dark blue shirt and a dark cap.

The forklift stopped. Backed up. Then turned onto Frank's row. There were big white letters on the one guys dark cap. They said "Security." The security guy called something in on a radio attached close to his shoulder. He held up his hand for Frank to halt. He had a flashlight in his black utility belt on one side. On the other side he had a gun in a holster.

Frank slowed.

Behind Frank, at the far end, another forklift turned into the row. Another security guy hung on the side of that one.

A lot of security guys for one bakery. But maybe they were worried about corporate espionage. Maybe H.C. & Sons had a secret million-dollar recipe they needed to protect from the French and Germans.

Frank looked left, looked right. Saw an open stocking location ahead on the ground. The pallet there wasn't full, just a couple of bags of sugar. Furthermore, Frank could see daylight on the other side.

"I need you to stop," the security guard said.

Frank dashed for the pallet, scrambled over the sugar and found his way blocked by another pallet partially stacked with boxes full of cinnamon. Almost a dead end, but not quite. There was just enough space to slip past the boxes.

The forklift accelerated down the row toward the spot where he'd scrambled in.

Frank wormed his way past the boxes and spilled out onto the cement lane on the other side.

Behind him, the forklift's rubber wheels screeched to a stop. "He's on the other side!" the guard called. "Aisle four!"

"Roger," someone called out of the man's radio.

Frank ran down the aisle, heard the whine of the forklift backing up on the other lane, knew the second forklift was doing the same. He suspected they might have others. Heck, they might have a whole fleet of traveling security.

Frank reached the intersection, jumped to the next row back and kept running, but the aisle was too long. Way too long. It was going to be like playing against the rooks in chess. Sooner or later they were going to corner him.

Frank looked left, looked right. Looked up. The shelves were stacked seven levels high. They towered over him. He saw an open pallet three levels up. He leapt to the second level, grabbed the vertical support, then hauled himself up to the third level, careful not to step on the boxes and leave a bootprint. The mostly empty pallet was perfect. Too perfect.

The forklift reached the intersection of the cross lane back on aisle three. The rubber tires squealed to make the corner.

He climbed up to the next level and then the next, working the supports like a gorilla, and stepped onto the location two levels above the empty one.

The forks appeared down in the intersection behind him, and Frank slid into the location alongside a pallet of stacked and wrapped vanilla cream fondant.

The forklift stopped. The security guard hopped off and ran through the intersection, continuing along that crossing lane, probably so he could look down all the rows. He came back a few moments later.

Frank quietly wormed back farther.

"Go slow," the guard said.

The forklift headed down Frank's row. Just below Frank's position it stopped. He heard the forks lifting. Heard them pause at the empty bay on the third level. Hear them rise a bit more.

"You can't be in here," the guard called. "Come on out; it's dangerous with all these forklifts." He sounded so reasonable. He sounded like any security guard would when someone unauthorized needed to be escorted out. Maybe this wasn't the lair of a drug lord and slaver. Maybe the Goroza names had been stolen. Identity theft *was* big business. Perfect for someone like Ed. Hector, Flor, and José could all be upstanding citizens.

On the other hand, since when did bakeries need multiple guys to guard the Twinkies? One guy would have been plenty.

The top of the security guard's dark cap rose into view. He was standing on the forks, probably against all safety regulations, checking the shelf on the fourth level, the one above the empty one.

One more level and he'd see Frank wedged along the side looking back at him like a raccoon caught between the garbage cans.

Frank should have brought the submachine gun. He thought about shoving the pallet out onto the guy's head. But he was alongside it with no leverage. And he couldn't huck the buckets at anyone because they were wrapped tightly with industrial plastic.

The guard's cap sat there a moment more, and then he said, "Nada." A moment later the fork motor whined and the guard's cap descended from view. A little after that the forklift's electrical engine revved and the driver and security guy moved on.

If these guys followed normal protocol, they would be calling the cops right about now. In a town like this they probably had a four-minute response time. Maybe shorter. If the cops showed up, things were going to get a lot harder. He wriggled forward, slowly peeked out, watched the forklift roll down the lane, the guard scanning the shelves.

He looked the other way. The lane was clear. But the forklift had round convex rearview mirrors, giving the driver a wide and tall view. If the driver had any brains at all, he'd be checking those mirrors; he'd notice movement.

So Frank carefully slid back, then over the strut to the shelf behind his, and across the tops of some bags to carefully peek down the lane on the opposite side. A security guard on foot stood way down at the far end watching. The second Frank popped out of his hiding place, the guy would see him, call it in, and they'd all converge. He'd lose precious seconds climbing down to the floor.

He pulled himself back into the center of the shelf. Each pallet location was separated by nothing more than a diagonal support strut. And while the locations all had pallets in them, the bags and boxes and buckets didn't fill the whole space right to the top. There was a gap. And at the end of the gap was a lane that ran right back to the docking bays.

Frank turned and wriggled in a good soldier belly crawl across the tops of the boxes and buckets until he came to the crossing lane. He peeked out. To his left, the lane ran to the back of the warehouse. Nobody that way. To his right, the lane ran to the loading dock, to the dude with the desk in the painted yellow square and the blue door that led outside. The guy at the desk in the yellow square was hunched over filling out some form. A truck driver stood next to him waiting.

Now or never. Frank wormed out of the row five levels up, high above the lane. Then he climbed down the metal shelving to the cement floor. Aisle five with the forklift crossed behind him. Aisle four with the security guard standing watch at the far end crossed in front of him. He was going to have to cross aisle four and two others to get to the wide loading dock and the blue exit door beyond.

Frank headed for the dock and door. He crossed aisle four, saw the security guard spot him, saw him call it in. Frank hurried his walk. He passed the next aisle watched by a forklift guard combo. Passed the next. Walked out from the rows of shelves onto the loading dock floor.

Up ahead the guy at the desk handed the driver a slip of paper. The driver walked to the blue door, opened it. The bright light of afternoon shone in. Then he exited and shut the door behind him.

Sam said over the Bluetooth in Frank's ear, "A police cruiser just entered the parking lot. It's heading fairly quickly toward the front door."

"Keep an eye on it," Frank said. "Let me know where the officers go."

In the warehouse, the desk guy turned around and spotted Frank. He frowned. "Hey," he said. "What are you doing out there? I told you to walk on the path."

Behind Frank in the warehouse someone began to run. A couple of forklifts beeped down the aisles at high speed.

Frank said, "Dude, I got lost."

The guy was clearly annoyed. "You with White Transport?"

White Transport, the truck that had been parked in the bay next to the stairs. That was probably the truck that belonged to the driver who'd just been standing here. Frank was about to answer, when a voice came over the intercom at the desk.

"We've got a code four."

The guy at the desk looked down at the intercom. Looked back up at Frank and narrowed his eyes. The guy at the desk wasn't some skinny pencil type. He wasn't fat and slobbish either. He was a guy who looked like he could take care of business. Like maybe he'd taken care of business a time or two. He stepped to the left and blocked Frank's path to the door.

"What are you doing here?" he asked.

"Leaving," Frank said.

"I don't think so," he said and slipped his hand into his pocket.

Frank didn't wait to see what surprise he had there. He headbutted the guy in the face.

The guy reeled back.

Frank rushed him, put his foot behind the guy's leg, and shoved.

The guy tripped and slammed into the cement floor all akimbo, which made it very easy for Frank to stomp his gonads.

The guy groaned, curled in on himself, and rolled to the side.

Frank strode past and opened the blue door.

"The officers are going in the front door," Sam said.

Back in the warehouse, a forklift with its security guard attachment rounded the corner into the lane leading directly to the loading area.

Frank exited the building and shut the blue door behind him.

The police cruiser was parked right in front of the main entrance some distance down the front of the building to Frank's left. To Frank's right the White Transportation semi and trailer was pulling out. Frank leapt over the step railing, ran around the back of the semitrailer and up alongside the trailer of the slowly accelerating truck to the front. The round drum gas tank had a step built into it to make it easy to access the passenger side door. Frank hopped up onto the step and steadied himself. He looked up into the mirror and saw the driver watching the road in front.

The semi's motor rumbled and the vehicle picked up speed. Back at the truck bays someone shouted. If they were shouting for the driver, he didn't hear them. Frank didn't think he could hear them. The guy was listening to some book on tape so loudly Frank could hear the narrator through the door.

The road out of here curved just a little to the left, which kept the semi between him and the front of the building. A few seconds later the driver braked at the entrance to the main road facing the bakery. He waited for a group of cars to pass, then gave the truck some gas. The diesel engine rumbled; the dark exhaust rose out of the tall exhaust pipes, and the truck lumbered out into the intersection to make a left-hand turn.

This time the driver did notice Frank in the mirror, but he was in the middle of the intersection. This was no place to stop; he had to continue forward. He began the turn, but before he could buzz down the window to holler, Frank leapt off the step, ran to the curb, and into the parking lot where Sam and Carmen waited in the minivan. He opened the door just as the semitrailer rolled by out on the road. Back at the bakery across the road, men were fanning out across the front of the building, some running round back, others to check the parking lot. The cop was talking to the old gal from upstairs.

Frank ducked in the van and slid the side door shut.

"That was close," Sam said.

"We're not out of Dodge yet," Frank said.

"Did you get anything?"

"Nothing," Frank said and sighed with frustration. He pulled the folded photographs out of his pocket. "Just some high-quality mug shots. A fragment of an address. We've got nothing."

Carmen was sitting in the front passenger's seat. She held her hand out for photographs, and Frank let her take them.

"What do we do?"

That was a good question. They could wait here and hope to waylay that old secretary when she left and wring the truth out of her. But who knew when the shift ended? She was probably calling Hector right now, which meant the element of surprise, their biggest weapon, had just been blown.

743 Lu—what was that?

Lupine? Luna? Luke? Ludwig? Lucifer? Lucky? Lube? Lugworm?

Yeah, they lived on Lugworm Drive.

Or had that U been an O? Frank pinched the bridge of his nose then drew his hand down his face.

Carmen unfolded the photographs. Looked at the first and second. When she saw the third, her eyes went wide. She looked again. "Mi madre," she said in shock.

"What?" Frank asked.

"The woman."

"What about her?"

Carmen held the unfolded photograph up and turned it around so they both could see. There were two faces looking back at them, Carmen's above, the woman's underneath in the photograph. She said, "The woman that came for my sister."

Just then Pinto took his phone off mute and the sound of the plane came in. "Look out your windshield, coming out of the bakery's parking lot. Is that what I think it is?"

Frank looked. It was a two-toned Nissan with cola glass. It stopped at the entrance to the main road. The Hispanic driver looked both ways, then made a right turn.

"Is that it?" Sam asked.

Frank said, "I believe that's the dent I made in the side panel with Jesus's head."

The two-toned car sped up and merged with the traffic.

The license plate started with VAG. "Those first letters were on the car they took Tony in."

"You want me to follow?" Pinto asked.

"You'd better believe it," Frank said, then turned to Sam. "Let's get this thing moving. I think we've got ourselves a lead."

25

Tail

SAM BACKED OUT of his parking stall and drove to the exit.

Across the road the Twinkie guards and police officers were still doing a search. Even though Frank was in the back seat with tinted windows, he still ducked down.

Sam made his left hand turn and accelerated along the main road.

A few moments later Carmen said, "We're good. You can sit up now."

Pinto cut in. "The Nissan is turning left at the light."

"Got it," Sam said.

Frank looked back at the bakery and verified that nobody was following them. Then he turned back around. "You're sure that's the woman?"

"I'm positive," Carmen said. "Look at the birthmark on the side of her neck."

Frank hadn't noticed it at first, but there it was like half of a small flower.

"How is it possible?" Frank asked. "Out of all the people in Colorado we find her."

"There are dozens of slave sites between here, New Mexico, and the western part of Texas. But they're run by only a handful of trafficking organizations. We got lucky."

"We've been living right," Sam said.

Frank said, "Plan A—we take the driver of that car and beat him until he talks."

"Plan B?" Sam asked.

"I don't think we've gotten that far yet."

The Nissan went through the intersection. Sam rolled up a number of seconds later to a red light.

Pinto said, "He's running south."

They waited for the cross traffic making left turns. Then waited for the cross traffic going straight through.

"He's easily a mile ahead of you," Pinto said. "Taking a right."

The light turned green and Sam hit the gas, made the left-hand turn, accelerated down the road.

"Watch it," Frank said. "Last thing we need is a ticket."

Sam let off the accelerator a bit.

"You got him, right Pinto?"

"I got him," Pinto said.

It took about ten minutes before they finally were able to see the Nissan ahead of them. The driver made a left off the main drag and then a quick right past a 7-11 and an auto parts store into a residential neighborhood. It was an older neighborhood with smaller houses. A little run down, but a few of the houses had conscientious owners. He parked in front of a bungalow and ran to the house and banged on the door.

A cholo opened the door.

"That's one of the slave sites," Carmen said.

"How can you tell?" Sam asked. "It looks like all the other houses."

"There are a couple of profiles for these places. When they're in the city, they're often at the edge of a residential neighborhood, usually next to a business area, or a road that gets more traffic. There's easy access from behind, maybe an alley; in this instance a parking lot. I guarantee there's a gate in the back fence. And then you have the windows—the blinds are always down. You'd think they were vampires."

"They're worse than vampires," Frank said.

Sam drove past the house.

Carmen said, "That's the door watchman. They've already done a telephone interview. But they'll do another screening here. Where are you from? Where do you live? How did you hear about us? If the cochino passes, the watchman lets him in. He pays the money to the

260 · John D. Brown

ticketero who gives him a playing card or maybe a poker chip. Then he waits in the living room on the couch with the other men. When it's his turn, he chooses a girl, but sometimes there are only two in the house, so maybe he doesn't have much choice. He gives her the card, they go to one of the rooms, and then he rapes her.

"In his mind, it's not rape, right? It's business. Because the girls aren't tied up; they're working off the cost of the coyote; they're making an investment in their future. It's Walmart—high volume, low price. The girls are making it rich. But they're not. They're forced to service sometimes thirty to forty men a day. And they keep nothing. She gets maybe five or ten dollars a card. But then the padrotes charge her hundreds for condoms, more for room and board, for shampoo and clothes, more for protection. So much she'll never pay the debt."

"I'd wager most of those customers know exactly what they're doing," Frank said.

Back at the house, the door watchman yelled something to those inside, then he hustled down the front porch and out to the Nissan with the first guy.

Sam slowed and pulled to the side of the road.

The two cholos got into the car and drove back out of the neighborhood.

"Go around the block," Frank said. "We'll catch them on the main road."

They did catch them and followed them to a second house much like the first. It couldn't have been more than a mile and a half away. This one was down the street from a church.

The second watchman joined the other two men in the Nissan. On his way to the car, he made a show of his gun.

"They're gathering their forces," Frank said.

"Or going out for food," Sam replied.

They followed the Nissan to an auto shop and picked up another guy. This one pulled the gun out of his waistband before he got into the back of the car.

"That's four guys with guns," Sam said. "We still going with plan A?"

"We'll follow them and see," Frank said.

They followed them onto I-25 which runs straight through Denver. Half an hour later they were running south, leaving the Denver metropolis behind.

To the west, the Rockies rose up and towered over the landscape. Here the land stretched out in gentle hills with very few trees. They traveled down I-25. Before they reached Colorado Springs, the Nissan exited the freeway and headed east into the country. There were plains, plains, and more plains, as far as the eye could see. And then they started seeing hillocks covered in patches of ponderosa. They were close to the Black Forest area.

Pinto had been their eye in the sky this whole time. It had allowed them to keep out of sight, to follow the Nissan with more than a mile between them. But Pinto came on the line. "I'm going to have to drop down and fill up the plane."

"How long?" Frank asked.

"I'll be back in forty-five."

"Roger that," Frank said.

Sam sped up. A few minutes later they spotted the Nissan way up ahead, and Pinto flew off. Sam closed the distance until they were maybe only a half a mile back. The area was pretty here. Miles of pines and meadow and more pines. They followed the Nissan into a little town; on the way out the Nissan turned down a road flanked by pines.

Sam was slowed by a truck hauling hay and traffic coming the other way. He finally made the turn, sped down the road, but the Nissan was nowhere. They came to a T with a little gas station and bowling alley on the other side.

They looked left, looked right. There was nothing on the road.

"Crap," Sam said.

There were some teenage boys in the parking lot by the bowling alley. They were lounging up against a big yellow pickup, talking to some girls in a Volkswagen.

Frank said, "Lets go talk to those kids."

Sam drove across the road, but the teens were packing up. They were in their cars and moving before Sam could get to them. He rolled

262 • John D. Brown

down his window but they motored over to the bowling alley and exited the parking lot there.

"Should I chase them down?"

"Pull up to the front," Frank said. Sam drove past a car at the pumps to the front by the ice chest. Frank took out his phone and found their position with GPS. The little town they'd gone through was Calhoon. He Googled Calhoon with Lupine and Luke and Ludwig, but didn't find anything. Tried Lucifer and Luna. Even tried Lugworm. Nothing. He got out of the van and went inside the station to the stout blond woman at the cash register. There was a rack of gum on the counter. Frank took out a package of bubble gum and put it on the counter. "Got a question," he said. "I'm looking for the Goroza place."

The woman shrugged and shook her head, rang in the bubble gum.

"The owners of the big bakery," Frank said.

"I don't live around here," she said.

A twenty-something guy standing by the candy bar aisle had been listening to the conversation. "You talking about that place on Lullaby?"

Lullaby, of course. "Why, yes," Frank said.

The guy gave the woman at the counter a look.

"What?" Frank said.

"Nothing," the guy said.

"No really," Frank said.

"Just take a left out of here," the guy said. "Head down the road. Lullaby's a couple miles down on your left."

Frank turned to the woman. "What's he not telling me?"

The stout blonde said, "That's that place with the grotto, right?"

"Yeah," the younger guy said.

"Ah," the woman said and dismissed him. "They're Catholics. They've got this grotto thing with the statue of Mary in it. They light candles. Prayers. That kind of thing."

"It isn't always Mary," the young guy said.

"Oh, no?" Frank asked.

"I haven't seen it, but some say they perform other rites."

The stout woman rolled her eyes. "Don't listen to him; he doesn't even have a job. Nothing to do but think up weird things."

Another car pulled up to the pumps. It was a man and woman with bicycles riding in a rack up on top.

Frank motioned at the road. "So I take a left, go a couple miles, and then another left."

"You got it," the guy said.

The price for the bubble gum appeared on the register display. Frank handed the woman two one dollar bills. She made change, and Frank picked up his gum.

"Have fun," the guy said.

"They're bakers," Frank said. "They make frostings and snack cakes."

"See," the stout woman said.

Frank left the two behind to argue about the propriety of talking about your neighbors and walked out to the minivan. He Googled 743 Lullaby, Calhoon, Colorado. A moment later he was looking satellite view of a big old rambler with wooden shingles, a long drive, and a swimming pool. It was a pretty big spread nestled in the middle of huge swaths of ponderosa pines.

There was a barn, what looked like another smaller house, and some outbuildings. There were adjacent fields and corrals ringed by white post fences. One field looked like a place to ride horses. Frank zoomed in. Sure enough, the satellite had captured someone on a horse in that field. Frank zoomed out and then a bit more. A little farther away a stream ran through the pines to a fishing pond.

Sam said, "What is that? Forty acres?"

"A regular gentleman's ranch," Carmen said.

"Let's get down the road," Frank said. "Make sure this is the right place."

They found Lullaby right where the guy at the gas station said they would. It was a country road running through a landscape of pines and prairie grass. The land on the right of the road was fenced off. About a mile down the road they came to a newer section of fence. Every fifty feet the barbed-wire fence had a square No Trespassing sign.

"I think this is the start of their property," Frank said.

They passed pines and fields and a lot more No Trespassing signs, and then the entrance to the long driveway came into view. Alongside the drive was the riding field he'd seen from the Google maps with the white post fence. At the end of the drive were a bunch of SUVs. At the back to one side sat the Nissan.

"The troops have gathered," Frank said.

A number of men sat at a table on a shaded patio next to the house. Colorful chickens milled about the yard. Behind them a peacock sat on a fence post. Beyond the peacock, in the far corner of a field, stood a gaggle of ostriches.

Frank shook his head. "The Gorozas have got their fingers in all sorts of pies."

"Their oldest son has an MBA," Carmen said.

"Which goes to show that college degrees don't make a man smart," Frank said.

Sam continued a mile past the house then stopped along an empty section of road running through more prairie and pines without a single No Trespassing sign. This was probably some rancher's land used to graze cattle.

"Okay," Frank said. "That was the first pass. Now we need to do some close recon."

"We're just going to walk up?"

"We're going to drive up," Frank said. He put on his no prescription black-rimmed glasses. "It's a courtesy call to inform the owners of the property that Xcel Energy will be conducting a gas line survey in the area. If all goes well, I'll get in and check their furnace."

"What am I going to do?" Carmen said.

"You're going to take the binoculars; between Google terrain and this first pass I found the perfect spot for you to keep an eye on things. You're going to watch our backs."

"What about me?"

"You're going to sit in the van."

"Okay,"

Frank took out his bubble gum. "Have a piece."

"It's full of sugar; it will rot your teeth."

"You ever seen a bad guy blowing bubbles?"

"No."

"All right then. You're bored. You're in the van. You're blowing bubbles."

Sam took the gum, unwrapped his piece, and began to chomp. Then he put it in gear, made a three-point turn, and headed back toward the house.

26

Target

THEY COULDN'T JUST let Carmen off in full view of the house, so Frank directed Sam to drive about half a mile past the house and then pull to the side of the road. Carmen took Sam's binoculars, scrambled down the shoulder, over a fence, and into a stand of trees. Frank figured it would take her about seven minutes to get in place. So he and Sam got out of the van and walked around like they were doing something important. Frank's leg was still hurting, but he tried to loosen it up anyway. He brushed the stray Cheerios out of the van and moved the diaper bag and anything else that said this was a family vehicle into the trunk with the Cub Scout crap. With every Cheerio that fell to the ground he realized just how sketchy this plan really was.

They heard Carmen's hard breathing on the conference call as she ran. A few minutes later she said, "Okay, I can see the knocker on the front door and the labels on the beer bottles the men are drinking on the patio."

"How many people are there?"

"There are eight out on the patio. No, wait. Two more coming out of the house with plates of food."

"Is Flor there?"

"I don't see her. It looks like there are two sentries, one by the driveway, and another out back talking to a girl by the barn. That's twelve men."

"Who else is there?"

"There's a young girl serving drinks."

"Do you recognize any of them?"

"I see José. I see Hector. The rest I don't know. I wish I had a camera with a telephoto lens."

Frank wondered about her previous operation, how they operated, what success they'd had. "I bet you a penny this is their pow-wow," he said. "They're discussing Jesus's death, and how to react should the authorities trace anything to them. Probably some other contingency planning. And, of course, they need to plan the operation outside Hudson where we present ourselves for a four a.m. execution."

A lawn mower cut into the call. "I'm back," Pinto said. "We miss anything?"

"Christmas," Frank said and looked up into the sky. Pinto's plane was small and high up. "What do you see?"

Pinto said, "You've got a lot of people at the house."

Frank wondered if Ed was there. A big meeting like this, he ought to be there. "Carmen, can you see Tony?"

"No Tony," she said.

Pinto said, "Someone's on a horse ride south of the property. There's something down there, back in some rocky overhang. I think it's a statue."

"That's the grotto," Frank said.

"The rest of the area's clear. Everyone else is moving about close to the house."

Eyes in the sky, com-linked to the whole team, someone watching Frank's back—it was just like old times. Except not really.

"Any propane tanks?" Frank asked.

There was a pause while he checked. A moment later he came back on. "None visible from the air."

Frank said, "Carmen, you keep us apprised. Anybody new shows up, anybody changes locations—I want to know. Pinto, watch the wider area."

"Roger," Pinto said and muted his phone.

"Carmen?" Frank asked.

"Roger," she said.

Frank said to Sam, "It's time."

They got back in the van. Only then did Frank realize that the license plates on the van were Wyoming plates. Someone working for Xcel of Colorado would not be driving a Wyoming minivan.

Frank got back out and used his wrench to unscrew the bolts holding the plates. Then he put them in the back with the rest of the stuff and wondered what else he'd missed. "When we go down the driveway, don't turn around until it's time to leave. A missing front plate is less noticeable than a missing back one. And you busy yourself in the van, like you're taking calls and doing work. Get some paper and make notes."

"Okay," Sam said.

The sound of the Cessna roared into the call. Pinto said, "There are actually two riders. I missed the one. The riders have passed you. You'll see them on your right as you drive toward the house."

"Roger," Frank said.

Pinto muted his phone again and the sound of the Cessna cut out.

Sam turned the minivan round once more and drove down the road back toward the long driveway that led to the house.

The key was going to be getting inside the house to get as much a feel for it as he could. He had a flashlight in his tool belt. He figured he'd bluff them, tell them that the survey was prompted by contaminants, and that he needed just a few seconds to judge the color of their gas flame.

He figured that would work, unless, of course, Pinto had missed the propane tank. In which case, the Gorozas would tell him they had no natural gas and would immediately become suspicious. Maybe demand credentials.

The other problem was that Ed had probably already made sure they'd seen his picture. They would have wanted to know who had killed their son. They would want to make sure all their people knew. In fact, they probably had a copy of his photo and were passing it around to the men on the patio. Frank's face would be fresh on their minds. He just hoped the black-rimmed glasses and cap would be enough.

Frank shook his head. This was all such a long shot.

Sam slowly accelerated down the road.

"You okay?" Frank asked him.

"Capital," Sam said.

"You better put on some sunglasses," Frank said. "You've got the worst poker face I've ever seen."

Sam tapped a flat compartment in the ceiling of the van. It opened up to reveal a pair of sunglasses with big lenses and thick white frames—something only a woman would wear. "I don't wear sunglasses," Sam said, but he removed the glasses and put them on. He glanced over at Frank for an assessment.

"You look like an escapee from the Village People. Put 'em back," Frank said. "We'll have to hope nobody questions you. But if they do, just imagine your face is a frying pan."

"That's what they teach you in the army?"

"No," Frank said. "But it's the best we've got right now."

Up ahead on the right, the riders came into view. Frank hadn't noticed it before, but there was a trail about thirty yards off the road that ran through the ponderosa and prairie grass. The horses looked like fine animals, well-muscled and sleek. One was the color of pale sand with a black mane and tail. A girl rode on it. The other horse was black as night. Its tail was bobbed, its mane braided. It looked like a show horse. An older woman rode it.

Sam slowly caught up to them and passed. Frank caught a glimpse of the older woman's face before she moved back into the pines.

"Plan change," Frank said. He looked down the road. Saw the perfect place. "See that big dead pine a ways down?"

"Yeah."

"Get this thing down there quick and pull over. We're getting out. We're going to hop the fence and hustle out into that field."

"What's going on?"

"That was Flor Goroza on the lead horse. Probably just finished praying for her son in that grotto."

"And swift vengeance on the ones responsible for his death."

"We're going to do it here."

"They're on horses."

"Barging into a house is like storming a castle. Riskiest thing there is. Taking someone out in the open, away from all those beer drinking guns—dude, this is our opportunity."

"Maybe the desk jockeys came through," Sam said.

"What would Pinto say?" Frank asked.

The lawn mower cut in. "Pinto would say that you'd better speed up, or you're going to miss this window."

"Okay," Sam said, screwing up his courage. "Okay." He accelerated, sped down the road toward the pine. Frank grabbed the clipboard and duct tape. He had his glasses on. Had his baby blue baseball cap. Had the tool belt. Operation Flor was a go.

"Right here," Frank said. "Turn it around so we're facing away from the drive; as soon as we have her we want out of this place." He glanced back. The riders hadn't appeared through the trees yet, but he and Sam didn't have much time before they would come into view.

Sam braked hard, moved to the other side of the road, and made a tight U-turn that put them right alongside the shoulder on the Goroza side of the road. Sam put it in park. "So what are we going to do? Jump out of some bushes? I don't see much cover."

"We're going to act like we're surveying. Like we own the place. We're going to talk loud. Gesticulate large."

Sam swallowed and nodded.

"We'll be back here in less than three minutes."

"Okay," Sam said again, obviously feeling his nerves. "Time to go get us a slaver."

He turned off the van and they both opened the doors and hustled off the road's shoulder to the barbed-wire fence. Frank gimped along, but he could bear a little pain for Tony. For those children.

They climbed over the fence into the Goroza's property. This particular spot was a nice swath of open prairie grass about a hundred yards long. At one end were the pines from which Flor would emerge. At the other was the last stand of pines before the land opened up on the open fields around the Goroza's house.

The horse trail was only a couple dozen yards up ahead. "Right here," Frank said. "Just walk."

Sam slowed to a walk. He was breathing hard, looking all wide-eyed.

"We own the place," Frank said.

"Right."

Frank patted his belt. The duct tape was still there. This was going to work.

At the end of the field, the riders flashed between the trees.

Frank said, "They're going to come talk to us. When I grab Flor's reins, you grab the reins of the second rider. You're going to need to pull her off the horse. We'll duct tape them both. Then we'll take Flor with us."

"I've got a bad feeling, Frank."

"This is your first dance. Of course, you do. We all get a bad feeling the first time out."

"I know, but it's kidnapping."

"It's Tony. It's those children."

Sam blew out a big sigh.

The two riders began to emerge from the trees.

"Showtime," Frank said. "Pace with me." He strode off fifteen paces like he was measuring something. Then he turned his back to Flor, pointed down. He spoke loudly. "This spot here is where the pipe's coming through."

Sam got into his role. He pointed out to the road. "Over that hill, then run it the rest of the way out past the house. All these trees will have to go."

Frank nodded. He spread his arms wide. "We're talking a swath twenty feet wide for all the equipment." He acted like he'd just glimpsed the riders out of the corner of his eye, looked at them bold as you please, then he stepped off another ten paces and pointed from his current spot to the previous one where Sam stood. "We're talking this wide," he said loudly.

Sam nodded. "I think that will work." He was getting into his role.

Flor was now only a few dozen yards off, looking at them from atop her horse with some annoyance. Of course, from the photo Frank had seen, that could be her happy face. She had shorter hair than in her photo and a good amount of blue eye shadow. The second rider was much younger than Frank had first thought. She looked young enough to be Flor's granddaughter.

Frank pointed at the riders and said loudly, "Let these folks pass." Then he turned over his clipboard and began writing and diagramming, making notes, ignoring Flor like she was some kind of tourist.

When they got close, he looked up and smiled. "Hello," he said.

Flor gave her reins the slightest tug, and her splendid black horse stopped. The girl behind stopped her horse as well. They were amazing animals. Even Frank could see that. Flor held a black leather riding crop in one hand. Behind her were two saddle bags. In the bags were tall candle glasses. The wax had all burned away; the glass was smoky.

"Who are you?" Flor demanded.

Frank took on happy helpful tone. "Well, Ma'am, my name is Clarence Thomas. I'm with Xcel Energy." He folded his clipboard under his arm and walked toward her. "We're out doing a survey. Is this your land?"

"I don't know of any survey."

Frank continued with the happy helpful worker bit. "Well, Xcel Energy is always looking to develop domestic energy sources. And our geologists are thinking there might be something in this area."

"What are you talking about? Oil?"

"Natural gas." He walked right up to her. "Natural gas is our future. There's a big old fault that runs parallel to I-25. Every so often a secondary fault will shoot off. Those formations are rich with gas."

Frank had no idea what he was talking about. He'd BS'd with a driller that worked for Halliburton a few weeks ago. He was making this all up from what he could remember of that conversation.

He glanced at Sam who had just realized he needed to be next to the girl's horse, not ten feet down the trail.

"So, Ma'am, we're just out doing a preliminary. But we do want to talk to the owners. Do you know who owns this property?"

"I own this property."

"Well, that's perfect. You're going to get a letter and a call. I can't promise anything, but if things check out, there might be a lease opportunity."

"I am not interested in trucks and drilling rigs ruining my land, Mister . . ."

"Thomas. Clarence Thomas. Like the supreme court judge."

"Whatever."

"Don't be too quick. Things aren't like they used to be. The way they drill now, they can go in from the side. Set up the rig a mile away, off your property, and go in sideways. You'll never even notice." Frank was waiting for Sam to get into position, but he was taking his time.

"Is that so?"

"There's a lot of good money to be made. Of course, this land might be dry."

"Well, today is not the day for me to talk. We'll wait for your letter and call."

Frank's golden opportunity was about to ride off. He looked at Sam.

Sam smiled broadly. He said, "You have got some fine horses here. Is this palomino a Morgan?" He walked up to the girl's horse and patted its flank.

"It is," Flor said, her face as bitter as old beer.

"Not as high-strung as an Arabian, but a much finer sit than the Quarter Horse. When I was a kid, our troop rode Morgans to get our equestrian merit badge."

"How nice," Flor said. "And now we need to go. Excuse us."

Show time.

Frank grabbed the halter of Flor's horse right by the bit. "I'm afraid that's not going to be possible."

Sam reached out and grabbed the halter of the girl's horse.

Flor's eyes narrowed. "Like hell," she said, then pulled back her riding crop and struck at his face.

Frank raised his free arm to block the blow, but Flor put her heels into her horse's flank, and the animal surged forward. The power of the animal was immense. The horse ripped free of his grasp, and then its flank slammed into him, knocking him to the ground.

Frank scrambled to his feet tried to gimp-run after her, but Flor was already galloping away. She had, what, a half a mile to the house? That would take that horse no time at all to cover the distance. They had to get out of here. Now!

"Sam," he said and turned.

But Sam had a hold of the palomino Morgan. His foot was in the stirrup. The girl was on the ground.

With a little hop, Sam rose up and swung his other leg over. He fitted his free foot into the other stirrup. Then he grabbed the reins with both hands and said, "Move."

"What are you doing?"

Sam kicked his heels into the horse's flanks and shouted, "Ha!" The horse surged forward right toward Frank.

Frank leapt off the trail. Sam flew past. He yelled and kicked the horse again. The animal surged again. Clumps of dirt and grass flew up from its hooves. Beyond them Flor raced for the trees. Sam yelled again and slapped his horse on the rump. The horse stretched out. Sam's baby blue work hat blew off.

This was not going to end well. Frank thought about the P90 in the van, abandoned that idea, then loped for all he was worth down the trail after Sam and Flor.

By the time Flor reached the trees, Sam had cut the distance between the two of them by more than half. He was raised up a bit out of the saddle, riding like a pro.

Flor slowed when she got to the trees. Sam did not.

He caught up to her in the pines, grabbed the reins of her horse, and pulled back. The animals bumped each other and tossed their heads and slowed to a jumbled walk.

Flor yelled something in Spanish and struck Sam with her riding crop. She struck him again.

Sam winced, grabbed the riding crop.

Flor fought him.

The horses wheeled.

She let go of the crop. A moment later she held a revolver in her hand. She pointed it at Sam.

Sam tried to grab the gun, but he was too slow. She fired it right at him.

The muzzle flashed. The sound cracked through the trees. Loud enough to hear back at the house. Loud enough to hear for a couple of miles. The horses startled, jerked to the side. And Sam fell from his mount, dragging Flor with him.

They landed in a heap. The horses shied away, dragging their reins.

Lord, no, Frank thought. *Sam!*

He ran as fast as his dumb leg would allow and covered the last few yards of the open field and entered the pines.

Sam was trying to get up, holding his arm. Flor was on her hands and knees, looking for something. Then she saw it and rose unsteady to her feet.

Frank lengthened his stride. His tool belt bounced at his waist. His shin protested mightily. He was only a few dozen yards away.

Sam got to his feet, blood running down his arm.

Flor scrambled two paces and bent down to reach for her gun.

Frank lowered his shoulder and charged.

She came up with the revolver, wheeled it round. Then she heard Frank coming. She turned to face him, but he was already upon her. He struck her in a full-body tackle. She was a small thing. It was like tackling a grade-schooler, like taking down a bird.

The revolver flew out of her hands, and they slammed into the ground, his large bulk hammering her.

She cried out in pain.

Frank rolled her onto her stomach. Then he pulled the duct tape out of his belt and tore off the end. He brought both of her hands behind her back and wrapped the tape around them tightly four times. Then he rolled her over. Her eyes were full of anger and pain. She snarled at him, said something he thought might be Spanish but just as easily could have been Demon.

He tore off another strip of tape about six inches long and pressed it down over her mouth. Then he turned to Sam.

Sam was covering his upper arm, face twisted up in pain fear. His blood was soaking his shirt, dripping off his hand.

Frank ran over to him. "We got to get out of here."

As if in reply, the girl who Sam had pulled off the horse started shouting in Spanish through the pines. She was somewhere between Frank's location and the Goroza's, running for the house.

"She shot me!" Sam said.

"Let me see that," Frank said and pulled Sam's hand away. The blood welled up. But not as bad as it could have. The bullet had grazed him, cut along the outside and into the muscle.

Frank tore the hole in Sam's shirt wide. Tore the whole sleeve off. Then he wiped the wound, had Sam put some direct pressure on it with the torn sleeve, and then tore off a large section of duct tape.

Sam pulled the bloody sleeve away, and Frank applied the duct tape, trying to butterfly the wound shut. Then he tore off another piece and wrapped it round the other way. Duct tape had saved more than one man's life out on the front lines. That should hold until he could get Sam to a hospital. In the meantime, they had Flor.

Except they didn't. She had gotten to her feet and was running away.

Frank chased her down. Then he picked her up and tossed her over his shoulder.

"Get to the van!" he shouted.

They hustled back through the pines and out onto the grassy field, Sam holding his arm, Frank hobbling along with his load.

The girl was still yelling in the distance, but now men were yelling back.

Frank's leg was killing him. He walked-jogged the last few yards to the fence. Sam pressed the top wire down, and Frank stepped over.

Back at the Gorozas, an automobile engine roared to life. Then another.

"Get the side door open!" Frank said.

Sam climbed over the fence, up the shoulder, and rushed to the van. Frank followed behind. Sam flung the side door open. "I can't drive with this arm," he said.

"Put the keys on the seat!" Frank said and unloaded Flor onto the floor of the van.

Down the road, a black SUV came barreling out of the Goroza's long driveway and skidded onto the road.

Sam threw the keys on the front seat and ran around the front to the other side.

The SUV's motor roared, and the vehicle straightened out and headed toward them. One of the Goroza's goons hung out the passenger's window with something that looked like an AK-47. A moment later he started firing.

Didn't the idiot know he was as likely to hit his boss as one of them?

Bullets whizzed past, striking the van, thudding into the ground.

Maybe he didn't care. Maybe Flor wasn't the head of this organization. Or maybe he was just an idiot with a gun.

"Get in!" Frank roared. "Get in!"

Frank attempted to move Flor's legs and shut the door, but the moron in the SUV let off with another round that kicked up dust on the shoulder near Frank. They had to get out of here fast. He left Flor where she was, tore open the driver's door, and jumped in.

Sam hopped into the passenger's seat.

"The keys!" Frank yelled.

Sam pointed. "The seat!"

Frank fished the keys out from under his kiester, found the right one, and shoved it into the ignition.

A bullet zinged into the side of the van.

Frank turned the key. The van's engine started, warning tones ringing about the open doors. Then Frank threw it into drive and floored the accelerator.

The little minivan's engine roared. The van shot forward. The open side door rolled back in its track with a bang.

They shot down the road, picked up speed, then there was a thump, like something had fallen to the ground. Frank glanced in his driver's mirror and saw Flor Goroza tumbling on the asphalt behind him.

"She wriggled out!" Sam said.

27

Backup

FRANK BRAKED HARD. The anti-lock brakes kicked in and pulsed. The front of the car angled down. The sliding door flew forward in its track and slammed shut. The van stopped, and Frank threw it in reverse and floored it.

Flor climbed to her feet.

He had to hand it to her—she was one tough old bird. She began doing an old-lady jog back to the driveway, her hands still duct-taped behind her.

Beyond her, the SUV accelerated toward them. The idiot hanging out the window kept firing. One of his bullets shattered the minivan's back window, spilling glass shards into the van and onto the road. Another shot ricocheted off the ceiling and spidered the front windshield.

Frank continued in reverse. "Get the P90!" he ordered.

Sam reached between the seats to the back and picked up the submachine gun.

"Snug it up to your shoulder, more toward the center of the chest."

Sam brought it up, aimed the gun.

Frank lined the back of the minivan up with the SUV, pressed the gas, and, for the second time today, played chicken.

"Fire right at the bottom of the grill of that SUV!" he shouted. "Fire at the bumper!" He knew Sam would shoot high. Everyone did when they were learning. So if he told him to aim at the ground, Sam might put a few into the cab itself.

Sam said, "Where's the safety?"

"The selector's right by the trigger. Push it down. But don't go all the way; that's full auto."

The next moment there was a huge roar—a hailstorm-tin-roof-ear-blast; one long deafening drum roll of shots; fifty 5.7 millimeter narco killers singing out of the back end of the minivan, followed by a click.

"That was full auto," Frank said.

"Crap!" Sam said.

All the rounds in one go. And half had probably been put right through the roof of the minivan. Except the SUV suddenly careened off the road. It bounded off the shoulder at speed, crashed through the barbed wire, and slammed into a massive ponderosa pine tree. The SUV crumpled with a crunch of metal and glass. The tree shuddered. A moment later a number of pine cones the size of shoes rained down around the vehicle.

"Cartwright," Frank said. "You ride horses *and* shoot. Maybe you *are* the Lone Ranger."

Flor was still running back toward the driveway. She was making good time.

Frank continued in reverse, aimed for her, and then he gave the van some gas. She was only one reflector post away.

But then two more cars full of goons with guns came roaring down the driveway and skidded out onto the road. They straightened up and headed right for him.

"There's another magazine on the seat," Frank said.

Sam shifted around. "I don't see it. I don't see it."

Frank looked down. It was not there. All the accelerating and braking had flung it to the floor. "It's got to be under the seats!" he said.

Sam dropped down and started looking around, meanwhile the cars were coming. One was a Mercedes. The other was the cola-glass Nissan.

"Pinto," Frank asked. "Anymore vehicles?"

Pinto's voice came in with the roar of the Cessna. "No, they all piled into the SUV and the two behind you now."

"Roger," Frank said and floored it.

The minivan's motor whined in reverse. Frank aimed for the Nissan. Except the Nissan didn't want to play. It braked next to Flor. The back door flew open. A guy got out. Flor jumped in. The guy shut the door behind her, and the Nissan reversed and spun around and headed back for the house.

A moment later the Mercedes and the minivan flew past each other. The guy who had gotten out of the Nissan pulled a semi-automatic pistol out of his pants and started firing at Frank and Sam.

Frank kept it in reverse. He turned into the driveway, fully intending to grab Flor, but saw three men with assault rifles down at the end, standing in a line across the road, protecting the place.

Obviously, not all of them had piled into the vehicles.

The men parted for the Nissan.

Frank's heart sank. There went Tony's get out of jail free card.

The men raised their rifles.

Sam was scrabbling around on the floor by the back bench. "Ha!" he said and came up with the second magazine. "Got it!"

The men on the road opened fire.

The bullets whistled around the minivan. They punched holes in the back. One zoomed into the interior and tore the magazine right out of Sam's grip.

"Whoa!" Sam shouted and held his hand.

"We need some help down here!" Frank said.

"What?" Pinto said.

Frank threw the minivan into drive and floored it. "I was talking to God."

He careened back onto the road.

A bullet slammed into the side of the van. Another pinged off the engine block.

The van's motor whined.

The guys on the driveway kept firing.

Frank was devastated. He was angry. If he'd just grabbed Flor right when he'd taken the horse's halter, none of this would have happened!

"We've got company," Sam said.

Frank looked in the rearview mirror. The Mercedes they'd passed on the road had turned around and was coming after them.

Sam fetched the magazine from the floor and tried to fit it into the slot on top of the gun. "I can't get it it!" he said.

"Of course, not. A high-velocity round kind of has that effect on things. Can you get a round out?"

Sam struggled. "The thing won't go down." He banged it on the floor, but no bullets came out.

The minivan raced along the road. The guys in the Mercedes behind them rolled down their windows. They leaned out with their guns. They did not open fire. It appeared they were going to come along side, get close, trust the accuracy of point-blank range. A much better plan, especially if you sucked at shooting moving targets. Or maybe they wouldn't come alongside at all. Just move up close to the back end and shoot through the missing rear window.

Frank had the gas pedal against the floor. The speedometer showed eighty mph. Then eighty-five.

"Pinto," Frank said. "What's ahead of me?"

"Nothing. That road runs straight for five or ten miles."

"What are we going to do?" Sam yelled.

"I don't know," Frank said. "We need a gun."

"We got Cheerios and a bunch of idiot rocks," Sam said in disgust. Then he sat up straight. "We've got potatoes!"

"Vegetables aren't going to do much at this point," Frank said.

They were hosed. No question about it. Their only option now was to turn this thing into a demolition derby, but Frank had the funny feeling the guys behind weren't going to cooperate.

Sam leaned over the back bench and fished out the big white PVC tube with his good arm. Then he fished around some more and came up with a can of spray. He said, "You ever been hit by a potato going 250 miles per hour?"

Frank looked into the rearview mirror. "I don't believe I have."

"Why don't we see what an Idaho Russet can do," he said and reached down between his feet and came back up with the brown plastic bag of potatoes that had been sliding around since Sam first picked him up.

Up ahead the pines petered out and gave way to pure prairie. Behind them the Mercedes was coming up fast. Frank glanced at his speedometer. They were going 100. It appeared that's all this thing had in her on the flat.

They weren't going to outrun the Mercedes. And this was far too fast for any aggressive driving techniques. In a very short time they were going to have to slow down. Frank said, "If you're going to do anything, you'd better make it quick."

Sam tore open the bag and fetched a potato out. He crammed it into the mouth of the tube. Then he unscrewed the top of another tube attached below the main one and pulled out what looked like a long section of broomstick. He rammed the potato down with it, like a man loading a musket.

They sped down the road, the prairie fields flying past on both sides.

The Mercedes was only a few car lengths back and gaining.

Sam fiddled with the back end of the cannon, brought up his aerosol can.

"Lysol?" Frank asked.

"Nothing better," Sam said.

He sprayed the Lysol into a hole, fiddled with something again, then brought the cannon up with his good arm and laid it across the back seat.

One of the goons hung out of the Mercedes passenger window with what looked like a Mac10.

Sam turned a little knob. There was a thump from the spud cannon. A moment later something hit the hood of the Mercedes and careened out into the field.

The goon in the Mercedes let loose with his Mac10. Bangs and bullets and a few that plowed into the back of the van.

"Freaking Betty Crocker!" Sam cursed.

"You need something harder!" Frank shouted.

"I'm on it," Sam said, his voice full of anger.

Frank felt the steering get a bit squishy. One of those bullets had hit a tire; he was sure of it. He let off the gas. The guys hanging out the windows of the Mercedes had big grins on their faces. One of them flipped him off.

Laugh now, Frank thought.

Sam brought the cannon back down, grabbed another spud, then opened up a plastic ice cream bucket and pulled out something black and squarish about the size of a golf ball.

"Sam! We're running out of seconds."

"Just need a little bit of metamorphic," Sam said. He jammed the rock into one end of a spud, shoved the spud in the tube, rammed it home. He slid the cannon back up across the back of the bench, fiddled and did the Lysol thing.

The Mercedes was now close enough for the gunmen not to miss their shots, but far enough back to avoid him if he slammed on the brakes. So he'd have to slam them, put it in reverse, and ram them. Total long shot. No way was it going to work.

Sam sighted down the tube.

The gunmen took aim.

Sam twisted his little knob. The cannon thumped. The potato with its rock warhead flew out the back end of the van and smashed into the windshield of the car right in front of the driver. 250 miles an hour of rock backed up by Idaho potato. The windshield spidered into a hundred lines. Turned completely white.

The driver jerked the wheel; the Mercedes swerved.

One goon fell out and struck the road at speed. The other hung on for life.

Now was a good time, Frank thought. A very good time.

He hit the brakes. Not completely, but just enough.

The Mercedes rushed toward the back end of the van. The driver tried to swerve to avoid the crash. He overcorrected, sideswiped the van. Frank gave him a nudge.

The Mercedes careened off the road. It went down the shoulder in a cloud of dust, fishtailed, then came back up again at a bad angle.

It was going to T-bone the van.

Frank stood on the brakes with both feet, shoved the pedal to the floor. The front of the van tilted down; the anti-brakes pulsed. Sam came flying from the back seat with the spud gun and smashed into the console.

The Mercedes hit the asphalt ahead of them almost sideways. It had probably been going somewhere around eighty miles per hour. But asphalt doesn't give like dirt and grass. The law of inertia exerted itself, and the Mercedes rolled. It bounced, caught air. A huge leap. Rolled again, tumbled, glass and plastic flying everywhere.

One of the passengers flew out a window, the force tossing him in a high arc, his legs and arms wide. He sailed forty feet above the ground, out over the road, over the barbed-wire fence, and into the field. He crashed to the ground at a fatal angle on his back and head that made Frank wince.

The car crashed down the shoulder, rolled again, and landed on its wheels straddling the fence.

Frank and Sam came to a stop.

Sam fell back from the console.

"You okay?" Frank asked.

"Holy crap," Sam said.

"I'm going to go check it out," Frank said. "We need to change the tire. Get the jack."

"That guy in the field," Sam said in shock and horror. "Did you see him, his back . . ."

"That man wasn't wearing his safety belt," Frank said. "You can get a ticket for that around here."

"Holy crap," Sam said.

"Nice work with the spudzooka," Frank said.

"Holy crap," Sam said again.

Both of them got out of the minivan. Sam took in the bullet holes and broken glass.

Out on the road, the guy who'd been the first to fall out was moaning, but not doing much else. Frank ran down to the Mercedes and looked inside. The airbags had deployed, but it hadn't saved the occupants. The driver slumped over the wheel, his face a bloody mess. The one guy in the back who hadn't been thrown was upside down. Frank looked for the guns, but didn't see them. He turned. The guy in the field wasn't moving. He wasn't going to move. Not lying at that angle.

Frank took stock. Carmen had spotted twelve men. There had been two in the SUV that crashed into the tree. Four in the Mercedes. That meant the Goroza's had six guys back at the house. And now they were all on their guard. All armed to the teeth. On the other hand, Frank had Sam, the spudzooka, and a whole sack of potatoes with optional rock warheads. Somehow he just didn't think that was going to cut it. Even if Pinto turned his Cessna into a dive bomber and dropped pipe wrenches on their heads.

"Carmen," Frank said. "Report."

"José and Hector are on their phones."

They were probably calling in reinforcements.

"Another man, he looks like a brother, is talking to Flor and the girl who was riding with her. Two guys are watching the driveway. The other sentry is up and watching the back."

"Okay," Frank said. "It's way too hot to touch right now. But that could change in five hours. At three a.m. they might think they are safe. Carmen, you keep an eye out. Pinto, how much gas do you have left?"

The sound of the Cessna joined the call. "I'm good for a while. But you've got company."

"How many?"

"One car coming south along your road toward the Goroza's. It's a cop, lights flashing."

Frank thought about this. There was nowhere to hide along this stretch of road. So the cop would show up, freak, call in backup. Frank would tell him that there were armed men who had shot at him at the house down the road. The cop would proceed and tie up the whole house. He and the others would do a full search. He'd find AK-47s. Maybe other stuff. Who knew what was hidden in the house and vehicles?

But even if they took the Gorozas to jail forever, that wouldn't get him Tony back.

"Frank," Carmen said. "I see him. I see Tony!"

"At the house?"

"They've brought him out. They're pointing to documents on the table, shouting at him. They're handling him rough. He doesn't look so good."

Tony was at the house.

This changed everything. He wanted to shout hallelujah. "Roger," he said. "Do you see Ed?"

"No."

But Tony was there. And the police were just a few miles away. In fact, Frank could see the flashing lights now. Operation Tony was about to take a positive turn. "Sam, you need to call 911. Conference them in. You need to do it now."

There was no response.

"Sam." Frank looked back. Sam was on one knee behind the van, the jack and lug wrench lying on the asphalt. "Sam!"

But Sam did not respond. Anything at all could have happened when he slammed into the console. He might have broken a rib, punctured his lung.

The cop car was coming fast. Frank hurried back toward the van as fast as his leg would allow.

The cops reached the scene before he did. They never turned on the siren. Just braked hard. The passenger door flew open and a young blond cop with a weak moustache jumped out with a shotgun and pointed it at Frank. "Get down on the ground!" he roared. "Get down on the ground! Get down on the ground!"

Frank held his hands up to show he wasn't armed. "There are men with AK-47s just down the road. They tried to kill us."

"Get down on the ground!" the younger cop shouted.

"Officer," Sam said and crawled out doggie-style from behind the van. His face was a little pale. He was probably experiencing some mild shock.

The young guy swung his shotgun and pointed it at him. "Get down!" His freckled face was red.

Sam raised a hand in submission.

"On your face! Spread eagle!"

Sam lay down on the asphalt.

The older, heavy-set cop opened his door and slid out. He wore those prescription glasses that darkened in the sun and lightened indoors. They were a light amber, halfway between light and dark. "This is just procedure, boys," he said. "No need for alarm. I'm sure you understand."

Frank got a sudden bad feeling.

"You," the big one said and pointed at Frank. "Get over next to him. Once we've secured this area, we'll take your statements and sort it all out."

Frank said, "There are six armed men down the road."

The big cop nodded. "That's what you said."

"Move!" the young one shouted.

Frank did not like the big guy's nonchalance. You see five dead people and a minivan shot to pieces, you don't mosey about. He remembered what Carmen had said about trusting American police—how had these cops gotten here so fast? Frank's bad feeling went from a breeze to a tornado with full-blown purple and black thunderheads. But Frank didn't have anywhere to go. If he charged, the young guy would shoot him down for sure. And what was Sam going to do?

"Pinto," Frank said.

The young one pointed at Frank. "I think that one's going to cause too many problems."

"You going to cause us problems?" the big cop asked Frank.

"No," Frank said, looking for anything that he could use to cause a problem. But there was nothing, so he walked over to Sam, knelt down, and lay spread eagle on the asphalt.

The younger cop walked in to cover him with the shotgun, but he stayed far enough away to avoid any sudden moves.

"Put your hands behind your back," the big guy said.

"Behind your back!" the young one repeated.

Frank moved his hands behind his back. "Tell Yosemite Sam there he can stop yelling."

The sound of the Cessna came on the call. "What's going on?" Pinto asked.

"Mayday," Frank whispered.

"Be quiet!" the young one said.

The big man knelt down behind Frank. He cuffed one wrist, then the other. Frank hated the hard metal. Hated that click. Memories of cement walls and the smell of prison hit Frank like a hammer.

The big officer moved to Sam and cuffed him. Then the two officers searched them both. They took the BlueTooth units and the phones. They took Sam's wallet and change.

The big officer got up, breathing a bit hard. "Okay, boys. On your feet. Time to get into the car."

Frank and Sam climbed to their feet.

Frank said, "I think one of those guys might still be alive."

"Could be," the big officer said. "Those types are hard to kill. Kind of like cockroaches."

Sam said, "They were chasing us. Shot my van to pieces. You're going to need to call for backup."

The younger cop with the shotgun grinned.

"Son," the big cop said, all friendly like. "We *are* the backup." Then he opened the rear door of his car. "Watch your head."

28

Gorozas

FRANK GOT INTO the car behind the driver's seat. The back bench was a hard plastic, baby blue, three-seater that looked like it might have been super-sized from some toy collection. The plastic, of course, made it easier to clean when dirt bags vomited or pissed or defecated in the back. It was not very comfortable, especially not with your hands behind your back and a workman's tool belt around your waist.

There was a wall behind the front seat. The bottom half was metal, backed by steel plate. The top half was split in two with thick bulletproof plexiglass behind the driver and a square of steel mesh behind the passenger's seat. There was no way to unlock the doors from the inside.

The cops escorted Sam to the other side and shut him in. Then the two of them got back in the car, the big guy behind the wheel and the younger guy in the passenger's seat.

"We're going to take a drive," the older cop said. He started the engine. Normally, a police officer would immediately radio in the accident and the people apprehended. This officer did not.

Sam looked surprisingly calm despite his bloody arm.

Frank said, "You okay?"

Sam looked up. "I've got a feeling this isn't going to end well."

"We're going to be fine," Frank said.

"You sure are," the young cop said.

That weak scrub of hair on his upper lip was beginning to really annoy Frank. "You get that hair above your lip off the floor of a barber shop?" Frank asked.

"What did you say?"

"I think you boys should call this in."

The blond cop shook his head like Frank was a bit slow in the head. The older cop put the patrol car into gear and slowly drove away from the wreck. He drove down the road right back to the Goroza's house, slowed, turned in the driveway, and headed down all leisurely, like he was stopping by for lemonade.

Two of the Goroza's men were standing partway down the drive with their assault rifles. They parted, and the older cop buzzed his window down, then slowed and stopped between them. He looked up at the guy on his side and said, "We have two packages for Mrs. Goroza."

The guy looked in the back.

"We won't be long," the older cop said.

The man stood back and waved them on. He brought a radio up, clicked it, and reported it in Spanish.

The big cop let off the brake, and they slowly rolled down the driveway. Frank figured the older guy was the one who'd been corrupted first. It took some cash to payoff a law enforcement officer. Took less if that officer had been foolish with his money. Frank figured the older one had been foolish. Figured maybe he'd gotten sick of trying to rise up in the ranks. Then he'd gone and corrupted Yosemite Sam's pasty blond brother.

The older cop parked the patrol car in front of the garage. Then he and his partner got out. The big guy had a nice name tag above his right breast pocket. White letters on a black background that said R. Lyman. Officer Lyman walked around the garage to the front door. Yosemite Sam's brother stayed by the car.

Frank thought Sam might break down at this point. Thought he might be thinking of his wife and young children. Thinking about what might happen to the wonderful life he'd had ahead of him right up to the point that he'd gotten on that horse and chased Flor down.

Frank said, "This is going to get a little rough. But it ain't over until the fat lady sings."

Sam said, "Pinto's got a camera. I hope he's catching all of this."

"You ever done any fighting?" Frank asked. "Any martial arts in your youth maybe?"

"I have some Krav Maga DVDs."

"Some late night infomercial aerobics routine?"

"It's totally legit." Sam sighed. "But all they've been doing is gathering dust. I only watched one."

"Well, think about what you learned on that one." The truth was that watching some DVD could never train you in self-defense, but Sam didn't need to hear that right now. "Do you hear the fat lady singing?"

"I do not," Sam said.

"Then this isn't over, is it," Frank said. "You stay alert and keep your eyes on me. If I say Zulu, I want you to go all Mossad. You get as Krav Maga as you can be. You fight like Satan and his minions are upon you, because, in fact, they will be. And they will not take prisoners. It's us or them. On Zulu, the Cookie Man goes Jekyll and Hyde. Do you hear me?"

"Loud and clear," Sam said.

"All right," Frank said. "Now run that DVD through your mind."

Sam's heartbeat was racing. Frank could see his pulse banging away in the vein on his neck. But Sam had shown some mettle. He'd shown a lot of mettle. Frank hoped he could hold it together just a little longer.

He didn't expect Sam to go commando. He might not land a blow. But he could distract them. And when seconds mattered, a distraction could make the difference between walking out alive and having your head sawn off with a bowie knife.

Morale wasn't everything in battle, but it was close. You could have the best weapon systems, the most highly-trained men, but if you lost morale, the whole thing was going to swirl the drain. Frank had his dreams. He had his fears, mostly for Sam and Tony. But now was not the time to dream dreams or entertain fears. "Now is the time to focus on the mission," Frank said. "On nothing but the mission. And the mission here is to find Tony, destroy any opposition, and then get the heck out of Dodge."

"What about those children?"

"Keep it simple, Sam. We can help them better when we go to the cops with our tale and Pinto's photos. Now run that DVD."

Frank ran his own movie. He was going to require some mobility with his hands. Frank wriggled on the Barbie bench, brought his cuffed wrists down to his feet, struggle a bit, and then brought them up in front of him.

Sam tried to follow his lead, but the man was a little too big around the waist to fold as flatly as the space required, and neither his tool belt nor his injured arm was helping.

"You're all right," Frank said. "I bet the cops are going to want their cuffs back. I'm betting they take them off."

Officer R. Lyman came back around the garage. His light sensitive glasses had grown a few shades darker. He and Yosemite Sam's cousin ordered Frank and Sam out of the back seat. Then they marched them around the house to the patio.

The patio was sheltered by a high roof. It commanded a fine view of the property, which included stables, another barn-looking building, a bunk house, the riding corral ringed by nice white-post fence, and a swimming pool enclosed by a white, wrought-iron one.

On the patio, Flor Goroza sat at a table, her face and arms starting to show some very nice bruises. She was smoking a cigarette, blowing the smoke out her nostrils. Some gauze was wrapped around an arm that she must have scraped in her tumble.

There were three men with her. Two more men stood back by the sliding door to the kitchen. They were tatted up, and their heads were shaven.

One of the men with her was José, Flor's dried-out, cigarette-ash husband. The next was Hector. He stood about six feet, three inches. He could have played football. He certainly weighed well into the 200s. His dark hair was raked back. A smile played across his face.

The third man sat at the table; he had a strong familial resemblance to Hector and Jesus. He was older than Hector, not anywhere close to José. He was shorter, dressed in a suit with a white shirt that was open at the collar, displaying a nice gold necklace. He had the air of an exacting man who was used to being obeyed.

Frank did the math. Two out on the drive, two by the kitchen door, and the three Gorozas—that was seven. Plus wasn't there a sentry watching the back? That could be eight, which meant that Carmen hadn't seen everyone, or hadn't counted them right.

Flor turned to Officer Lyman and said, "Leave them here."

Officer Lyman replied, "Let me suggest you send someone to clean up that mess on the road before it's called in. You wouldn't want it tracked back."

"Wouldn't you be the one to respond?"

"You want paramedics and another squad car and a fire truck? As good as I am, it's highly unlikely I'll be able to make four bodies and two cars vanish before their eyes."

Flor looked over at the third man sitting at the table. "Amador," she said. "Take care of this."

Amador nodded his head at one of the men back by the house. The man immediately opened the sliding door and disappeared inside.

Officer Lyman took a handkerchief out of one pocket. He wiped the cuffs. Then he pulled his cuff key out of another pocket, wiped it, and set the key on the table next to Flor. He folded the handkerchief and shoved it back into his pocket. "Good day," he said. "Officer West and I now have an appointment with a doughnut." Then he turned around and walked back toward his car. He saluted Frank and Sam as he passed. "Have fun in Hell, boys. Save me a seat at the sauna."

Flor fingered the key, then slipped it in her leather vest pocket. "My son is dead."

"That was Ed's fault."

Anger filled her face. "I don't want to hear your lies."

"It's the truth."

Amador reached behind him and came up with a wooden baseball bat. "We'll have the truth soon enough. You're going to tell me who killed my little brother."

"Not here," Flor said. "It will never come out of the stone."

"You give me my nephew," Frank said, "and I walk away. This is your last chance."

Flor's face pulled back into a threatening glower, showing her teeth, "You killed my son, then come in here making demands?"

"Ed brought me in. It is Ed who got your son killed."

She stood up and spit in Frank's face. Then she stepped back and sicced her boys on him with a nod. Hector came at him from one angle, Amador the other. Frank backed up and ran into Sam. Then Hector lunged.

Frank tried to dodge, but Amador jammed him in the gut with the end of the baseball bat.

Frank gasped.

"Hold him," Amador said.

Hector grabbed Frank. Hector was not only big, but he was also strong. He locked his arms through Frank's elbows and then behind Frank's back.

Frank struggled to free himself.

"Hold still!" Amador said and put down his bat.

Frank raised his foot to stamp down on Hector's, but Hector was wise to that move, and Frank missed.

Then Amador pulled back his fist and struck Frank in the jaw with a huge right hook.

Frank's head whipped to the side. He tried to wrench away, but Amador came in with a left jab straight to his eye. He connected. Pain exploded in Frank's face, and his head jerked back. Amador wound up and went for Frank's nose.

Frank turned his head, letting his cheek bone take part of the blow. Amador connected. Pain shot through Frank's nose. Blood whipped out, a drop spattering the light stone floor and another staining Flor's shirt.

Flor looked down. "Gah! I said the pig shed."

Amador struck Frank once more in the gut. His fist felt like an iron post.

Frank tried to struggle free, but Hector held him fast.

"Give me my nephew," Frank said.

Flor rolled her eyes in disgust and exhaled two streams of smoke out her nose. "Get them out of here."

Amador picked up his bat. "Tell us what we want to know, and maybe we'll go easy on you."

Yeah, because drug cartels were known for their gentlemanly sense of fair play.

Hector released Frank and shoved him forward.

Frank turned. "You do not want to do this."

Hector pulled a hand gun from the back of his waistband and motioned with it toward a narrow walkway at the back of the patio that ran alongside the pool fence. "Move."

"Where's my nephew?"

"You'll be together soon enough," Hector said.

Out in front of the house, the patrol car made its way back down the drive. A moment later the Goroza's cleanup crew followed in an SUV.

Frank turned to the walkway.

The pig shed was most likely part of the barn that stood farther out, across from the corral.

"So what happens in the pig shed?" Frank asked.

"What do you think, pendejo?" Hector said with a smile.

"Cupcake parties?" Frank offered.

"We slaughter the family pig."

"The shed doesn't sound like such a good place for a pig." Didn't sound like a good place for Frank or Sam either, but the patio wasn't the place to fight. Too open. However, the walkway that ran alongside the pool fence was not. That nice piece of ground was just over three feet wide, flanked by the fence on one side and bushes on the other. It was just a little bit wider than a hallway in a normal house, which would force them all to walk single file.

Frank marched to the narrow walkway, making sure to get there first. Amador filed in behind him with his bat. Next came Sam, then Hector, then José bringing up the rear. Flor stayed back on the patio with her cigarette.

Frank could feel his lip swelling, his eye puffing. The swelling was already making it so he couldn't open his eyelid all the way. He felt his aching teeth with his tongue. Amador packed a wallop.

The narrow walkway was paved with stones. Not cement look-a-likes but real slabs of red sandstone. It went well with the line of red-orange daylilies that grew just inside the pool fence. It went well with the white fence. Somebody had done some color coordination.

Frank took a few steps down the path, then slowed down just a little. He felt the line stack up behind him.

Amador rammed the end of the baseball bat into his back. "Move."

Frank flinched. He looked around and said, "This is quite the place."

"Amador," Hector said. "I believe he's trying to chat us up, break the ice. Maybe he's got something to offer."

"You got something to offer?" Amador asked.

"Let me think," Frank said.

"He's going to think," Amador said.

"Better be quick," Hector said. "It only takes so many blows to the head, and then the brain doesn't think very well anymore."

The narrow walkway was about twenty-five feet long. It didn't feel like such a confined space because the bushes and pool fence were relatively open and only chest high. But that feeling of freedom was an illusion.

One of the fundamentals of military doctrine was to seek to use a more powerful force to engage a less powerful one. In this case, the enemy had more numbers. So the easiest way to eliminate that advantage was to line them up so you only had to fight them one at a time.

Frank looked ahead at the pig barn. He figured now was probably as good as it was going to get. He slowed again.

"Move," Amador said again and popped him in the back of the head with his bat. The blow was hard enough to make Frank's jaw clack.

Frank took a step forward, then used that leg to pivot and spin around. He didn't go for the bat. He lunged instead, his two hands locked together, and speared Amador in the throat with his knuckles.

"Zulu!" Frank shouted.

Amador's eyes went wide. He released the bat, letting it clatter to the ground, and clutched at his throat.

Hector shoved Sam out of the way and aimed his gun at Frank.

Frank pushed the wheezing Amador at Hector.

Hector pulled the trigger. Fire shot out the muzzle, and the bullet took Amador in the chest. Then it took some of what should have been inside and blew it out his back. A smattering of blood struck Frank's arm.

Amador went down to his knees, opening a clear shot for Hector.

Hector's face screwed up in rage. He yelled.

Frank lunged out of the way.

Hector fired and missed.

Frank pivoted and sprang at Hector, but his foot landed on the baseball bat and rolled underneath him, causing him to stumble.

Hector swung his gun over, took careful aim.

Then Sam got his Dr. Jekyll on and came flying at Hector from the side, yelling like a mad man, hands cuffed behind his back. He barreled into the big man with his shoulder, knocking him one step to the side.

Hector turned to strike Sam, but Sam arched back like a snake and slammed forward with his forehead into Hector's face. Right into his mouth.

Hector stumbled back into the pool fence.

Sam charged, drew back and struck again. This time his forehead connected with Hector's nose. The nose folded over to one side, and blood began to pour out like water.

Sam pulled back, struck again. Pulled back, struck.

Hector lunged to the side to escape the mad attack.

Frank snatched up the baseball bat with his cuffed hands.

Sam charged Hector again, but Hector side-stepped and clocked Sam in the side of the head with his pistol, knocking Sam to his knees. Hector pointed the gun at him.

Frank rushed forward. Brought the bat up and around to chop down in a two-handed swing that stuck Hector's gun arm just above the wrist. The blow made a loud woody thump, hammering the arm down and knocking the gun into the red-orange lilies and mulch.

Hector cried out and grabbed his wrist.

Frank pulled the bat back in the best two-handed grip he could manage and swung for the benches. He swung for Hector's head.

It was a home run.

Hector crumpled to the ground.

José ran for the gun. He tried to leap over Sam, but Sam struggled up and tangled himself in José's legs in a sort of body block.

José crashed into the paving stones. He rose, but Frank leapt forward and punted José in the gut.

José oofed; his eyes went wide.

Frank kicked him again. Hard. Then he reached down and picked up Hector's nine millimeter Glock. Same model as the one Jesus had.

He searched Hector for another weapon. Searched Amador. Found nothing. Searched José, but José wouldn't have been going for the gun if he had his own.

Frank said to Sam, "Don't let him get up." Then he walked back to the patio.

Flor was on her feet, alarm all over her face, her cigarette still in hand. "Ricky!" she screamed. "Ricky!"

Frank raised the Glock. "Give me the key," he said.

She turned and ran for the sliding door.

29

Tony

FRANK DID NOT shoot her. He needed one of these dirt bags alive so they could tell him where Tony was. So he fired a warning shot, shattering the glass door, sending shards to the patio and kitchen tile.

Flor squeaked but kept running.

Frank went after her, but she didn't make it to the patio door. Instead, she tripped one of the other chairs that had been brought out for the meeting they'd been holding, stumbled into a gas grill, and then Frank was on her, bad leg, broken nose, and burning rib cage.

He grabbed her by the hair with both cuffed hands then swept her feet out from underneath her with a booted sweep kick.

She dropped to the patio floor.

Frank planted his knee in her back, searched her quickly for obvious weapons and found none.

"Sam!" he shouted. "Get over here!" He brought the Glock up and scanned the pool, corral, and immediate areas around the fields and barns for any threats. He saw none and turned back to the house.

Sam ran onto the patio.

Frank laid his gun on the table, well out of Flor's reach, then searched her vest pocket. He pulled out the cuff key. "Come here," he said to Sam.

Sam walked over, turned his back to Frank, and presented his cuffed hands. Frank unlocked him.

Sam rubbed his wrists, then took the key and uncuffed Frank.

"What do you think? One or two more goons?"

Sam looked around. "I don't see a soul."

It was true. Save for the ostriches and horses out in their fields, nothing moved. But the old bag had been calling for Ricky. "Watch the house and those buildings," Frank said. Then he turned to Flor. "Where's my nephew?"

"I don't know about your nephew."

Frank took her wrist and twisted it painfully behind her. She cried out.

"We saw him. Where is he?"

"You're going to pay. You have no idea."

"I think I do. I hung out with your kind of people for six years."

He twisted her arm harder.

"He's in the cellar," she spat.

"You're going to show me the way." Frank yanked her wrists behind her back and put the cuffs on her. Then he hauled her to her feet.

"I want to see my boys. I want to see José."

Frank turned to Sam. "How's Hector doing?"

"Not so well."

Frank said, "He's not doing well, Flor. He shot Amador. Shot his own brother." He said to Sam, "Take your pair of cuffs and handcuff José's wrist to Hector's ankle. That way we can be sure both are still around ten minutes from now when Flor goes to visit them."

Frank held Flor by her arm and watched the area around the house while Sam ran back to the walkway. He swung José's leg closer to Hector and cuffed them together. He jogged back and said, "It barely fit around his ankle."

"Is he dead?"

"I don't think so," Sam said.

"There," Frank said to Flor. "After you take me to Tony, maybe we'll let you make a 911 call. Maybe you won't lose all three sons on the same day."

Flor's anger was all shot through with worry. Frank wondered how such a monster had any feelings at all.

She led them out to the stables. Around back was a shed. The shed had a padlock on it, but the lock was hanging open. Sam removed the lock and opened the doors. There were bags of fertilizer and some kind of feed. At the back end, a wooden door had been set into the floor. It didn't have a knob. Only a handle and a huge sliding bolt that secured it to the metal frame. Sam slid the bolt back, then pulled the door up to reveal a set of wooden stairs going down into the dark. They were narrow and steep.

Frank spotted an electrical switch on the wall above the door with a hose of aluminum housing running into the ground. He flipped the switch and a light turned on in the room below. Frank gave Flor to Sam and walked down the narrow steps.

Tony sat against one wall on a bench much like the one in the house they'd been held captive. His face was puffy and bruised all over, but he was alive. He struggled to his feet. On the dirty cement floor lay three zip-ties. Two looked like they'd been busted, Frank-style.

"Hey, buddy," Frank said.

Tony's shoulders slumped in relief, and then his face scrunched up like he was going to cry.

Frank went to him and took him in a large, but gentle embrace. "You're going to be all right." He stroked his hair. "Thank the Lord God. You're going to be all right."

"They've got those kids in the bunk house."

"Okay, we'll go up and see what we can do."

"Did you get Ed?"

"I didn't see him."

"He's here."

Frank said, "We're going to go up, head for the driveway, and ride out in one of the cars there. We're going to call this in. We can use the Evil Queen's phone. I think I'm going to duct tape her to the fence."

He and Tony walked back to the stairway. Frank put his foot on the first step. At the top of the stairs, Sam was facing the entrance of the small building with both hands raised in the air like he was being robbed. Flor was nowhere to be seen.

Frank froze.

Tony ran into him. "Sorry," he said.

Frank motioned for him to be silent. There was only one reason why Sam would be reaching for the stars.

"Frankie," Ed called out. "We know you're down there. Come on up. We need to have us a chat."

Frank's mind raced. How many of them were there? How many had guns? Where was their exact placement? He slowly moved up the stairs, taking them two at a time, placing his feet at the edges to minimize squeaking. He reached the sixth stair, keeping himself low, keeping his head below the line of the floor above him.

"Jockstrap," Ed called all friendly. "We can work this out."

Frank popped his head up and then ducked back down. There were three of them just inside the shed, the sunny dirt lane at their backs. Two had assault rifles. They might be the two that had been in the driveway, although Frank had thought they went to clean up the crash site. They might have been two that were watching the back of the property. They might have been Ed's men. It didn't matter. They were standing just inside the shed by the doors. Flor was standing with them, the one guy working on her cuffs.

"Looks like you've got yourself cornered," Ed said. "Ran yourself right into a box. Pretty much like I thought you would."

Frank moved back to the base of the stairs. It would indeed be foolish to try to shoot it out with them from there.

"You know, you owed me a favor. Then you got out and turned your back on me. I was coming to give you another chance. Forgive us our debts, as we forgive our debtors. Me and you, like old times."

"There never were any old times," Frank said.

He walked back into the room, taking little steps, heel to toe, to avoid any sound. He silent-walked past the restraint bench Tony had been sitting on and stopped about three feet from the back of the room and looked up at the naked floor boards and the spiderwebs clinging to their corners.

"I talked to management," Ed said. "I was looking out for you. Flor was willing to take an eye and a limb of your choice. We might have to

304 · John D. Brown

up that now, but your buddy, Mr. Sam there, and Tony can walk away. There doesn't have to be any blood. Come on up, Frank. Be a man and pay your debts."

The words of a psychopathic two-headed snake.

One of the men above took a step. Frank pegged his position. He pulled the Glock out of his pocket. Held it up and quietly released the magazine. He needed to know exactly how many shots he had left. There were little holes in the side of the magazine. A Glock 19 with a standard magazine held fifteen rounds. But the magazine hadn't been full when Hector shot his brother. It looked like Frank was down to nine shots. Not a lot for a shoot-out.

He slid the magazine back in place. It locked with a tiny click.

Ed raised his voice. "Frank, I'm starting to get impatient. Get up here now."

The man above Frank moved again. The boards creaked.

Frank pointed the Glock right where he thought the guy was. Then he pulled the trigger three times. Three bangs, three muzzle flashes, three holes in the subfloor in a line spaced about five inches apart.

A man cried out.

Frank ran for the stairs.

The men above shouted angrily, then let loose with their guns, shooting into the floor. The sound of the shots thundered in the shed like the world was coming apart. Dust and splinters rained down into the room. The bullets smacked into the concrete below.

Frank reached the stairs. Sam was huddled off to the side behind a wheelbarrow that had been stood on its end.

The deafening barrage continued.

Frank leapt up the stairs three at a time, his gun up and close in a two-handed grip, not worrying about the noise because nobody could hear anything but the cracking guns. He kept low until he was almost to the top.

One of Ed's gunmen ran out of rounds, and the noise dropped.

Frank popped up and extended his gun.

The men looked up.

Frank aimed at the man still shooting, pulled. The gun banged and kicked. He aimed, pulled, and the gun banged and kicked again. The two shots nailed the guy in his chest. He stumbled back. Frank swung his aim onto the second man.

The second man held a spare magazine in his hand and obviously knew he didn't have the time to shove it home because he charged Frank with a yell.

Frank aimed, pulled. The gun banged. He aimed, pulled, and the gun banged again. The second man crashed into a shelf containing bottles of pesticide, then fell to the floor, the bottles falling on top of him.

Ed pointed his gun at Frank. He stood at the mouth of the shed about fifteen feet away. "Drop it!" he shouted.

Frank did not drop his gun.

"Kill him!" Flor snarled. She was standing back from the mouth of the shed behind Ed and to the right. In the direct sunlight she looked like a hag with blue eye shadow.

Ed's face was all screwed up in a rage. "You stupid mother. This is *your* fault. You should have just given me your car."

"Kill him," Flor said through gritted teeth.

Ed fired three times. Three loud bangs. Three bright muzzle flashes.

Frank aimed. Pulled the trigger.

The gun banged and kicked. Ed rocked back a step. Blood blossomed on his chest. He looked down, felt his chest, and pulled a bloody hand away. "Frank," he said, like being shot was a surprise. He tried to bring his gun up again.

Frank pulled the trigger again. The gun banged, and the second shot took Ed a few inches from the first.

Ed's face screwed up in pain and dismay. He dropped his gun. His legs buckled underneath him, and he fell to his knees on the floor.

Frank walked forward, his gun trained on Ed the whole time.

"Buddy," Ed said and struggled for breath.

"I told you not to mess with my journey, Ed. I told you not to mess with Tony."

"I saved your life," Ed said. "We were brothers."

"We were never anything of the sort."

Flor fired a pistol. The round took Frank in his ribs. The sound, the pain—it sent a shock through him. He lost his grip on his gun, and it thumped to the floor.

She was holding a petite .22 caliber revolver. Where she'd pulled it from, Frank couldn't guess. Some gun owners scoffed at the small .22 caliber, but let them take a shot in the side and see how innocuous they thought it was then. It felt like someone has sliced his insides with a knife. And if she'd hit an artery, he'd be joining Ed real soon.

She pointed the revolver at his center mass. She was too close to miss. Too far away for him to reach her before she pulled the trigger. Furthermore, there was a riding lawn mower in his way. She'd get another couple of rounds off easily before he would be able to grab her.

"Ricky!" she yelled.

Frank was going to have to charge her or dive for his gun. And do it all with a sharp pain running through his side like a shard of glass. He set himself, and then it was too late because Ricky finally showed. He was of average height wearing sunglasses and a loose silk shirt with a bright floral print on it. Another son or Flor's bodyguard? He held a nice nine millimeter. He pointed it at Frank.

"Ed's right," Flor said. "I'm not going to kill you. I'm going to flay you alive. And then I'm going to flay your nephew."

Ricky took aim at Frank's knees.

A shot rang out from the yard, somewhere behind Flor and Ricky.

Ricky jerked, stumbled forward, dropped his gun.

Out in the yard Carmen walked into view. She held an AK-47 rifle to her shoulder, pointing it at Flor. She must have taken it from the guys in the SUV that had barreled into the tree. "Don't move," she said.

Ricky moved; she swung the rifle and shot him again. This time he went all the way down.

Carmen turned the gun on Flor.

The witch of Lullaby Lane glanced about like she might run, but saw it was hopeless. She dropped her little revolver and raised her hands in the air. "Don't shoot!" she cried. "Don't shoot!"

Frank picked up his gun and winced at the pain in his side. He could drop her. One bullet was all it would take. He had two just waiting. He might have three.

"Sam," he called. "Are you okay?"

No response.

Frank's ears were still ringing from all the shooting. "Sam!"

"I'm okay," Sam said.

"Come take these guns." Frank kicked Ed's gun away because even though he was down, Ed was not dead yet. And sometimes dying men surprised you.

Sam got up and moved forward. "Holy crap," he said.

"Tony!" Frank called.

"I'm coming," he called from the room below.

Carmen walked up to Flor and leveled the rifle at point-blank range.

"I've got money," Flor said. "I can pay you. What do you want?"

"I don't want your filthy money," Carmen said.

"You want a piece of the action? There's a lot of money to be made." She looked over at Frank. "We ship a lot of product. I can give you a territory. You're obviously far more capable than Ed."

"Get down on the ground," Carmen said.

"I'm offering you a fortune!"

"Down!"

Flor knelt.

Carmen said, "Eight years ago you visited a little town in Monterrey. You took my sister. And then you killed her."

"I never killed anyone."

"You brought her north, promising a princess American life. And then you killed her."

Flor narrowed her eyes in disgust. "Nothing in life is free. I offered her a chance if she would work hard. A chance to have what I have. You want something, you have to fight for it. That's what I did. That's what everyone does. That's life. She was not a fighter."

"On your belly," Carmen said.

Flor narrowed her eyes in disgust. "You think you can kill all these men and not rouse the anger of their brothers?" She looked at Frank. "They're going to come after you. The organization will come after you. You're going to be taken out with the garbage."

"They can send all the garbage men they want," Frank said. "Now get on the ground."

Flor lay face down on the dirt. "I can give you protection."

"Turn your face this way," he said.

She complied.

"Listen to me," she said.

Frank pulled the duct tape from his belt. His side cut him with every move. It was making his eyes sting. But he ignored the pain, ripped off a nice big strip of tape, and sealed her mouth shut.

He sat back. "I think that's the best thing I've done all day."

"What are we going to do with her?" Sam asked.

"We're going to bind her wrists." He motioned at Tony to come forward. "Wrap her up tight."

Blood trickled down his side. He could feel it gathering at his belt. He reached over and gingerly felt the wound. "Gah," he said in frustration and anger. He'd gone all tunnel vision and ignored Flor. It was a beginner's mistake.

Tony came forward and took the tape and began to bind Flor's wrists. When he finished, Frank pulled up the side of his shirt. His side looked terrible; it was scraped and raw with huge dark bruising from his tumble on the snowmobile. Just up from the bottom of the rib cage, the bullet had made a small bloody hole. "Get a strip over this."

"Ooh," Tony groaned in sympathy.

"Come on," Frank said, knowing a tape bandage wasn't going to fix it. The round had hit him in the ribs, where all the vital organs were. Someone was going to have to open him up to stop the leaks there.

Tony carefully smoothed a patch of silver tape over the wound.

Sam walked over to Ed and felt his pockets. He found Frank's red phone in Ed's vest. He found his own phone in Ed's pants pocket. He leaned over and looked Ed in the face. "Not my phone," he said. "Not my wife, and not my friends." Then he caught a whiff of Ed's blood pooling on the floor and retched. He retched again and then hurried out into the sun.

Tony walked out of the shed into the light holding the assault rifles and Ed's tiny-hands semi-automatic.

"I'm going to get the children," Carmen said.

"I don't know how many more Gorozas there might be," Frank said. "It's like whack-a-mole. So keep your eyes peeled."

Carmen nodded. Fierce, tough-as-nails. La Matanarcos. But that didn't really capture who she was. She needed a new name. Maybe La Loba. The she-wolf, the mother wolf.

"Keep them safe," Frank said.

Carmen ran to the bunk building.

Frank was almost deaf from all the gun fire, but he thought he heard something in the distance. He listened.

Sirens.

He thought about Officer Lyman and West. The best place to take them would be in the driveway as they entered the property. But then he saw the flashing lights through the trees. There were a lot of lights. A lot of cars and SUVs, which meant this wasn't a Lyman and West operation.

The sirens grew louder. Then the vehicles raced along the front of the property beyond the horse ring, lights flashing. There were patrol cars and patrol SUVs, and was that green pickup a game warden's vehicle?

Someone had put a call out. Pinto. He must have gotten through. If he'd narrated the shootings to the 911 dispatcher, the local authorities would have called everyone in range for help.

The cars did not turn into the drive, but stopped out on the main road, a whole row with flashing lights. The officers piled out. Some stayed behind their vehicles. Others moved left and right. Most had rifles.

They were going to set up a containment perimeter. That's what he'd do if he were coming upon a house or property with an unknown number of gunmen inside.

They were also going to run his information. They would find out he was an ex-con. Frank could count at least three felonies he'd committed over the last twenty-four hours. And that didn't include any of the men he'd shot in self-defense. Prosecuting attorneys didn't generally have a reputation for giving ex-cons the benefit of the doubt. And as much as Frank enjoyed male companionship, he really didn't want to check into another fine state facility, even if it was in the great state of Colorado.

The officers who were staying with the cars had their rifles to their shoulders, using the top of the squad cars or the hoods of the SUVs for elbow rests, using the scopes to surveil the place. The officers moving left and right, rushed down the road. Then a number began to cross the barbed-wire fence and skirt the fields. He figured they'd have a pretty good perimeter established in about three minutes. Three minutes was plenty of time to run, especially since the cops didn't have any air support, yet.

30

Anything You Say

FRANK COULD RUN. Not very well with his wound, but he could. A lot of men would. But Frank wasn't the running type.

He looked over at Sam. There was a big red area above his brow where he'd done the forehead of death on Hector.

"We're almost there," Frank said. "But keep your eyes peeled for stray Gorozas wanting honor and glory. I don't want to get shot yet again after having won the battle."

"Amen to that," Sam said.

Tony pointed at the house. "She's got them!"

Carmen was exiting the building, leading a number of children out of the door. He saw the older girls that had been at the stash house. Saw others. He waited. The last two out of the house were the little boy and the little girl. They were holding hands like brother and sister. Like the fact that they had each other made them more safe.

Hallelujah, Frank thought.

One of the cops used the bullhorn atop the roof of his car. "Lay your weapons on the ground, then walk into the field toward us."

Carmen was looking out toward the field, looking back toward the woods. Frank knew she was thinking about running. It would be cleaner that way. It would be safer. She had a bounty on her head. The last thing she needed was to be identified and then detained; it would be like big flashing arrows over her head, letting those hunting her know exactly where she was. They'd all be waiting for her when the authorities released her. If they released her. She could be tied up in court for some time. She could be deported back into the arms of the Mexican police that she thought so highly of. If not, she would be sitting there in jail for anyone with connections to take a crack at.

Her testimony would have been valuable for his case, but her testimony just might also get her killed.

"Carmen," Frank called. She looked at him, and he motioned for her to leave.

She hesitated.

"Sam, Tony, go help those children," Frank said. "Double-time!"

Tony and Sam ran toward the children.

"Go!" Frank called.

Carmen held Frank's gaze for a moment, and then she nodded. She slipped around the corner of the bunk house, hopped a white fence into the wide ostrich pasture, and ran for the pines.

"Lay your weapons on the ground!" the cop ordered. "Come to the field on this side of the house."

Frank turned, scanned the buildings. The children needed to get to a safe area. Needed to get away from the houses that might be hiding someone who just might think this was the end, and a hostage would be his ticket out.

Back in the field the ostriches spooked and took off running. Beyond them a handful of officers with rifles filtered through the trees.

Frank looked for Carmen and saw her disappear into the pines.

He turned back to the situation at hand.

"Lay your weapons on the ground," the cop with the bullhorn repeated.

Frank held his gun up for the cops to see, then placed it on the ground. Over by the children, Sam and Tony did the same.

Frank walked away from the shed. He stopped by Flor. His side was really beginning to hurt, but he hauled her to her feet. "I think you're going to enjoy this party," he said.

It's astounding just how much can be communicated through the eyes. Flor smoldered a black malevolence straight from the pits of Hell. She was definitely going to want payback. He probably should have killed her when he had the chance. No, not probably. He *definitely* should have killed her.

Sam and Tony pointed the way for the girls and escorted them over the fence into the riding field toward the police cars.

"Hey!" Frank shouted after them. "Wait for our lawyer to make your statement."

They didn't respond.

"Tony!" Frank called. But Tony and Sam were focused on the children and the multitude of flashing lights.

The girl who had been riding with Flor came out of the house with her hands up and walked toward the field with the others.

Frank scanned the windows of the Goroza's fine home and bunk house and barns and wondered how many more were there. Then he escorted Flor forward. He kept her right in front of him, turning as he walked to keep his eyes on all the structures, using Flor as a shield. It was like they were dancing, except it was nothing nearly so graceful or quick. And every step cut his side.

Frank walked her out to the gate of the field. Walked her through. Nothing but the peacocks and horses moved. He walked her all the way through the field until they were almost to the other side where the line of police waited with their flashing lights. By the time he got there, he was having to grit his teeth against the stabs of pain.

"Stop there," the cop with the bullhorn said.

Frank stopped.

"Step apart from each other."

This was the moment anyone back in one of the Goroza buildings with a high-powered rifle would have his shot.

Frank stepped a few paces away.

"Now turn around slowly with your arms raised."

This was all standard procedure. They just wanted to make sure he wasn't hiding anything behind his back.

Frank tried to raise his arm but could only do it halfway. "I've been shot in the side."

"Turn," the cop said.

314 • John D. Brown

Flor and Frank turned. It really was like Dancing With The Stars.

"Thank you," the cop said. "Please kneel and wait as the officers approach."

They had done the same with Sam and Tony and the children. They pretty much had to. The police had no idea what was going on here and who the bad guys where. Many criminals tried to evade arrest by playing the victim or innocent bystander. For all the police knew, Frank was a killer with a gun hidden in Flor's pants.

Frank knelt and put his hands on the top of his head. Flor, of course, was constrained.

Two officers approached. One to take Frank into custody and the other to cover with his gun should Frank try anything funny.

The officer who approached Frank said, "We're detaining everyone until we know the area's safe."

Frank said, "Ms. Goroza there is the one you want to be careful of."

"Put your hands behind your back."

Frank did.

The officer cuffed him. "Let's get you back behind the cars and look at your wound."

"You're going to have to clear the buildings," Frank said.

"We have a SWAT unit coming."

"Did you get the three that were north of here?"

"We're looking."

"And officers Lyman and West?"

"You can tell me all about what happened here when we get you to a safer area."

"You don't need these cuffs," Frank said.

"Maybe not. Now come this way." The officer led Frank over the fence to the patrol cars. The other led Flor Goroza toward a different vehicle.

Frank walked past a couple of officers holding their rifles and then alongside the car where Sam sat cuffed and alone in the back. Tony was a few more cars down in a nice white SUV, but the officer led Frank across the road to a third patrol car. They wanted them all separate for safety, but also to get separate stories. The officer asked Frank to stand,

and then he lifted his shirt to assess his injuries. "Your side is pretty beat up," the officer said. "I assume the tape is covering the gunshot wound?"

"Yes," Frank said.

"We've got paramedics coming. Do you feel dizzy, light-headed?"

"I'm okay," Frank said.

The officer opened the passenger's side door so Frank could sit down. Then he scooted around the front and slid into the driver's side. "While we're waiting for the paramedics, let me get your story. What's your name?"

"Frank Shaw."

"Is there anyone else on the property?" he asked.

"I'm not sure. I think there might be."

"Why were you holding that gun when we came up? Had someone threatened you?"

The officer seemed concerned for Frank's welfare, and he probably was, but Frank also knew the officer was digging for information. The more time that passed, the more the quality of information from a suspect dropped until the attorneys showed up and advised their clients not to say a word. Right now this was an official detention, not an arrest, which meant the officer didn't have to read Frank his rights. But they would move toward arrest soon enough.

Anything he said or did could and would be held against him in a court of law. He had the right to remain silent. He had the right to an attorney. If he couldn't afford an attorney, one would be provided.

"Mr. Shaw?"

The officer's name plate said "Banks."

Frank said, "You recording our conversation?" Being a patrol car, it wasn't considered an invasion of privacy to make such a recording because it wasn't reasonable to expect you would have any privacy in such a car. All of which meant that the officer didn't have to get permission to record.

"This patrol car can record what occurs inside."

Frank said, "Did you get a 911?"

"We received a call from a pilot."

Behind them, the sound of a buzzing airplane motor grew loud. A white Cessna roared over their heads. Close enough you could see the rivets on the underside of the wings and the two yellow stripes running down the sides. Two men in the front. A happy canine in the back.

Frank nodded and watched as Pinto banked Yolanda above the pines. Out in the fields the horses and ostriches looked on, watching the spectacle.

The officer with Frank said, "Mr. Shaw, you want to tell me what happened here?"

The district attorney would make the decision to charge Frank based on the reports of the officers. And while Frank had nothing against Banks, he'd heard far too many stories in jail about incomplete and inaccurate police reports. Yes, the stories were from criminals, but not all were lies. Cops made mistakes. They had their biases. And there was the fact that Lyman and West had been corrupted.

Frank said, "I want to tell you exactly what happened, but we're going to have to wait for a lawyer. We need to make sure everything gets in the report."

Banks nodded. "We need to get this situation under control. It will help us if we have more information."

"I understand that," Frank said. "What you need to know is that the Gorozas were running a slave operation. There were at least twelve armed people when we arrived. There might be more. Two others working with the Gorozas were officers Lyman and West."

"And what brought you here?"

Banks was smooth, unassuming. Frank assumed he easily got most people to talk. Frank said, "That will be in my official report."

Banks nodded. "Let me look you up in the system. What's your current address?"

Frank gave him his address and social security number. A moment later Banks whistled. "Manslaughter, Pleasant Valley, California?"

"That's me," Frank said.

"You know I'm going to have to take you in. If nothing else, we've got a felony possession of firearms."

"Yeah," Frank said. He wondered how many Goroza associates, or those wanting to please them, were already in the system.

"Are you sure you don't want to get your side of the story out? I think it will help your case. A show of cooperation goes a long way."

Frank sighed. If the officer transcribed something wrong, misunderstood, or missed a part, it could give the complete wrong impression. "I want to comply. I just want to make sure it's full and accurate," Frank said. "I think I'd better wait. What you need to know is that you guys need to be careful going in."

Office Banks nodded. He clearly wasn't pleased, but he didn't push. "I think it's best if you wait in the back seat. Can you get up?"

"Yeah."

"Then I'll come around and open the door."

Officer Banks came around and opened his door and helped Frank into the back. It was much like the back of Officer Lyman's and West's car. A steel and plexiglass wall between him and the front seats. Officer Banks reached over and buckled him in, and for the second time today, Frank had the pleasure of sitting on a plastic seat. Except is wasn't a pleasure—every other move to get here had sent a stab of pain through his side.

Banks shut the door, then went to confer with other officers.

Frank craned his head around looked back at the vehicle Sam sat in. Sam was nodding and talking, gesticulating with his hands, the officer with him writing it all down.

Frank sighed. Sam obviously hadn't gotten the memo back at the shed. Or maybe Sam, being the honest fraud dog he was, would never imagine how things could go wrong.

Anything you say or do can and will be held against you in a court of law. Please, Sam, say the right things.

An armored SWAT truck rumbled down the road. It was black and large and looked like it belonged in the Army. "Sheriff" was written on the side in huge fat white letters. The driver stopped momentarily, talked to an officer in charge. Then he proceeded forward and turned into the drive and approached the house.

Frank risked more pain and turned in his seat again, hoping to catch Sam's eye, but he was focused on his conversation with the officer.

As Frank waited, the SWAT team lined up in good order and cleared the house and outbuildings. More police arrived until it seemed like the Goroza's house had become the venue for a cop convention. There were state troopers, folks from the county sheriff's office, municipal police in cars, municipal police in SUVs. There was the SWAT, a K-9 unit, and, of course, the game warden, who'd been joined by two park rangers.

Down at the house, an officer walked out the door carrying a computer. Another hauled away a small filing cabinet. Meanwhile, the officer with the dog went inside. That was a drug dog, for sure. Despite his situation, Frank smiled to himself. This place was going to be a beehive for quite some time.

Four ambulances showed up. Officer Banks led one paramedic team to Frank. The man and woman pulled Frank's shirt up, peeked beneath the tape. A few moments later they were helping him into the back of their truck.

Officer Banks got in the back with him. He said, "We'll get you patched up, but I think you all are going to be spending at least a night or two at the El Paso County facility in Colorado Springs."

"Charges?"

"Felony murder seems likely."

Felony murder was the law which said that if someone died while you were committing a felony, even if you didn't intend for that person to die, you were guilty of their death and could be charged with murder. And it didn't matter if you were the one actually committing the felony or the one aiding—both were principals in the crime. Sam certainly fell into that category, as did Pinto, Heber, and Carmen.

"Tony isn't guilty of anything," Frank said.

"We'll see. You sure you don't want to get your side out? There are a number of dead men up the road. A couple on the property. A few others who look like they aren't long for this world."

"Those men were shooting to kill us," Frank said.

"And you shot back?"

"It will be in my report," Frank said.

* * *

The ride to the nearest hospital was quick. They ushered him into the ER, took an x-ray, told him the bullet had hit a rib at an angle, broken the rib, and lodged in the muscle tissue that held his ribs together. He could see the bullet—a bright little lump on the x-ray.

The doctor explained that had it gone between his ribs, it probably would have cut straight through the top of the liver or the bottom of his heart and into a lung.

"Your rib did its job," the doctor said.

"My rib hurts like hell," Frank said.

"I'll pull the bullet out. You're going to be fine."

"Yeah," Frank said, patched up so he could live the rest of his life between cement walls with men like Edward Meese and the Gorozas.

They pulled the bullet out, wrapped his torso, cleaned and stitched his leg, then handed him over to Banks who had been waiting the whole time. On the way out, Banks said, "We're relocating you to the Criminal Justice Center in Colorado Springs."

For some reason the name reminded Frank of the League of Justice that Batman belonged to. "Am I going to get to meet Aquaman and The Flash?" Frank asked.

"I don't think so," Officer Banks said.

Frank could already smell the inside. He could feel the fluorescent lights. Feel the miles of concrete and razor-wire fencing penning him in.

He'd been looking forward to real French toast this weekend, made with fat slices of challah or brioche because a recipe he'd read said that those breads, and Frank had never seen such bread before, were the kings of French toast. He'd been looking forward to smothering those slices of king with real butter and real maple syrup from maple trees, not any of that faked-up corn crap. He'd had French toast a number of times in the Pleasant Valley facility. Every time it had tasted like plastic.

Frank asked, "You guys have a five-star chef, right?"

"Sure," Officer Banks said, "the legislature was very excited to hear we were spending tax payer dollars for Wolfgang Puck to run the correctional eats. It's nothing but five courses all the way."

"Can't wait," Frank said. "Do you think you can keep the three of us together? The last thing we need is some MS-13 moron getting the idea that one of us alone would make a good target."

"We can talk about that when we go down. You'll have an initial appearance before a judge in twenty-four to forty-eight hours. Then a date for the preliminary hearing will be set."

They got onto the interstate that led through the fine city of Colorado Springs, heading in a south-westerly direction, into the sun which hung low in the sky.

Frank looked at the stores he would not be able to visit. The parks. The movie theaters. The grocery stores. The sidewalks. A free man could lie down on a sidewalk if he so desired. He could roll around in the grass like a dog and stare up at the sky. He could run hill and dale. He could climb trees. He could buy a Coke at three a.m.

An arrest wasn't a conviction. But it did mean you were in the system. It meant you were heading down the river. And now he had put Sam and Pinto and Heber—men he hardly knew, good honest men—into his boat.

Officer Banks left the interstate and cruised through the city on a main road. Then he made a few turns, and a structure that looked like some medieval tower loomed up in front of him. It looked like the French Bastille, except there wasn't one inch of frill. It was gray and round and flat-roofed with a handful of small slot windows. A big tombstone of a sign out front proclaimed "Criminal Justice Center."

When Officer Banks opened the back door, Frank almost couldn't bring himself to get out of the car. He paused. Officer Banks waited. Then Frank climbed out and surveyed the place.

Formidable. That's what this place was. And it was a county jail. What did the state prison look like? He said, "Tony's a good kid. Sam's

Mr. Nice Guy. Please think about putting in a good word so they don't get shunted off into some holding cell inhabited by a serial killer."

"I can't promise anything."

"The Gorozas were in with MS-13. News travels fast. At the very least Sam and Tony should be separated from anyone affiliated with that gang or its allies."

Officer Banks nodded. "Come on; we need to get you processed." Then he took Frank's elbow and escorted him forward.

Frank took in a breath of air, looked at the blue sky. The door buzzed. Then Officer Banks opened the door, and Frank walked in. A moment later the door clicked shut behind him and locked.

31

Five-Star Accommodations

BANKS LED FRANK past the locking doors that hummed with electricity to a uniformed woman who asked him a number of questions and officially booked his arrest. She led him to another woman in blue who took his fingerprints with a scanner. When the scans didn't come out clean, the mistress of fingerprints gave him a squirt of hand lotion, told him to rub it around, and try it again. He did, and the prints came out just grand—he could see it on the monitor. From fingerprinting Frank went to a man who took his picture against the height wall chart.

Then came the inmate property technician who sized Frank up, then gave him an orange jump suit, white socks, a white undershirt, and white prison briefs. He folded them all up in a nice bundle and placed a pair of fine prison bright orange Crocs on top.

Frank was taken to a room where two "technicians" asked him to undress. When he was naked, they asked him to turn around, bend over, and cough. Frank knew the drill and complied, six years of memories running in his head. They asked him to put on his new clothes. He did. They bagged and tagged all his belongings and took them away. Then they gave Frank to two correctional officers who led him to his holding cell and explained the rules as they went.

This was a modern facility, which meant his cell was not one of the old time cages with open bars. Instead, it was an enclosed room about ten feet by fifteen. It had a thick metal door with a narrow window about six inches wide and three feet tall running up one side. The window was made of plexiglass.

There was a slot in the middle of the door for passing food trays and other items. Inside, the walls were covered with sheets of stainless steel. Attached to the stainless steel walls were four narrow bunks. Up against one side of the room was a metal toilet and sink combo. A large man with large dark bags under his eyes and large dark hair that stood up on his head and looked like it hadn't been cut or washed for eight months was sitting on that toilet. His prison jump suit and briefs were down around his knees. His undershirt was hitched up above his large hairy belly. He looked over at Frank and scratched his face and didn't say a thing. A moment later he grunted and let loose with something that sounded like a rototiller. This man was obviously at ease with public dumping.

Frank turned to the officers with him. "I'm going to need to make a phone call."

The one nodded. "We'll get you in. Give it forty-five minutes, maybe an hour."

"Thank you," Frank said.

"Shower's in the morning," one officer said. "Then breakfast. You should get your initial appearance sometime tomorrow afternoon, but it might be as long as the day after next."

Frank didn't want to wait for the day after next. Every moment Tony and Sam were in here was a risk. The guards left him there with Big Fart who looked like he was on that toilet for the long haul. Frank took a bunk and sat back, his arm bandaged close to his side. The painkillers were doing a splendid job.

He studied the stainless steel walls and rivets. He thought about Sam. Thought about Tony. Thought about those children.

Thought about Carmen heading for the pines.

* * *

What seemed like three hours later, the two officers who had walked him in opened the door. "You still want to make a call?"

"Yeah," Frank said and stood.

"We going to have to restrain you?"

"Nope," Frank said. What was he really going to be able to do with his side?

They escorted him down the hallway outside with its shining floor and gray walls, around a corner, and through an electrically locked door to another room. The jail had a contact visitation area with chairs bolted to tables and tables bolted to the floor. Behind it was a non-contact visitation area with a class wall and phone booths and stools at each booth. To one corner of the contact visitation area were a number of booths with phones that connected to the outside world. A clock on the other side of the visitor's window indicated it had indeed been about three hours.

Frank made his call, knowing he was being recorded. He called Kim. She picked up on the third ring.

He said, "Have you heard from Tony?"

"Frank?"

"Have you heard from him?"

"Is he okay?"

"Tony's just fine. Where are you?"

"I'm waiting at the airport."

"Okay, I want you to listen. Here's what been going down. Tony was kidnapped by Ed Meese, one of my meat head cell mates. This was yesterday. We freed him. The problem is there was some shooting."

"Oh, my Lord," Kim said.

"Hang on, Sis."

"Oh, my Lord, Frank."

"He's all right."

"Frank."

"Kim, we're going to need a good lawyer."

There was a pause. She was trying to get a hold of herself. "We?"

"It's a long story."

Anger thickened her voice. "Frank, I swear."

"We need the lawyer to talk to the prosecutor before he gets too far down this path."

"What path is that?"

"Kim, I don't have a lot of time. I just need you to focus and listen. Later on you can chew me up one side and down the other. Get a pen out." He waited. "You got a pen?"

"Yes."

"I'm in the county jail in Colorado Springs. It's called the Criminal Justice Center. I believe they've taken Tony to a juvenile detention center. We need to meet with a good lawyer ASAP. Tony's going to be fine. But we don't want him to spend an hour more in detention than is necessary. The police are already working to support a number of charges and present them to the county prosecutor. We need someone on our side talking in the DA's other ear."

"Frank, this is beyond the pale."

"Kim, you get a lawyer and get yourself down here. I'm in with my neighbor. His name is Sam Cartwright. He's probably called his wife, but it's best if you coordinate. He's in the phone book in Rock Springs."

"Why is it the women are always cleaning up after the men?"

"I think that was something to do with the Garden of Eden."

"Uh, huh," she said. "You talking about that frame job by Adam?"

"No comment."

"I'm going to get Tony out. You, on the other hand, I just might leave to rot."

"I can understand that," Frank said.

She sighed. "Colorado Springs. This is not how I wanted to spend my vacation days."

"The mountains are lovely," he said. "I'll make it up to you."

"That's what you always say."

He realized it was what he always said. And instead of paying his debts, he just borrowed more.

The officer tapped the back of his wrist indicating time was up.

Frank said, "Got to go, Kim."

"You drive me crazy," she said. "It's like battered wife syndrome."

"I love you, Kim," he said and ended the call.

326 • John D. Brown

When the officers dropped him back at his holding cell, Big Fart was back on the toilet.

"What is it with you?" Frank asked.

"Beans," he said. "I got me some bad beans."

Frank walked over to him, then reached down to the toilet paper roll and removed about five feet.

"What are you doing?"

"Making sure I'm not left high and dry by you and your industrial beans."

"Fair enough," he said.

Frank wrapped his paper up and turned to his bunk. "Good Lord," he muttered and looked up at the ceiling, "I would account it a great favor if you could turn off my nose."

Big Fart grunted and started up with the rototiller again.

Maybe the nose was too much to ask, Frank prayed silently. Let's just do the simple thing and help Kim find an attorney with some brains.

Frank turned to Big Fart. "If you flush when you let loose with your cannon, it will suck some of that stink down the drain."

"Okay," Big Fart said, then reached in his shirt and scratched his chest. When he did, the sleeve of his jumper pulled up a little higher. Frank didn't know how he'd missed it before, but there, on his upper arm, was a tattoo for MS-13.

Frank's alert level ticked up to orange.

Had Banks sold him out? Or was it the guards? Or was this all a simple oversight?

More importantly, had Big Fart received any communication while Frank was on the phone to Kim?

Big Fart didn't looking like he was plotting a murder, but he wouldn't. He'd wait for when Frank was least suspecting it and only then pull out his shank.

Frank was tired, but he did not sleep. Not until far into the night and then for only an hour or so. He was awake the next morning when the PA system out in the hall announced it was time to rise. A few minutes later the detainees started taking turns going to the showers. When Frank's turn came, he was up and ready to go. Big Fart was sitting up, looking as rough as when he went to sleep.

The officers let them down the hallway with the shining floor and gray walls to the showers. It was an open shower with eight heads. A number of detainees were already there. Frank disrobed in front of another officer and put his clothes into a plastic bin along with the others. The soap was white soap. The shampoo was white shampoo. He couldn't take a full shower, not with his injuries and bandages. So he made do with a wash cloth while the others washed and rinsed in silence. He made do making sure to take a shower head that would allow him to keep his back to the wall. When he finished, he walked out of the shower area past Hairy Big Fart, took a white towel from many on a shelf, dried, then placed the towel in a laundry bag on wheels, and dressed again.

The whole time Frank remained in code orange. When you lived in prison, you always had to know what was going on in your surroundings. There was nothing going on here now, but that could always change in a heartbeat.

Big Fart finished his shower. A little while later, the two of them were escorted back to their high-rent bungalow.

Frank sat. Big Fart rolled onto his side and went to sleep. A little while later an officer came by with two styrofoam trays. Breakfast was something called cracked wheat in a paper bowl with plastic wrap over the top. It was basically a gruel of shattered wheat kernels. There was milk in a little box on the side along with a package of sugar and a banana on its way to going black. It appeared Wolfgang Puck was really losing his touch.

Frank woke Big Fart. They ate, then waited for the officers to come back with the garbage bags. The officer opened the slot, took their garbage, then closed the slot back up. Frank went back to counting the rivets in the stainless steel walls and listening to Big Fart breathe.

Sometime later another officer showed up at the door. "Visitor," he said. "I think it's your lawyer."

"Hallelujah," Frank said.

Once again he was escorted back to the visitation room. To his surprise, he found Sam waiting there, sitting at one of the tables.

"I don't think orange is your color," Frank said.

"Dude," Sam said.

"Not quite the Hilton, is it?"

"They have me in a room with eight guys. I swear half of them are on meth."

"Any of them have tattoos like Jesus Goroza?"

"No."

"You'll be all right. Stay alert, stay calm. Don't talk about cookies."

"Are you kidding?" Sam said. "I've already collected half a dozen recipes."

Frank grinned. "You're going to get out, Sam."

"I'd better."

The officer with Frank pointed at the electric door that led from the outside into the visiting area. "Your visitor is here. You have fifteen minutes. The only touch you may have is a hand shake. No hugging, kissing, or lap sitting."

Frank nodded. A woman walked through the door. She was dressed in a dark skirt and woman's suit jacket. Her blonde hair was pulled back smartly in a pony tail. She looked like she was in her thirties.

Both Frank and Sam stood.

"Let's hope the cavalry has arrived," Frank said.

The woman walked over to their table. She looked at Sam. "Mr. Cartwright?"

"Yes."

She looked at Frank. "Mr. Shaw?"

Frank nodded.

"I've been retained by Mr. Cartwright's wife and Mr. Shaw's sister to represent you. My name is Melinda Cross. I work for Brindley, Brindley, and Fiss. Let's sit and talk."

They all sat.

She didn't have any paper or pens. No folders. She'd certainly been searched before coming in and had probably been asked to empty her pockets. She was a fit woman, not some glamour gal, but fit and all business, which Frank put in the plus column. She said, "I've been able to look at the police reports."

"They gave them up?" Frank asked.

"They were happy to. You just have to ask politely. Now, what I want to do now is make sure I have your side of the story to verify the police didn't leave important parts out."

"Okay," Frank said. "But before we go further, I need to know what your credentials are. How many cases have you tried?"

"I've been practicing for almost ten years. I've represented hundreds of clients. Assisted on even more cases. Don't worry, your sister was thorough."

"How well do you know the DA and judges?"

"I've been practicing here, in these courts for eight of those years. I know how these judges operate. I know the DA."

Frank was feeling better by the second. "Okay," he said. "What do you want to know?"

"I want to hear the whole story. Start to finish. And we don't have a lot of time, so I suggest you get talking."

Right to business. That was good. Frank nodded and said, "At about 2:00 p.m. yesterday in Rock Springs, Wyoming, I and my nephew Tony returned to my house from Cowboy Donut where I had just made an application for work. I always lock my doors, but my front door was unlocked. I saw signs that the door had been forced. We entered the house and found Ed Meese waiting in my living room with a handgun."

Frank continued. He told the story of what happened with as much significant detail as he could remember. In the military, he'd learned how to give an accurate report. Ms. Cross listened intently, interrupting him just a few times to ask questions. When he finished, she asked Sam to add his point of view. When Sam finished, Frank said, "This is self-defense, right? We did the best we knew how with the threats at hand."

She looked up at the clock on the wall and then back down. "We have

330 • John D. Brown

three minutes. I need you to listen to me. Here's what you're facing, Mr. Shaw. One count of arson, one count of felony possession of a firearm, one count of attempted kidnapping, three counts of felony murder."

Frank blinked.

"Mr. Cartwright. You are facing one count of attempted kidnapping and three counts of felony murder. If convicted, you're both looking at multiple life sentences."

"Life?" Sam said in shock.

"But—" Frank said.

"Those are the charges the police are sending to the DA based on reasonable cause." She turned to Sam. "I really wish you wouldn't have told your life story to the officer on the scene."

"I'm not the kind of guy to hide things."

"We would never want to hide anything. But we do want to make sure we control the information to make sure it is accurate. I've already identified at least three key things that did not make it into the police report."

Life, Frank thought. The whole rest of his life lived in a cement box. Sam's too.

"What about Pinto and Heber?"

"Based on your testimony, they were accessories to the kidnapping, and so are facing that charge plus the felony murders."

"You've got to be kidding me," Frank said.

"Mr. Shaw, do you want me to sugarcoat it?"

"No," Sam said.

Ms. Cross said, "The prosecutor, when deciding whether to file charges, sometimes has a very limited perspective. He will only have the police reports and the accuser's testimony. In this case, Ms. Goroza. I want to make sure he considers her credibility, and that of those with her. My hope is to get this thrown out in the DA's screening process. I have a meeting with him in an hour. Maybe I can present evidence to him that the case isn't as strong as it appears at first blush. Then I have to meet with the DA for Weld County where the arson and other shootings took place."

"They're not going to try them together?"

"I hope not. Our best bet is to convince them to try this as a number of separate incidents. Try this as one, and I think you're screwed."

"But they kidnapped Tony," Frank said.

"I know, and I've got to convince them you weren't taking the law into your own hands, that you weren't involved with the Goroza operations, and that you weren't trying to hide evidence with the arson. And I've got to do it in two counties, pulling information from police departments in two states."

Frank slumped in his chair. *Focus.* "They've got me in with a guy sporting an MS-13 tattoo. We need that changed. And we need to make sure Tony isn't set up with anyone affiliated with that gang or anyone with any ties to anyone potentially associated with it." Jails could sometimes be as dangerous as prisons, sometimes more dangerous, because everyone went into the jail to await their hearings and trials and sentencing. From the hardest of the hardest killers to the moron who shoplifted a box of Twinkies. Tony needed to be with offenders who would not be tempted to do a favor for the Gorozas.

"I'll work on that," Ms. Cross said. "Right now they're still thinking about whether he should be charged with anything."

"Charged?" Frank said.

"You claim he was kidnapped. You need more than claims in court. They're going to have to sort it out, find some evidence to suggest that's true, that he wasn't just part of your gang like Ms. Goroza suggests."

Frank sat there a moment trying not to be stunned.

"What about bail?" Sam asked. "If they go forward, they'll set a bail, right? I'll still be able to go back home."

"With these charges, bail is likely to be set at a million, maybe a million five for each of you. And that's just in the El Paso court. The bail bondsman is going to want ten percent up front. Then she's going to want collateral for the bond. Can you get $120,000 in cash for the fee? From a family member or friend? Do you have a million in assets you can put up as collateral?"

A beat passed.

"No," Sam said.

"It's very difficult for anyone except drug operators and the very rich to post bail in these situations. The county police, the state Attorney General, and the U.S. Attorney are all conducting investigations. If this isn't dismissed, you're going to be in this facility for probably at least three or four months before your trial."

"No," Frank said. That was three or four months for the Gorozas to try to get at Sam, Tony, Pinto, or Heber. If there wasn't someone already here, they could easily have someone commit a crime to get in. Something with only a year or two attached to it. Frank might be able to survive a hit. Pinto might as well, but Sam? Tony?

"Sam," Frank began to apologize.

Sam shook his head. "We did what we could, Frank. They would have killed him."

Frank nodded, but knew this wasn't over. He turned to Ms. Cross, "You tell the DA that if he puts us in here, he's painting a huge target on our backs." It was not at all uncommon for someone inside, who was in for the long haul, to do a job to provide for someone on the outside—a wife, a son, a mother, a daughter. "Did they bust the other slave sites?"

"There has been no news of other busts."

Frank wondered for a moment if Carmen had been telling the truth. Was she part of a vigilante group? Or had it all been a sham? But there was no reason to disbelieve her report.

"Leave me in," he said. "Let the others out. They had nothing to do with this."

"Unfortunately, Mr. Shaw, that's not the way of the American justice system."

32

Ms. Cross

FRANK AND SAM were led back to their respective cells. Frank entered his room in somber silence. The door behind him slid shut with a soft but heavy thunk. Big Fart was still asleep.

Frank prayed. Normally, he'd do a hundred push-ups and a hundred sit-ups and a hundred air squats and a hundred squat thrusts. But that wasn't going to happen with his side. He rinsed his head in the small metal sink behind the toilet and sat on his bunk. He made a mental list of everything he needed done on the outside. Made a list of what he needed to do in here. But that only took about five minutes, and he was staring at the ceiling and walls again.

During his previous six years inside, he'd learned to divert his mind by memorizing and reciting poems and pithy quotes. He tried to run the poetry and pith through his mind and found he couldn't do it. He just couldn't.

Night came, but they did not turn the light in the hallway off. The only reason he knew it was night was because they announced it was bedtime. Frank dozed. Then his warning horns sounded. He woke with Big Fart bending down toward him.

Frank twisted, kicked him in the belly, slugged him in the groin.

Big Fart grunted.

Frank darted up and got around behind the big man. He stomped the back of one of Big Fart's knees.

The big man went down.

A couple of kicks and Frank could kill or incapacitate him. But if

Frank did, his act of self-defense would count against him. Fights while in jail tended to only add to your sentence. And right now he couldn't afford anything that might undermine what Ms. Cross was trying to do.

Big Fart tried to climb to his feet, but Frank swept his feet out from underneath him. He fell again to the floor.

Frank drove a knee into Big Fart's back, then grabbed his hand, twisted it hard, bringing his arm up behind his back.

Big Fart struggled, but Frank pressed, forcing the arm up higher into the pain position.

"Dude!" Big Fart said.

"What are you doing?"

"I needed some butt wipe."

"Do I look like a toilet?"

"Toilet's out, man. I was just going to borrow some of yours."

Frank twisted the arm up a little higher. "And after you'd borrowed it, were you going to put it back in my pocket?"

"Get off me," Big Fart growled.

"Show me your other hand."

"Let me go," Big Fart threatened.

"Show me your hand."

Big Fart finally relented and stretched out his other hand. There was enough light from the hallway coming in through the plexiglass for Frank to see his hand was empty. Frank kept his grip on the man with one hand and patted him down with the other. It was slow going. In the end, he didn't find a shank or garrote, but that didn't mean anything. It only took eleven pounds of pressure on a guy's neck to throttle him. It only took one good punch to a guy's voice box while he was sleeping to almost incapacitate him.

Frank said, "Big boy, you and I might end up as buds, but right now I don't know you. You come on my side of the room, and I'm going to take it as a threat and respond accordingly. You understand me?"

"Come on, man."

"You want butt wipe, you ask. Understand?"

"I understand."

"I'm going to let you up. And you're going to go to your side of the room. Okay?"

"Fine," Big Fart said.

Frank pushed up off Big Fart and stood back far enough that the man couldn't take a swipe at him.

Big Fart stood, breathing hard, a big lug illuminated by the light from the hallway. His eyes told the whole story. If he hadn't been planning something, he certainly was now. Soon enough he'd communicate with someone from MS-13. They'd share Frank's story. And then Big Fart would come with a shank.

Big Fart spread his hands wide. "No hard feelings."

"No hard feelings," Frank agreed.

Big Fart turned like things were all okay between them and went back to his bunk. But things were definitely not okay.

You had all types in prison: morons, jerks, sociopaths, bullies, cowards. Frank's modus operandi had been to respect the other man by following a simplified version of the golden rule—don't mess with me, and I won't mess with you. That worked okay man to man. But that didn't work too well when a gang had it out for you.

Frank needed to get out of this place; and he needed to do so quickly.

* * *

Breakfast was passed through the slot in the door. It was a hard-boiled egg, toast, and an orange. When the officer came back for their trash, Frank politely asked for more toilet paper. Lunch came a number of hours later. It was gray turkey slices on white bread with a square of cheese, a squirt package of mustard and mayo, and a fruit cup. Big Fart scarfed his down in about three seconds and looked for a moment like he was going to eat the styrofoam tray.

About an hour later, two officers arrived and told Frank he was being taken to see the judge. This was the initial appearance where the judge would likely set bail. And the fact that he was going meant Ms. Cross had not convinced the DA to drop the charges.

A cold hardness settled along his bones. It was like a darkness had found his room swept clean and come back to say hello.

The officers asked Frank to put his hands through the slot. He did, and they cuffed him. Then they opened the door and asked him to come out. One officer watched Frank while the other cuffed Frank's legs. Then they put on the chain belt and cuffed his hands to it.

They led him down the hall and through an electric door out into the sunshine. They led him to a bus with four others cuffed up in seats like he was. He passed an officer with a shotgun and took a seat. They waited for two more. One of them was Sam, who wasn't saying much. Then they shut the front door and drove out. It took them about ten minutes to arrive at the courthouse.

Frank and the others were led in a line out of the bus to the side of the courthouse. They moved along in their orange jumpsuits and orange Crocs. Somewhere a restaurant was grilling meat. Frank's mouth began to water. Then he was shuffling through a side door into the air-conditioned building, and the smell of meat faded behind. They filed down a hallway and into a court room.

The judge and the recorder sat up front. There was a US flag and one for the state of Colorado to one side. There were two tables up front about fifteen feet from the bench, one for the defense, one for the prosecution. Behind them were maybe thirty chairs set up in two groups facing the judge. Ten were occupied. Frank and Sam were led to the jury seats along with the other prisoners and told to sit.

The prisoner next to Frank sighed. "Oh, great. Judge Ellis. We're all screwed."

Frank looked at Sam. "You get a hold of Kim?"

"I did," Sam whispered.

Frank nodded. Not much else to say, and you didn't want to draw a judge's reprimand for disturbing the proceedings with a lot of chatter.

The judge processed a woman in an orange jump suit who was being charged with burglary. The judge had seen her before. He gave her a lecture and set bail. He processed a thin bald man charged with assault. He processed three more. Each one was led out a side door when the judge finished with them. Ms. Cross stepped into the room just before the judge called Frank and Sam forward.

Frank looked at her expectantly.

She shrugged.

The judge tapped on his screen and looked at his court schedule. He finally looked up. "Ms. Cross," he said. "You're representing Misters Shaw and Cartwright?"

"I am, your Honor."

"Bailiff, please escort Mr. Shaw."

The bailiff escorted Frank in his chains to a pulpit that stood between the tables for the prosecution and defense. Ms. Cross came to stand with him.

"Mr. Shaw," the judge said. "This is not your first offense. I see here that you spent time in California for manslaughter."

"That is correct."

"Mr. Shaw, you have the right to remain silent. You have the right to have an attorney present now and during any future questioning. If you cannot afford Ms. Cross or any other attorney, one will be appointed to you free of charge if you wish. Do you understand these rights?"

Frank's heart sank. They *were* charging him. "Yes, I do, your Honor."

He looked over at Sam. *So sorry my friend.*

The judge turned to the bench for the prosecution. "Mr. Andrews, you may proceed."

Mr. Andrews said, "The District Attorney will be pursuing a charge of felony possession of a firearm. It carries a sentence up to two years in prison."

Frank waited for the list to continue.

Judge Ellis said to Frank, "You know the law concerning felons and guns?"

"I do, your honor."

"And yet you still, as it says here, retrieved the P90 from the pond up in Weld County."

"I did, your Honor."

The judge nodded. "This is only an initial hearing to make sure you hear what charges are being pursued, understand your rights, and be given the opportunity to post bail. You will have a chance to formally enter a plea of guilty or not guilty at your arraignment."

"Yes," Frank said. He again waited for the list of charges to continue.

Mr. Andrews shuffled a few papers and said, "There were other charges the police recommended, but based on the reports and evidence obtains thus far, the DA feels Mr. Shaw acted in great part in self-defense and the defense of others in immediate danger. Those charges will not be pursued at this time."

The DA's words hung in the air.

"I'm not being charged?" Frank asked.

Ms. Cross smiled.

Judge Ellis said, "You should know that last night the police located and searched twelve other Goroza properties where there was reasonable cause to suspect slaves were being held and prostituted. Mr. Andrews has informed me the state will be pursuing many charges in conjunction with those operations. I believe this was a hornet's nest you walked into, Mr. Shaw."

"Yes, your honor," Frank said.

The judge nodded. "Mr. Shaw, illegal possession of a firearm by a felon is itself a felony. I'm setting bail at thirty-five thousand dollars." The judge asked a clerk for some information. When the clerk replied, the judge turned back to Frank. "Your arraignment is set for September 30th. You will make your plea at that time."

"Thank you, your Honor."

"Mr. Cartwright," the judge said. "We'll take care of the two of you together."

The bailiff escorted Sam down to the pulpit.

"Mr. Andrews," the judge said.

"With regards to Mr. Cartwright, the prosecution has reviewed the police reports and testimonies of the witnesses. We find insufficient evidence to pursue any charges at this time. We recommend Mr. Cartwright be released."

For a moment Frank couldn't believe his ears.

The judge looked down at Sam. "I would admonish you to be careful in the future. We are a nation of law. We rule by law, not by mob. Do you understand?"

"Yes, your honor," Sam said.

The judge motioned at one of the corrections officers that had come in with them. "Officer, you may remove his cuffs. Mr. Cartwright, you'll travel back to the justice center. They will return your clothes and belongings and you will be free."

The officer moved forward with a key and unshackled Sam who rubbed his wrists like the cuffs had burned.

Sam and Ms. Cross turned and walked toward the courtroom's main doors, Sam a free man. Frank was led out of the side door back to a holding room with the others. About fifteen minutes later Ms. Cross found him. She was accompanied by a guard.

"What happened?" Frank asked.

"We got to the DA early," Mr. Shaw. "It didn't hurt that the police have been investigating the Goroza's for some time for drugs. You blew the lid off, which, I think, disposed the DA's office toward you. But even that isn't the whole story. Late yesterday evening, I came into possession of a trove of well-detailed documents. Somehow that information was not only sent to the DA's office, but also to a number of activist organizations and news outlets. The Governor started receiving calls. It appears a friend rallied the troops in your cause."

"Who gave you the documents?" Frank asked.

"Who do you think, Mr. Shaw?"

There was only one person he could think of. "Carmen," he said.

Ms. Cross shrugged. "I went out to the restroom, came back, and they were sitting on my secretary's desk."

"The Matanarcos," Frank said. "I think I'm in love."

"They've also released your friends in the plane. The question now is whether you can post bail."

"It depends," Frank said. He couldn't, but Kim could. The question was whether she was inclined to save his hide. "I need to make a call."

"We'll work on this charge," Ms. Cross said. "I'm thinking we might be able to talk the DA into probation. Of course, you have another DA with charges to clear in Weld County where the Goroza's house went up in smoke. I'm going to make sure he gets this information; I think it's going to help the DA up there."

Frank nodded, but knew this wasn't over until it was over. Ms. Cross left. The others that had filled the jury seats with Frank joined him one by one. Then they were all led back to the jail bus and traveled back to Aquaman's lair.

He might not survive the hit that would be put out on him, but the others were all free. And that was a positive thing.

33

Crème Brûlée

FRANK POSTED BAIL the next day with Kim, Tony, and Sam sitting in the courtroom seats. Ms. Cross revealed that upon consideration the DA in Weld had decided not to press charges. He had decided Frank was not trying to hide evidence of the killings, but calling for help.

"Was that DA conducting an investigation against the Gorozas as well?"

"District Attorneys have a lot of discretion in what cases they will pursue and what charges to bring," Ms. Cross said. "Slaves fighting for their freedom isn't the kind of thing most law and order types are going to go after."

"I just don't believe it."

"Believe it," Ms. Cross said. "It's the American justice system. And the media. And politics. Remember: this case came to the attention of the governor."

"And you didn't have anything to do with that?"

"Your sister will get my bill," she said and smiled. "And the governor and media will continue to hear from the advocacy groups."

"Has Carmen come in?" Frank asked.

"Carmen is a ghost."

That was good. That meant the cartel couldn't threaten a reporter or Ms. Cross here to make them divulge Carmen's contact information.

"You are not a ghost, Mr. Shaw. I think you need to go into the witness protection program."

"I'm not going to hide," Frank said.

342 • John D. Brown

"Famous last words," Ms. Cross said.

"I'll think about it," Frank said.

They walked out of the courthouse. A gaggle of reporters with cameras and microphones turned toward them, then came up and got in his face.

A woman reporter asked, "Mr. Shaw, is it true you saved five young girls? Can you tell us what happened?"

"No comment," Frank said and tried to push past.

"Mr. Shaw," another reporter said, "some people are saying you're a hero."

"No comment."

A reporter stuck a microphone in Sam's face. "What about you, sir? The public needs to know."

Inane questions from inane minds.

"The public doesn't need to know anything at this time," Ms. Cross said.

Frank gently pushed through. It wasn't Frank's humility that was bugging him; it was all those cameras, all of them capturing his face, clear as day. Capturing Sam's and Tony's and Kim's as well. Were they streaming this live? There was good reason why the identities of Special Forces, Rangers, and SEAL teams were kept hidden. There was a good reason why those who killed people in criminal organizations should be too. Flor was going to get a hold of this tape. Flor or someone who owed her a favor.

Earlier this morning, the state and federal prosecutors had met with Frank and asked him if he would testify in court against the Gorozas as well as officers Lyman and West. He'd agreed. They'd offered him witness protection. He was beginning to think it might be a good idea.

The reporters began to follow them, and then Ms. Cross announced she would make a statement about the case. All cameras and microphones turned toward her. It was enough of a bone to distract the dogs; enough to let Frank and the others escape. The four of them hustled to the parking garage where Kim's rental car was, got in, and drove out the exit on the far side.

Frank looked at Tony in the front passenger's seat. He had agreed to testify against the Gorozas as well. "How you doing, buddy?"

"You think the Gorozas will come after us?" he asked.

"I think it would be wise to take precautions."

"Lord," Kim said. "Is your crap ever going to end?"

"That's a hard one to call," Frank said.

* * *

Frank went with Sam to retrieve his minivan from the police. Someone had changed the tire. And despite the broken glass and bullet holes, it was drivable. Sam sighed about the van, made a joke about it being well-ventilated, then called a glass company who came out and installed new glass in two sides while they waited. The glass guys couldn't install glass in the back window because too many bullet holes had damaged the frame, so Frank and Sam went to a Walmart, asked the folks for some old boxes, and duct-taped a piece of cardboard across the back. They used the pink tape. They used it on the bullet holes as well. When they were done, the baby blue minivan looked like it had chicken pox.

And that's how they drove home, the wind whistling through a number of bullet holes anytime they went above fifty. About eight hours later they rolled into Rock Springs. Sam drove into the gas station where the Nova was still parked and pulled up alongside the old car.

Sam said, "There she is."

"You were a lifesaver, buddy."

"I was the chauffer."

"You were more than that."

Sam shrugged, took on a lofty tone of false humility. "I suppose you're right. I was rather spectacular."

"Watch it," Frank said. "Cockiness kills."

"Small doses also attract women."

"You're married."

"That's right, and my wife's going to kill me. I'm going to need all the alpha male aura I can get."

"Good luck with that."

"I'm thinking I should butter her up first with chocolates and roses."

"You'd better get a lot of them."

Sam nodded, then got this wise look. "Maybe you go in first, pave the way."

Frank shook his head. "Oh, no," he said. "That's way above my pay grade."

"I thought you military types never left a man behind."

"Sometimes the Lone Ranger has to go solo. Tonto will be by to pick up the pieces. But you can tell her I accept full responsibility for the van."

"I enlisted the van willingly."

"I still owe you a van."

"You're handy," Sam said. "We'll figure it out."

They said their good-byes, and then Frank climbed out and stepped over to the Nova. He unlocked the car, slid in, and put the keys in the ignition. She started up with a roar.

He drove home and found the light on. He opened the door. Tony was sitting at the table eating a mixing bowl full of Golden Grahams cereal.

"Do you know how good this is?" Tony asked around a mouthful of the cereal. "I've been craving the grahams."

"Where's your Mom?"

"She stepped out for some groceries."

Frank walked over to the table and grabbed a couple of grahams out of Tony's bowl. Then he sat down across from him, watched him take another spoonful.

"Buddy," Frank said. "I can't tell you how sorry I am you went through that."

Tony shrugged. "Things happen," he said and kept munching. After such an experience, many folks would be traumatized. Afraid of shadows. Frank didn't see that. What he could see were gears whizzing in the boy's head. They were doing calculus.

"What are you thinking?"

Tony poked his cereal down into the milk. "Mom says we should un-list our phone number."

"That sounds reasonable."

"Maybe move."

Frank sighed. He truly had thrown a wrench into their lives. "I don't think anyone knows where you live, but we don't know what Ed left behind."

Tony said, "These morons piss me off. They drag me into their crap, and now I'm the one that's got to run and hide?"

"That's life sometimes."

"Who says?"

"Thousands of guys willing to cut your head off."

Tony shrugged.

Frank said, "You don't want to take them on mano a mano. One guy against who knows how many. Sometimes the best action is to exfiltrate and retreat. In a couple of years you can join the FBI."

Tony shook his head. "The FBI didn't break this case."

Frank saw where his teenage white hat calculus was leading him. "You're not Batman."

"No," Tony agreed. "Batman's a fiction. But the Yeti—who knows what he'll do?"

Frank chuckled. "Right."

But Tony was not laughing. He pulled a black jump drive out of his pocket and placed it on the table.

"What's that?"

"It was on Ed." He pulled another drive out of his pocket and placed it next to the first. "That one was in the stash house."

"And?"

"Mostly crap."

"But not all?"

"We'll see," Tony said.

"Dude," Frank warned.

"Look," Tony said. "I'm not going to be a victim. You're either

346 • John D. Brown

playing offense, or you're playing defense. I intend to be the guy who is a step ahead."

"At this point, you are not on their radar. You're not a target. There isn't any offense or defense to be played."

"Oh? Then why am I changing my address?"

"Because Flor might want to use you to get to me. But you start messing around, and you'll be the one they're coming after."

"Bring it on," he said.

The boy was going to get himself killed. Frank was about to explain that fact in baby letters when he realized what was going on. "Tony, you listen to me. You weren't a victim. You were a prisoner of war, a soldier caught by the enemy. You performed your duty heroically."

"Heroically? I was helpless. A big wuss who couldn't do anything without his computer."

"Oh? Well, who was the one who originally freed Carmen? What have they identified now—thirty-seven slaves? None of them would have been freed without you. And who was it in that field that placed himself between the pickup and Carmen fleeing with the children on that snowmobile? If you hadn't done that, Ed would have caught them. He would have taken Carmen and the kids right there and driven off; those children would still be slaves, and Carmen right now would be dead. Do not disrespect your service."

Tony took another bite. Mulled it over. Took another.

"Don't go wasting yourself on some futile charge into the enemy's machine guns just to prove a point. You're a soldier. Get trained. And when it's time, you go into battle with intelligence and a team to back you up."

Tony munched.

"You listening to me?"

"Yeah," Tony said.

That was not quite the commitment Frank was looking for.

* * *

Later that night Sam called to report that Pinto and Heber were home and doing just fine. Then he invited Frank and family over for barbeque. Frank and family went. It was an ambush. Julie, Sam's wife, ganged up with Kim, and the two of them gave Sam and Frank the third degree. Frank told them they could slap him if it would make them feel better. They opted to chew him and Sam out some more. When it was over, they all played Canasta, Sam's kids running around and making a racket. Frank told himself this is what happens when the Lone Ranger settles down and gets married.

When it started getting late, Frank scooted his chair back from the kitchen table and stood to excuse himself.

Sam walked him to the front door, then said, "Hang on. I've got something for you."

"Does it involve sprinkles?"

"It's way better than that," Sam said. "Don't move." Then he walked down the hallway to his den, retrieved his surprise, and came back carrying something in a closed fist. He held out his hand. "I want you to have this."

Frank looked down. It was not a plate of baked goods. It was about the size of a golf ball, brown with a white stripe running through it. He said, "You want me to have a rock?"

"I want you to have a rock," Sam said.

"You're feeling pastries are now too close to the dark side?"

Sam smiled. "You put it on your pillow or chair. You get up; you go to bed; the rock is there. It reminds you that God is happy to chat."

"Yellow trucks?" Frank offered.

"Yellow dump trucks," Sam said. "Full of rocks."

Frank sighed. "It's always something with you, Cartwright, isn't it?"

"Take it."

Frank took it and slipped it into his pocket.

"You know, the Lord worked through you."

"Really?" Frank asked. "I don't remember getting any instructions or a contract."

"Why would he give you instructions when he was confident you knew what had to be done and would take care of it? It's like *World of Warcraft*; you ever played that game?"

"No," Frank said.

"It's on the internet. So you could be playing against people in China or Bulgaria. You've got opposing players from all over with virtual armies of orcs, elves, men, or trolls. All those fantasy races. As a player you set your orcs or men to a task, and then let them do their stuff. They go off and fight, build, whatever. You only redirect when they're out of line or doing something useless. Or you need resources to take care of something quick."

"You're telling me life is like a Play Station?"

Sam shrugged.

"We're all little orcs and humans running around with no will of our own?"

Sam thought for a moment, rubbed his chin. "Maybe life isn't totally like *World of Warcraft*." Then his eyes lit up. "Maybe it's like a bakery."

"Oh, brother," Frank said.

Sam grinned. "Enjoy your rock."

When Frank got home, he walked over to the shelf in the kitchen where he kept the jar of blood money. He set the rock next to the jar.

The next day Frank called Walmart. They said he'd been put on probation and to get his lazy butt into work. He reported to the Wally man that evening. He took a couple of Tylenol for the pain and worked his shift the best he could.

During the weekend Frank relaxed. On Sunday night, he came home to find a big squarish envelope and three red roses tied with a pink ribbon on his kitchen table. He opened the envelope. It contained a photograph of five girls and a little boy lined up in a row in front of some building. They were laughing, smiling, looking at someone just outside the frame. All he could see of that person was her arm and some of that dark lovely hair done up in a braid. Frank knew those children. He knew that hair. He knew that arm.

He turned the photograph over. It said in pencil, "You came for them." Underneath that was today's date. Underneath that was a capital C with a period.

Frank went outside, looked up and down the street, looked around the house to see if the rose-bringer was there, but she was nowhere to be found.

He walked back into the house and stood the photograph next to the rock which sat next to the jar. He stepped back and looked at the trio of objects catching the kitchen light. He stood there for some time.

* * *

On Tuesday, Frank called Cowboy Donut, just as he said he would. Ms. Mary Rogers invited him down for a second interview. His face looked like marbled meat, but he'd made a promise, so he drove down in the Nova with Tony riding shotgun.

Frank left Tony in the car, walked in, and smelled the fine doughnuts and coffee. He told the gal at the counter he was there to see Ms. Rogers, and she pointed him to the back office.

The door was open. Frank cleared his throat and knocked.

Ms. Rogers looked up. She examined him up and down. She shook her head. "Your face looks like a train wreck. What is it with you? The ex-con gig wasn't bad enough? Now you want me to hire Frankenstein?"

"This face will be a hit at Halloween," he said. "And that's prime doughnut time. My good looks are going to make you a million dollars."

"So what happened?"

Frank shrugged. "Nothing much."

"Is that so?" she asked. She hit a few keys on her keyboard, then turned the monitor so he could see it. It was a news website. The headline said "Ex-con Becomes Hero." Right below it was his picture. He was wearing an orange jumpsuit outside the Colorado Springs court house. Along with the fine photo, the first paragraph told everyone who read it the city and state he lived in.

The media was going to get him killed.

"Who is that?" Ms. Rogers asked. "You and Pillsbury have another brother?"

"It's a big family," Frank said. "Long story."

"I know. It's ten pages. I read all of it. Seems to me you're a bit of a high risk."

That was the truth. He nodded and thought he'd save her the breath. "Well, I appreciate your time, Ms. Rodgers."

"Where you going?" she asked.

"I—"

"I'm a business owner, Mr. Shaw," she said. "I take risks. This whole shop was one big gamble. An informed gamble, but a gamble nevertheless. You called me when you said you would. That showed some responsibility. You showed up here looking like a herd of cattle stampeded your face. That shows a willingness to work. Shows some grit. I like grit. Given the activities of the last few days, a lot of folks would take time off, think the world owed them something, but not you. So I'm going to take a risk on you, Mr. Shaw. Are you ready to work?"

Frank had a five year plan. That plan required cash. "Work's my middle name."

"Excellent," she said. "I'll see you tomorrow. Five a.m. sharp."

Frank nodded. Working the night shift at Walmart and the morning here was going to turn him into a complete vampire. But he could do the vampire. For a little while at least. It was a lot better than being dragged behind a bus.

He said good-bye and walked back past the gal at the counter and out of the shop into the sunshine.

Tony was still sitting in the car, getting ready to make his sales presentation for Yeti Inc.

"So?" Tony asked.

"So I am now officially a doughnut guy."

Tony faked a sentimental sniff. "My baby's all growed up and got himself a job."

"Watch it," Frank said.

Tony flipped down his laptop. "Now I'm going to show you how real money is made in the new economy. I need you to give me an introduction." Tony got out and started to walk to the shop.

"Right," Frank said, then took a big breath and gazed about at the town and the hills in the distance.

"Hey, you coming?"

"Just a sec," Frank said and lingered by the car. The DA in Weld County might end up sending him to jail. Flor, the evil baker, might put out a hit on him. Anything could happen: Frank might walk off the curb and die of a heart attack. But that was all in the future.

Right now he was filled with the electrical thrill of being a free man. One with a Wally job *and* a doughnut job. A man with the means to get some assets. A man living and breathing someplace other than inside a cement box. He had the telephone number of Ms. Cross, and, if you counted being roughed up by drug lords, he'd already had a first date with Carmen.

He gazed out across the landscape. It was a glorious day in dirt land. There was the dirt and rock at his feet. And the traffic motoring by that smelled like diesel. And the dirt hills dotted with sagebrush in the distance. And the sun shining down out of a wide blue sky. And over it all, the Wyoming wind was blowing, rolling across the unfettered land for miles and miles, as far as the eye could see.

The End

Dear Reader

I HOPE YOU enjoyed the ride. If you did, please consider leaving a review at your favorite bookseller's website, even if it's only a line or two. Leaving a review not only helps your fellow readers, it also helps me continue to bring you more books.

Your review means a lot.

And it will probably usher in world peace.

Author's Note

THE TYPES OF slavery depicted in this story are real and occur in every nation on this earth. A good portion of my research was based on actual busts of criminal organizations with operations in Colorado, Texas, Georgia, Nevada, and California.

If you want to learn more, please go to the website for the Department of Homeland Security at www.dhs.gov and look up the topic of human trafficking to see how you can identify and report suspected incidents of this crime. For those looking for a broader treatment on the subject, while there are many good texts, I found *The Slave Next Door* by Kevin Bales particularly helpful.

Finally, if you want to get more involved, become an abolitionist by supporting Operation Underground Railroad (www.ourrescue.org), a private group of former CIA agents and Navy SEALS who are running operations across the globe to free child slaves, or www.freetheslaves.net, an organization dedicated to doing just what its name says.

Acknowledgements

THIS STORY WAS inspired by a fine old brother in my church in Ohio who was one of those salt of the earth folks who also happened to have at one time been a bank robber. When he got out of prison, he determined his life would change. He married a good Methodist girl he met at a church dance, went into the laundry business, and never looked back. It was my privilege to record his life history. Not a single event or detail in this book is about him. But I can tell you that his story deserves a book. Hopefully, my character Frank ends up doing as well in life as he did.

A number of folks provided excellent feedback on early versions of this story. **Alexandria Brown, Anne Squire, Amy Lamborn,** and **Caitlin Blasdell** (my agent) provided helpful reader responses. **Edie Ogilvie** provided a sharp-eyed edit. **Kip Motta** provided expertise on the details of flying Cessnas that included an aerial tour over the Caribbean blue waters of Bear Lake. **Gary Ogilvie** and **Mark Lee** shared insights only those who have been cops in small western towns can. **Larry Correia** kept me honest with my guns. And **Marcus Custer** not only helped me develop Frank's backstory in the military, but also brought the special perspective of someone who has seen and done much both in Special Forces and Homeland Security.

A few other folks helped in my initial general research for the story by taking time to sharing their experience and insights. These include **Brad Torgersen** on general military culture, **Gary Bergesen** on Special Forces, **Judson Roberts** on organized crime, **Sean Linnae** on Special Forces, and **Stephen Gehrke** on how things are run in the Utah state prison. Of course, any errors in the text are mine.

For the cover I'm indebted to **Shai McDonald**, a very flexible and accommodating artist, **Devon Dorrity**, who helped me put it all together, and **Isaac Stewart** for good beta viewer response.

Finally, a huge amount of thanks goes to **Nellie**, my excellent wife, who provided insight and support every step along the way.

By John D. Brown

Thrillers

Bad Penny

Awful Intent

Epic Fantasies

Servant: The Dark God Book One

Curse: The Dark God Book Two

Raveler: The Dark God Book Three

Glory: The Dark God Book Four (in planning!)

Shorter Works

Bright Waters

Loose in the Wires

The Scent of Desire

From the Clay of His Heart

Don't Miss Out!

Join the many readers who have asked to be notified when the next book is out at by signing up at **johndbrown.com**.

About the Author

JOHN D. BROWN lives with his wife and four daughters in the hinterlands of Utah where one encounters much fresh air, many good-hearted ranchers, and the occasional wolf.

Feel free to drop by his website **johndbrown.com** to post comments or just say hello. He always enjoys hearing from readers.

Made in the USA
Columbia, SC
28 October 2017